Seven Dirty Words

Charlotte Howard

Cover design Shannon Yarbrough, St. Louis, Missouri

The characters and events in this book are fictitious.

Rocking Horse Publishing
All on the Same Page Bookstore
11052 Olive Blvd.
Creve Coeur, Missouri 63141

Visit our website at www.RockingHorsePublishing.com

First edition: January 2013

ISBN 10: 0-9884933-3-0
ISBN 13: 978-0-9884933-3-9

i

DEDICATION

This book is dedicated to Rich. Thanks for the research tips!

ACKNOWLEDGMENTS

If I were to sit here and type out the list of names of people who have supported and helped me over the years, the acknowledgments would be longer than the book! Thank you to everyone who has inspired and encouraged me to write.

Thank you to my best-friends and sisters-in-crime, Dee & Sian, for giving me so many Tequila-induced memories to draw from. Thank you to my mum for showing me how a cup of tea can solve every problem. Thank you to my husband, Rich, for believing in me.

Chapter One

I died for a short while the first time we met. There was no fluttering in my chest, no somersault of my stomach, no burning in my loins. My heart literally stopped. He was tall, at least six-foot-four, and dressed in a pair of worn indigo jeans that perfectly matched his intense stare. A silk black shirt covered what I imagined to be a ripple of hard muscle, and opened at the top, showing a dusting of tight, dark curls. His thick neck led towards a razor-sharp, square jaw line, a straight nose that had clearly never seen the ill effects of rough play, and deep, hooded eyes. Hair that could have been straight had been styled with a slight wave. I was sure it was dark brown, but it could have easily been black, and had shots of silver-grey streaking through it.

My face was lined up with his toes, or more precisely, his pristinely polished black patent chukka boots. Palms down in the thick mud beneath me, I pushed up and let my eyes glance at the man in front of me. He looked none too pleased to see his clothes spattered with flecks of dirt from where I had landed and splashed him.

I struggled to get to my feet as my own boots dug into the ground, slipping against the wet grass. Eventually I found my knees and leant back, looking up at him. I forced a grin on my mud-covered face, but he didn't return it. Finally able to stand without landing on my backside, I wiped my hands down the sides of my bare thighs.

His glare speared through the apology that I tried to splutter, words failing to come from my vocal cords. In the distance, I heard someone call my name. Looking over my shoulder, I could see my teammates beckoning me to rejoin the group. "Sorry," the word leapt forward.

A dark eyebrow flicked upwards. "Are you going to pay for that?" he asked, snapping each word as though he was talking to some insolent child.

"It's a muddy field, you're watching a rugby match," I countered, my eyes narrowing. "Try stepping away from the lines."

"You've got a mouth on you." A smile twitched at the corners of his lips. I've got a mouth on me? What the hell was that supposed to mean? I was about to make some loud comment about him being arrogant and conceited, but the captain of the team had already reached my heel.

"You coming?" Lou tugged on my elbow, throwing a smile towards the man who loomed over me.

"Yeah," I said, racing back into the game.

"Who's your friend?" Lou asked, nodding towards Tall, Dark, and Smoldering.

"I haven't got a clue, but he wasn't impressed by my skidding halt!" I laughed, tossing her the ball.

We finished practice at two o'clock, as we did every Saturday afternoon. I listened to the laughter and loud chattering of my teammates and friends, as I scrubbed at the mud that caked my arms, legs, and face. Warm water pummeled at my aching muscles. I rubbed away the sweat with a floral-scented shower gel. I made a point of using feminine-scented products, since I lived in such a masculine world.

Not only did I play rugby, a game that my mother always told me was unbecoming for a woman of my standing, but I also lived with two men and worked in an office where I was the only female. I was also incredibly single. My exes were exes because they found it impossible to deal with, and those non-conquests refused to believe that I wasn't a lesbian. Saying that, it had been over a year since I'd even tried to get anyone into my bed….

As well as girly soaps, I also keep my hair long, although it was usually tied into a loose bun, and I wear makeup every day. I can't help my physique, unfortunately. I am shorter than average, standing at only five-foot-three, and while I do have what would be classed as an hourglass figure, I am also plagued by quite thick thighs and strong arms. This is not helped by my exercise regime.

2

Once a week I play rugby, nothing serious, simply for fun, but I also attend mixed martial arts classes on Mondays, go swimming at least twice a week, and hit the gym on Tuesdays, Thursdays, and Fridays. When I'm not at the gym, swimming, or taking part in a game where my backside is often handed to me on a platter, I like to go for long jogs or ride my horse. Except for Sundays. Sunday is my day of rest. Not because I am religious in any way, shape, or form, but because I have been socially trained to accept that this is the day that I do nothing.

After the game where I slid on my face for several feet until coming to an abrupt stop at his feet, I decided that I would forego our usual routine of drinks down at the local pub and, instead, head home to nurse the scrapes and scratches that marked my elbows, knees, and chin.

Walking back to my Golf, I saw Tall, Dark, and Smoldering leaning against a tree. His arms were folded tightly in front of him, and he had a chukka resting on one of the many boulders that separated the car park from the fields.

I threw a nod and a smile towards him as I rummaged in my jean pockets for my keys, dumping the battered and muddied holdall next to the wheel.

"Good game?" he asked, but when I looked up, I could see he wasn't pointing the question in my direction. A stick-thin, terribly young blonde had appeared by his side and kissed him on the cheek. She clutched a hockey stick in her right hand, and handed him a pink rucksack with the other.

Part of me felt almost embarrassed that I had wanted him to be talking to me. The rest of me bundled into the car and headed home.

I should probably point out that my home was not a shabby apartment in some dingy area of town. It was actually an old farmhouse at the edge of a well-to-do village, nestled in the heart of Hampshire.

As I said earlier, I live with two men, and no, neither of them are gay. I have sometimes questioned the sexuality of my brother Mark, what with his flair for style, and his love of shopping and spas, but then again I have also been introduced to the many girls that have graced our home for a single night.

The other man to reside with us is Daniel Turnbull. Danny is gorgeous in every sense of the word, but may as well have been my other brother.

3

I've known him all my life, since he and Mark are best friends. He is also ultra-macho to the point of being a Neanderthal. It would not surprise me if one day I caught him dragging the lifeless body of some poor girl he'd clonked over the head to drag back to his cave.

On this day, when I arrived home, both men were sitting in the living room, feet resting on the coffee table, beer bottle in one hand, Xbox controller in the other. "Jeez," I muttered, as I tried to resist sniffing the air in fear of my gagging reflex reacting to the scent of primal male. Unfortunately, when you live with two men under the age of thirty, it is impossible to avoid the stench of sweaty socks, stale beer, and cheesy nachos. Combine that with the fact that it was the height of summer, and you have one highly stink-filled house.

I dumped the holdall next to the washing machine and looked around the kitchen. Bowls filled with the residue of the morning's breakfasts, an empty milk bottle, several empty beer bottles, used newspapers, and layers of shed clothes were scattered around the room. "We seriously need to tidy up," I yelled through, knowing full well that the only reaction I would get would be an annoyed grunt or two.

The dishwasher door fell with a clatter, as I peered in and realized that it was still full of dirty pots from two days ago. The stench of old food was unbelievable, and my head snapped backwards with such force I'm surprised I still have neck bones. Ripping open a packet from under the sink, I aimed the blue-and-yellow tablet at the little box in the door before slamming it shut and pressing the white button. It whirred and chugged noisily as I ran the water in what little space I could find in the sink and began to sort through the pots and rubbish, attempting to find a clean spot.

Peeling a pair of boxer shorts from the back of a chair, I grimaced and flung them towards the holdall by the washing machine. "Disgusting men," I chuntered in revulsion, even though I knew that our living arrangements were as much my fault as they were theirs. But that didn't stop me from blaming them.

"Stick the kettle on," called a voice from the front room, grating on my final nerve. A deep growl vibrated in the base of my throat as I stormed into the room and began yelling several obscenities at them.

"All right, chill, Butch!" Mark laughed. He knew I hated that school nickname. I wanted to throw something at my brother's head, but I knew that Mother would only chastise me for having put him in the hospital with a split skull yet again. Golden boy could do no wrong. Fortunately, our father always took my side when it came to arguments, so we were evenly defended.

Danny saw sense and ducked into the next room to make tea for everyone. That is the glorious, if not slightly annoying, thing about living in England. We are the country that truly believes, without any shadow of a doubt, that a simple hot beverage can solve all issues. Arguing kids? Cup of tea. Problems at work? Cup of tea. World war, mass hunger, and poverty? Have a cup of bleeding Rosy-Lee.

I marched after him, spitting my annoyances out as he busied himself by the kettle. Throwing dirty clothes towards the washing machine, chucking empty packets in the bin, did nothing to soothe my frustrations.

"Bad game?" Danny asked, in an attempt at small talk.

"Not really," I grunted, sinking into the one chair that no longer had clothes, newspapers, and pots covering it.

"Go on, then."

"Go on, then, what?" I asked, squinting to emphasize my annoyance.

"Go on, then, tell us what your problem is." By this time, Mark had joined us, shoving everything off the chair opposite me so that it landed on the floor. I glowered at him like an angry cat threatening to hiss and spit.

"Jesus H. Someone's pissed you off," Mark groaned, almost in a mocking manner, if that's possible.

"No," I said, my brows furrowing into a tight knot at the top of my slightly snubbed nose. Confusion settled in. Was someone pissing me off?

"Seriously, Butch, we know you far too well. Spill it."

"Nothing!" I snapped, perhaps too quickly.

"What's his name, and what did he do?" Danny this time, his voice getting deeper as though ready to go into full-blown protective mode. I rolled my eyes and tried to ignore him.

"Sis, you have to tell us now." Mark leant forward and grabbed at my hands. I pulled away and threw him a "What the hell?" look. He laughed and fell backwards into the seat again. Danny plonked a mug in front of each of us. The cream-colored liquid sloshed over the sides, giving me yet more to clean up.

"Okay, okay," I relented, picking up the mug and sipping at the cool drink. Danny always added too much milk for my taste, but it was still welcomed, helping to massage away the aches and pains that gripped at my muscles from the match earlier. I proceeded to tell them all about TDS, even though I wasn't sure why he was the one in my head. I could have come up with a thousand excuses for my foul mood: rough game, annoying bad drivers, untidy house. But the truth was that he was still at the front of my thoughts. He had riled me in a way that I had never been riled before.

"Sounds like you're in L.O.V.E!" cooed Mark, ridiculing me. I wanted to slap him, but couldn't reach, and didn't dare throw lukewarm tea across the room, so I settled for a scowl.

Downing the rest of my drink, I turned to the holdall and dirty clothes piled on top of it, shoving them all into the machine before filling it with powder and liquids to get rid of the muck and smells. "You two can finish the kitchen," I yelled, as I went up to the private sanctuary of my bedroom.

Chapter Two

Lying back on my bed, covered in its teal geometric-patterned sheets, I let my thoughts trail towards TDS. There was a desperate part of me that wanted to know who he was. I'd seen him talking to some blonde, but she had looked far too young to be his girlfriend. Saying that, anything was possible. His daughter, perhaps? He had seemed familiar to me, although I was positive I hadn't seen him at the field before. Perhaps he lives nearby? I pondered before pulling myself up to sitting and flicking on the television.

The news played with all its depressing glory. Images of a war-torn Middle East shattered the screen as the newscaster warned of "flashing lights and images that some may find disturbing." I'd been too hardened by computer games and movies to find anything sickening about the dead bodies that piled high outside a crumbling building, except for the fact that this was real and not Hollywood. But it was the reality that tugged on my heart, not the images themselves.

As I was thinking of switching it off, the next reel started. A piece about entrepreneur Vance Ellery donating hundreds of thousands to the local hospital began, and there, taking up all twenty-six inches of the screen, was TDS.

Glued to the item, I sank back into my pillows and watched as his beautiful face broke into a smile. He shook hands with a few locals, members of the council, and hospital board. The voiceover introduced his daughter, Bianca, and on walked the blonde. I felt smug, knowing that my assumption had been correct.

"Mr. Ellery has told reporters that he intends to stay in the Brookfield area over the next few months," announced a gorgeous, but overly made-up, brunette reporter, before the camera panned around to TDS.

"Sport has always been important to my daughter." He cast a loving smile down at the blonde before deep blue eyes glanced back at the cameras and crowds. "And she has convinced me that Brookfield has many budding Olympians and athletes." A cheer rose from his audience.

"Yeah, but you're a year too late to sponsor Team GB," I snorted towards the television.

"So I have decided to work with the local community to improve the area and provide much-needed sports and play equipment that will benefit all of the families who live here." Another cheer from the crowd, another snort from me, although my ears pricked when he began to mention the sports pavilion. "The facilities on the playing fields are inadequate," he shouted, above a roar of agreement. "And my first act will be to improve the changing rooms and gymnasium."

"What are you watching?" Mark asked from the doorway.

"Get out, this is my room." I threw a book towards him, but he ducked, and it sailed over his shoulder into the hallway for me to pick up later.

"Who is that?" He marched in, arms folded, and plonked himself on the end of the bed.

"TDS," I smiled, with a sigh.

"Oh, my God, Butch!" He jabbed me in the ribs.

"Fuck off calling me that." I jabbed back.

"Okay, okay! I'm sorry!" He laughed, holding his hands up in defense. "But he is hot."

"Pity he's an arrogant fucker with it."

"Such dirty words from such a pretty girl," he teased, using the sentence that our mother often scolded me with.

"Prick," I retorted, shoving him off my bed.

"I'll let you get back to your fantasies. Dan's cooking spag bol for dinner if you're interested."

"I'll be down in ten," I called after him as he thumped down the twisted staircase. My eyes shot back to the screen, but the clip had finished and was back on the aging reporters who sat behind the red desk. I reached for the remote and switched the TV off before rolling off my bed.

Danny wasn't a bad cook, but he wasn't great either, so his spaghetti bolognaise came from a jar. I preferred Mark's homemade version, but after a good match I was so hungry I ate without complaining about the burned garlic bread or dry meat. I listened to the lads talk about the late-night clan match they had planned on the Xbox.

"Joy. Another night being locked in my room with earplugs," I groaned, slurping up the last strand of sticky pasta.

"Join us," Mark said, knowing full well that I would rather gouge out my own eyes than play on one of their shoot-'em-up war games.

"Think I'll pass. The mare needs riding; perhaps I'll do that instead." I left them to wash the pots, and headed out the back door, stopping only to pull on my muckers and padded jacket.

For mid-June it was decidedly chilly by seven o'clock, despite sunset still being a good hour and a half away. The breeze danced around me, but failed to get past the jacket and my jean-clad legs. I strode down the crazy paving path with purpose, towards the metal gate that separated the garden from the paddock and stables.

Georgia, my grey Arab mare, stood with her head hanging over the dark wooden door, whinnying as I neared her. Grabbing a brown synthetic saddle and bridle from the stable next door, I tacked her with ease and efficiency before mounting and steering her down the tarmacked drive that went down the side of the house and out through the front gates.

It was only a gentle and short hack, once around the village, up to the playing fields, and then back to the house. But it was what I needed. The fresh air whipped away any memories of TDS that lingered, so by the time I

9

was home, I had a big grin on my face and was ready for a bath and the soft comforts of my bed.

Georgia tucked gratefully into a huge net of hay as I removed the tack and brushed her down. I swear, if she'd been able, she would have purred beneath my touch. Pressing hard into the plastic cover that protected the light switch, the stable was sheathed in darkness. I loved being able to stable her in my back garden, and had my parents to thank.

You may have realized by now that Mark and I come from a wealthy background. My father, Stephen Holmes, does something with banks and money, so has plenty of it. I've never worried myself about getting involved or asking questions about what it is he actually does. All I know is that he works in the city, resides in the country with my mother, and pays for the little luxuries that our jobs can't afford.

However, to speak to us you wouldn't have known about our overindulged bank accounts. My father had made a point of ensuring we had friends within the local community and were not tied to only the rich stock that my mother circulated within. Mother had tried to object, but her children's happiness was all that was important to her, so she reluctantly encouraged us to play with the other children. Unfortunately for her, despite the good education and expensive boarding school in Kent for six years, we also sound as though we grew up in the village of Brookfield.

My father has jokingly suggested that I join the armed forces before, thinking that I would be quite suited to the life. My mother frowns, tuts, and scorns us. "A girl with your heritage should not know all seven dirty words," she would tell me, on a regular basis.

Mark and I had decided to leave home and claim a little independence when I was twenty-one and he was twenty-four. But we're not that independent and had moved into a farmhouse that is owned by our parents. It used to be rented out to an older couple until they decided it was too big for only the two of them.

Knowing it would be too big for us to manage as well, Dad suggested we take in a lodger. He insisted it be someone we know, and someone he trusts, so it only made sense that the lodger be Danny, whose mother works with Dad. That was five years ago.

I'd like to say that was it, that we were one happy little unit, surviving on our meager wages, but supplemented by our parents. Unfortunately, that was only a small section of my life.

Sunday was, as I've said before, my day of rest. I fully intended to simply muck out Georgia's stable and spend the rest of the day chilling out, reading a book. However, my plans were rudely interrupted by an invitation to lunch at my parents' house.

Mark managed to get out of it by conveniently having a photo shoot that had suddenly appeared in the diary. My eyes narrowed as I heard him gushing false apologies down the phone to our mother. He tossed the cordless handset to me before leaping over the back of the sofa and racing out of the room with a childish giggle.

"Prick," I muttered, quietly, I'd thought, but unfortunately, my mother had heard me demeaning her little boy, and I was in the firing line. "Yes... No... I'm sorry, Mum... Yes, I'll apologize to Mark... Yes, I'd love to come to lunch this afternoon." Damn it, he was going to pay for this.

Lunch consisted of deliciously cooked roast chicken with all of the traditional trimmings. As usual, my parents insisted that I was not eating healthily enough, and so piled my plate so high that I thought I might need a Sherpa in order to find the top.

I tucked into as much as I could manage, but pushed almost a full plate aside, much to Mother's disgust.

"You'll waste away, Paige," my mother cooed at me.

"Mum, I'm really not hungry!" Looking down at the plate, all I could see were calories I would have to work off tomorrow. I found it hard enough keeping a slim figure without my mother's interference.

"And you look so pale," she continued, to my annoyance. I struggled not to groan like a moody teenager, excusing myself to use the bathroom.

Unlike my brother, I wasn't naturally blessed with an easy-to-keep build, tanned skin, or drop-dead looks. While he had taken every positive aspect of our parents' DNA, I seem to have been lumbered with what he deems as his "leftovers." In fact, we were so different that some people failed to believe that we were even related, let alone brother and sister.

I looked in the gilt-framed mirror, my reflection staring back at me with a vacant expression. Hazel eyes, medium-to-dark brown hair, and a snubbed nose. Average looks, marred by the many injuries I'd received over the years. An ever-so-slight bump in the middle of my nose was courtesy of a riding accident when I landed, face first, on a jump pole as a teenager. A thin white scar on the underside of my jaw was the result of a rugby match when I'd landed with my chin on another player's boot. A thick white scar split through my right eyebrow where I'd been kicked during a sparring match, even though we had both been wearing pads and headgear. And that's solely my face.

Perhaps I shouldn't be so surprised that my parents were against my chosen activities. Still, they were supportive enough, and my father attended any major matches or competitions. Mother chose to stay at home, unable to watch her youngest child get pummeled into the ground, although she had been more understanding of my choices over the past year.

Taking several deep breaths, I walked back into the dining room of Holmes Manor, ready to face the rest of the meal, which ended without incident.

It was while relaxing in the drawing room, with Mother reeling off the list of most eligible bachelors, that I noticed the newspaper lying front page up on the sideboard. I glanced down at it, and there was TDS, looking all smug and superior, staring back up at me with those penetrating eyes.

"Oh, isn't he wonderful?" Mother's voice was creamy smooth as she looked down at the same paper.

"He's replacing a pavilion, not finding a cure for cancer," I grumbled unnecessarily. Mother shot a look at me as if she could read the thoughts that even I didn't know I was having.

"Precisely," my father joined us.

"I don't see you offering the council money to renovate the old place," Mother snapped. My eyes widened as my parents started into a debate of politics and finance.

"I think I do plenty for this village already! I fund many functions, I have donated thousands to local charities, and I am on the local council!" Dad was right; he did do an awful lot for Brookfield and the surrounding areas. He held fundraising summer balls and Christmas parties each year, sponsored as many charity events as he knew about, and was an active member of the parish council.

Being involved in village life and the community was something that had rubbed off on me as well, since I was now on the board of trustees for the local sports council. Knowing that I was, at some point in the near future, going to have to speak to and possibly work alongside TDS only served to irritate me further.

"He's still a very nice man." Mother's pout turned downwards, forcing her bottom lip forward and out. Dad instantly swept to her side, kissing it back in, making me want to gag, as any daughter does when her parents show signs of affection for each other. They may gripe and argue, but they did truly love each other.

"Yes, he is," Dad agreed with a warm smile.

I had a great respect for my parents' love and tolerance for each other, especially considering the two different backgrounds from which they came. My mother was born into old money, with rich ancestors that could be dated back to the last century and probably beyond. She had been a debutante when she met my father, and my grandfather had instantly disapproved of any budding romance. My father was wealthy, but he was of new stock and not the blue blood that my grandfather had sought for his eldest daughter.

Dad's father was a builder, and a successful one at that. He had a habit of buying near-derelict homes and restoring them to a former glory and beauty. He also created half of Brookfield. Holmes Manor had been one of his projects, which he had then given to my father, his only son, as a gift for graduating university and landing himself a prospective career within the world of banking. I had never known a home other than Holmes Manor.

"He's an arrogant bully," I interjected, as my mother continued to spout Vance Ellery's many redeeming qualities.

"And how would you know, Paige?"

"I met him at the playing fields yesterday. He stood right on the sidelines and then moaned when I tripped and splashed his bloody Wranglers in mud," I exclaimed, my arms waving around wildly.

"I don't think men like Mr. Ellery wear Wranglers," Mother giggled.

"Whatever he wears, he's still a prick," I grumbled, wrapping my arms tightly around my chest. My mother instantly started chiding me for my language.

13

"So you wouldn't be happy if I told you he was our guest of honor at the ball then?" My father smirked.

Chapter Three

The next day I woke before either one of the boys, who remained snoring loudly with pig-like grunts occasionally echoing down the stairwell, while I hurriedly munched on toast smothered in blackberry jam and gulped at piping hot tea.

I dressed in a knee-length, dark grey pencil skirt, white blouse that ruffled down the center, and matching grey jacket. My dark brown hair was loosely twisted into a chignon and clipped in place, and I had applied my makeup with the precision of an artist. Ready for the day, I headed to work.

I worked on an industrial estate on the edge of Brookfield, in a brick building as grey as my suit. It's two stories high, but is still overshadowed by the warehouses that surround it.

Dad had not been overly happy when I told him I'd got myself a job working for a company that custom builds body parts for cars. But he did not try to deter me either. He knew how important it was for me to have my independence. He'd also shown an inordinate amount of pride when I went back to work after having had so much time off recently. I had only been back a few months.

Fortunately for him, I work in the office, mainly in the sales team, and not actually getting my hands dirty. I leave that for Saturday afternoons.

The job is one more thing that causes bigoted (and often hopeful) men to think that I am a lesbian. Even my co-workers had questioned my sexuality before, but mainly because I hadn't slept with any of them. Hadn't. Past tense. A couple of Christmases ago, we'd had a party in the office, got totally bladdered, and I had ended up in the back of my car with Alek Zubek, one of the mechanics. Mainly to prove a point.

Since then, every single man in the office and workshop had tried it on with me in some way or another, and each one had been rebuffed.

The comments had simmered over the past twelve months, and half-hearted advances had all but come to a stop. The guys had started to look at me as though I was some broken doll, glances that I'd tried to put an end to by flirting with them all. For a month now, things were beginning to take a turn towards the norm.

That day, I couldn't concentrate on any of the innuendo-filled comments, though. All my mind could whirl around was the fact that my father had decided to invite TDS to his summer ball, a ball that I was expected to attend whether I liked it or not.

"So when are you going to let me give your bodywork some detailing?" came a voice from behind me. I swung my legs down from the desk and removed the biro I'd been absently chewing on, turning to see Greg Bertin towering over me.

Any woman with half a brain wouldn't stand for his blatant sexual harassment, but the fact was that I enjoyed receiving it as much as he enjoyed dishing it out. I was so used to being ignored by men that I welcomed any attention nowadays. Plus, he was married, so no real threat.

"Well, it's true that the Golf could do with a paint job," I replied with a coy smile.

"Come on, what's eating you?" He nudged my keyboard sideways and perched on the end of the desk.

"Men. You're all shits." There was a laugh in my voice, but a nervous one. Why couldn't I get him out of my head? Every time I was left alone with my thoughts, every time I closed my eyes, all I could see, feel, was TDS shadowing me with that intense glare of his.

"That, we are," he laughed back, before standing and moving behind me. His hands, rough from manual labor, with the smell of grease etched into the pores, gripped at my shoulders and began to rub at the knots. I leant my head to one side, feeling the bristles of his naked arm against my cheek, and moaned in relief.

"How are you getting on?" he asked sympathetically.

"I'm fine. Please don't keep asking me."

Greg was an amazing boss, and extremely understanding in situations where I'd otherwise have been let go. But he was also as fussy as a mother hen.

"This is not me getting any work done," I complained half-heartedly.

"You weren't doing anything anyway," he retorted, leaning forward to stare at my screen. A blank invoice stared back.

The phone rang, forcing me to pull away from his grasp. "Hello, Bertin Body Shop, Paige speaking, how can I help?" I asked in my friendliest and most professional tone.

"'Tis moi!" I recognized the voice instantly.

"Hey, Mark, whaddya want?"

"Has Mum told you about this summer's event?"

"If you mean, have I been told how Tall, Dark, and Twatish will be there, yes."

"Cool. Well, Danny and I are going to be hunting out DJs, wondered if you wanted me to pick you anything up?"

16

It is probably wrong on many levels that not only was Mark straight, but he was my brother and knew my exact dress and shoe size. But that didn't stop me from agreeing without hesitation. We hung up with our usual "Bye, Bitch," "Bye, Butch," send off.

I swiveled around in my seat, but Greg had already gone back down to the workshop. I stood up and walked over to the large plate-glass window that ran the length of the office overlooking the main floor.

Below me, several men worked tirelessly on cars and at machines, building bespoke, and expensive, designs. I was in awe of the yellow fireworks that shot out from grinders, the cold blue flame from blowtorches, as they welded together strips of metal. Sometimes when I watched over them, I half-expected them to burst into song, like life was a musical being played on some giant screen.

The phone rang again, and I answered with the same welcoming manner. It was a new customer who wanted to meet with Greg, who was not only the owner, but also head designer and a brilliant artist to boot, about a custom build for his Mitsubishi Evo.

"We actually have a cancellation this afternoon at one-thirty, if you'd like that, sir," I offered, tapping out the details onto the screen. "Great! We'll see you this afternoon, Mr. Jackson."

Glancing down at my watch, I realized it was already ten o'clock, and time for my scheduled tea break. I kicked back from the desk and wandered out of the door, down the metal steps that led into the workshop, and through a side door into what was termed as the "Staff Room."

Greg was leaning on the coffee machine, waiting for it to splutter out the thick, dark, bitter liquid. "Filled your one-thirty," I said, choosing the kettle and a tea bag over the crappy vending machine. "It's an Evo," I smiled, knowing that the Evo 8 was one of Greg's preferred cars. He grinned back at me, his wide smile taking over his heart-shaped face.

Running a hand blackened with oil through his dirty blond hair, he hammered a fist on the side of the machine. "Damn thing," he moaned.

"Tea?" I offered, lifting up a second tea bag.

"Yeah, go on, then."

I made tea for us both, but rather than sitting amongst the old gym-style lockers and stench of grease, petrol, and engine oil, we went back into the office. I had made a vain attempt at personalizing the space and making

17

it appear more feminine by adding potted plants and scenic paintings, but at the end of the day it was still only a metal and glass box that overlooked a body shop.

"Why do you work here?" Greg asked for the umpteenth time, as he slurped at his tea.

"I enjoy it," I said, with my usual reply.

"Nah," he shook his head. "That's not it. You have a degree in psychology or whatever."

"Sociology," I corrected him, with a giggle.

"Whatever." His eyes widened comically. And yet you choose to spend your day on a telephone surrounded by men who wouldn't know suave and sophisticated if it bit them in the arse."

"Perhaps that's why I work here."

The truth was that I had grown up surrounded by men who were couth and genteel, and being rebellious by nature, I had found myself heading in the opposite direction, much to my mother's disappointment. More recently it was a safe haven as well.

"You kickboxing tonight?" Greg asked, downing the last few murky dregs.

"Yu-huh," I nodded between slurps. Monday nights are MMA nights, but I didn't try to explain the difference.

"You're certainly not like any girl I've ever known," he teased, leaving me with the dirty mugs. I tutted with disapproval, but ignored them and turned back to my computer.

My lunch break was from twelve until one, but that day I had been running late and didn't leave until twelve-fifteen. I grabbed a sandwich from a café on the estate, bringing back several orders for the guys who insisted on working through lunch and seemed to prefer their bread with an oily aftertaste.

As I got back, plastic bags in hand, I noticed a tall young man, about my age, standing by the entrance to reception. "Hi, can I help?" I asked, dumping the food on the tall yellow desk.

"Matt Jackson." He introduced himself as the one-thirty appointment. I peered out the window and saw a brand-new Mitsubishi parked out in front, instantly wondering how I'd missed seeing it on my return.

"Oh, yes, please take a seat, I'll grab Greg."

18

Matt Jackson stood at least six-foot-three, with a shock of inky black hair that was closely cropped at the sides and longer on top, but styled neatly into a row of short spikes from his forehead to crown. His eyes were a deep blue until they were almost as black as his hair, and he was, to say the least, gorgeous.

I swallowed hard, taking him in, as I dialed through to the office and called Greg. Looking up from underneath my lashes, I hoped I was being subtle as I stared at him. No such luck. He threw me a wry smile that twisted his thin lips and gave him even more sex appeal. "Your one-thirty's here." My voice came out as a harsh whisper. My throat suddenly felt dry and sore.

Leaving to head back to my desk, I glanced over my shoulder one more time at the Adonis in reception before walking through caveman central and into my not-so-feminine office.

I tried to make myself look busy, tapping noisily at the keyboard, as Greg showed Mr. Jackson through into his own private room at the back of the office. I couldn't help but catch sight of his reflection in the metallic edge of the monitors. Even that distorted view made him look stunning. My breathing quickened as I realized he'd caught sight of me watching him like some perverted stalker. My cheeks reddened and grew hot with embarrassment.

They were in there for a good hour or more, their laughter seeping out from the gaps under the door. I wanted to listen to what they were saying, but then again, I am ridiculously nosy. I jumped as the door burst open and the two men walked through in such a jovial fashion.

"Paige will take your contact details, and I'll give you a ring in the morning." Greg led Mr. Jackson towards my desk.

Shit. Compose yourself! I scolded myself, adjusting my skirt and twisting to face him with a beaming smile. Shifting sideways, I offered him the chair next to me and proceeded to take all the details I needed. He held out a hand. I took it. His palm was soft, yet his grip was strong. My heart began to thud against my rib cage to the point that I thought it may break free and suddenly grow wings.

"Thank you, Paige," he said with a smile, which only worsened the now-painful thumping in my chest. My stomach twisted into a tight knot as I watched him walk out, and a sudden rush of heat sank between my legs.

"Control yourself, girl," I hushed at myself.

Suddenly the rest of the day seemed to fly by, and I was looking forward to beating several shades of shit out of the pads.

I got home late, well past ten o'clock, as was usual for a Monday night. After finishing work at half-six, I headed straight to the gym where my classes were held. Part of the Monday ritual was to spend half an hour chatting to the other students before the lesson, which finished promptly at half-eight. Shower and change at the gym took another half-hour for me, which always confused the other girls, who were either finished in fifteen or didn't bother using the facilities and went home. But for me, it was all part of being feminine in ways that I otherwise wasn't.

By nine o'clock I was in the car, adjusting my lip gloss, and driving back towards the farmhouse, which could take anywhere between half an hour and an hour, depending on the traffic.

As I sauntered through the door, throwing my gym bag towards the washing machine, I could hear the boys on the Xbox mid-throe of clan match. They were both swearing loudly, cursing all manners of racisms towards the Americans and French they played against. None of it was serious, but simple retaliation for the equally slanderous comments that they were receiving via headset. Boys. Do they ever grow up?

"I'm home," I said, even though I knew they wouldn't notice, and went straight out the back door to say good night to Georgia.

When I finally made it up to my bed, Mark had laid out the dress he'd chosen for the summer ball, a turquoise satin number that would stop above my knees, with long, lacy sleeves. He'd matched it with a pair of silver sandals that had crystal-covered straps. It was stunning.

Chapter Four

Tuesday morning was painful, which surprised me. It's usually the Wednesday that hurt after a good session on Monday nights. I clambered out of bed as my alarm went off at six-thirty, and pulled on my tracksuit bottoms and a hoodie. Every movement wracked at my muscles, sending searing shots of electricity down my spine, arms, and legs. Stiffly, I straightened up and moved carefully down the stairs.

Downstairs was empty apart from empty beer bottles and pizza boxes. I gathered them up to dump in the recycling boxes as I went to see to Georgia. I threw a slab of hay over the door before gathering the tools I needed to muck out her stable. She munched gratefully, with a slight whinny. I inhaled deeply, expecting the normal aroma of sweet meadow hay and comforting scent of greasy horse hair. But all I got was an overwhelming urge to vomit.

Diving towards a bush that grew up the side of the stable, I let my stomach contents fall onto the greenery. Where the hell did that come from?

As I opened the stable door, Georgia ambled out slowly, with about as much urgency as a snail. I pushed her to the side and moved in behind the grey mare, pulling a wheelbarrow loaded with a fork, shovel, and stiff-bristled broom.

Normally it would only take me twenty minutes at the most to clean her stable out and bed it back down. But for some reason, each fork-load felt extraordinarily heavy, straining my neck and shoulders. I cried out in a whimpered agony as I managed to shift the last pile into the green barrow and pushed it out the door.

Walking back to the house seemed like such a long journey, and the melodramatic part of me wanted to fall onto all fours and crawl back. But I managed to stiffen myself and trundle into the house.

"Jesus H. You look like shit, Butch," Mark exclaimed, jumping off his seat and reaching for me before I fell into a crumpled heap at his feet.

"I feel it."

"I hope you're not going to work this morning. I'll call in for you."

"No." I stopped him before he could reach for the phone. "Better if I do." I knew how much Greg hated it when partners or parents called in sick for the guys. I grabbed the receiver and punched in his home number, knowing he wouldn't have left for the workshop yet. I explained how suddenly crap I felt, and he replied with a sympathetic understanding.

"Think I'll go back to bed," I groaned, stripping off to my underwear and dumping the ammonia and muck-laced clothes by the machine.

"I'll bring you up a cuppa," my brother offered.

For all his jibing about my outward appearance, Mark really was the best big brother a girl could ask for. He took care of me, and I needed him.

Falling back into the soft sheets, I didn't even bother climbing back into my pajamas. I lay naked, apart from my sports bra and pants, staring up at the white ceiling.

Mark knocked on the door before entering, a courtesy he only ever gave me when I was feeling ill. He laid a cup of hot, sweet tea on my nightstand and placed a plate of warm, buttered toast next to it. "I haven't got anything on today, so I'll take care of you," he sighed, sitting on the edge of the bed, running a hand through my hair. "You're burning up," he said, handing me a couple of tablets. "Take these. I'll ring the docs."

"No, it's only a cold."

"Unlikely," he scoffed. "More like full-blown flu."

"They won't do anything," I tried to argue, but my throat was sore, leaving my voice raspy. Mark grabbed the remote and switched my TV on. Yet another news program played in the background, but I wasn't really listening to it, and certainly not watching. The bright screen hurt my eyes.

Realizing my sensitivity, Mark stood and drew my curtains together; I rarely closed them when I went to bed. "Seriously, Paige, you look like death. I'm calling Mum."

That was possibly worse than calling the doctor. Mother always worried and become paranoid whenever one of us was sick. I tried to stop him, but I was too weak to follow, and he marched quickly out of the room.

I think I fell asleep, but I'm not sure. All I know is that my mother appeared at my side within what felt like minutes, and I was incredibly drowsy. I fought to keep my eyes open, my forehead and upper lip felt damp with sweat, and I could taste the salty beads at the corner of my lips.

"I've called for the doctor." My mother's voice sounded comforting, reaffirming the fact that I was delirious.

"No, Mum, I'm fine. It's just a cold," I started. But either she ignored me or my voice was so hoarse that she hadn't heard me. I closed my eyes as a cold, damp flannel was placed on my brow. It was soothing, and I welcomed the icy touch, easing away the stabbing pain behind my eyes and temples.

The next voice I heard was deeply masculine, and almost every other word was followed by a "hum" or "tut." "She has an infection, but it is viral," he assured my mother.

I opened one eye and stared up at the grey-haired man peering down at me. I closed it again. "Make sure she takes paracetamol every six hours and drinks plenty of fluids." His voice was calming, yet still stern. "Unfortunately, there's not much more I can do for her, I'm afraid. But you did the right thing calling me, Mrs. Holmes."

Had I been more sober, I would have argued the necessity of calling the doctor out, wasting money.

Their voices all seemed to drift above me as I fell into a deep slumber. When I woke, I found my Mum sitting in a chair by my bedside, watching the news.

"Ow," I moaned, gripping my head and pulling myself to sitting. "Mum, what are you doing here?"

"Keeping an eye on you. I'd like you to come back to Holmes Manor if you're up to the drive."

"Mum, I have a cold, I'm not dying. I'll probably be fine tomorrow," I argued.

"I've ordered the boys to tidy up," she said, ignoring me. "It's no wonder you get ill, with all this dirt. Hannah will be coming over to look after Georgia."

I groaned loudly. Hannah was my mother's yard manager, and also one of Mark's many exes-slash-currents. I still struggled to understand why Mother needed Hannah, considering she only had one horse, who she barely rode. But it appeased her, and one thing my father is good at doing is spoiling my mother. I didn't really mind. Hannah loved Georgia as much as I did.

"She'll come with the box today and take Georgia back to Holmes Manor until you're feeling better."

"No, Mum," I tried to argue, but as with anything with my mother, resistance was futile.

Two hours later, Hannah rolled up in a horsebox and loaded the refined Arab into the back. She mouthed an apology with a sympathetic smile as I was bundled into the back of Dad's Mercedes along with a suitcase of clothes that Mark had thrown together.

"Bitch," I griped at him as he slammed the boot shut and walked past the window. "I have a fucking cold."

"Let Mum have her fun. She never gets to baby you." Normally I would have fought him, but the germs that circulated my veins had somehow blocked my ability to return with a comeback. I didn't want to be fussed over. I had only just relinquished myself from Mother's nurturing grasp.

I pulled my jumper's sleeves around me tightly and turned my head away from him in defiance. Mark laughed at my impetuousness before Mum sidled in beside me, wrapping an arm around my shoulders as though I was twelve years old and being sent home from boarding school again.

The car rolled to a stop outside Holmes Manor only a short while later, followed by Hannah and the horsebox. Stepping out, I looked up and took in my childhood home and all its glory.

Some may have called it imposing, but as I looked up at the sandstone bricks, the massive white windows, and brown tiled roof, all I saw was a flood of sweet memories. I rarely came home much, apart from the odd insisted Sunday lunch, and the compulsory functions.

Speaking of functions, I could already hear the commotion coming from the back of the manor as a hired event organizer ordered around staff, getting ready for the summer ball. Mother ushered me inside, demanding Arthur, my father's driver, bring in my luggage.

Dad was in the drawing room, sitting on the leather sofa, reading from the pink pages of a broadsheet.

"How are you feeling, Pumpkin?" he asked, but not looking up once to face my pale and sweaty appearance.

"Like shit."

"Such dirty words from such a pretty girl," my mother scolded, pushing me into the room.

I sat down next to my father and curled up into a tight ball, my head resting on his crisp white shirt. I inhaled deeply, taking in the comforting scent of spices and musk from his aftershave. He turned and placed a gentle kiss on the top of my head, and I closed my eyes, happy to be home.

Mother woke me with a cup of tea. I was alone in the drawing room, lying on my side and stretched across the leather sofa. Someone had covered me in a cashmere lilac blanket. "Thanks, Mum," I murmured, as she placed the cup and saucer on the floor by my drooping hand.

"Not a problem, dear," she cooed, with all the love that only a mother can feel. As much of a pain as she was, she was still my mother.

"It might be an idea to move up to your room soon, sweetheart. I've had your bed laid out. Only Mr. Ellery is stopping by to discuss some business with your father."

At that, my eyes shot open, and my body sprung to a sitting position. The sudden movement caused a wave of hot pain to surge over me, forcing me to double over, and for bile to rise in my throat. "Bed, now," Mother ordered, in a tone that was not to be trifled with.

She helped me up, gripping my cup and saucer in one hand, and guided me into my old room. "I've spoken to Mr. Bertin, who has agreed that you should have the rest of the week off."

"What? Oh, Mum," I groaned, although I wasn't sure if it was her action or the pain in my ribs and stomach that were causing the wail to seep from my throat. I sat down on the bed, laid out in pale pink sheets, and felt the comforting deep softness of the covers and mattress envelope my hips and thighs.

"No arguments. I know you like your independence, but I still have to look after you."

"Why is Mr. Ellery here?" I asked the question, although I didn't particularly want to think about TDS being only feet away from me.

"He's the guest of honor at your father's summer ball this year, and they're going to be working together in order to raise funds for that sports pavilion you love so much. Mr. Ellery is considering sponsoring your rugby team as well." It meant a lot that, despite their thoughts towards my chosen sports, my parents still supported everything I did.

I smiled gratefully, although the thought of TDS having anything to do with my rugby team made my heart stop as suddenly as it had when I first landed at his chukkas.

25

"Get some sleep." My mother's soothing voice calmed my nerves and restarted the beat inside my chest. "Come down when you're ready and we'll get you something to eat." She left me with a kiss on the forehead.

Chapter Five

I woke a couple of hours later to hear male voices chatting and laughing below me. Steadily, I stood, straining to hear the topic of conversation. I heard the words "Money", "Sport," and "Pavilion" mentioned, and knew instantly that TDS was in my childhood home.

There was a sudden yearning inside me to see him again. But, glancing in the full-length mirror by the door that led to my en suite bathroom, I saw that I was in no fit state to be speaking to handsome older men.

Disheveled was an understatement. My hair was a bird's nest, my eyes had marked purple rings underneath them, and I could already smell the stench of sweat and sickness leaking from my pores.

I dragged my feet towards the bathroom, letting the water run until it was almost scalding. My body trembled with a cold that only I felt. A hot shower was desperately needed. Clouds of steam billowed over the top of the glass doors, informing me that it was now ready to cleanse away the illness that stuck to me like goose grass.

The powerful jets of water were welcomed by my aching muscles, smoothing over the knots and lumps across my shoulders as well as any masseuse. It hurt like hell, but I rolled my neck around and around, rotating my shoulder blades, and stretching out the tight tendons.

Stepping out of the glass confines, I caught sight of my naked body through the mist in the mirror. I reached out and wiped a towel over the screen, examining myself. An angry red line slashed across my stomach. It was a scar that held much more than damaged tissue. The memories that came with it were more painful than the wound itself. My eyelids fell and fought against the tears. Wrapping a towel tightly around my chest, it hid the unsightly marks from view.

I dressed in a pair of dark low-slung jeans and a tight neon-pink vest before pulling my black woolen cardigan over my shivering frame. My hair was scraped back into a bun at the back of my aching skull, with loose tendrils of outgrowing fringe framing my oval face; a far cry from my usual maintained appearance.

Shoving my cold feet into the leopard print ballet pump slippers, I made my way downstairs, hoping to catch a sneak peek at TDS. But there was no sneaking or peeking to be had. I stopped on the bottom step as he and my father were leaving the drawing room.

"Ah, Paige, darling. I believe you've met Mr. Ellery." My father beamed.

TDS held out a hand for me to shake. "Miss Holmes." His face smiled, but his voice didn't falter once.

I stayed on the step and took the hand and gave it a gentle tug. "Mr. Ellery." I returned his false gesture. At least at this height I came to below his chin rather than level with his feet.

"My daughter has come home to stay with us while she recovers from a virus," my father explained. TDS took a step back, obviously fearful that I may be contagious.

"Oh, I'm fine. It's just a cold."

"Mr. Ellery!" My mother beamed, marching into the hallway and taking him into a fake hug of air blown kisses. "You must stay for lunch,"

"Thank you for the offer, Mrs. Holmes, but I really must get on." His voice was gruff and unforgiving.

"Nonsense! We can't have our guest of honor starving!" It was pleasing to know that even TDS was unable to fight my mother.

Dad and TDS walked outside while my mother ordered an array of sandwiches to be made. I tried to convince her that I would take mine back up to my room, but she insisted that the fresh air would help to clear out any lingering germs. Reluctantly, I sat on the decking with my father, mother, and TDS.

The decking was on a slight rise to the rest of the land, right outside the dining room. From it you could see across the grounds, and I watched as the event organizer, a short woman with a halo of frizzy blonde hair, shouted and screamed at workmen and staff.

"It's going to be the best summer ball ever," my mother announced proudly. It was also the same statement she made every year.

I rolled my eyes and bit into a ham sandwich, wishing that my parents would accept that adding mayonnaise and cheese to such a snack would not be as low-brow as they felt it was.

"Your father tells me that you are quite the sportswoman." TDS was trying to be polite and friendly, although his manner was still stern. I suspected that, as a father, he was probably quite strict.

"I enjoy sport, yes."

"Martial arts and rugby are not exactly ladylike sports."

"Perhaps I should only wear ankle-length dresses and corsets too," I bit. My mother gasped in horror. My father coughed and spluttered, although neither should have been shocked by my comments. A flicker of a smirk crossed TDS's lips, but it could have been a trick of the light, because no sooner had I seen it than it had disappeared again.

"If you'll excuse me." I stood and dusted the crumbs off my jeans. "I'm suddenly feeling extremely sick." I attempted to march away in defiance, but my weak knees trembled, so it was more of a stagger.

"Mrs. Holmes, thank you for a lovely lunch," I heard TDS say as I re-entered the house, but no more could be heard after I closed the door behind me.

Walking into the drawing room, I grabbed at one of the many leather-bound books that decorated the wall and sat down on the leather sofa. Flicking open the pages, I wasn't really reading the words. My anger steadied from a raging boil to a gentle simmer, and then I heard his voice again. "Miss Holmes."

I turned and saw him standing in the doorway. I looked around for my parents, but neither were present. I really did not want to be alone with this man. There was something about him that unnerved me.

"Your mother is in the kitchen, and your father is overseeing the readying of the ball. I said I would see myself out," he explained, invading my thought process. I was suddenly very aware of how naked I felt without any makeup on. He neared me, and stood at the arm that I was leaning against. His indigo eyes bore down into me. I gulped hard at the heat that seemed to radiate from his thighs, so close to me. "I would very much like to discuss the plans we have for the sports pavilion, since you have such a vested interest in them."

I swallowed again, although less obvious this time. "Perhaps when I'm feeling better," I heard myself saying.

"I hope you're feeling better soon." Was that a smile or a smirk? There felt like a sudden pull in the room, as though he were capable of telekinesis. The air relaxed as he turned to leave. "I'll call you later on in the week."

Mother entered into the room shortly after he left and commented on the sudden color that painted my cheeks.

"Yes, I'm feeling much better," I mumbled, before retiring to my room with the book I had no intention of reading.

Wednesday was a better day. I woke refreshed, but still sore. My throat was burning, but my eyes and sinuses felt much clearer. I floated down the stairs into the kitchen and informed my mother that I would be going back to the farmhouse, but she soon put a stop to that.

"I have asked Sophie to take Larry and ensure that that place is spick-and-span before you return."

An involuntary grunt rumbled in my throat. Sophie and Larry were two of the many people my parents employed to keep Holmes Manor clean and tidy. Sophie was a perfectionist and, I suspected, someone who suffered from OCD. I dreaded to think where my things would be when I was finally allowed to return home.

"Mum, seriously, I think Mark and I can handle it."

"I don't think you can," she said with a forced laugh. "I had to wipe my feet leaving that place. Your father paid good money for that house, and you two have left it in such a state that it may be declared derelict."

"Oh, don't be so melodramatic," I argued pointlessly. In the end I conceded to staying another couple of days, since Greg had insisted I take the rest of the week off when I had finally rung him earlier.

"Good." My mother was jubilant with her triumph. "Oh, and Mr. Ellery rang."

A shiver shot across my shoulders and up my neck at the mention of his name.

"He will be returning this afternoon with some plans to go with your father. He'd also like it if you could join them and give him your opinion, if you're feeling up to it." I could see the question behind my mother's confused expression, although I was equally bewildered. He'd slammed my choice of exercise, yet treated me like an equal when it came to decisions that weren't mine to be made. Talk about conflict. I didn't respond, instead making noises about ringing Mark.

I took the phone up to my room, hiding behind a closed door. "TDS is fucking here," I shot down the receiver.

"Really?" Mark exclaimed. "He's there? Right now?"

"Well, no, not right now. But he was here yesterday and he's coming back today, with fucking plans for the sports hall that he wants my opinion on."

"Ooh, sounds like someone has the hots for you."

"Except he's about the same age as Dad, and a misogynistic prick."

"There's obviously chemistry between you two and it's been ages since you had a good fucking. I say go for it."

"For a big brother, you're not exactly worried about who I sleep with," I almost spat.

"I do worry, but I also know that you could kick my arse, so are perfectly capable of looking after yourself."

"Oh, be warned. Sophie and Larry are on their way over with a cleaning crew, by the sounds of it," I added as an afterthought.

"Fuck-a-duck," Mark said under his breath. "Better stash the porn."

I laughed. It was nice to laugh.

"Okay, see you, bitch."

"Bye, Butch."

I showered and made an effort that day. I was determined that TDS would see me in my most feminine state and not as a rugby player, or dying swan. By eleven o'clock I was dressed in a pale green summery dress, dotted with lilac and navy flowers around the hem. It ruched around my ample chest, but fitted across my slender waist and wide hips, showing off my best bits and hiding my worst. It stopped level with my knee, meaning that he couldn't see my wide thighs.

I pulled a white cotton shrug over my shoulders, hiding my strong biceps. I painted my face with kohl eyeliner, lashings of black mascara, and a slick of glittered gloss, using plenty of concealer to hide the purple bags and shadows.

Slipping my feet into a pair of white leather ballet pumps, I skipped down the stairs, fluffing my hair around my shoulders.

"Glad to see you're feeling better, darling." My father kissed my cheek as he passed the stairs, heading into the study next to the drawing room. I followed him, with a smile firmly fixed on my lips.

"Mum says that Mr. Ellery wants to show me some plans." It came out as more of a question than a statement. My father hummed a reply, but didn't really answer, so I sat in one of the velour coated chairs opposite his antique oak desk. "I don't quite know exactly how I can help."

"He needs someone on the inside, if you will," my father explained, as he searched through the drawers.

"That sounds almost mysterious," I teased, leaning back and kicking my feet onto the wooden panels. My father glowered at me until I let my feet drop to the floor.

"You have more pull with the sport committee than either of us do. We may have the money, but you have the connections. He's going to draw up some ideas for you to give to Louise."

"So all you want me for is my friends." A half-hearted sigh sank my chest. Dad straightened up and cast a cynical frown on me before looking towards the door. My mother was walking through, arm linked in arm, with TDS.

He was wearing a light grey silk woven suit with crisp white shirt and navy tie, which seemed to bring out the shots of deep violet that streaked his irises.

"Miss Holmes," he greeted me, before shaking my father's hand. "So, let's get to business."

He pulled several spread sheets from his briefcase, all of which forced me to stifle a yawn. "Are you sure you need me?" I complained, desperate for another round of painkillers.

"If you're not up to it, darling…" my father fussed, but didn't finish the sentence.

"Sorry," I apologized meekly. "I thought I was feeling better." I felt like I should curtsy before leaving TDS, but settled for a crooked smile and went to fetch the drugs.

I was in the living room, channel-hopping and wrapped under the lilac cashmere, when TDS strode in with meaning. "Miss Holmes," he nodded. "I'd really like to discuss these plans with you."

I threw a look of contempt up at him. "And I'm really not feeling very well."

"You look much better than you did yesterday." Was he seriously trying to say that I was feigning my illness? Of all the arrogant⸺ "But I understand. Why don't we discuss it over dinner, say, Friday night?"

My eyes narrowed at the request. Here I was in all my un-glory, and TDS loomed over me, asking me out on a date.

"Fine," I yielded grudgingly. "Eight?"

"Seven," he ordered. I suspect if I'd said seven, he would have said eight to get his own way. I nodded, and let my stare move back to the flickering screen.

Chapter Six

Thursday was pretty much a non-event, apart from a phone call from Greg, who was excited about this project on the Evo. It was going to make him lots of money, Matt Jackson had more of it than sense, and he was looking forward to me coming back and drawing up the contracts. Yeah, yeah, yeah.

Friday, and I really was feeling much better. The virus was clearing away, swept out by the fresh air and fussing from my clucking hen of a mother. I packed my suitcase and asked Hannah to take Georgia back to the farmhouse. A panicked phone call from Mark assured me that Sophie had indeed moved everything to where she thought it should belong, as opposed to where it actually did.

"Are you sure you should be going back?" My mother, ever the worrywart, tried in vain to smother me in cotton wool and bubble wrap.

"Positive, Mum." I kissed her cheek reassuringly. "Mr. Ellery is picking me up at seven, and I thought I'd ask him to take me straight back to the farmhouse. I'll come and get my bags tomorrow. Just so you can see that I'm still alive," I added.

"I can't help but care."

"I know, I know. But I am twenty-six."

"I'm not sure I like you having a meal with Mr. Ellery either."

"It's a business dinner, Mum. It's not a date. Trust me, I have no intention of doing anything other than eating a nice meal, paid for by him."

"Okay." She placed her lips against my cheeks.

My mother, Elizabeth Holmes, or Lizzie to her close friends, was beautiful in every sense of the word. It was from her that both Mark and I got our hair- coloring from. She had a deep green gaze that neither of us had inherited, and a smooth oval complexion. I had her face shape and milky skin, whereas Mark had taken our father's square and tanned look. He also had Dad's chestnut eyes, while mine had been a mixture and come out boringly hazel.

At seven o'clock, I was dressed in an elegant and simple black dress that stopped halfway down my thighs and was ruffled going over my hips and bust. The hem that lined my chest was decorated with large crystals, emphasizing the sparkle and glitter of my lip gloss. I'd swept my hair into a crocodile clip, letting it spill over the top like a brunette fountain, and wore a thin black shrug, large silver hooped earrings, and a dainty necklace with a diamond heart pendant.

I'd managed to carefully cover the scars using concealer and foundation, filling the gap in my eyebrow using a pencil. To the outside world, I was unmarred.

"You look as beautiful as your mother." TDS smiled, although I knew the compliment was aimed at her, not me. "I've booked a table at Matieus."

I was impressed. Matieus was a relatively new, but ridiculously expensive restaurant where prices were not deemed necessary for the menu. If you had to ask, you couldn't afford it. Mum and Dad dined there regularly.

As I stepped out into the warm summer- evening air, TDS opened the Jag's door for me. "Chivalry isn't entirely out of your repertoire then?" If he thought I was going to let his comments from less than a week ago slide, he was in for a long night.

He climbed in beside my slightly nervous frame and turned to face me. I took him in: his sight, his scent, his aura.

He was dressed in black trousers that matched his look perfectly, with a dark blue shirt opened at the top button. Almost casual, yet still smart, with a pair of patent black oxfords finishing the look. His too-long hair was styled into the same waves I'd noticed on Saturday.

Breathing deeply, I could almost taste the sandalwood and musk from his aftershave, with an underlying note of citrus fruits, maybe from a body wash. A sudden rush of electricity shocked my core. My thighs instinctively tightened.

"We should start again," he purred. His voice was so smooth, it could have been made from chocolate. As clichéd as that sounds, it's true. He reached out and placed a firm hand over mine, which clutched at the handbag as though my life depended on it. "I would first like to apologize for my behavior when we first met." Well, that will do for starters. "My name is Vance Ellery," he re-introduced himself.

I stayed rigid beneath his touch. "Paige Holmes," I managed to say, despite my dry mouth.

"Nice to meet you, Miss Holmes. I have to say, you are nothing like your first impression."

"What's that supposed to mean?" I snapped harshly, whipping my hand away as though he were about to abuse it.

"I've never met a woman who enjoys the rougher games." There was a tone underlying his words, one I did not appreciate. I edged away towards the door. He chuckled. "I apologize. That didn't come out the way I meant it to sound."

"Really," I chuntered, turning away from him.

"My daughter plays hockey," he started, and the sudden image of that frail young blonde by his side shot from the recess of my memory. "But that's as rough and tumble as she gets. She plays it to appease her brother, I think."

"You have a son?" I heard myself asking.

"Yes, it's his restaurant we're going to."

"Oh!" I snapped my head around to meet his burning gaze. "But you're not married."

"No. Divorced."

Relief swept through me. I didn't appreciate the idea of being taken to dinner by a married man. Even if it was a business meal.

The car pulled up outside Matieus, and TDS stepped out to open my door for me. I thanked him and began to walk towards the door. He caught up with me in two strides, gripping his hand around my elbow. Even with my six-inch killer heels, he still towered over me.

As we found the entrance, a waiter resembling a penguin waddled over and greeted him by name, instantly whisking us to the most intimate corner of the room. The table could have fitted six or seven people around it, but it was laid only with two places. TDS sat next to me. He rudely clicked his fingers and ordered a bottle of wine.

"Oh, I'm not sure I should." I tried to decline, but he was having none of it, insisting I try at least one glass.

"So, the sports hall…" I spoke up, loudly, trying to shift the air of tension that seemed to hang around us.

"Do you honestly think I brought you here to discuss sports?"

" "Yes." I swallowed a large mouthful of the wine. Boy, it was good. Crisp, fruity, and dry. If I'd been a connoisseur, which I'm not, I would have guessed elderflower, sloe, and raspberry undertones.

The air between us tightened, disturbing my wine-tasting ideals. "Well, it's not." His voice became deep and almost threatening. My fist clenched around the stem of the glass as I sipped at the cool liquid again.

"This is good," I responded, trying to change the subject.

"Paige." As he said my name for the first time, I felt my pelvis weigh down. A surge of heat ran to my most feminine parts. I liked hearing him use my name, I realized. He looked at me, gripping a finger under my chin, forcing me to return the gaze. "Since you landed at my feet, I've wanted to see you again."

"And yet you were so callous," I mocked

"I've apologized. I wasn't expecting…" He stopped, pausing as though searching for the word. "That." His dark, groomed eyebrow flickered. Letting go of my chin, he ran a hand through his silver-streaked locks, reminding me that he was old enough to be my father. But that didn't stop the heat that pulsated in my veins.

"What?" I pushed, wanting to hear his voice, wanting to feel his breath against my skin. Mark was right, I needed a good fucking.

"I don't know." His shoulders relaxed with a heavy sigh, leaving me confused. "As soon as you landed at my feet, looking up at me with those big brown eyes, I knew I wanted to fuck you."

Shocked, I nearly choked on my wine to hear such a harsh word leave his luscious lips. Lips that I wanted to kiss, hard.

"It's no coincidence that I'm working with your father on this project. But I wasn't sure how else I was going to get close to you."

"How did you even know who I was?"

"I have my ways."

"And now you sound like a stalker." I finished my glass, watching the liquid empty from the bowl, refusing to look at him.

The waiter arrived with the menu, but TDS waved him away. "I'm not sure I'm hungry for food," he growled.

"Well, I am." I grabbed at a menu and opened it.

"Paige."

"No, Mr. Ellery." I came over all formal, refusing to give into those primal urges that screamed in my brain, and between my legs. "You wanted to discuss sports, we're discussing sports. Unless, of course, you want a physical demonstration of what I've learnt during the past year I've been practicing mixed martial arts."

I shot him a look, which he instantly understood. He took the other menu before the waiter scuttled back into the kitchen. I wasn't about to give into his power games, but if he wanted to play, I would sure as hell give him a run for his money.

We ordered steak, although he did have the gall to ask if I would prefer a salad. "Steak, rare, with plenty of garlic butter," I demanded to spite him. "With thick cut chips, side salad, and garlic bread," I added, handing back the menu. "I wasn't even aware that such dishes existed in haute cuisine," I said, with a smile sharp enough to slice him to the core.

"You'd be surprised what they can cook up when asked." His voice was brimming with an emotion I couldn't place. Anger, perhaps? I decided to dismiss it.

When the dish arrived, it was haute cuisine despite my queries. The steak had been shaped with a fluted cutter, piled high and decorated with wisps of something long, thin, and green. Beside it were three dots of garlic butter, two thick cut chips, and a curl of peppery rocket. I raised an eyebrow. For too long had I been living off pub lunches and takeout.

But nevertheless, I sliced into the bloody meat and bit into it, savoring the delicious metallic taste. "Good steak," I said, chewing to one side. He looked disgusted at my obvious lack of manners, and I felt pleased by this. "So your son owns this place then." I decided to be at my most ill-mannered. Mark would have been proud.

"Yes, he does." He sounded repulsed, and my subconscious laughed haughtily.

"And what are your plans for the pavilion?" Less of the small talk, and down to business.

"Well, I..." he stumbled over the words. The inner laugh grew louder.

"Mr. Ellery, are you unprepared?" I asked, my head cocked to one side as I took a final bite of my steak.

He beckoned over for the waiter and whispered something to him before turning back to me. "I think it's time I take you home."

And I win! TDS succumbs to my bad nature. My subconscious laugh became evil and sadistic.

The car pulled up and I thought he might actually push me in rather than be as genteel as he was earlier. Before I'd even managed to adjust myself, his lips were on mine, his tongue hungrily parting my lips. His hands whipped into my hair, pulling me further into him. I should have fought him, or at least tried, but I found myself kissing him back.

I opened my mouth, inviting him further, as his hand slipped down to the small of my back. I leant into him, my own hands reaching around the back of his neck, fingering the tendrils of hair that reached over his collar.

"You are infuriating," he growled with such sexual awareness.

"And you are an arrogant fuckwit." I wriggled out of his grip. "How dare you come to my parents' home and use my father to get me into your bed. I wouldn't fuck you if my life depended on it." My voice grew louder, but the driver continued to act as though he were deaf.

"Yes, you would. And you will," he promised.

"Only in your dreams. You're old enough to be my father," I retorted with a snort of disgust.

"Perhaps that is precisely what you need," he countered. Still recovering, I couldn't think of a comeback, so kept my lips tightly pursed. The corner of his lips flicked into a sly grin. His hand moved over mine. It was warm, and sent a shot through me, hitting the pit of my stomach with such force I thought I might die.

"Next time, Paige," he simpered, as the car stopped outside the farmhouse.

"Not on your life," I snapped, heading into the safe confinements of my own territory.

Chapter Seven

"So how'd it go?" Danny asked, as I marched past the living room door.

"Fucking bastard, fucking twat!" I spewed as many obscenities that my brain could conjure up.

"That good," Mark joined in.

"Oh, Mark, he is a complete… See. You. Next. Tuesday." I spat the words out, as they left a distinct pungent taste in my mouth.

"Whoa." Danny threw his hands in mock defense, a look of shock twisting across his face, distorting his wide jaw. "You hate that word."

"Yeah, well, that's how mad he's made me." I twisted on my heel and stormed into the lounge, collapsing on the cream sofa. I hadn't even noticed how clean, sparkly, and tidy the house looked.

"Vance Ellery lives up to his infamy," Mark laughed.

"What's that supposed to mean?" I shot the words across the room with such vehemence that I may as well have been pissed off with him.

"Don't tell me you haven't done your research! Mum sure has. She rang me in tears earlier, really didn't want you to go out with him."

"What?" My brow furrowed, and my cheekbones rose so much that my eyes practically disappeared.

"Vance Ellery," he shook a magazine open and read from the pages, "known for his womanizing ways, has been spied with high-fashion model Eloise Dangers draped over his arm at the restaurant Matieus. If you want a table at Matieus, you'll have to join the year-long waiting list, but not if you happen to be the owner's father."

This, I already knew, although thought the "year-long waiting list" was a slight exaggeration. A couple of weeks, perhaps, but certainly not a year.

"But how would you feel about allowing your father to eat in your establishment with your current girlfriend? Mr. Ellery's son was unavailable for comment."

"Chauvinistic, two-timing, son of a whore!" I screeched, grabbing the magazine and letting my glare burn through the glossy paper. Mark and Danny both laughed in unison. "Oh, fuck off," I spat, jumping up to my feet. I kicked off the heels before they snapped, and stomped loudly up to my room, fuming with envy and hate.

I lay on my bed, looking up at the same spot on the ceiling that I always stared at when thoroughly pissed off. How dare he! He accused me of humiliating him, but the truth was he saw me as yet another floozy to use and abuse. Worse still, he was going through my parents to do it!

I hated him for his violent torment of my emotions. I hated myself even more for letting him sink so deep into my core. I'd shared less than a few words with him, yet there was something, more powerful than I could describe, pulling me towards him.

Salt-filled tears glistened at the corners of my eyes.

41

"It's because he reminds you of him." Mark's voice came from the doorway. I rolled over and spied my guardian angel casting a look of concern over my wretched body.

"Is it? He doesn't look anything like him."

"He has that power, that pull. It's obvious. Mum can see it too. That's why she's scared for you."

I rolled away from the agonizing memories that threatened to break the barriers I'd spent so long building up.

"Stay away from him, Butch." Mark bent down and kissed my head, sending me into a rolling slumber where I dreamed of better things.

Saturday morning started with a phone call from Mother. "I was so worried about you," she cried in fits and sobs.

"Oh, for goodness sakes, Mum, it was only dinner. I'll be over later to pick up my bag and get Georgia sent back." Seriously, this woman needed therapy. "I'll tell all then!" I promised, although what I told her would be a spate of lies to steady her.

As I pulled up in my Golf, I could see a familiar black car at the front, directly by the stone steps. Instantly I knew TDS would be behind the doors.

Mother threw a worried glance towards the study door. Sweeping an arm under hers, I led her to the kitchen and made us both a cup of tea. "Honestly, Mum, nothing happened." Although it was true, I sensed that she could read the underlying falseness of it all. "We ate, I went home. We talked about sport and his family, nothing else."

"He's bad news, Paige," she muttered, her shoulders trembling.

"Then why do you let him in the house?"

"Your father insists I'm being silly. Mr. Ellery has a lot of money and a lot of sway."

"Mum," I elongated the word, sitting down beside her. "Less than a week ago you were happy for them to do business, and were even encouraging me to get involved. What's changed?"

"You read things in magazines, and when you're a mother, you can sense them too."

"Oh, for God's sake, not this again," I groaned, rubbing my hands over my face. I'd heard it all before. Prospective boyfriends would be welcomed with open arms, but no sooner had they introduced themselves that Mum "sensed" they were no good and rushed them out the door.

I took her white knuckles in my hands and rubbed them with my palms.

"I'm fine, Paige," she scolded. "I'm worried about you." Her dark green eyes searched me, tracing over my entire face. "It's only been a year since…" and she stopped. She couldn't say the words any more than I could.

"And I'm fine." I wasn't, but you don't tell your mother that you still wake up in cold sweats, that you can't bear to see your own naked reflection, or that you still need the safety and strength of living in a masculine world.

"Look, I promised Greg I'd stop in and do a bit of paperwork since I've been off all week." I planted a firm kiss on her cheek. "He's nothing like him." I forced a smile. "He's just a very wealthy arsehole. A bit like a rash; itch at it and it'll get worse. Ignore him and he'll eventually go away."

"He's only here for a couple of months." My mother smiled back. I wasn't quite sure who she was trying to reassure.

"Precisely. Ask Hannah to drive Georgia back. I need the ride." I called good-bye to my father as I walked past the study door, but didn't wait for the response.

Throwing my suitcase into the boot of my Golf, I drove towards Bertin Body Shop. I enjoyed working on Saturdays when it was quiet, but glancing at my ticking watch, I felt I should show my face at the rugby pitch. Even if I had no intention of playing today, I should at least show my girls some support.

"Oh, hey, you didn't really have to come." Greg stood at the threshold that separated his office from the space I called mine.

"Yes, I did. I've got so much to catch up on."

"Are you feeling better?"

"Much, thanks. How's it been?"

"Busy. Just remember to take it easy." He stepped sideways, and out walked Matt Jackson.

"Oh, hello." I was a little bit surprised that Greg would work on a project at the weekend. He must be putting up a lot of money.

"Hi, Paige," he smiled, and I couldn't help but feeling warm at the fact that he remembered my name.

"I've drawn up the designs, Paige, if you wouldn't mind filing them." Greg took Matt's hand and shook it firmly before turning back to me. "Any changes Mr. Jackson wants to make…" His voice trailed as he slid back into his office.

My glare tapered in confusion. He didn't usually involve me in such things, I was simply a glorified secretary-cum-saleswoman. "Take a seat." I took the bait and unrolled the designs. "Wow." I gaped at the extravagant display of colors and sweeping lines that took over the page. "This is going to be fabulous!" I couldn't help but show my excitement for the possibilities.

"Isn't it?" Mr. Jackson looked equally pleased. "Your boss is a very talented artist."

"Hmm. Pity he doesn't believe me when I tell him that. Have you seen his prints? No, of course, you haven't. Nobody has."

"You know, I'm actually looking for some new artwork. Perhaps you could show me?"

"Oh, I couldn't. I've seen his sketches, and that's his," I pointed to the painting on the side wall, "but other than that, I don't know where he keeps any of it."

"Such a shame. What about you? Do you paint?"

I laughed. "The most I can draw is a stickman. I'm afraid I'm too athletic to be artistic." I shot a worried look at my watch. "Which reminds me, I'm really sorry, but I've got a rugby match at one."

"You play rugby?"

"Yes, well, I play at playing rugby. Nothing serious, I just like the exercise."

"I play too."

"Really? You should come watch." As soon as the words left my mouth, I felt like scrambling to push them back in, but it was too late. They were out there for all and sundry to see.

"I'd like that," he replied. Damn it. Too late to backpedal now!

I stood up, brushing down my jeans and grabbing my handbag. "Would you like a lift?" Seriously? Will I ever be able to control this gob of mine?

"That would be great."

We climbed into the Golf and I drove at a steady speed, much slower than my usual rush, towards the fields. When we got there, Lou was already there, ready and dressed, clutching the Gilbert ball in the crook of her elbow. "Didn't think you were coming!"

"I wasn't going to; still feeling a bit rough," I called back, reaching into the back of my car, tugging out my holdall. I smiled towards Mr. Jackson before chasing over to the changing rooms.

When I came out, wearing navy shorts and a matching rugby shirt, I could see that Mr. Jackson was quite clearly standing on the sidelines in a familiar spot. When I first caught sight of him, I felt my heart stop in the same way it had a week earlier. Tall, elegantly poised, and dressed in jeans, an open-necked shirt, and work shoes... I swallowed hard and tried to shake the imagery my mind conjured. Flashbacks of the past week shot to the forefront of my mind.

Closing my eyes tightly, I chanted my mantra of breathing instructions. "In through the nose, out through the mouth. In with the good, out with the bad." Once my heart re-started, I jogged onto the field and grabbed at the ball before throwing myself full-swing into the practice match.

I was enjoying the rush of adrenaline, smell of pheromones, sweat, and mud, and feeling content when the elbow connected with my jaw. All I saw was a blur of white and navy blue before Jasmine, our best hooker, plowed into me.

The ground beneath us slipped away, despite the lack of rain. I fell sideways, my knees collapsing underneath me as though they were made of tissue paper. The rock- solid angle of her elbow jabbed into the corner of my jaw.

I heard the skin splitting and the bone crunching before I felt it. The loud sound of clicking and blood pumping echoed in my ears. I landed with a thud. My face pressed into the muck. I tried to inhale, instead getting a taste of blood and torn grass. I tried to stand, but there was something on top of me. No, someone. The girls had piled onto me, not realizing what had happened. Pain seared through the line of scar tissue that already traced my chin.

I let go of the ball, feeling someone grab at my fingers, my shirt, and my thighs. Fingers grasping all around me. Legs burrowing into my ribs. I screamed.

Suddenly, the pressure released from my lungs and I gasped for air. I took in hungry mouthfuls of precious, sweet oxygen.

"Jesus Christ, are you okay?" I heard a man calling to me, as I tried to push myself up to standing. But I was still weak from the virus. I tried to open my eyes, and that was when I realized it wasn't only my jaw that was bleeding.

The feeling of sticky warmth dripped over my lids, closing them together. I rubbed at them, but my fingers throbbed. "Fuck!" I yelled, shaking my hands violently.

"Shit, Paige, I'm so sorry." That voice, I recognized. Jasmine reached out and grabbed my arm, yanking me to standing.

"No biggie." I shook my head. Hair stuck to my brow and jaw. "Just another scar." I tried to laugh, but my chest hurt. I could already feel the skin bruising.

"You should stop," said the male voice again.

"Yeah, he's right." Lou this time. I still couldn't see clearly, although I knew my eyes were open. Light fought to break through the fog. "Hit the shower." She clapped a hand on my back, forcing me to cough and splutter a mouthful of blood. The iron taste flooded my senses. It was overpowering. I nodded, knowing I'd had enough for the day.

"Here, let me." I felt a hand take my arm, but it was too big to be one of the girls. I peered through the blood and mud and saw a friendly face. Mr. Jackson helped me until I was steady before walking with me towards the pavilion.

Chapter Eight

I didn't rush the shower. I embraced the warmth of the water, the strength of the jettisoning stream. Leaning with my hands against the cold tiles, my head hung towards the ground, I let the powerful surge beat away the taut muscles and congealing blood.

Once I felt clean, I walked, naked, back into the female changing room. "Shit!" I yelped, grabbing for a towel as I realized that Mr. Jackson was still there.

He'd helped me, unnecessarily, I should point out, all the way to the lockers. I thought he'd left after that, but he'd stayed. Had he seen me showering? Had he watched? Suddenly, I felt highly vulnerable.

"Sorry," he mumbled, his cheeks burning almost fluorescent. "I needed to make sure that you were okay."

"I'm fine," I snapped. "I've had worse." I pulled the towel tightly around my bust with one hand, while the other shot down to cover the scar I hated so much.

"I'm not sure I'm happy to hear that." It was an attempt at a joke, to lighten the mood.

"Sorry." I shook my bad manners and ingratitude. "Thank you." Lifting my hands, I wrung the water out of my hair over the tiled floor. "Excuse me." I pushed past him to reach into my locker, pulling out my underwear. I turned my back to him, wishing that he'd leave me to dress.

"I should…" He pointed over his shoulder towards the door.

"Yeah, you should." I waited until he'd left before dressing and readjusting myself.

Staring at the reflection in the mirror, I examined the wounds. There was nothing truly new, just old wounds re-opened. Wasn't that how I'd felt the night before? Re-opened? The irony was not lost on me.

I sucked on my front teeth. At least the bleeding in my mouth had stopped. Reaching for the first aid kit we kept by the mirrors, I emptied its contents onto the side, taking the Steri-Strips and lining them over the cuts.

I threw a wave towards the girls who were still playing on the field as I left, hoisting my bag up over my shoulder.

"Glad to see you're okay."

I jumped at the sound of his voice. "Jeez. I wasn't expecting you to stay," I laughed.

"I had to check you were still in one piece. You should get those checked."

"Nah." I waved him off. "Like I said, I've had worse."

"At least let me drive you home. You've had a knock to the head. You could be concussed."

"I've spent the week fighting flu. This is nothing."

"Then I'm definitely driving."

"Thank you." I smiled and handed him my keys. I was definitely concussed. I do not normally go about giving my car keys and address to handsome strangers.

He drove with undisturbed caution, winding down the streets of Brookfield, navigating his way, with my vague directions, towards the farmhouse. I kept my eyes closed, fighting the waves of nausea that ebbed over me with every bend in the road.

"I'm not usually this pathetic," I tried to speak, but the words got caught in my throat.

"Nearly there." His voice was a gentle lull.

The car rolled slowly to a stop. My eyes remained closed until I heard the creaking of my door being opened. Looking up, he stood with the light casting a golden halo around his dark hair. His hands reached down to me, gripping around my bicep as I pushed myself out of the deep seat.

I fell through the front door, stumbling over my own feet. My head was swimming, but my body was drowning.

"What the hell happened?" Mark's voice ripped through the humidity and tension.

"I'm fine," I shushed at him, as my skull tightened and my temples throbbed.

"She got caught underneath a ruck," Mr. Jackson explained.

"And you are?" Danny had joined us in the kitchen and sounded far more protective than he needed to be.

"Matthew Jackson. I was watching the match."

"Thank you, Mr. Jackson," I murmured through the saliva that seemed to fill my mouth.

49

"Matt, please." He bent down at my knees and looked up at me from under thick, long lashes. "You really should go to the hospital."

"I've had…"

"Worse, I know," he said with a chuckle before standing up.

"Mark, Danny, this is Mr. Jackson. Mr. Jackson, my brother, Mark, and housemate, Danny." I attempted to make introductions, blinking against the pain. With my hands firmly planted on the table, I stood and shook away the trembling that rippled through my shoulders and hands.

"Sit," ordered Danny, pointing at the chair.

"Fuck off," I threw back at him. "Shit, my bag."

"It's in the car." Mr. Jackson walked out of the kitchen. I knew he had my keys because I heard the jangle of several key rings.

"Who is he?" Mark asked. If I hadn't known otherwise, I would have sworn he was attracted to Mr. Jackson, which I couldn't have blamed him for. Matt Jackson was indeed a fine specimen of man, and could easily have been found plastered on posters advertising underwear or aftershave.

"He's a client from work," I explained, reaching for the painkillers that we kept in a drawer by the microwave. "My head is killing me!"

"I'm not surprised. You look like you've lasted five rounds with Mike Tyson."

"Except you still have ears," Danny added. I narrowed my eyes and threw him a "ha-ha" smile.

"Seriously, I'm fine. I just got knocked around and then this bloody virus has left me feeling weak as a kitten."

"I think a kitten could kick your arse right now. Sit." Danny forced me into a chair and knelt by me to inspect my wounds. "Well, at least you're used to stitching yourself together."

The door thumped opened as Mr. Jackson returned with my holdall.

"Oh, thank you ever so much. I don't know how to repay you." I grimaced through the pain that had now dulled to a throb.

"You could convince your boss to give me a discount." He winked. My scarred eyebrow automatically began to rise, and fell as quickly as the Steri-Strips pulled at the hairs and skin. I winced against the stinging tug. He stifled a laugh, but failed to stop the smile from leaping to his kissable lips. "Honestly, there's no need. I'm glad you're home safe. I'm sure I'll see you next week."

"Oh, how will you get home?" I stepped forward, suddenly realizing that we had driven in my car, leaving his at the garage.

"I was about to go to the pub for a late lunch. I have some business to attend to, and I'll get a taxi from there."

I nodded, and walked to the door with him. "Well, thank you again." Closing the door behind him, I found myself ambling into the living room and falling into one of the sofas, kicking my aching calves up onto my brother's lap.

The boys were back to watching some low league football match. I joined them, my eyes following the white ball as it was passed from player to player, but never reaching the goal lines. Wriggling down, I pushed my legs into Mark's hands. "A massage would be nice," I grumbled.

"What about Mr. Jackson? I'm sure he's good with his hands," he protested, but still ran his hands under my jeans and gripped at the aching muscles, pushing away the rigid knots that had begun to form.

"He is cute, isn't he? But he would never be interested in me. Men like him never are."

"God, you're blind."

Danny cursed as the ball was finally shot into the back of the net, but at the wrong end of the pitch. He reached for his bottle of beer and took a long swig. The cool liquid looked inviting, but I could never stand the taste of beer.

"I wish you were right," I sighed, closing my eyes. My head hit the cushioned arm of the sofa, instantly enveloped by the plump softness. "It's been a year since anyone showed me any serious interest." And with good reason.

"What about your TDS?"

"Him." I emphasized the word with vehemence and disgust. "He can go straight to hell and stay there."

Mark chortled as he pushed my legs down. "You're done."

"Thank you." I sat up and tucked my massaged legs underneath me. I faced the television and tried to concentrate on the game, but failed miserably. My head was still sore, and now filled with the thoughts of TDS and Mr. Jackson merging together. I was in for some seriously fucked-up dreams.

I spent most of Sunday in bed, nursing the purple and yellow that now patterned my ribs, back, and legs. My right eye had swollen and looked ferociously red, but at least it hadn't closed like the last time. Mark rang Holmes Manor, and Hannah agreed to help with Georgia for a while, until I was healed.

By Monday I was feeling much better and headed into work, ready for the comments about how bad the other guy must look.

Sitting at my desk, I gulped down two ibuprofen with a cold swig of water from the bottle that sat by the keyboard.

"Shit, what happened to you?" Greg exclaimed, handing me a thick pile of invoices.

"Rugby," I stated firmly, not wanting to go into any more detail in case he managed to eke it out of me that I hadn't been alone. The last thing I needed was my boss realizing my attraction to his new client.

"No sympathy then. Can you get those posted out today, please? Oh, and give Matt Jackson a ring. I have his quote ready, but I'd like to finalize a few details before I send it out."

I nodded, not really wanting to speak to him. But since I couldn't think of a decent excuse, I chewed on my bottom lip and waited for him to answer the phone. I praised God when the answer machine clicked and whirred into action, leaving a brief message for him to contact Greg.

Sitting back with my morning cup of tea, a buzz in my handbag alerted me to a text message. It was from Mark, reminding me that I still hadn't tried on the dress, and he needed to know it fitted since the ball was this Saturday. I cursed myself under my breath.

I hadn't told Mum about my new appearance, and wasn't sure that red, purple, and yellow would coordinate with the blue-green satin that Mark had picked out for me. Still, I had a few days to recover.

I decided to forego the MMA lessons that night, thinking with my current injuries I'd probably be sent home anyway, opting for a hot bath instead. The dress, of course, fitted perfectly and looked fabulous, despite the person wearing it. I was going to need some serious camouflage makeup.

Sitting down on the bed, admiring my reflection for once, I heard the phone ring. Danny sounded angry when he answered, but I couldn't make out what he was saying. My bedroom door slammed open, smacking against the wooden bedside table.

"Jesus, Danny!" I jumped, clutching at my chest as though I had narrowly avoided a heart attack.

"Your TDS is on the phone. He wants to talk to you," he snapped, thrusting the receiver towards me. "By the way, you look gorgeous."

I smiled at his compliment. Danny never complimented me.

With a deep breath, I lifted the phone to my ear. "Hello?"

"Paige, it's Vance Ellery."

"Hello, Mr. Ellery, how can I help?" I tried to sound nonchalant, but my voice was brimming with anger.

"I wanted to apologize for the way I acted."

"And you decided to wait a week to tell me this?"

"I thought we needed to make sure the air was clear."

"What can I do for you, Mr. Ellery?"

"I'd like you to be my guest at your father's soiree."

"No." I was blunt, to the point, and proud of myself for not faltering at the sound of his lusciously sexual tones.

"Miss Holmes," he growled. "You are certainly challenging."

"It's not a challenge. It's a rebuff." I was about to hang up on him, but something made me hesitate. Jeez! Even his voice had a magnetism about it that I couldn't fight.

"Miss Holmes, I would be honored if you would join me at the Brookfield Summer Ball." Now he was being formal. It made me furious, but something about him was incredibly difficult to resist.

"Fine," I relented. "But it is not a date. I am arriving with you, and I will be leaving alone."

I heard him chuckle as though he were placating me. "I will pick you up at six."

"I'll be ready at seven."

Chapter Nine

I managed to avoid Mr. Jackson over the next week, since he arrived when I was either on my break or at lunch picking up the orders. I even managed to hit the gym several times, although my personal trainer did warn me about overdoing it and insisted I stick to simple exercises until my ribs were fully healed. So when Saturday finally arrived, I was actually in quite a good mood and looking forward to the ball. I had almost forgotten who would be accompanying me. Or more to the point, who I would be accompanying.

Standing in my bedroom, facing the mirror, wearing nothing but a black thong, I traced my finger across the red line that ran from my hip. Unlike my other scars, this would never fade. My shoulders sagged under the invisible weights as I fought the memories.

"He'll be here soon." My big brother's voice appeared from the doorway. Instinctively I reached my arm across my breasts and stomach to cover what little dignity I still possessed.

"Go away." I kicked out at the door.

"Call me when you want your hair done," he said from behind the wood as it closed inches away from him.

The turquoise dress clung to my bust and hips, accentuating my natural curves. I pulled on the sandals and hoped that my painful ankles would hold up long enough for me to walk from door to door.

My eyes moved over the dressing table, searching for the colored concealers. It was like painting by numbers, using greens to cover the red swelling, lilac to hide the blue bruises, and beiges to even out my overall skin tone. I looked ghoulish before the thick layer of foundation was applied.

Teetering on the heels, I moved cautiously down each step, clutching at the wooden banister to steady myself. At the bottom, Mark and Danny were smartly dressed in black and white dinner jackets, and I couldn't help but notice how handsome they both looked.

"Heartbreakers," I teased, flicking my head towards my brother. "Chignon, please."

With dexterous fingers, Mark had clipped my hair into place in seconds.

"Is he here yet?" I asked, peering over the kitchen sink towards the end of the drive.

"You sound almost eager." Danny grabbed my clutch bag and handed it to me before placing a kiss on my cheek. "And you look sexy as hell."

"You don't look so bad yourself."

"I know." He grinned widely, destroying that air of elegance and grace, and replacing it with cockiness. "Hopefully there'll be some tall blonde model in need of a shoulder to cry on." His elbow nudged into Mark's ribs, who coughed and rubbed the sore spot.

"Hopefully she'll have a sister," my brother added.

"Boys." I rolled my eyes.

"Well, we'll see ya there." Mark planted a kiss on my forehead and ducked out of the doorway, shortly followed by Danny. I watched as they both sauntered down the drive, elbowing and jibing each other, ruining the appearance of suave sophistication. It was like watching a pair of teenagers headed to the end-of-year prom.

I glanced at the clock. It was six-thirty. I'd got ready early, despite telling TDS that I wouldn't be ready before seven. I couldn't be sure if he'd arrive at the time he'd stated, or I had.

At six-forty-five, a long black limo pulled up and a well-dressed chauffeur stepped out, walking towards me. I walked into the wall of summer evening heat, and wondered if the wooziness was because of the humidity or the bruising that hid behind my thick layer of makeup.

"Miss Holmes." The driver took my elbow and led me towards the car after I turned to lock the front door.

The sun was still awake, but had started its decent into the thin horizon beyond the trees that encompassed the village. A bright orange light hit my eyes, causing me to shield myself against the burning glare as I bent towards the backseat of the car.

As the sunspots dissipated, I saw him - TDS in his all his magnificence.

He was dressed in an expensive dinner jacket, with jet black waistcoat and bow tie. His silver-streaked hair had been slicked back, revealing more nut-brown than aging grey. In the dim light that dotted around the car, his eyes looked as dark as his suit.

"Thank you." I forced a smile as he handed me a glass of English sparkling wine, a single strawberry lying in the bottom of the fluted bowl.

"You look divine," he purred. "I would once again like to apologize for my behavior last week."

"So you should." I sidled closer to the door, wanting to put as much distance between us as I could.

"That looks painful." He pointed towards the cut above my eye.

"You should see the other guy," I said, echoing the comments I'd received from work. He chortled, and it was a delicious sound that sent waves of electricity coursing through me.

"Thank you for giving me a second chance." He moved closer, gripping his own glass of bubbly. I threw my head back and downed the drink in one gulp, thrusting the glass in his direction. He smiled at my ill manners as though amused by the contempt I held for him. "I'm looking forward to this evening."

Shifting in his seat, his knees moved to point towards the front of the car, his eyes following and looking straight ahead. My shoulders and chest relaxed, as I breathed heavy with relief. They tensed when he shot a look at me, his eyes glistening in the sparkling light. "It should be an event to remember."

I was grateful when the car stopped outside my parents' house. Stepping onto the gravel, the sound of wheels crunching at the small pebbles mixed with the soft string music that sang and danced from behind the house, creating an expensive ambience of elegance and grace.

The sun had dipped behind the line of trees by the time we found ourselves underneath the white marquee, drinking imported champagne and nibbling on thin slithers of toast topped with crème fraîche and caviar.

The chatter of finance and charity filled the air, until my mother's call flew over the crowd. "Paige, darling!" She waltzed towards us, arms open wide, but she threw a look of disapproval towards TDS, as he sauntered to mingle with the crowd. "I'm so glad you could make it. When Mark and

Danny arrived without you, I was so worried. What on earth has happened to your beautiful face?" She cupped my chin and examined the wounds.

"Please, Mum." I shuffled out of her grip. "Don't make a fuss. It's nothing. I fell at rugby last week. I'm fine. Don't cause a scene."

"Elizabeth, let the poor girl breathe." My father arrived to rescue me from Mum's vice-like fingers. "I hope you had them looked at," he added.

"She wouldn't let me take her to the doctor's." A voice I recognized came from behind me. Swiveling around on a thin stiletto, I came to face Mr. Jackson. I tried to hide the gasp, which sort of turned into a choke.

"You were there, Mr. Jackson?" I thought my mother was about to reprimand him, but she seemed to stop herself.

"Hi, what are you doing here?" I asked.

"Oh, my father, he insisted," he waved a hand towards the crowd of people. "He likes me to make an appearance at these functions."

"You two must talk more." Mother ushered us away as though we were annoying birds, trying to steal her seeds. "Perhaps he'll distract you from Mr. Ellery," she whispered in my ear as we left.

"Sorry about her." I pursed my lips together tightly.

"Mothers are always over-protective. Mine's just as bad."

"Is she here?" I looked over the blurring faces of people.

"No, she lives in France."

"But your father…"

"Oh, he lives wherever the money is."

I nodded as though I understood, but to be truthful, I was confused. TDS caught my eye as he talked to the blonde I now knew to be his daughter. His thick brows knitted into the bridge of his nose, so I tossed him a smile to let him know that I hadn't forgotten him.

"I really should," I said, gesturing towards the gathering, "mingle."

"Yes," he laughed. "I know what it's like. But please, save me a dance."

"I will. Thank you, again, for the other day."

"I take it you're feeling better?"

"Much!" I called back to him as I wandered back to find TDS.

Reaching his side, I couldn't help but let my gaze fall over Mr. Jackson. He was so kind and warm, and genuine, not at all like the intense TDS, who was now talking to Philip Branning, a member of the local parliament, about something tedious and financially related.

I struggled to hide my boredom, lifting the back of my hand to cover a stifled yawn.

"Can I discuss something with you?" TDS moved a hand to the small of my back, leading me away from the party.

"And I was just beginning to enjoy myself."

"We got off on the wrong foot, and I intend to rectify that." He circled me around to a more private, secluded area of the garden. It was blanketed in shadows now that the sun had tucked itself behind the horizon. My chest tightened, and my hands curled into fists, ready to defend myself. Positioning me in front of a wrought iron bench, he guided me to sit before placing himself beside me. "You are a very attractive young lady."

I pushed my shoulders back, straightening my spine.

"And I'd like to get to know you better. I have a proposition for you."

I coughed, and tried to search for Mark, Danny, or my father.

"A position has opened up in my office."

"I already have a job."

"Yes, Bertin Body Shop. You must find it tedious."

"Actually, I enjoy it very much. It suits me."

"But with your brains and experience, you should be doing something more…" He searched for a suitable word. "Challenging. I'm in desperate need for someone to run my HR department. My manager has just been placed on maternity leave, and I have no reason to see her returning."

"Why would I want to go into HR? I love my job."

"Working for me would bring you a wide range of opportunities, ones you can't get from living and working in Brookfield."

"Mr. Ellery." I turned to face him, trying to hide the anger that now simmered beneath my skin. "I am perfectly happy with my life. I have a job I enjoy, friends and family close by…""You're trapped."

"I am not!" I snapped, although my voice broke at the truth. He was right, I had been feeling trapped recently, but not by my career choice.

"You need to break out and face your fears."

"And what do you know about my fears? You don't know me."

"I know of you, Paige." His hand reached forward, gripping at my thigh. I should have felt violated, but I didn't. I should have wanted to slap him down, but everything inside me was urging him to move higher.

"What do you know?" My voice faltered, failing me. His succulent lips were merely inches from me. I felt my bottom lip tremble in anticipation.

"Paige, darling?" My mother's voice called, breaking the tension that was rigid between us. I jumped to my feet and moved from under his grasp.

"Sorry, Mum." I straightened myself up and walked back to the party. "I just needed some fresh air."

Chapter Ten

I tried to relax, I tried to enjoy the event, but I couldn't. My mind was racing, each thought hurting more than any bruise. What had he meant when he'd said he knows of me? Everything that had happened had been buried by my father. I didn't want to think about it. I'd spent a year fighting those unwelcome thoughts. Twelve months, three weeks, and one day, to be precise.

Danny whisked me into a swaying waltz as the string quartet played something classical, although there is no point in asking me to name the tune. A tap on his shoulder stopped us. "May I?" TDS stood, holding a hand out. Danny looked at me, his gaze searching mine for permission to put him on his backside. I shrugged and took the hand of TDS.

"Your friend doesn't like me."

"He's protective, that's all. He sees me as his little sister."

"We didn't get to finish our conversation."

"There's nothing to be finished." He twirled me around and the satin rose up my thighs, revealing a small purple line. I reached down to cover it. "I'm not working for you." I looked up and caught his glance resting on the hem of my dress.

"Is there any part of you that hasn't been beaten recently?"

"My knee is working perfectly fine, as you'll soon find out if you don't move that hand off my arse."

His hand slipped up again to find the nodules of my spine. Looking around his arms, I saw Mr. Jackson chatting to my mother. He was standing by an older gentleman I presumed to be his father. They were happily laughing, and I found myself wanting to be in on their little joke.

"I wish you would reconsider. I would like to see more of you."

I raised a painful eyebrow at his underlying suggestion.

"Keep wishing." I stepped back as the music finished, and let my heels click across the makeshift dance floor, heading towards my mother and her guests.

As I reached her, I heard my father's voice boom out across the crowd as he spoke into the microphone. "Thank you all for joining us on this glorious evening. I hope you have all helped yourself to the champagne and appetizers. A buffet is being laid in the dining room, so please feel free..." He waved a hand towards the double doors that were swung open and guarded by silver-service staff.

"Later on, we will be announcing the winners of the silent auction. Please bid generously, as the money will be going towards the hospital and also towards rebuilding the sports pavilion. As you are all aware, my daughter is on the board of trustees for the sports community."

My cheeks reddened and burned as he directed the crowd's gaze towards me. I lifted a hand, silently cursing him for the embarrassment.

"And we are both working with the council and Mr. Vance Ellery, to improve the facilities of the local playing fields and halls, encouraging our young people to become more active," he continued. A gentle round of applause waved over the garden. "Now, enough of my boring speech." A tittering arose. "Please enjoy yourselves and spend lots of money!" He stepped down and walked towards me, pulling me into a bear-like hug. "Where's your brother?"

"Probably chasing skirt. He and Danny were determined to find blonde model sisters."

"He's such a cad," laughed my father towards TDS, whose arm was now encircling my waist most uncomfortably. "I'm glad you two are getting along." My father winked. "Have you introduced Paige to your daughter yet?" And there it was, the reminder that he was old enough to be my father.

61

"No, not yet." He twisted and turned, spying over the sea of faces. "Bianca!" He waved towards the stick-thin blonde who skipped across, weaving in and out of the bustling men and women.

She was wearing a bright purple shift dress that barely covered her curvaceous backside. I was surprised that Danny and Mark hadn't left drool marks on the cotton fabric.

"Hi." She beamed with a grin that had clearly been created by an artistic dentist.

"Hi." I held out a hand and shook it firmly. "So you live around here?" I asked, trying to find some subject for small talk.

"I go to Brookfield Girls," she nodded.

Brookfield Girls School was a private education boarding establishment that I had managed to avoid as a teenager. I already knew the type that went there: overly-wealthy Daddy's girls who belonged to old money and pompous, arrogant families. She fit the standard quite well.

Mark and I had been sent off to boarding schools in Kent, which I had been only too happy about, desperate to escape the claustrophobic confinements of Brookfield. Yet, after we finished university, it was exactly where we had both ended up. Back at home.

Bianca continued to gabble about how wonderful life was, bringing me back into the conversation when I heard her say, "OMG!" I mean, come on! Who talks in textspeak? Widening my eyes, I searched around for who or what she was OMG'ing about. She waved her hands frantically, blonde curls bobbing up and down as though they were springs finally free from a restricting cage. "Look, Daddy!" She gripped TDS's arm and yanked him beside her.

I stepped sideways and let him sweep past me.

"Mattie!" She jumped to the point that I was half-expecting her to spill out of the top of her dress. This girl was like an overly-wound poodle. I spun my head around and saw Mr. Jackson striding towards us. Great, this was all I needed.

"Hi," he smiled down at me. I felt overly short, crowded by too-tall women and equally looming men. My chest began to tighten. My mantra began. Breathe in, breathe out.

"Paige, have you met my son?"

That woke me up.

"Son?" I repeated the word back to TDS.

"Yes. Matthew, this is Paige Holmes…"

"We've met," he interrupted, holding a hand out to me. A wave of calm ebbed over me. "She's working on my car."

"Well, not me personally. The company I work for," I corrected him. "You didn't tell me you were Mr. Ellery's son."

"I didn't see the need." Our gazes were fixed, as though the rest of the world could have fallen apart and neither one of us would have noticed.

"No, Matthew prefers to use his mother's name." TDS stepped in.

"I'd rather succeed on my own laurels than on my father's tailcoats." His deep glare shot towards his younger sister. Suddenly it made sense. The reason he had looked so distractingly familiar when I saw him by the sidelines. How had I missed it?

Of course, Matieus – a variation of Matthew! Oh, I'm such an idiot! I could have kicked myself, but I gritted my teeth into a fixated grin and listened to the banter, deciding to bite my tongue against any dumb words that may fly out at any given moment.

So he owned a restaurant in the area, was having work done on his car at a garage I worked for, his sister went to school here, and his father was doing business with mine. It seemed like suddenly fate had sprung her surprise. She should have slapped me in the face with it, though, since clearly my brother was right and I was too blind for my own good.

"If you'll excuse us," I heard TDS saying as he took my elbow, disturbing me from my own chastising.

"If I'd known…" I pointed back to his children, who were still mingling with the crowds, and had now been joined by my own brother and housemate.

"I hope this changes nothing."

"There's nothing to be changed."

"Miss Holmes," he sighed heavily. "I find you highly attractive. I will fuck you." There it was. That harsh word that, when spoken by him, managed to send shockwaves straight down to the apex of my thighs. "Come with me now." He pulled me towards the line of trees only meters away from the center of the party. Caressed by shadows, we were hidden from sight.

63

His lips were on mine, his neck arched to reach me. Automatically my hands shifted up to his head, entwining in the dark strands. His tongue probed, tasting the champagne and caviar. Violent pulsations of lust beat at my skin.

A hand darted over my ribs, and I winced as he found the soft, tender spots of bruising. "You should get these looked at." His head dipped to my neck; feathery kisses tickled my surface.

I wondered if I may actually melt beneath him as his touch became light, his fingertips dancing over the sensitive, wounded skin of my jaw. I felt utterly powerless. And it scared me.

"Please stop," I begged, but my voice was weak, and sounded more like a mousey squeak than actual words.

I felt him hard against me as he pressed my back into the trunk of a towering spruce. It prickled through the satin fabric, and for a split second I worried that my dress may be ruined. "I want you." His words were urgent, powerful, and filled with lust.

The moonlight fell through the canopy, splitting across his face. That indigo glare stoked a fire I thought had long died. His hand slipped to the hem of my dress, feeling his way beneath the thin fabric.

In the distance I could hear the chortle of the party, music playing softly on the warm breeze that danced around us.

He kissed me again, hard, moving his thigh between my legs, parting them while his hand felt for the thin strap of my thong.

"Please," I tried again. "I can't." He heard me this time. Pulling away. Something flickered in his eyes. Anger? No. Not anger. A heavy mix of frustration, lust, and confusion. "I'm sorry." The word trembled against my lips, fluttering like a dying butterfly. Common sense and logic told me I had nothing to apologize for, but in the depths of my despairing heart, I felt pity for the man before me.

I had spurred him on and led him down a path I knew wouldn't and couldn't lead to anywhere but regret.

"Don't," he whispered, placing a thick finger against my lips. Gentle pecks dotted the corner of my brow, narrowly avoiding the torn tissue. Smoothing down my dress for me, and readjusting himself, he looked at me with such intensity that I felt glued to the spot. I physically couldn't move away from him.

"I'm sorry." The word came again, stronger this time, but still with a cry tingeing it.

"No. I won't have you saying that to me."

I was confused. Tears brimmed against the walls, threatening to burst if he was kind to me.

"Please, Mr. Ellery."

"Vance. You know me well enough to use my first name."

"I don't know you at all." The harsh truth stopped us both. Neither of us knew the other. We were strangers caught in a whirlwind of pure lust and sexual tension.

"Then let's fix that." He stepped towards me and placed a kiss upon my lips. But it wasn't fervent or hungry like the others. It was compassionate and gentle. "I will pick you up tomorrow evening and take you out for dinner."

"Not to Matieus. I couldn't,"

"No. Not to Matieus. Somewhere more private, where we can truly get to know each other."

I smiled in agreement. It seemed odd to be so wanting of this man, someone who only moments ago I had detested with such a passion that it burned me. But I guess that is the power of driven lust. Hate one minute; desperate, aching need the next.

Returning to the crowd, I was expecting my brother, at least, to want any dirt he could dig. But nobody had even noticed we'd disappeared. Or, so I thought until my father spoke out over the crowd, announcing the silent auction was coming to a close, so everyone was to place their final bids. I was wandering over to see what was on offer when I felt a presence beside me. I turned to see Matt Jackson with concern etched into his clenched jaw and deep eyes.

"Please be careful," he said bluntly.

"Excuse me?"

"My father. Be careful."

"I appreciate your concern, but I can handle myself." I turned back to the table laden with items donated by stores, companies, and individuals.

"It's not that." His head bowed as though he were almost ashamed.

"Look, if it's the age difference..."

"No. No, nothing like that."

65

"Then what? Mr. Jackson, I…"

"Matt," he corrected me, with a smile that he tried to hide as soon as it flashed across his softening jawline.

"Matt, I like him, and by all accounts, he likes me too." I placed a friendly hand against his arm, hoping to put his fears to rest, and mine.

Part of me was scared that he may close his account with Bertin and take the car elsewhere. Since Matt Jackson had walked into the office, Greg had been excited about the new project, and money. As much as he hated to admit it, Greg was on the verge of having to take on more repair work than custom body builds. He was also facing the possibilities of making staff redundant, including myself. I couldn't let that happen.

He sighed heavily, gazing down at me before moving his glance towards the star sprinkled sky. "That's what worries me. You're a nice girl, and I'm afraid he'll ruin you."

I coughed a laugh, turning back to the table. "Trust me, I'm already ruined."

"You don't understand. Be careful, please. Don't let him pressure you into anything you don't want to do."

"Wow, you make him sound like some sort of sex-pest. You feel that much respect for your own father?"

"There's a reason I don't use his name. And it has nothing to do with laurels."

"Nothing has happened. Nothing is going to happen." I tried to assure him. "He wants to get to know me, and to be honest, it has been so long since anyone showed me that kind of attention…" I stopped myself from going any further. Yet again, I was about to spill my life story onto the lap of a man I barely knew. "There is nothing between us. It's just business."

"Okay." He nodded, breathing heavily as he signed an amount and his name against an item on the table.

Chapter Eleven

I woke on Sunday with the hangover from hell. After TDS Junior had tried to warn me from his father, I'd spent the rest of the night avoiding both them and Bianca, who reminded me of a Duracell bunny on speed. I had enough baggage of my own. The last thing I needed was to get involved in their deep-rooted family issues.

Heading for the champagne, I had steadily become more and more plastered until Mark and Danny managed to maneuver me to my old room. It was there that I woke.

If bruised eye sockets, jaw, cheeks, and ribs weren't bad enough, I now had the ache and throb from dehydration and too much alcohol combined with it.

When I did, finally, manage to peel my lids apart, and gently rubbed away the sticky sand that clung to the corners, I found a cup of tea sitting on the bedside table. I doubted my mother had put it there, since her morning routine consists of being pampered to the utmost extreme before floating around the house, ordering the staff. I could only think that perhaps Sophie had left it for me.

Not truly caring about the identity of my savior, I pulled myself up and drank at the sweet, hot liquid, letting it soothe the rough paper that had once been my tongue and throat. Betraying myself, I let my thoughts trail to the night before in an attempt to fill in the blanks. TDS was firmly in my mind. I could still feel his fingers trailing across my hypersensitive skin. I could still feel his breath, hot with anticipation, opening my pores. I hated him for the way he made me feel.

It was eleven o'clock before I dared to face the harsh light of day, and even harsher attack and lack of sympathy I knew I would get from my family. By all accounts, Danny and Mark had found a couple of possible mates, skulking back to the farmhouse not long after I crashed.

Grateful that my mother insisted I kept some clothes in my old wardrobe, I dressed quickly and bundled the dress from the night before into my old school rucksack that still hung on the back of my door.

"Did I make a complete idiot of myself?" I asked my father meekly, as he drank his morning coffee in the drawing room.

"You upset your mother," he said with a smirk. "And you owe me twenty-five thousand pounds."

"I did? I do?"

"She was hoping you'd be more feminine last night."

"I'm guessing I wasn't."

"Most ladies use glasses to drink champagne. They do not grab a bottle and ask for a straw." I could see the smirk widen. He always found my antics amusing. It had always been difficult to rebel against my father.

"So why do I owe you twenty-five grand?" I sunk into the seat beside him, resting my weary and painful head against his soft arm, inhaling the comforting spices.

"You bought a romantic weekend for two in the South of France."

"Oh." It was all I could muster.

"Don't worry, you offered it to me and your mother as an anniversary gift."

"Well, at least I remembered this year. Check do?" I lifted my head and kissed his cheek, his morning stubble grazing my lips. "Does Mum hate me?"

"The holiday appeased her. I think you're forgiven." He kissed my cheek in return before folding his paper and standing up. "A check will be fine. Arthur will drive you back to the farm when you're feeling more human. Can I suggest a shower?" He wrinkled his nose in mock distaste.

The farmhouse was still blanketed in darkness, with no curtain twitching. I tried to be quiet as I stepped into the kitchen, but failed as my keys fell with a clatter into the metal bowl in the center of the table. Tiptoeing through the house, I sneaked upstairs and into the bathroom.

The water from the shower head hit the tiles with full force, steam and mist puffing like thick smoke from over the glass doors. I stripped out of the hoodie and jeans I'd found at Holmes Manor and threw all of the clothes into the sea grass hamper by the sink.

Near-scalding heat was welcomed as it washed away the stench of stale alcohol and blanked memories. The scab from my chin softened and fell between my breasts before swirling with the soapy bubbles down the drain. With the wound now open, exfoliating became particularly painful. I tried to be gentle, but it still stung like crazy to wash properly.

I tried to concentrate on my breathing, letting the aromatherapy of lavender and tea tree clear my senses. Breathe in through the nose, out through the mouth. In with the good, out with the bad. It was a mantra my yoga teacher had taught me years ago, and one my psychiatrist had confirmed would be good for controlling the panic attacks.

Stepping out into the steam-filled room, I wiped away the condensation from the mirror and peered at my reflection, as I did every day. The bruising had settled into a mottled brown and yellow across my jaw and brow. Opening one side of the towel, I could see that my ribs were slowly turning back to a pale peach rather than purple and blue. If it hadn't been so painful, I would have thought the mixture of colors looked like a pretty rainbow.

That red line still scratched across my pelvis, though. I hid it beneath a white shift dress with a brown leather belt that accentuated my narrow waist but full bust and hips.

Two o'clock and my stomach began to grumble against the lack of food. Well past lunch and the boys were still in their beds. I peeked around

Mark's door to check that he was still breathing. A tumble of naked arms and legs stretched across his still body.

Danny's bedroom door was firmly shut. I didn't open it in fear of the aging creak disturbing him and his guest.

Making my way back downstairs, I raked my fingers through my damp hair, deciding whether I was brave enough to try and apply makeup to the freshly washed grazes across my face. It probably wouldn't do me any harm to have one day without a layer of powders and oils.

Two slices of toast and a cup of tea settled my growling hunger . I was sipping the last few dregs when Danny appeared from the hallway. His disheveled look, with bed-fussed hair and stubble-lined cheeks, chin, and neck, were nothing I hadn't seen before.

"Anything for me?" he asked, noticing the crumbs on my empty plate.

"You were asleep." I threw back the last of my tea before dumping the plate and mug in the sink. "Good night?" I asked, noticing the lack of mate behind him.

"I guess." He yawned, flicking the kettle to re-boil.

"You didn't pull then?"

He shook his head. "But Mark did."

"I noticed."

I found it hard to believe that he'd come away without a night's conquest. There had been plenty of eligible young models accompanying their fathers and friends, and Danny wasn't exactly shabby. With light brown hair, strong bone structure, and grey eyes, I had to admit that he was handsome. Leaning against the counter, his toned muscles were obvious. From his strong upper arms, to the abs and muscular V that led into his boxers, there was nothing that wasn't attractive about him. Sometimes I felt a pang of incestuous lust for my brother's best friend. I'd known him for too long to be sexually aware of him, but at the same time, who could ignore the obviousness of his beauty?

"Who'd you fuck?" And there it was. The reason I wasn't attracted to him.

"Nobody, not that it's any of your business." I sat back down at the table, grabbing a magazine and pretending to be interested in the celebrity gossip.

"It's been what, a year?"

70

"None of your business," I sang, trying to ignore him.

"It's been a year, Paige." He sounded more serious.

I shot a glare at him. "None of your fucking business," I repeated angrily through gritted teeth.

"You can't let him rule you."

I could feel the heat in my cheeks rising as he spoke. My phone buzzed, cooling my temper. "Hello?" I answered, although I already knew who was on the other end, since his name had flashed across my screen. "Hello, Mr. Ellery." I threw a sneer at Danny, hoping he'd back off now. "Yes, that would be lovely. I'll see you at six."

"He's not right for you." Danny shook his head.

"None of your…"

"Business. I know."

Mark finally rose at three. His friend, and I use the term loosely, was some Swedish modelesque female. She was a typical stereotype – tall, blonde, skinny, and beautiful. I was almost disappointed when it transpired that she also had a PhD in Astrophysics, and was grateful when she was ushered into a taxi and sent home so that I was once again the more intelligent member of the household.

Timekeeping was obviously going to be one his bugbears. With the sun still fairly high in the sky, although it had begun its descent, I'd opted to remain in my white shift, but coupled with it was an animal-print jacket and patent black killer heels, and added a thin layer of makeup. I moved into the seat, trying to avoid the burning in my ears as Danny tattled on us to Mark.

"How's your head feeling this morning?" he asked, not unkindly.

"When you live and work with men, you learn to drink like one."

"You are an enigma, Paige Holmes," he chuckled.

It was then that I noticed how good he looked. Light strands of silver peppered through his mahogany waves almost gave him an air of authority and wisdom. His indigo eyes were perfectly set off by the dark blue silk shirt he wore tucked into silver-grey slacks. My eyes shot to the ground and I saw those black chukkas that I had been acquainted with a few weeks earlier.

"So where are we going?" I asked, clearing my throat.

71

"I thought we would go to the hotel where I'm staying and order room service."

"That's a bit presumptuous of you."

"It's all entirely innocent. There is a portfolio I'd like you to glance over before I show it to your father. We agreed last night that since you are on the board of trustees, it makes sense that you are brought further into the plans before we submit them."

"I hate business. I'm on the board because of my name, nothing more."

"Then we'll just eat."

The hotel was as palatial as its name. Richart Courts was outside of Brookfield, surrounded by acres of luscious green pastures, and providing everything your heart and wallet could desire. From luxurious spa treatments to a round on the 18-hole course, it was a mecca for the wealthy.

Of course, TDS had the royal suite that took over half of the top floor. The two-bed apartment was bigger than the average flat and decorated in silver-veined marble, creamy pillars, and gold-leaf filigree.

I should have felt awkward as he showed me around, seating me in the sunken lounge area. Most other women would have at least been in awe of his unmistakable affluence. But I wasn't. I felt almost comfortable. I didn't even shrink under his shadow as he sat by me. It would have been easier to pull away from him if I'd been even the slightest bit intimidated by his power and strength.

He held a menu out to me, and watched as I glanced down the exquisite list.

"Your friends don't like me, and neither does your mother."

"My mother doesn't like anyone who shows me any interest," I said, matter-of-factly. "It's not you. Please don't take it personally. They're overprotective. Mark is my big brother, it's his job to hate you, and Daniel is his best friend, so it's his job to agree with Mark."

He seemed to be comforted by that, but I wasn't sure how long he'd be pacified by my excuses. I wondered if I should broach the subject of his son having equal displeasure for our friendship. Before I could open my mouth, his hand was on top of mine, reaching for the menu.

"Have you made a decision?"

"Not really." My voice was unusually quiet. I swallowed against the pressure that built up in my chest and stomach.

His fingertips stroked the back of my hand, his gaze firmly fixed on mine. He leant forward, and as he did so, my pelvis became heavy with the heat that swelled between my legs. Jeez, what this man could do to me with a single look

"I want to get to know you, Paige." The sound of his voice vibrated over my skin, sending sparks of pure unadulterated lust driving down into the pit of my belly.

I'd been starving when his limo stopped outside the farmhouse. But now there was only one thing I was hungry for, and it wasn't food.

Chapter Twelve

I'd promised myself that we would simply talk. After the night at my parents', when I'd pushed him away so harshly, I'd promised myself I wouldn't go back on that. But now, as he edged closer to me, I could feel my eyelids become heavy, my lashes fluttering like frantic wings against my cheeks.

"You don't have to be afraid of me," he hushed, as a hand moved away a stray wisp of hair that fell over my vision.

"I'm not afraid," I stuttered.

"Then why are you shaking?"

Looking down at my hands, I could see them firmly gripping into the tops of my thighs, trembling as though I was on my own private earth and it was quaking at the core.

"I've been thinking about your proposal." Business. Talk business, and shake away the stupid crush.

He moved back, a weirdly amused smiled wavering on his lips. Leaning into the arm of the sofa, he lifted a hand and let his index finger graze across the impression.

"I really don't think…"

"Don't turn me down." He stopped me, but didn't move. Nothing changed, apart from the heat in his darkened stare. "At least consider it. Tell me you'll think about it, but don't turn me down."

I had the sudden impression that TDS was not used to hearing the word "No." I wasn't in the mood to argue. My head was still feeling ever-so-slightly wobbly. So I nodded. "Okay, I'll think about it. But I'm not saying yes either."

"Good. That's settled then." He stood and reached for the phone, speaking to whom I assumed was reception, and ordered two steak sandwiches and a bottle of red wine.

"Nothing's settled," I tried to interrupt, but he simply held up a finger, stopping my words from reaching him. "Oh, my God!" I jumped to my feet in defiance. He may not be used to being turned down, but I was not some pet to be ordered around.

Slamming the receiver down, he was by my side within a split second of me standing. "We're not finished here."

"Yes, we are." Each word was as strong as the next. I stood firmly, back straight, chin up, lengthening my short stature as much as I possibly could.

He bent towards me, his lips so close to my ear that I could feel his warm breath brushing away the strands of hair that covered it. "You need to be fucked."

"You can go fuck yourself," I whispered back, pushing past him.

"What happened?"

The question stopped me from reaching for the door handle. My hand faltered mid-air. "Nothing." I denied him the truth with my words, but the tears of pain and anguish broke through my façade. He was by me again, moving so swiftly that he would put a ghost to shame.

"You don't have to tell me, if you don't want to." How could he be so harsh one minute and so understanding the next? A contradiction was more predictable than TDS. I was beginning to think that TDS Junior had a point.

"We all have our secrets." His hand moved my hair over my shoulder.

"I'd rather mine stayed that way."

"At least join me for food. No more talking about fucking." He moved a hand towards the sunken lounge, guiding me back to the sofa.

"You said you wanted to get to know me."

"And I do."

"My personality, not my body?"

"Yes."

I nodded in gratitude. "I'd appreciate that." Sitting back down, my fists clasped over each other against my knees.

TDS stood by the bar, pouring two tumblers of vodka over ice. "You need a drink." He handed me the glass before sitting back down. "So tell me about your personality."

"I get the feeling you're not used to this any more than I am," I stated, ignoring the question.

"A beautiful young woman being in my hotel room? Yes, I am used to that. That same beautiful young woman wanting to talk rather than…" He stopped himself from using the "F" word. "No. I'm not used to that."

"Do you always get your own way?"

"We're supposed to be talking about you."

"I want to get to know you too."

He sighed heavily, tossing the sharp, clear liquid down his throat, seething as the burn hit him. "Yes, I do."

"And your family accepts that."

"My ex-wife couldn't, so she left me. My daughter is blinded by her love for her father, and my son, as you have probably guessed, hates me."

"I can't say I'm surprised."

"Don't believe all you read in the papers, and don't believe all he says either. He may be my son, and I will love him for the rest of my life, but remember that he is my son. Apples and trees."

He placed the empty glass on the table in front of us, his hand brushing past my naked calves. I caught my breath as he moved back to his position, his eyes never leaving mine. "What about you? Your family clearly cares for you, and yet you ignore their advice and agree to meet me anyway?"

"I thought we were here to discuss sports and money. You wanted me to look at a portfolio of designs."

He laughed again and reached for the briefcase by the side of the sofa. Opening the clasps, he pulled out a thick pile of documents. "Feel free." He handed them to me, and I pretended to be interested in the contents. "What do you think?"

"I think I should take these and show them to the board, and then we'll arrange a meeting between them, you, and my father."

"Where do you find the time?" he mused, shaking his head with what looked like pleasure. "More to the point, why do you find the time?"

"I don't know what you're talking about." I handed him the papers back and finished the last of my vodka.

"You keep yourself busy for a reason."

"I like being active."

"No." He shook his head and got up as a rap sounded against the timber frame. "This isn't being active. This is hiding."

I straightened myself again, refusing to give in to his prodding.

The steak sandwiches were deliciously mouth-watering. Greedily, I tucked into the sub, ignoring any thoughts of being demure. He smiled, watching me fill my empty stomach. He found me amusing.

Empty plates on the table, he reached forward and took my hand. There was that shot of electricity again. I pulled away from him.

"Why fight the inevitable?" His voice was a loud purr. Moving towards me, his lips were on mine, tasting the savory flavors of my tongue. I didn't fight him as his hand crept up my waist, brushing over the healing ribs. I didn't stop him as he cupped my breast, his thumb and forefinger teasing my nipple until it became painfully erect. But as his other hand found the hem of my dress…

76

I shuddered, instinctively moving backwards. "No." The word came to my lips before I could stop it.

I felt his shoulders weigh down as he pulled away, his dark violet-blue eyes contemplating me. "If you don't want to do this, I won't force you." The honesty of his words caused my breath to catch in my throat. I hadn't expected him to be understanding without an explanation. "But it won't stop me from wanting you."

"It's not that I don't want to," I cried, unable to stop the sudden well of tears that spilled out over my lashes. "I just can't."

"Tell me why."

"I can't," I repeated, shaking my head almost violently.

His hands were around my face, soft and gentle, warm against the rough scars. "Then don't. Let me." His lips reached mine. Pliable kisses placed upon my bottom lip, trailing towards my chin. He kissed the red and white line. His hands rested against my shoulders, not moving.

His mouth moved to my cheek, caressing the tears before they reached any further. He went to my brow, the tip of his tongue tracing over the stinging cut. I inhaled sharply against the pain. "Let me," he whispered, as his hands slid down my arms, stopping at my waist. "We'll take it as slow as you want to go."

I knew it was an act. This man was unable to feel any form of kindness. He was brutal in every part of his life. But as the softness of his palms stroked the naked skin of my thigh, revealed by the hem of my dress, I felt myself succumb to him.

Relaxing into his touch, he scooped me up, his mouth never leaving mine, and moved with ease into the bedroom, as though he could sense how uncomfortable and visible I felt in the lounge.

Laying me down on the bed, he kissed down over my dress, never once moving under the fabric. He reached my thigh, and his hand slid down until it removed my shoes, placing them neatly by the bed. Closing my eyes, I allowed myself to trust him.

Before I could breathe, his lips were on mine again. He lay by my side; a hand gripped behind my knee as he lifted it to him. His warm palms reached beneath the fabric of my dress. I gasped, unsure. "Let me," he said again.

I nodded, holding my breath as he found the curve of my buttocks. His fingers moved under the thin satin of my pants, pulling them to the side. My own hands stilled at the back of his head as I waited for him to move.

He lifted his head away from me. "May I undress you?"

It was an odd question, but I appreciated the sentiment behind the words. "Yes," I replied. He lifted my dress over my head, throwing it into a heap by the shoes.

I was suddenly aware of how naked I was. Dressed only in my white bra and pants, I could feel the slickness of his silk shirt against my skin.

As he lay back beside me, his erection pressing into my thigh, he reached into my bra and let me spill out over the metal and fabric confinements. "You are beautiful." He kissed the top of my cleavage. "Why do you hide?"

My hand shot down to cover the red scar splayed across my abdomen. He looked down at it. "That's nothing to be ashamed of." He moved my hand, bending his head to kiss along the keloid bump.

"You don't understand." I trembled beneath him.

"Then make me. Tell me what happened."

"No." I gripped underneath his chin and pulled him back to my mouth. "Make love to me, please," I begged. "No fucking; I need you to make love to me."

His kiss was hard and hungry. His hand massaged the plump flesh of my breast. He was solid against me, as though starved of attention, which I doubted was the case.

Moving his hands behind me, he unhinged the clasp of my bra with one-handed expertise before slipping down and moving my pants over my hips. Soon both pieces of underwear were on the floor.

I reached between us and tugged at the zip of his trousers, revealing him into my hand. He kicked off his clothes, pulling the shirt over his head without undoing the buttons, and he was as naked as I was. The soft curls on his chest were darker than the espresso and platinum of his head. I raked my fingers through them as his hand moved slowly down my center. He found me soft, wet, and wanting.

"Wait…" He stopped and moved off the bed, shuffling through the contents of a side table. I heard the rip of foil, and within seconds he was back at my side. An urgent growl left his throat as I guided his sheathed member towards me. He filled me fully, moving with an ease and slowness that I appreciated.

He was gentle. I will always remember that. It was not at all how I had expected and, perhaps, dreamed it would be with TDS.

There was a respect between us, as he moved inside me, throbbing against my wall, but never once quickening the pace. His hands beneath me nipped at my buttocks as he came, exploding inside me as I returned his joy.

We lay naked for a moment, basking in the gloriousness of it all, before he moved into the bathroom to clean himself. Part of me, the part that rejected all intimacy, waited for him to ask me to leave. But he didn't. He held me in his arms, kissing my head until we both drifted into a deep slumber.

It was possibly the best night's sleep I'd had in over a year.

Chapter Thirteen

Acutely aware that I hadn't planned on staying the night, and only had yesterday's pants to wear, I woke early and asked that TDS take me home so that I could change before work. I was fortunate in the sense that Mark and Danny had left equally early for a photo shoot in London that morning, so breathed a heavy sigh of relief when I arrived at an empty house.

"I'll call you to arrange that meeting," I said, getting out of the car, thankful that I'd managed to avoid the "Walk of Shame." "Make sure you do." TDS handed me a plastic file, brimming with papers. There was no lover's kiss good-bye or lingering looks as his driver pulled away. I felt innately content at our departure.

Quickly changing into a smart black trouser suit and a clean set of underwear, I threw the plastic file on my bed, with every intention to take it to either my father or Lou later on. Then I remembered it was Monday. "Shit, shit, shit." I searched under the bed for my holdall. Where the hell had I put it? The sex had been so damn good that my mind had cleared, and I'd forgotten where I kept my gi and pads. With seconds to spare, I remembered tossing them into the bottom of my wardrobe.

How I wasn't late for work, I have no clue, but by eight-thirty I was sat at my desk sipping at a cup of tea, pretending that I hadn't been rushed at all. The day whizzed by, and at half six, I was in the local gym, chatting to the other girls, waiting for our instructor to arrive.

Tyler Byrne was tall, slim, and deceptively strong. To look at him, you would have described him as gangly, standing at least six-foot-three, if not taller, and all arms and legs. He reminded me of a newborn foal, or perhaps a giraffe, the only difference being that he was sure of his footing. The shock of orange-red hair he kept closely cropped was a complete contradiction to his temper. Far from being fiery, Tyler was possibly the most relaxed person I had ever met. I'd known him for years, and had been only too happy to help build up his clientele when he'd informed me he was starting MMA classes in the area.

Dressed in a red gi, his black belt was tied around his waist, emphasizing the leanness of his build. He checked the newcomers' belts before standing in front of us and calling for our attention. With a bow, we immediately jumped into back-guarded stance as we began our drills. My own belt was an electric blue, but my fitness levels were still being rebuilt. I jogged lightly on the spot while others raced into the ground, and I had fallen back to press-ups on my knees as opposed to the edge of my toes. Still, I was proud of myself for having got this far in such a short space of time.

When I finally got home, there was a message from my mother that had been left with Danny. I managed to decipher his scribble through the tiredness and sweat that ruined my vision. She wanted me to go for dinner the next evening. Great. I knew exactly what this meant: another lecture on my unbecoming behavior and language.

Tuesday was as boring as Monday. Nothing remotely interesting happened, apart from I'd noticed the lewd comments drizzled rather than poured.

Being the dutiful daughter, I changed my routine and headed for Holmes Manor rather than the gym that evening. My mother was eagerly awaiting my arrival, martini in hand, but my father was nowhere to be seen.

"Business," was mother's only explanation. This wasn't unusual. He often worked late, and with this new plan involving TDS, I figured he was probably too busy to breathe, let alone socialize.

She handed me a glass of orange juice. "Oh, don't look so appalled," she said, taking a sip of her own, alcoholic, drink. "I think you've had more than enough to drink over the past few weeks."

I knew she was referring to my behavior at the summer ball, but for this, I was prepared.

"You need to be more careful. You shouldn't be drinking on your medication," she continued.

"I stopped taking the pills weeks ago. Don't worry, it's all been okayed by the doctors," I added, trying to reassure her. She didn't look convinced, but knocked back the rest of her martini. Way to support me, Mum, I thought glumly.

"Paige, darling, I wanted to talk to you." She turned her knees towards me, taking my hands in hers. "I couldn't help but notice how close you and Mr. Ellery were the other evening."

"Mum." I elongated the word into a whine.

"I can't help worrying about you, darling." She tapped my hand, giving me that sympathetic smile.

"I know," I sighed heavily.

"What about his son? Don't you work with him now?"

"He's a client at the garage. I've met him a couple of times."

"He's available, and hard-working, and ever so handsome. He obviously likes you."

"I thought you liked Mr. Ellery," I mused.

"He's fine enough, but he's not for you, sweetheart. He's far too old, for one thing."

"He's younger than Daddy," I pointed out.

"Only just, which is precisely the point. He has children your age."

"His daughter is much younger than me. She's still in school."

"Now you're being facetious. Matthew is more appropriate."

"Appropriate?" The word leapt from behind my teeth before I could stop the high-pitched squeal coming with it.

"Paige, please don't be like that. Matthew is a lovely boy. He's done very well for himself. Your father and I really think you two should see more of each other."

"Oh, good, I'm glad you've been discussing my love life," I snapped sarcastically.

"It's not like that, darling. We're worried about you. You've become very closed towards advances." She held a hand up to stop my rebuttal. "We know why, and of course, we don't blame you. But we do feel it's time that you started coming out of your shell a bit more. Stop spending so much time at the gym." She grabbed the top of my arm. "You're an attractive young lady, but these   scars…." She let go. I winced at the nipping from where her fingers had been. Mother sighed, and pulled me into a gentle hug. "It's not healthy. I read an article…"

Here we go. Mother was always reading and then reciting articles she'd read in her most recent magazine. And of course, we were all expected to suddenly change diets and lifestyles to accommodate these newfound "health benefits."

"It said that fitness and exercise can become addictive," she continued, falling silent as Rosa, her cook, walked in the room to announce that dinner was ready.

We moved into the dining room, and Rosa served us a dish of pork casserole with vegetables. I picked at it, not all that hungry, under my mother's watchful scowl. To appease her, I chewed on mouthfuls of the tender meat. Despite my reluctance to eat, it was delicious. Rosa was a highly talented cook. I needed her to replace Danny and his spaghetti bolognaise.

"Have you spoken to Dr. Franklin recently?" she asked, placing her knife and fork down as she spoke.

"I spoke to him a few weeks ago when he agreed to me going back to work."

Mother raised an eyebrow, realizing that there was a time difference between me returning to Bertin's Body Shop and actually getting permission from my psychiatrist to be working again.

"I had to, Mum," I bleated. "I was getting so bored, cooped up in that old house. Danny and Mark have been so busy with weddings recently…"

"You could have stayed here." She cut me off, before lifting the fork back to her pouty lips.

"I know, and appreciate that, I really do."

"But you need your independence, your space, your life. I know. Dr. Franklin did explain it all to us." She said it with such a heavy heart that I couldn't help but become overwhelmed with guilt.

We finished the last of our meal in silence, returning to the lounge as my father came home. He bustled in, kissing us both on the cheek before jumping up the stairs. Sometimes I had to wonder if he really was closing in on his sixties or whether he was a teenager trapped beneath dark grey hairs and a warm brown gaze.

When he joined us, he had changed from his usual black suit, crisp white shirt, and garishly bright tie to a pair of beige chinos and sky blue polo shirt. "Are you playing golf this evening?" I quizzed humorously.

"You get your hilarity from me." He grinned, leaning back into the armchair and flicking through the Financial Times.

"Mum was just telling me how you two think I should see less of Mr. Ellery," I said deliberately, my eyes firmly fixed on my mother's face as her lips pursed into a tut.

Father put his newspaper down and passed her a half-cocked smile and a "leave the poor girl alone" stare. "We are concerned about your well-being," he said, contradicting his expression. "Have you spoken to Mr. Ellery recently?"

I've done more than that, I thought. But it wasn't quite the admission you make to your parents. "I met with him the other day. He gave me some paperwork to pass on to the committee."

"And that was it?" my mother interrupted.

"Yes, Mother, that was it," I lied.

"I do think that you should see Matthew again," she said persistently. "In fact, why don't we organize a dinner party?" she announced excitedly.

"Lizzie, I'm still recovering from the summer ball," my father groaned, picking up his paper once more. I stifled a giggle as Mother turned to him and began to bat her lashes, begging him to reconsider. I had always been in awe of my father, but even more so with the power that my mother wielded over him.

"We need to find a suitable partner for Paige," she pleaded.

"I am right here, Mum," I complained at her talking about me as though I was suddenly invisible. "And I am perfectly capable of finding someone myself. When I'm ready."

"There you go. You heard her. When she's ready," my father emphasized. I was beginning to hate my brother for having been able to get out of these tête-à-têtes so easily.

"Sweetheart," Mother purred , ignoring my father completely. "Humor me. Let me organize a lunch, at least, and we'll invite Matthew, and you two can get to know each other."

I growled in defeat, realizing that there was no point in trying to stop her from starting on this quest. She was determined, stubborn, and obstinate, and all the other adjectives that are commonly used to describe myself.

Chapter Fourteen

"Oh, good, glad to see you're here." Greg grinned as he walked through to the office on Wednesday morning, seeing me with my face firmly in my palms. I was still trying to get my head around my mother's impulsiveness. He dropped a pile of invoices on my desk. "Matt Jackson's stopping by this morning with the Evo. I said you'd drop him off at the rental place."

"What?" I exclaimed, jumping out of my skin as well as my seat.

"It's only ten minutes down the road. Don't worry, you can still have a lunch break and I won't dock your pay." Greg sidled away from me, as though fearful of my sudden burst of anger. "What bit you? I meant what I said, if you need more time…"

"No, I'm fine, sorry." I sat back down, resting my head in my hands. "It's just that he came to my parents' fundraiser the other night, and…"

"You two didn't do the horizontal mambo, did you?"

"You have such a way with words, Greg. No, we didn't. But we didn't exactly leave on good terms either."

"Paige, he's a client. The customer is always right and all that jazz. Shit. I should make you take him out for lunch."

"No! Anyway, you don't need to. My mother has decided to invite him over for lunch one day. I'll make it up to you, I promise," I grumbled.

"It's not me you need to apologize to."

"I promise, Greg, I won't screw this up for you."

"Seriously, Paige, perhaps you should take some time."

"I'm fine, honestly." My teeth were gritted. "I don't need any more time."

"If you insist, but don't mess this up, or no more Mister-Nice-Greg." He turned on his heel and marched into the office. I winced as the door slammed behind him.

Fuck. I shouldn't have said anything. I should have avoided the whole bleeding thing. But how was I going to keep a straight face around Mr. Jackson? I'd spent the night fucking his father. No. Not fucking. Making love. TDS had made love to me. Something I didn't think would be within his repertoire.

I spent the morning watching the clock. Each minute ticked by slower than the last until finally the bell from reception rang. I made my way down the metal stairs, my caution having nothing to do with the five-inch spikes attached to my feet.

Matthew Jackson stood with his back to the desk. He was wearing jeans and a leather jacket, making him seem casual and instantly putting me at ease.

"Hi," I managed, cringing inwardly at the endless possible memories that he would remember and I had mysteriously forgotten in my drunken state. I wondered if I should have warned him about my mother's impending invitation.

"Paige," he beamed, as though pleased to see me, despite our previous conversation. I relaxed with relief as his friendly demeanor settled my nerves.

"Shall we?" I motioned towards the door and the racing-green Golf sitting outside.

It amused me how his looks were darker than TDS's, yet he was so much lighter in manner. His pleasantness lay easily with me, although a small slither of subconscious was aware that it could be a false sense of security.

I tried to ignore the fight between the muscles in my neck and shoulders as he climbed into the passenger seat beside me, his naked arm barely inches from mine. The prickle of goose bumps forced each hair to become boldly erect. Despite the June heat, I turned the air conditioning off, hoping that he would assume I was cold.

Pulling out of the car park, I drove towards the rental office, a short drive away from Bertin Body Shop. I'd been hoping for a quick, easy journey, no more than fifteen minutes tops. I hadn't been expecting the mid-morning rush to block the roads leading out of Brookfield.

"It's normally such a quiet village." I flashed a grin towards him as the car rolled slowly behind the line of traffic that followed a huge blue tractor.

"Gives us time to have a chat." He smiled back.

My brain cursed while my conscience laughed loudly.

"Congratulations, by the way."

"What for?" I tried to concentrate on the cars overtaking the tractor. If I could get close enough…

"The trip to Nice. I hope you and…"

"Oh, I've given it to my parents. It's their anniversary soon." I clawed my way through the sentence, desperate to stop him from asking who I was planning on taking away with me on such a romantic trip.

"I see." Was that a smirk? What was it with the Ellery family and their smirkiness?

"Did you win anything?" I tried to fill in the hazy blanks.

"No," he said bluntly. "My father seems to win anything I aim for."

Ouch. That hurt. I couldn't see any way of avoiding this next topic.

Shooting the car forward, I closed in on the bumper of the tractor.

"You seem to be doing pretty well for yourself."

"Not bad, I guess." His smile was softer this time, as though contemplating his many accomplishments. Pride, but not arrogance, flooded his strong features.

The traffic light, the only frigging lights in the village, turned red, forcing me to stop. The smell of burning diesel choked through the car, and I had no choice but to turn the fans on in order to clear the air.

"What are you doing for lunch?" he asked, as we both glanced towards the clock. It was one o'clock, and I was getting hungry.

"I usually grab a sandwich."

"How about joining me instead? I know this fabulous little restaurant not too far from here."

"I don't know if I should," I murmured, revving the engine as the lights hit red and amber.

"Please," he urged. "I'd like to talk to you."

"That sounds ominous." Green for go! I felt like praising God as the tractor went right and I went straight ahead.

"What about getting a car?" I was so close to the rental office, and even closer to having some space to breathe.

"You think I only have the Evo?" It was stupid to even ponder the possibility of such a man owning a single car. Still, he could have said something before this unnecessary trip!

"I guess not."

"So take me to the restaurant instead. I'll clear it with your boss. He likes my wallet too much to argue."

"Fine," I conceded, hoping beyond hope that he would steer clear of any conversations concerning his father.

We arrived at Matieus, and I was almost taken by surprise when the waiter directed us to a private room at the back, until I remembered who owned the restaurant.

Before we'd even sat, I was presented with a bottle of white wine. "Oh, no, I really shouldn't. I have to drive back."

"Yes, she will." Mr. Jackson gave the waiter a nod. "Make yourself comfortable. I will be back in a minute." He stepped out of a door marked "PRIVATE" in large bold letters on a golden plaque. Moments later, he returned with a huge smile on his face. "That's settled. I have spoken to Mr. Bertin, and he has agreed to allow you the rest of the afternoon off so that you may wine and dine with me."

"That doesn't sound like Greg." I stumbled over the words.

"As I said, he likes my wallet. Please order what you like. I know the owner," he said with a wink. There was something about him that made me feel utterly at ease. He placated every worry I had, unlike TDS, who violated my subconscious and stole all of my common sense.

"I have to admit that I got you here under false pretenses." He spoke softly, treading with caution around the sentence. His confession weighed on my heart. Perhaps he wasn't so unlike his father after all.

"Mr. Jackson, please." I don't quite know what I was begging for. Mercy, maybe?

"No, don't. Let me speak my piece, and then you can take it or leave it. And it's Matt."

I prepared myself by gulping at the cold glass of wine, letting the alcohol steady my nerves.

"I need to know what your intentions are with my father."

"Excuse me for being dense, but why is my relationship with Mr. Ellery any of your concern?" Anger boiled beneath my skin. How dare he!

"You don't know my father, Paige."

"And you don't know me." I slammed the glass down with such force I thought it might shatter into a million pieces.

"No, you're right. I don't. I apologize for being so forthright." Apparently it was something he and TDS had in common. "But..." But. There's always a but, and it was usually me at the end of a joke. "Forgive me," he said, shaking his head with a smile. The waiter walked in, carrying two plates piled with crisp salad I wasn't even aware we'd ordered.

I waited for him to leave before turning to my host. "I appreciate the business that you're giving to Greg, and I hope that what we say today won't affect that." Be professional. Breathe in, breathe out. "But it's none of your goddamn business who I spend my private time with. Whether he's your father or not, it's my life." Control slipped away from me like dirty water swirling down into the depths of a drain. Fury swept over me like a ferocious tsunami of self-preservation, pride, and contempt. If I'd been able to look in a mirror, I suspect that my hazel gaze had turned into a blackened stare.

The wounds above my eye and along my jaw began to simultaneously throb. I fought the tears, grasping for self-control. My subconscious scrabbled for iron supports to hold the wall in place.

"You slept with him, didn't you?" He said it so simply, so calmly, that I hated him for it.

I stood up, throwing my napkin down with purpose. "Thank you for lunch. It was..." I paused. "Enlightening."

Grabbing my handbag, I turned and marched out of the room, swinging the door wide in order to make a scene. How dare he treat me like some common slut! Did he not know who my father was? Bastard. Fucking men.

I could have easily driven back to the body shop, sobbed into Greg's shoulder, and tried to convince him that Jackson's money wasn't needed. I had money; I'd keep him running, if I had to, although it was money I'd hoped never to touch.

I could have gone to my mother and father, begged them to intervene and console me with promises of ruining the Ellerys, which I knew they had enough power to do. Although I suspected my mother would have been cross with me more than them.

Instead, I found myself driving back to the farmhouse, hoping that Mark and Danny had returned. But it was empty, shrouded in darkness from where the curtains had still not been opened. I was home, on my own. I was alone. And alone, for me, was a precarious place to be.

Chapter Fifteen

The tequila bottle hadn't been touched in a year. Dust gathered on the glass shoulders, which I now drew into. T. D. S.

Twisting the red cap, I poured the clear liquid into a short tumbler, knocking back the burning drink in one gulp and inhaling sharply as it hit the back of my throat. Another shot went down.

A fist pummeled against the back of my eyes.

I fell into the sofa, lying on my side, staring into the darkness. Slithers of yellow light tried to creep through the closed curtains.

Another shot.

Another fist.

No, wait. The knocking wasn't in my head. I ignored it.

Another shot. I fought the urge to vomit.

Another fist against the doorframe, this time coupled with a voice.

"Paige!" he called through the wood and glass. "Paige, let me in!"

I rolled onto the floor, my knees and palms digging into the rough-cut pile. My stomach tensed as the contents forced their way into my esophagus. I swallowed it back down, which may sound revolting, but I was in no fit state to be cleaning half-digested salad and tequila from a mushroom-colored carpet.

Gripping hold of the hard edge underneath the cushions, I used the sofa to help me stand. Criss-crossing my legs, I stumbled to the front door. There was no need to peer through the windows to see who would be standing there.

His taut knuckles hammered on the wood, and I waited for it to splinter. It didn't.

"Paige, please." He said the word, but there was no begging in his voice.

Matt Jackson continued to holler through the door.

"Mr. Jackson," I grumbled, opening the door wide enough for me to peer through a small gap and use the frame as a leaning post.

"Jesus-fucking- Christ." He barged through, forcing me backwards. I felt his hands grasp at my waist, stopping me from landing flat on my backside.

"Is this how you handle every situation? Getting wasted?" He sounded angry, and I was left confused, until I remembered that the last time we'd had a difference of opinions, I had solved it by drinking several bottles of champagne.

"Works for me!" I giggled, falling into his arms. "Oh, Mr. Jackson," I flirted drunkenly.

"Shit." He scooped me into his arms and carried me up the stairs. "Which one is yours?"

I shrugged, forgetting where I slept, and mumbled something that sounded nothing like, "I don't know."

Knocking through each door, he eventually found mine and dumped me on the soft mattress. "Well, your Daddy was much more of a gentleman about it," I chided, pointing an accusatory finger at him.

An arm hung loosely over my head as I lay in a crumpled heap. The stale taste of alcohol nauseated me. I gagged, but managed to contain the phlegm and vomit.

"I can't leave you like this. When will your brother be back?"

"How did you know where I lived?" I asked, my voice wobbling more than my head.

"I followed you. I was worried."

"You followed me? But I have your car." Pieces came together like I was digging a jigsaw from under the sofa.

"I have more than one, remember?" He sighed heavily, sitting on the edge of the bed. My head dropped onto his lap, and he stroked his fingers through my hair. "What is your mystery, Paige?" he sang, not really asking the question.

"Your Dad asked me the same thing."

I heard him tut and guessed that he looked away from me.

"You don't approve of me fucking your father?" I asked into his thigh.

"No."

"Why?"

"He's not good for you, Paige. He destroys everything he touches. He's dangerous."

I closed my eyes and don't remember anything else that was said.

When I woke, I was alone. I rubbed at the hangover, my second in a matter of days, and glanced at my watch. I couldn't make up my mind if it was seven in the evening or seven the next morning. Either way, I needed to be sick.

My head was firmly down the toilet bowl when I overheard voices from downstairs. Mark and Danny were home. There was a third voice too, one I recognized. "Oh, fuck," I swore at myself as I remembered why I was getting drunk and how I'd got into my bed.

Stripping out of my clothes and jumping into the shower, I washed away the stale tequila, and hoped I was in there long enough for him to have disappeared. I even took the time to scrub my teeth, removing that furry scale that always builds up after alcohol and sleep.

I was tiptoeing back to my bedroom, towel firmly in place, when Danny appeared at the top of the stairs.

"Wow. You really know how to fuck up."

"Screw you," I sneered before reaching for my door. His hand gripped tightly around my wrist, nipping at the skin, causing me to wince. "Ow, get off." I pulled my hand away from his. He'd never hurt me like that before. He'd never seemed this angry before. "What?" I tossed the word at him as though it were a ball and we were playing Piggy-in-the-Middle.

"I thought you were doing good."

"I'm fine."

"Clearly, you're not, Paige. Mark and I are worried about you. Perhaps it's time to call Dr. Franklin again."

"Screw you," I repeated, but with more vehemence this time. "I am absolutely fine."

"No. No, you're not." He shook his head as he walked away.

My head was spinning. I sat on the edge of my bed and cried into the palms of my hands. Perhaps Danny was right. Perhaps I was a fuck-up. Perhaps I did deserve everything that had happened to me.

Reaching into the bedside table, I pulled out the business card I'd kept as a reminder of how well I was doing. I hadn't had any intention of ringing the number ever again. But now, as Dr. Franklin's name stood out prominently against the glossy card, I wondered if maybe I wasn't quite as ready as I'd thought I had been.

I pulled on some jeans and an old shirt that only ever got worn when I was either mucking out stables or decorating. Even the feminine strength that I relied so heavily upon over the past year was fading. My façade was shrinking away like a dying moon. Once so brightly lit, it dwindled in the darkness of my depression.

Creeping like a reprimanded, sullen teenager, I found Mark and Danny in the living room. They were both on the sofa, with fury etched into their tight jaws and furrowed brows. Sometimes I wondered if they couldn't pass for twins.

"I'm sorry," I whimpered, my voice sounding pathetic.

Danny tutted loudly, pushing past me, his heavy feet thudding up the stairs. I turned my pitiful look to my brother. His arms were folded tightly across his chest, but his expression had softened. "I'm sorry, Mark," I cried, needing to hear the sympathetic comfort of his words. I sank into the cushions beside him and rested my head on his tense bicep. "I really am sorry."

"I know you are." His words were monotone, as though he didn't truly believe in them.

"What did Matt say?"

"He was worried about you. He said to tell you not to worry about the account, so I suppose at least your job is safe. I'm not sure about your sanity, though."

That stung. Mark had stood by me through everything, he was the pillar that supported me in my darkest moments, but now that strength was beginning to crumble beneath my selfishness.

"Danny and I --"

"I know." I stopped him from going any further, handing him the card with Dr. Franklin's number. "I'll ring him in the morning."

"You should get some sleep."

"You won't tell Mum and Dad, will you?"

"They have a right to know. If you're going down that road again, Paige... "

"I'm not. It's a blip. I made a stupid mistake and now I'm paying for it." I stood and walked towards the door.

"One question," he asked . I stopped and turned to face him. "Is what Matt Jackson said true? Did you sleep with his father?"

"Mark, I..."

"It's not any of my business who you're shagging, Paige. Be careful."

My room was shrouded in silence, thick curtains barring out the light and music that comes with a typical summer evening. My chest hurt like hell, more than any hangover could. Greg was going to fire me for sure. He'd been so understanding, giving me nearly four months off to heal physically, followed by a cut workweek to ten hours for another two, slowly building back up to a full-time job. I'd only been back properly for a few weeks, and already I'd had a week off for flu, and then tomorrow I was headed in with a hangover.

Dr. Franklin had said, if I needed more time, to ask and he would sign me off. Greg had been unsure when I'd said I wanted to come back to work so soon. But he knew it was precisely what I needed. Routine. Security. Everything that had been snatched away from me.

I'd thought that if I threw myself into work, into getting fit, I would heal. But Danny and Mark were right. I wasn't ready. I was pushing myself too soon, too quick. Something had to give before I broke beyond the point of no return.

I collapsed into a pathetic heap under my duvet. With the heavy curtains hanging to block out the rest of the day, I quickly found sleep.

I was surprised that I woke on Thursday without any of the expected repercussions, apart from an excessive amount of guilt weighing heavily on my shoulders and mind. I could have called in sick. Again. But that would have been weak, and I had to prove to myself that I was much stronger than that.

I have to say that further surprise lay in store for me, when I arrived to see Matthew Jackson already in reception. I blushed a deep shade of crimson as I sidled past him, mumbling, "How can I help?"

"I've come to see you."

"Mr. Jackson, I really don't know if this is the right time or place."

"I had to make sure you were okay. You were upset and angry. And how many times do I have to ask you to call me Matt?"

"Mr. Jackson! What a pleasant surprise!" Greg burst through the back doors, clutching a mug of hot tea. "Was there a problem with the designs?" he added, seeing the odd expressions slapped across both our faces.

"No. None at all. I was wondering if Paige would be so kind as to have lunch with me again." I deeply wished he would stop being so kind to me. I didn't deserve it.

"Yes, she'd love to," Greg answered for me, casting a concerned glance in my direction.

It was bloody typical that at that point I felt the vibration of my mobile through the pocket of my grey suit jacket. Subtly, I dipped in and checked the flashing screen. Three highly unwelcome letters glared up at me in neon green. Fuck.

"Will you excuse me, please." I darted into the back office and answered my phone, seconds before the answer machine kicked in. "Mr. Ellery, how can I help you?"

"Have lunch with me." Blunt, to the point, and obvious. Everything that I expected from him.

"I can't. Not today." Or I could, but it would mean having to turn your son down, who has arrived in my office.

"Then dinner."

Could I really date father and son at the same time, on the same day? I decided that I couldn't. Even I wasn't that immoral.

"No, not today." I didn't say I couldn't have dinner with them both! But not on the same day, that's all.

"I need to see you again, Paige."

"Mr. Ellery." It struck me that he had only asked me once to call him by his first name, and hadn't insisted when I refused. "I'm working. But I'll be free at the weekend."

"You'll be free tonight," he demanded. Bloody cheek of it! Yet I was almost powerless to resist. He took my silence as a "yes." "I'll pick you up at eight." Click.

CRAP!

Chapter Sixteen

To say I was nervous of my lunch appointment would have been an understatement. I was terrified. The last time he'd bought me something to eat, I'd ended up screeching at him like some wild banshee before consoling myself with half a bottle of tequila, the consequences of which I was still suffering. Not physically, although a headache had begun and I did feel slightly nauseous, but emotionally I was a wreck. I had now arrived at the conclusion that tequila is evil.

My eyes watched as the second hand moved around the clock's face at an ever-slowing pace. At one point I could have sworn it went backwards for a second. If you'd looked close enough, I am sure you would have seen minute beads of sweat forming along my hairline, although, as I glanced in the cracked mirror on the bathroom wall, I could see that my makeup was fully intact.

Alek Zubek stumbled into me as I opened the door from the only restroom in the building. He grunted my name and looked down at the floor as I stepped by him. Clearly there were rumors going around the workshop, and none that he cared to listen to.

97

A small part of me felt sorry for Alek. He'd been the last man I'd slept with consensually before TDS. Greg had told me enough times about the torch that Alek held, but I couldn't feel the same way about him. To me, he'd been a drunken one-night stand, and my last good memory before the scars had been inflicted. I wanted to keep him that way.

I raked my fingers through my hair, scooping it back into the restraints of its bun at the back of my head, as I walked back to my little corner of the office. Looking back up at the clock, I could see that I'd managed to kill a whole ten minutes. Five left before Matt Jackson walked back into my life.

"Greg, are you sure you don't need me to work through today?" I called, trying desperately to find an excuse to blow him off.

Greg peered through the glass at me and scowled. "Do it for me. You owe me big time."

He was right. I did owe him, for a lot more than he would ever admit to.

At one o'clock, the throaty burble of Mr. Jackson's Audi R8 Spyder signaled his arrival. My head dropped backwards as I failed to think of any more excuses.

"Enjoy!" Greg called out to me with a smirk plastered across his face. He was wallowing in my misery.

With a groan of reluctance, I grabbed my handbag and jacket, and made my way to the forecourt.

Even though was nearing the end of June, there was a distinctly nippy breeze blowing about. I wondered if we were ever going to get the heat wave that had been promised by the Met Office. But my typically British thoughts of weather were soon cast aside as I caught sight of Mr. Jackson standing proudly, holding the door of the white car open for me.

His dark hair had been teased into spikes, but smoothed around the sides. His sapphire eyes glinted in what sunlight managed to peek from beyond the gathering clouds.

I was comfortably accepting of his disheveled appearance: almost-black jeans with deliberate shredded patches around his calves, knees, and thighs, held up with a grey webbing belt. A white t-shirt covered his torso and hung loosely around the waist. The look was completed with a pair of pristinely clean white trainers. He certainly didn't look like the owner of an exclusive restaurant, or the son of a man who had a hand in almost every business venture going. It was refreshing, and relaxing, to know that Mark and I weren't the only ones trying to escape our opulent stereotypes.

"I feel overdressed," I whispered, looking down at my own smart grey suit. "I'm guessing we're not going to Matieus."

He shook his head, and I couldn't help but feel a mixture of relief and disappointment. I was happy that I wouldn't have to face the staff I'd blown past in such a rage last time, but I did enjoy being wined and dined in a restaurant that turned down even the rich and famous.

"I thought we'd go somewhere a bit more private. Somewhere you can scream and shout at me without making such a scene." There was a hint of laughter in his voice, but the expression on his face was serious. I shrank into my seat with embarrassment, folding my arms tightly across my waist.

He laughed loudly. "Don't worry. I won't hold it against you. My father has that effect on people." His eyes softened as he smiled, but soon hardened at the mention of his father.

"Is this why you wanted me to meet you? To discuss your father?"

"No." He shook his head, his jaw tightening. He went silent, and it unnerved me.

Shuffling in my seat, I was grateful when he finally pulled up the driveway of a small cottage at the back of Brookfield. It was quaint, to say the least, with tumbling roses climbing over the stone walls and baskets hanging beside the front door, drizzled with red, white, and pink flowers.

"Who lives here?" I asked, taking in the fragrant scent of lavender and the humble buzz of the bees that danced around the purple flowers lining the path to the entrance.

"I do." He smiled sweetly.

"You?" I asked, shocked. It was certainly not the masculine ultra-modern bachelor pad that I would have envisioned him living in. "I didn't know you lived in Brookfield."

Brookfield wasn't a huge village, but it was certainly larger than those where everyone knew everyone else. In fact, there was debate as to whether it should have been classed as a small town instead. Still, it surprised me that I hadn't met Matt Jackson before, considering I'd lived there all my life.

"I moved in a few weeks ago," he explained, as though reading my thoughts. "Matieus is doing really well, and I'm thinking about expanding."

"Oh," was all I could muster as I stepped inside the little abode. "It's very…" I paused, looking around the cottage and taking in the wooden floors, aging furniture, and peeling décor. "Rustic?"

"It needs work," he laughed. I liked his laugh; it was comforting to hear. "But I haven't had the time. I've been thinking about hiring a decorator, but I prefer to do these things myself. "Hence…" He motioned towards his clothes. "But I did manage to rustle up something to eat." He beckoned me towards a door that led to a kitchen. White paint, light wooden surfaces, and large windows that overlooked the back garden made the room airy and naturally bright.

On the table in the center was an array of salads, fruits, and wraps. "You've been busy. Are we expecting others to arrive?" I looked around for hidden guests.

"No," he laughed again. "I enjoy cooking. It helps me relax."

"You must have been stressed." I dumped my handbag and jacket on the work surface and walked towards the table.

"I was worried about you." His voice was softer now, as he took my hand and turned me to face him. "I won't lie, Paige. When I found out about you and my father, I was jealous."

A surge of heat rushed down to my belly as he spoke my name. My cheeks flushed at the sudden arousal he spiked in me.

"But that's not why I tried to warn you away from him. Please, don't get angry, just listen. You didn't let me finish last time, and when I found you in that state…" His own fury apparent, I pulled my hand away from his. "He's no good for you."

"You keep saying that."

"He always wants what he can't have, and once he's got it, he throws it away. He cheated on my mother countless times. Three of my ex-girlfriends have fallen for his charms, including my ex-fiancée. He'll use you, abuse you, and throw you on the scrap heap with all the others."

"Is that why I'm here? You trying to get back at your father?" I stepped backwards and made to grab for my coat, but he was there, his hand on mine, his fingers curling into my palm. Dark blue eyes burned into me, stoking the fire in my loins.

"No." The word was said with such harshness, so fiercely, I was almost scared by it.

"Then why am I?" My own voice sounded weak in comparison. He took my hand and lifted it to his lips. I was afraid my legs may collapse underneath me as his warm breath brushed over my knuckles.

"I wanted to make sure you were okay," he said, and not for the first time.

"I'm fine." I cleared my throat, regaining my strength and taking back my hand.

"I know that's not true, Paige. People who are fine don't have a disagreement with someone and head straight for the bottle."

"Are you calling me an alcoholic?" My larynx tightened around the word.

"No." He shook his head, looking at the ground. "But there is something that you're fighting."

"Why do you care, Mr. Jackson?"

"You mean you can't feel it?"

"Feel what?" I picked up my coat and bag, turning for the door, desperate to escape the madness. But his hands were around my waist, tugging me into him. As my jacket and bag fell to the floor, his hands crept around the edge of my trousers, pulling me closer to him. His lips sank to mine, and I could taste his own desperation. I let myself relax into his arms as I returned the kiss.

He stepped back, but kept his hands on my hips with a gentle pressure. "I've wanted to do that ever since I met you."

"Mr. Jackson…"

"Matt." He kissed me again, but this time I pulled away.

"Mr. Jackson, this is all wrong." I closed my eyes as the words slipped from my lips. "I can't."

"Yes, you can. Forget about my father."

"He's asked me to dinner tonight," I confessed.

"I see." He let go of me and walked back to the table. The smell of food caused my stomach to rumble, but I tried to ignore it. "You know it's just sex to him, don't you? You're one more prize for his trophy cabinet."

"Please don't say it like that. I like you, I really do."

"But not as much as you like him. My father has that effect: all-powerful and Godly. I hate him so much." His fingers gripped into the table as the loathing vibrated out of him.

"I'll go."

"No. I need you to stay." He stood and took my hand, leading me back to the table. "I hate myself more than I do him."

"Why?" I asked, sitting beside him, his hands clasped in mine.

"When I saw you the other day, after you'd left, you were in so much pain,"

"Please don't blame yourself. Or your father, for that matter. There is so much more going on with me than either of you will ever realize."

"Then tell me."

"I can't." I shook my head violently, twisting towards the table laden with such delicious food, and none of it appealing to me.

"I'm a good listener," he encouraged. I swallowed hard at the memories and tears that threatened to explode out of me. I looked away from him, fighting the urge to reveal myself, my hand rubbing at the lump that had suddenly appeared in my neck.

He stood behind me, his hands relaxing into the muscles on my shoulders, and rubbed at the knots that formed. I should have stopped him, but there was something addictive about his touch. What was it with this family? Both men incited something inside of me that I was unfamiliar with. I battled the blockade, but I knew I was pointless. I needed some release. The words blurted out of me with such force I had little strength to stop them.

"I was raped."

Chapter Seventeen

His hands lifted off my shoulders, acting like a floodgate for the emotion that I'd spent a year bottling up. Tears streamed down my cheeks as though I hadn't cried since it happened. There was little point in holding back any longer. I'd said the words.

"Fuck." It was his word that was spoken after a period of stunned silence.

"He was someone who worked with my father. We met at last year's summer ball. Things went well. He asked me out to dinner, I went, and afterwards we went back to his house. I tried to push him off me. But I couldn't remember anything I'd learned in my classes. It was all a blank, like I'd been drugged, even though I hadn't. He pinned me down, and… On his

103

living room floor. And when he was done, he stood up, looked down at me, and said that I wasn't as good as he'd been expecting."

My head dropped, ashamed of the occurrence, ashamed of the words, and hatred for the shame. "Worse than that, I was left pregnant." A nervous laugh filled my words, breaking through the cries.

"Fuck," he said again, unable to rake through the dictionary of his mind.

"But there were complications and I got an infection." My hand shot across my waist. "There was a lot of scarring, and they had no choice." The words stopped. The tears fell. "I had to have a laparotomy. I can't have children."

"Paige, I am so…" His hands were clasped around mine. I looked up to see him knelt in front of me, with a look I was only too familiar with.

"Sorry? Yeah, I hear that a lot."

"I don't know what else to say."

"Nobody ever does. They just wrap you in this little bubbled world, and then pretend you're not there anymore. That's why I slept with your father, I guess. He was the first man to have shown me any real attention since, and I loved it," I admitted it not only to him, but to myself.

"Do you have any idea what it's like to be told not to be ashamed, that it wasn't your fault, and yet be surrounded by people who can't even look at you because they don't know how to react? Then your father noticed me. I wasn't the victim who can't have children anymore, I was a woman again, and I needed that."

"I had no idea."

"Why should you? It's not something I go around broadcasting. Oh, hey, my name's Paige Holmes, last year I was attacked by a friend of my father's and it left me infertile, wanna fuck?" I took my hands from his and stood to leave again. "I'm sorry if you think I'm being flippant, but it's my way of dealing with it. Now I really should go."

I dug through my bag to find the tissues and wiped away the mascara I knew would be lining my cheeks. Even though I'd said the words so mechanically, the memories were raw. Grating against me like coarse sandpaper, scratching away any dignity or self-worth that hadn't been ripped from my core.

"No, you don't."

"What?"

"You don't have to go anywhere. What you've said, it doesn't change anything. I understand some of it now, but that doesn't make me feel any different. I still want you, Paige."

"Why?"

"Because you are an attractive, intelligent woman, and I don't give a damn whether you're screwing my father or not. What I do care about is you."

"If you think you're going to rescue me, you're a year too late. I've been through it all already, and my life is finally getting back on track. People are finally beginning to forget about it, I've got my job and my friends, and…" And what? There was nothing else. No life, that was for sure. I woke up, went to work, and filled in my spare time running off the energy that could so easily be flooded by unwanted memories.

"You think sleeping with my father is going to help you recover?"

"Not really, but…"

"But what? He's an older man like that…" He searched the ground for the word that failed his lips. "That cunt." The severity of the word hit me as though I'd been slapped. He didn't seem to notice my surprise as he continued. "And you think by sleeping with him, it'll make it all go away?"

"I was hoping so." The sound of my voice was near silent as I tried to digest his rage. I didn't correct any of his assumptions.

"Has it worked?"

"No," I cried in great sobs, my hands clutching at my chest as I tried to keep my heart from breaking out of its bony cage. "Jesus, I can't breathe." I gasped for air, grappling for the sideboards, trying desperately to keep my legs from falling away. My mantra, what was my mantra?

My mind raced, searching through every drawer, but all it pulled out were pictures of his face, laughing down at me.

"Breathe." I heard the words in harsh whispers. Hands gripped under my arms. I tried to bat them away. Mark. I needed Mark. I dug through my handbag and fished out my mobile, but it tumbled out of my grasp.

"Breathe."

That was it. Breathe in, breathe out. In through the nose, out through the mouth. In with the good, out with the bad.

Breathe.

As I came to, I realized I was no longer in Mr. Jackson's kitchen. I was laid prone on a sofa, staring up at black beams stretching across the ceiling. Where was I? I rolled my head and saw Mr. Jackson by my side. "Breathe, Paige,"

"Shit." I pulled myself up, trying to sit, but his hands were on my shoulders.

"Are you okay?"

"I suffer from panic attacks," I explained, breathlessly.

"I can see that. Are you feeling better?"

"Yes, thanks." I took the glass of water he held out to me and sipped at it gratefully. "I'm really sorry,"

"You have absolutely nothing to apologize for."

"I should get back to work."

"You should get some rest. Your boss will understand if you let me talk to him."

"No. I need to work. I need to keep going, or he wins."

"I won't pretend that I understand or agree with you, but if that's what you want."

"It is."

"What about tonight? At least cancel my father."

"It's just a panic attack, Mr. Jackson."

"I really wish you'd call me Matt."

"Okay, Matt." I smiled, provoking a broad grin to erupt from my host. "Could you drive me back to the office, please?"

Greg was tied up with phone calls when I got back. I could hear him yelling down the receiver to a customer who still hadn't paid his bill, despite the umpteen invoices we'd sent to him. When he did finally emerge from the wooden box, he took one look at me and declared that I looked exhausted.

"Nothing a hot bath won't cure."

"How was your lunch date?"

"Boring and uneventful." My stomach growled in disagreement.

"Well, it's nearly five. You may as well head home. See you tomorrow?"

"See you "tomorrow." I forced a friendly and grateful smile.

I arrived home to find Mark and Danny both playing on the Xbox, as usual. Dipping into my bag, I realized that my mobile wasn't there. I tipped the contents onto the kitchen table, sifting through them frantically. No, it was definitely missing. Crap.

I looked at my watch. Twenty to six. My brain scoured through the events of the day. The last time I'd needed my phone was... when I tried to call for Mark mid-panic attack. I'd dropped it at the cottage. Double crap.

Grabbing the phone and my diary, I searched through until I found the number I needed. It rang several times before he answered. "Mr. Ellery, I'm ever so sorry, but I'm going to have to cancel tonight. I'm afraid something's come up."

"This is not good enough, Paige," his voice growled.

"I know, I'm so sorry, but I've really got to get this work done before tomorrow. Can we take a rain check?" I pleaded. The line fell silent. "Hello?"

"Fine. I'll see you on Friday evening instead. I'll pick you up at eight." Click.

With a sigh of relief, I searched for the number of Matieus and hoped that Matt was working that night. It was the maître-d' who answered before passing me through to the office.

"Paige, I thought you had a date with my father this evening."

"I do -- I mean, did."

"You canceled on him?" He sounded surprised. "He won't like that." There was an element of enjoyment in his tone.

"No. He wasn't happy. But I think I've left my phone at your place."

"Yes, it's in the kitchen." He paused as though he were thinking of the more rational way of returning it. "I'll pick you up in about half an hour and we can go and get it."

"I can drive myself."

"No, I'll pick you up," he insisted. Half an hour, time for a quick shower and to get changed.

I tried to race past the living room, but Danny came out and blocked my path. "TDS again?" he asked, with an obvious suspicion.

"If you must know, I've canceled on him."

"Oh." Glee settled in the suspicion's place.

"I've left my phone at a friend's, though, so if you'll excuse me." I squeezed past him.

"This friend," he quizzed, "wouldn't happen to be tall, dark, handsome, and the son of the man you're shagging, would it?"

"Fuck you," I threw back, jumping up the stairs.

I chose to change into a pair of jeans with a tight white vest, but of course, I was wearing those killer heels. The Audi pulled outside the house as the grey clouds tightened over the summer evening sky.

"I'm surprised you canceled on my father." Matt couldn't help but smile.

"I didn't cancel, I postponed," I argued.

"Have you eaten yet?" he asked, as my stomach growled again.

"No, I haven't had the chance."

"Then I am feeding you. No arguments."

"How can I resist?" I asked sarcastically as I swung my legs into the passenger side. I could feel him trying to catch a glimpse of my figure as he drove towards the little cottage. "So how long are you planning on staying in Brookfield?" I asked, attempting small talk.

"I'm actually considering moving in permanently." He cleared his throat and opened his mouth as if to talk again, but nothing came out.

"Go on," I encouraged.

"How are you feeling? After this afternoon?"

"Much "better." I smiled. "Thank you for being an ear and a shoulder."

"I'm glad you told me."

"I wish I hadn't. I'm sorry I unloaded my baggage and issues onto you."

"Don't ever apologize." His brows knotted across the bridge of his nose and his jaw tightened into a solid line, making him look even more like his father. "You have nothing to be sorry for. When you told me what that, that…" He couldn't find a word to describe him any more than I could. "What he did to you. I've never wanted to hurt anyone before. It's not in me to be violent, but if I ever found him, I would kill him." It was an honesty that I appreciated.

"You won't need to. My father saw to it so that he won't be seeing the light of day for at least another eleven years."

"Eleven years" He shook his head in disgrace, a feeling I knew all too well.

"It was a life sentence, because of the complications." It all came out so mechanical, a rehearsed script from my past. "But he only has to serve twelve years before he can apply for a license. My father also sued the crap out of him. I've got five million sitting in a bank account that I hope never to touch. I keep debating whether I should donate it to charity, but I'm not sure I want to taint anyone else."

Matt's eyebrows shot up as I mentioned the amount. I hadn't ever told anyone before, but he made me feel at ease. Perhaps my mother had a point after all.

We pulled up the driveway of the little cottage and I stepped out into the summer evening air, instantly wishing I'd brought a jacket. Wet spots landed on my bare arms. "Great," I muttered under my breath.

"Come on," Matt laughed, beckoning me over the front door.

Inside, the cottage was shrouded in the gloom cast down by the heavy clouds. Matt flicked on the light switches, creating a warm orange glow. "Here you go." He handed my phone to me.

"Thanks." I wasn't sure what to do next. Was that it? Was I supposed to go? He had promised me food, and God knows I was hungry.

"I don't know what I've "got." His voice was muffled by the space from the kitchen to the living room. I wandered around, examining the downstairs rooms. "We could order in." His voice was clearer. I turned to see him standing in the doorway, leaning against the wooden frame, still dressed in those torn jeans and that white tee.

"Chinese sounds good," I offered, falling into the sofa that was opposite an open fireplace, surrounded by red brick.

"Chinese it is." He disappeared into the kitchen again and I heard him mumbling into the phone, no doubt ordering from the only takeaway shop in the village. "It'll be here in about forty-five minutes," he said, reappearing.

"No TV," I noted.

"I don't really spend much time here, to be honest. I'm usually at work."

"That's refreshing. My brother and Danny are always glued to the bloody Xbox. Apparently they own a photography company, but I haven't seen much proof of them doing any work," I joked, and he joined me in chuckling.

"So Mark and Danny, are they…" he wavered on the assumption that so many did.

"No! No, Mark, I'd believe it if you told me he was, but Danny is heterosexual in every sense of the word."

"But you all live together?"

"I moved in with Mark a few years ago to get out from under my parents. Danny fills the empty room. I've thought about getting my own place, but after last year, it seemed the sane option to stay where I felt safe."

"I can't believe how strong you are, considering it was only a year ago."

"Yeah, well, that's me!"

"Sorry, if you don't want to talk about it."

"It's not that I don't want to." I took his hands in mine, and gazed into those deep blue pools. "I've never found anyone who's willing to listen."

Chapter Eighteen

The food arrived moments before the thick grey clouds blackened further. A rumble in the distance sent a shiver down my spine.

Matt dished out the noodles and rice onto two plates, thrusting one in my direction. We ate hungrily. "I've never seen a girl eat like you," he laughed.

"I'm starving," I said, in between mouthfuls of prawns and peas, trying to ignore the darkening room. A crash overhead started the storm's symphony. Fat raindrops splattered against the window, as the room lit with a sudden flash. Seconds later another rumble flooded the sky. I shuddered.

"Are you okay?"

"I don't like thunderstorms," I admitted, finishing the last of my noodles. The truth was, I was afraid of any loud noise.

"Don't worry, I won't force you out in this."

"I forgot to bring a coat," I grumbled, rubbing my arms as though it had suddenly got cold.

Matt stood and peered out the window. "It'll be a while before this is over." He picked up the plates and took them into the kitchen. I followed him, not wanting to be alone in the dark room.

As I walked in, I suddenly remembered the large windows, and saw the grizzly sky blanketing the village. My eyes widened in fear, as another flash filled the sky. Matt smiled at me.

"What's so funny?"

"You are," he laughed, nearing me. "I didn't think you were afraid of anything."

"Appearances can be deceptive."

"That, they most certainly can!" He took my hand and led me back into the living room. "Well, it looks like we'll be here a bit longer than intended." We sat back down on the sofa.

"And no TV to kill the time," I said, staring at the empty fireplace. "Look, if you want to get rid of me, I can make a mad dash to the car door. It's only rain."

"I don't want to get rid of you, Paige." As he said my name, I felt the hairs on my neck and arms stand on end. "But I'm not willing to share you either."

"You mean your father." I stumbled over the words.

"I know I said that I didn't care, but if I'm being honest, I do."

"Please don't ask me to choose. I'm not sure I can," I said candidly. As much as I enjoyed being in Matt's company, I couldn't deny the enigmatic force of TDS. I knew that the instant I saw him again, I would fall for his charms.

"I think you made that choice already."

111

"What are you talking about?" I wasn't aware of any choice-making.

"You canceled a dinner with him, to come and see me."

"Is that all this is? A pissing contest between the two of you?" I wanted to be angry, but my voice was mellow and controlled, surprising us both.

"I won't lie to you, Paige. I think you've been betrayed enough." Heat rose to my cheeks. "Yes, I want to hurt my father, but not through you. If I thought that seducing you would upset him, I'd have done it at your father's ball."

"Don't be so sure of yourself," I scoffed.

"I feel honored that you trusted me enough to open up to me." He ignored my mocking. "If you felt for my father as you do me, you would have told him, and I can assure you his reaction would have been different to mine."

I swallowed the lump of uncertainty that lodged in my throat. I hadn't considered how TDS would have reacted to my confessions. I hadn't considered telling him at all. Would he have listened to my cries, or would he have tossed me out like a used tissue? I suspected the latter.

The crash of symbols above the house grew louder, flooding the house with a bright white light. I heard a shriek seconds before realizing it was mine.

My shoulders began to shake before the tightness encompassed my ribs.

Breathe in, breathe out.

The acrid taste of bile rose to my throat.

In with the good, out with the bad.

I began to heave, gasping for air. My eyelids fell shut, the lashes fluttering against my cheeks as I searched for that tranquil place.

"It's okay," I heard the voice softly speak through the darkness. Hands were resting on my arms; gentle, kindly, and warm.

Inhaling deeply, the sweet rush of oxygen swept up into my nostrils.

In through the nose, out through the mouth.

"Slowly, Paige," the voice soothed. Arms wrapped around me. No, too tight. I shook my head harshly, pushing away at the tangle of limbs.

The crash grew louder. Cries threatened to break free.

"You're all right. I'm here."

I opened my eyes. "I'm sorry." I tripped over my own tongue, still reciting my mantra. Matt sat in front of me, his arms across my knees, hands still resting above my elbows.

"How many times do I have to tell you to stop apologizing? Are you feeling better?"

"Not really."

"Can I get you anything? A glass of water?"

I shook my head. There was only one thing I needed at that moment in time. "Can you hold me, please?"

Matt smiled, wrapping his arms around me. "When you pushed me away..."

"I couldn't breathe. When I'm having an attack, I need my space," I explained, closing my eyes and relaxing into his strength. My mind began to drift, and I wondered whether TDS would have held me and saved me from my panic.

The thunder continued to roll around, tumbling in its fight with the lightning and rain. My spine quivered as the fear began to subside.

His hands ran over my arms, brushing against the curve of my bust. That single touch caused everything in me to tighten and tense, and I was glad for the padded bra, hiding my obvious arousal.

"I should say sorry," he started with a deep breath. "You're not a pissing contest, and I'm sorry that I made you to feel that way."

"It's okay. I shouldn't have tried to play games between you and TD -- your father," I corrected myself.

"TD?" he inquired, sounding bemused.

"Oh, nothing. It's silly." I wriggled down, trying to avoid the conversation.

"No, I'm intrigued now. What pet name do you have for him?"

"TDS," I offered. "Tall, Dark, and Smoldering."

"You think my father smolders?" He was mocking me.

"I did when I first met him." This was embarrassing.

"But not now?"

"I'm not sure of anything anymore."

"Why not?"

"You." I turned to face him. His eyes had darkened so that they matched the sky.

"What did I do?" he asked, feigning innocence. I pulled from his grasp and sat up to face him. A bemused smirk crossed his lips.

"I didn't know who you were at first; I thought you were just some cute bloke wanting his car done up. But then, when I found out you were his son, it confused me. I was attracted to you both."

"Was?"

"Am. I am attracted to you both. I can't help it and I'm not going to hide my feelings for your father. I can't control myself around him."

"Not many women can. Don't worry, it's a magnetism I wish I possessed."

"Oh, no, please don't wish to be like him. You're so much more. He's just sex." I saw him cringe beneath the words. Of course, he would be uncomfortable discussing his father's sexual prowess, as much as I recoiled at the thought of my parents even so much as kissing. "But you," I continued, trying to hide both our embarrassment. "You're so kind and warm. I love spending time with you. I really do."

"But I'm not sex." There was no more teasing in his voice now. Seriousness spread across him.

"Why are you even pursuing this? You know that I've spent the night with him, yet you still want me as well?"

"Because since the moment I met you, I've wanted something much more."

"Even though you know about…"

"Yes." He stopped me from mentioning TDS further.

"Doesn't it bother you?" I probed further, delving deep into his skin.

"I've already told you it does," he snapped. He stood up, running his hands through his hair. The muscles in his back flexed beneath his t-shirt, a sight that sent shock waves coursing through me. How could I even be contemplating a man who was old enough to be my father when this stood before me?

He dropped to his knees beside me. "It bothers me a lot. But there is something about you." He lifted a hand to trace the line across my chin. "You stir something inside me that I haven't felt for a long time. I meant it when I said I felt honored that you told me." He leaned towards me, closing the gap between us. His lips brushed across mine. "Spend the night with me, Paige."

"I don't know that I should." My mouth trembled against him.

"Forget about him," he growled, his hand lifting to my arm, his fingers tracing the outline of my bust and waist. "He's not worthy of you." His kiss stopped me from responding.

A hand trailed down my spine, reaching the waistband of my jeans. I lifted my fingers to his hair, grazing through, as I pushed myself into him. He stood up and took my hands, pulling me with him. I looked up at him, reaching to kiss his jawline. Before I could stop him, he'd tugged the t-shirt over his head and tossed it into a pile on the floor. My eyes went with the white fabric as it landed. A finger under my chin tilted me into his hungry lips.

My hands moved over his chest. The hard muscle beneath my palms caused my stomach to clench. His touch found the curve of my buttocks, lifting me up to him. Turning me, he pressed my back into the hard wall, lifting me so that I could feel his erection pressing through his jeans and into my inner thigh. I gasped; my breasts swelled against him.

His mouth was on mine, his tongue searching desperately. I sucked on him slowly, savoring his taste. He moaned against my lips as he pressed me deeper.

In a swirl of fumbling, we turned to the sofa, and I was laid on the cushions as he tugged at my jeans, pulling them over my hips. He kissed my ankle, trailing his lips over my calf and thigh, stopping as he reached my hip.

Instinctively my hand fell to that spot.

His eyes fixed on mine, he moved my hand and lifted my vest, kissing along the angry red line. "I wish I could take it all away," he whispered into my skin. Tears rose in my eyes, threatening to burst the dam. "No, please don't cry," he hushed, darting up my body until his mouth was on mine. His hand slipped underneath the vest and found the cusp of my breast. He massaged gently, kneading at the plump mound.

I gasped loudly as his fingers found my nipple, teasing lightly. Dipping his head, he lifted the vest over me and took the stiff flesh in his mouth, his tongue circling the sensitive part. A hand slipped beneath us, biting into my buttocks.

His erection pressed into me, hard as iron. I couldn't take it any longer. Scrambling for his fly, I tugged at it until he was free and in my hand. I rubbed at him eagerly, desperate to feel him. I heard him moan as he throbbed within my grasp.

Hands fumbled into my pants, jerking them down to the floor. There we lay, flesh on flesh, skin on skin, basking in each other's heat.

Dipping between our bodies, he found me swollen with desire. I already knew how damp I was. He groaned, slipping a finger into me, his lips against my chest. My back arched to meet him, urging him into me, guiding him.

Hands moved beneath me once more, lifting me as I let him fill me. I felt him pulsate against my wall as I tightened around him.

Moaning against him, I buried my face deep into his shoulder, raking my nails down his back as he quickened, rocking back and forth before he shattered under my touch.

We lay still for a moment, beads of sweat mingling together. I could taste the saltiness of his skin as I kissed his bare shoulder. "Would you mind if I used your shower?" I asked humbly as he moved from me.

"Of course not. Perhaps I could join you?"

Chapter Nineteen

I checked my mobile to find a single message from my brother simply asking me to text him when I was alive. Hastily, I dialed the house phone and let it ring before leaving a quick message letting them both know that I was fine but got caught in the storm and that Matt would be bringing me home soon.

Matt stepped out of the shower in the house bathroom, wrapping a towel around his midriff. I sat on the bed, rubbing at my hair, watching small droplets fall around my wrists. "You don't have to go," he soothed, sauntering closer.

"Yes, I do. I have work in the morning, and I have no clean clothes here. The storm's stopped now."

"What are you going to do about…"

"Vance?" it was the first time I'd said his actual name for a while. Up until now he'd been 'your father' or 'TDS' in my mind. "That depends what it is that you want."

"I want you, Paige. I have ever since the moment I met you."

But how long will it last? I asked myself, not wanting to hear the answer out loud. How long before you replace me with someone who can give you a family of your own?

There lay the real reason behind my wanting TDS. Mark was wrong. It had nothing to do with him reminding me of that night and the power that he could exert over me. It had nothing to do with battling demons. TDS would never want me to have his children. TDS was safe, where security meant a life without the pressures of society. TDS was a quick fling, an affair to regain my control and self-awareness. I wasn't ready to wage a war against long-term yet. I wasn't ready to have that conversation.

As Matt drove me back to the farmhouse, I couldn't help but feel the tension divide us. I cursed myself for having succumbed to his and my wants and desires. The complex weave of lust strangled me as my thoughts drifted to the inevitable exchange that would come when TDS ensured I kept my date with him.

"Can I see you again?" Matt asked as I climbed out of the Audi. "I'd like to."

"You'll see me at work."

"I meant outside of work."

"I take it you haven't heard from my mother yet then?" I could tell by the confusion that knotted his brows together that he hadn't. "She wants to invite you over for lunch one day."

"I'd like to. Are you okay with that?"

"I'm not sure," I stuttered, tumbling down the spiral of lies and deceit I was slowly building around myself. Slamming the car door, I turned to walk up the driveway. What the hell had I gotten myself into?

Danny was at the kitchen table, his hands gripped around a cooled mug, his grey eyes watching as I skulked through. I tried to ignore him, dumping my bag in the middle of the table with a clunk to make a point that I wasn't bothered by his brooding looks.

"Where's Mark?" I eventually asked, pouring myself a cup of tea.

"He's got a date." Ah, so that was it. Jealousy. I did feel for Danny. He was always left in Mark's shadow when it came to girls.

I sat opposite him, and we watched each other, drinking our tea. It was as though we were competing in a staring match, fighting for that top-dog spot. Finally, I broke the glare to catch sight of the clock on the wall. "I've got work tomorrow. I excused myself, standing to go to bed.

"Paige." He stopped me from going any further. "If you ever need to talk, I'm here for you."

It was sweet that he cared so much, and I loved that I had two big brothers to look out for me. But I didn't need it. With a heavy sigh, I simply nodded before marching up to the sanctity of my own room.

I stared up at the ceiling, and for the first time, I noticed a small dark spot right within my vision. Had it been there before? I couldn't be sure, but it felt as though it had. A little dark spot that I could watch as it either grew or shrank, while my mind adapted to the complexity of the life in which I had become wrapped.

I don't remember falling asleep, but I must have done so, because at two-thirty I was wide awake, listening to Mark clambering up the stairs. Only it didn't sound like he was alone. There was a light giggle, far too high-pitched for my brother.

Peering around the door, trying to catch a sneak peek without being caught, I watched as a skinny blonde stumbled up the steps. She looked familiar, but I couldn't quite place the platinum curls and pointed, pixie-like features.

Wearily, I sunk back into the darkness of my room and collapsed on my bed, still fully clothed. I barely slept. The rest of the night, or morning, was filled with broken dreams swirling around my foggy mind. But at least they weren't the nightmares or terrors that sometimes plagued my sleep.

I couldn't even remember them when I woke with my alarm, but I was exhausted. Stretching and yawning awkwardly, I spent less than ten minutes in the shower before brushing my teeth and dressing in a knee-length black skirt and scarlet red shirt.

The blonde was in my kitchen as I reached for the bread to make myself some toast. Through bleary eyes, I could make out that she was petite in every way. "Hi," I stated bluntly, without the energy to even force a smile.

"Morning, Butch," Mark chirped. "You remember Bianca."

Holy crap! It was TDS' daughter, Matt's sister!

I don't know whether my mouth actually dropped, but if I'd been a cartoon character, I'd have been picking up my jaw from the floor. "Hi, Bianca," I elongated the words, fixing a grin, which could have easily been a grimace, across my lips.

I marched into the living room, finding Danny still in his boxers, half-lounging across the armchair with the news flashing images across the screen. "Do you have any idea who his date was last night?" I asked in a harsh whisper.

"Keep it in the family," he shrugged.

"You okay, Butch?" Mark asked, passing me a plate of buttered toast.

"What the hell, Mark?" I exclaimed, grappling at my cool as it slipped between my fingers. "She's like, fifteen!"

"She's eighteen, and she's fit as," he justified. "I'm not going to give up on that piece of arse just because you're screwing her father and brother."

"Oh, if only your parents could hear you two," chimed in Danny. We both shot him a look that shut him up immediately.

"For Christ's sake, Mark."

"Hey, this onus is on you. I'm only shagging one Ellery."

If I'd been a violent person, I'd have punched him square in the jaw, but it wasn't in me to hit my own brother. Fists clenched by my side, I screeched an "ooh" that sounded like I'd gotten something large and bulky stuck in my throat.

Grabbing my bag, I stormed out of the house, clambered into the Golf, and slammed my palms down on the steering wheel several times, screaming into the mirror.

An elderly gentleman walking his dog gave me a sideways glance as he crossed the road to avoid my temper. Yup, only your neighborly nut-job losing the plot here!

Marching up the metal steps into the office, I was lucky I didn't break a heel. No comments, no sideways glances, and the guys buried their heads into the engines and wheel arches as I swept through, with a dark cloud of fury close behind.

"Okay, Paige, it's time we talked." Greg sounded serious. My shoulders already ached from the pressure and stress mounting on them; the last thing I needed to hear were the words, "You're fired."

"Greg, I…."

"My office. Now."

Grudgingly, I stood and followed him like a scolded puppy. He pointed to the threadbare seat in front of his desk and began his lecture. My fists curled into tight balls on my lap, pulling at the hem of my skirt, wrenching out the tension. He spoke about his wife, and my father, and how they had all worked hard to make sure I still had a job. And while he completely understood and sympathized with my situation, he still had a business to run.

"I'm your friend, Paige, I really am. But I'm your boss first."

Tears hit the back of my lids as I closed my eyes, pushing back the tidal wave with weak barricades.

"I think you need some more time."

"Greg, I'm fine, I am. Please don't fire me," I blubbered.

"I'm not firing you, honey." He sank by my side and took my hands in his. "But you're clearly distracted. I'm worried that you came back too soon. You've had a hell of a lot to deal with, and you've taken no time to heal."

"I'm fine," I argued.

"Physically, maybe, but not mentally." He exhaled loudly before standing up and running his oil-stained hands through his dirty blond hair.

"I don't want to go behind your back, Paige. But if you don't take a break and get some help, I will speak to your dad again. I've contacted a temp agency, and they'll be sending someone over tomorrow morning. Please go home and rest. Talk to someone."

He touched my shoulder before sitting back in his own chair. "I blame myself. I pushed you too soon."

"No! No, Greg. It's not your fault," I exclaimed. It would have been so easy for me to blurt it all out then and there, to tell him about the landfill-sized mess I'd got myself into.

But perhaps he had a point. Perhaps I did need a bit more time to gather myself, to recover from the trauma.

My head dropped in a semi-nod. Last time my boss and my father spoke, it ended up with me being put under Dr. Franklin's care and prescribed a concoction of antidepressants, muscle relaxants, and painkillers that had sent me into a world of fantasy for two weeks straight.

The antidepressants still sat in my medicine cabinet, the seal cracked, but the bottle untouched in nearly two months.

I picked up my bag and made ready to leave. Forced onto sick leave again. My life was a complete and utter shambles. He was winning all over again.

The dark cloud of depression loomed above me, threatening to burst at any second. My mind raced around the past few weeks. TDS. Matt. Perhaps it was time to cut my losses with both of them.

It was Thursday. I still had a day until I was supposedly meeting TDS for a dinner which I suspected wouldn't be involving food. The knots in my stomach fought relentlessly.

I'd hoped that he would help clear away those dusty webs that clung to my every corner, but it seemed all he'd done was build more. Matt was the fly to his spider; breaking strands as he begged me to fight the attraction.

I still didn't know if I was even sure of TDS. One minute he was strong and powerful, dominating in every sense. The next, he was playing at being a lover, equal in all respects. But even when his arms had felt soft around me, I could detect that hidden authoritarian. I didn't feel safe around him. I felt out of control, and I had to keep my secrets concealed.

At least Matt was honest and straight. He'd shown his emotions, he'd helped me - encouraged me, even - to open up and lay myself bare to him. He'd been compassionate, angry for me, not at me, protective and sincere. But there was something lacking in him. He was the submissive to his father's alpha male. Of that, I was certain. But what did that make me?

What a mess. Unfortunately, it wasn't like my kitchen. I couldn't ask my parents to pay someone to clean up after me this time. This was down to me and me alone. It was time to take a firm hold of reality and shake it until my subconscious revealed itself.

Chapter Twenty

I should have gone home. Instead, I headed for the one place that showed my strength: the gym.

It had been a couple of weeks since I'd stepped foot over the threshold, but it still smelled exactly the same: a delicious blend of sweat, deodorant, and rubber. The gym was an old warehouse on the trading estate that had been converted to house a small dance studio which was also used for the occasional martial arts classes (although less often since Tyler had opened his new unit). Free weights, a few treadmills, bikes, rowing machines, cross-trainers, and two multi-gyms. It wasn't exactly luxurious, but it was exactly what I needed.

"I was beginning to think you'd fallen off the face of the planet," exclaimed Ken Marston, owner of the gym and my personal trainer. He was a bodybuilder and looked every part of it. From bulging biceps to tree-trunk thighs, he was pure and utter muscle. He was also not much taller than me.

"Work," I explained, not wanting to divulge any aspect of my life.

"I have half an hour to spare if you want a session."

"No, thanks. I have some energy I need to burn off."

"Sure, go ahead. Tyler mentioned you've missed a few of his classes as well."

As well as being my MMA instructor, Tyler was also Ken's civil partner. They'd helped me rebuild my strength after my surgery, and had probably been two of the reasons, alongside Lou, that I hadn't given up on my sports. They were more than simply gym staff to me. They were my friends.

I threw him a reassuring smile. "You know how it is. Work, flu, blah, blah, blah."

"Well, if you need me, just yell. I take it you haven't forgotten how to use the equipment safely?" he teased.

"I'm sure I can figure out," I called, as I pushed through the turnstile and waltzed into the changing room.

Sitting on the cold wooden bench, my head fell into the palms of my hands. Shoulders heaved heavily as I struggled to regain my composure. I'd managed to get as far as changing and shoving my belongings into the red metal locker before the frustration took over, exasperated by the events of the past fortnight.

"Pull you together," I chastised myself. "Get out there and prove them all wrong."

It took an inordinate amount of effort to make it towards the treadmill. I plugged in my iPod and switched it to my playlist, a mixture of rock, pop, and trance tunes that helped to block out the pain that surged through my tiring limbs.

The sting of lactic acid slowed me down as I tried to break through the wall, but I was still weak and hit it with a resounding thud. Slowing to a gentle jog, I grabbed a hand towel, mopping the sweat that drizzled down my face and neck.

"You're doing good there, girl." Ken's Bristol accent pushed past the music playing in my ears.

Yanking one white wire, I breathed heavily, reducing myself to a steady walk. "Thanks," I panted. "Think I'll call it a day, though." Taking a swig from the water bottle, I noticed the lack of sunlight at the top windows.

The showers at the gym were basic, but welcome. There is nothing better than hot water thrashing against the cluster of muscles and sinew that build after a good workout. The jasmine scent of the shower gel was calming, as I smoothed it over my body. My fingertips traced the red line along my abdomen. Greg was right. It had healed physically, but mentally the rips were still visible to anyone who cared to look deep enough.

I remembered what Matt had told me, had asked me. He had taken my past with the ton of salt it needed, but would his father, if I divulged the same details? Did I even want TDS to know of the history behind the scars? This one certainly didn't have the same flowery story of those that lined my jaw and brow.

Pulling on my jeans and flimsy teal tunic, I wrenched the holdall straps over my shoulders and headed back home.

Mark and Danny were out, no doubt visiting one of their many clients who insisted on evening consultations. The house was masked by the night, although they had thought to leave the landing light on for me. The golden glow from upstairs soothed away one of my many fears.

The kitchen phone flashed an amber warning that there was a message to be heard. I pressed the button as I scrunched up the clothes from my holdall into the washing machine. My mother's voice sang through the air, informing me that she had spoken to Matthew Jackson and had arranged a lunch on Sunday. I was to arrive promptly at twelve, and could I bring an array of clothes with me?

I rolled my eyes and groaned. It wasn't bad enough that she was forcing me to dine with the one person I now wanted to avoid, but she was determined to dress me for it as well.

Ignoring the plea to return her call, I fell into a deep sleep on my bed, refusing to wake when the boys returned. I didn't even roll out when my alarm finally alerted me to the next morning, but tumbled out of bed more than half an hour later.

"Work?" Danny pressed, noting that I was still wearing my grey pajamas, with ruffled hair and no makeup.

"No," I responded, not wanting to talk. But Danny wouldn't give in so easily. He flicked the kettle on, preparing for my sob story, and munched on a slice of marmite toast. Instantly, the smell of yeast extract caused me to gag. "Do you have to eat that crap?"

"It's good for you." He took another giant bite before preparing two mugs for tea. "Sit, and tell."

"What would you like me to tell?"

"Why you're not going to work, why there's a message on the phone from your mother, and why you've been acting like the only person on the planet who gives a shit about you." There was no point in trying to escape. I could tell that he'd been talking to Mark and my parents. Yet again, they had intervened on behalf of my sanity.

"Come on, Paige, if you're not going to tell your parents or Mark, then you have to talk to me. How long have I known you?"

"Twenty years?" I shrugged, not caring to remember the countless memories, I had growing up with Danny standing in my brother's shadow.

He placed the two piping hot mugs on the table and sat behind one of them, gesturing for me to join him. "Exactly. You know that I'm the closest thing you have to a best friend." Depressingly, he was right. Over the past twelve months, I had single-handedly managed to destroy most of my close friendships. Except his. He hadn't budged, no matter how hard I shoved him.

"So I'm not going anywhere until you tell me what the hell is going on with you," he continued. I sat down, my hands wrapped around the hot mug, taking in the warmth and letting it calm me.

"I don't know what's going on with work. Greg told me to go home or he'd talk to Dad again. I guess I'll need to get signed off." My head dropped with shame and guilt. I felt Danny place a hand on my arm, rubbing gently as the hairs prickled beneath his touch.

"What about you?" he probed, trying to catch my eye. I lifted my chin slightly and was immediately trapped by his cloud-grey stare. I wanted to tell him I was okay. I didn't want to admit my torment, but as he glowered at me, I knew I was helpless beneath his touch.

The tears burst like a waterfall rushing over a steep cliff. "I don't know what I'm doing," I sobbed, shoulders heaving against the weight of blame.

Dan sank back into the chair and tipped his head towards the ceiling. His hands rubbed over his face as he struggled to find the words. I cowered, ready for his barrage of how stupid I'd been, how fucked up I was....

"I take it you're going to let your mum down, then?"

"How can I? She's so desperate to see me act like a normal human being," I muttered, shamed by my own actions.

"Don't beat yourself up." He leaned towards me and rubbed a friendly hand over my arm.

"So what do I do?"

"I can't answer that one. I do know you need to stay away from Vance Ellery. He's bad news, Paige."

"I know," I said in a mousy whisper. "But there's something about him." As my thoughts drifted towards TDS, I couldn't help but fall into a trance, feeling his hands as they glided down my sensitive skin.

"He's not right for you," Danny snapped, breaking me of my dream. "What do you actually know about him?"

"Only what he's told me. He said not to believe everything I hear, and he's right."

"Is he? When are you seeing him next?"

"Tonight," I admitted, fighting down the excitement and the adrenaline beginning to seep into my veins at the mere thought of being in his presence again.

"Does he know? About what happened?"

I shook my head. "But Matt does."

"Doesn't that tell you everything you need to know? You're willing to tell his son, but not him. Paige, I think deep down you already know what you have to do."

I couldn't ignore his concerns, or the truth that spoke out so loudly and clearly. A voice of reason. Neither could I ignore the swell of heat that pressed against me whenever I thought of my TDS. I knew why everyone was against me seeing him, but they hadn't been the ones to feel his warmth as he made love to me, breaking my second virginity.

"Thank you." I half-smiled towards him as I sipped the comforting tea.

"Always here for you." He placed a sympathetic kiss on the top of my head, rubbing my shoulders. "But jeez, have a shower before you go anywhere," he teased, lightening the serious mood that had settled between us.

Finishing the tea, I slinked back upstairs to get dressed, ready to fight the day before TDS arrived in the evening. I didn't bother with a shower, slipping into my jodhpurs and a faded pink polo shirt before tacking my poor, neglected mare.

Hannah was at the stable, her abundant curls swept into a single band. She was about the same age as Mark, and one of his only staff-conquests that had stuck around. Of course, my parents had no idea about their history.

"Thank you for helping out." I tightened Georgia's girth before hooking one foot into the stirrup and hauling myself onto her back.

"No probs," Hannah grinned. "Is Mark in?"

"Yeah." I nodded towards the door. "He was still in bed. Feel free to wake him." I shouldn't have encouraged her crush on him, but at the same time, I hoped that she would distract him from Bianca Ellery.

"Cool." She nodded. "Take it easy. You got your mobile?"

"Oh, not you as well," I complained.

She lifted her hands in defense and stepped back with a cheeky smile. "I only do what I'm told, and since Mrs. Holmes is the one who pays my wage…."

"Yeah, yeah," I chuckled, showing her the strap around my arm that housed the phone tightly. "I'll be back in about an hour. Just need to clear my head."

"Take as long as you need." She jogged down the path towards the farm. I seriously didn't understand why Mark didn't date her permanently. The two were infatuated with each other, stealing glances and kisses when my parents weren't around. Only Danny and I knew about their relationship. Mark had ended it after a couple of months when he left for the university, but I was pretty sure there had been the occasional "sleepover" since.

Chapter Twenty-One

The village was quiet. Only the sound of the strong wind above my head as it rushed through the line of trees, and the occasional chirrup of small birds hunting for their breakfast, disturbed the peace. A brilliant blue sky was wrinkled with bleached clouds as the sun shone down, beating through the ozone. Even with the rays warming my bare arms, it was still cool for the end of June. Nevertheless, I was intent on enjoying what heat I could get, letting the brisk breeze refresh my thoughts and clear out those metaphorical cobwebs.

The clip-clop of Georgia's hooves echoed along the naked tarmac as we rode down a no-through lane reaching for the open fields that led towards the forest at the edge of the village. I enjoyed riding along the bridle paths that surrounded Brookfield. It often gave me time alone to collect myself, something I hadn't done since before my troubles began.

I wondered if I would remember the route I used to take, across the fields, into the woods, and over the private cross-country course that belonged to one of my father's neighbors. It was okay, though. He'd told me many times that I was more than welcome to use it as long as there were no competitions on that day. I couldn't see any boxes or 4x4s, so as we entered the field, I urged Georgia into a steady canter.

There was something comforting about the smell of grease and horse hair combined with the sound of thundering hooves as she hurried over the hard ground.

As we reached the line of conifers that separated the field from the small forest, the earthy aroma of pine waved over us. I took a deep breath, savoring the freshness of it all. We trotted down the narrow, winding paths, kicking up dirt as we hit the ground, softer due to the inability of the sunlight breaking through the thick canopy.

Oxers and brushes made from natural elements broke areas of the wood, but I decided against jumping around the course today. It had been a while since I'd done anything more than pop over a trotting pole, and I needed to rebuild my confidence levels, as well as my strength and fitness.

Rather than risking a fall and yet more injuries, I opted for a gentle hack, although Georgia seemed eager to jump. She flinched beneath me, her breathing becoming more erratic as we went round. I gripped tightly onto the leather reins, squeezing gently to bring her back.

It was the rabbit that did it.

I saw the flash of brown fur moments before Georgia fell onto her hind legs, bringing her front hooves close to her belly as she reared up in fright. Leaning forward, I gave her the reins, urging her back down. As her front feet hit the ground, her back legs shot beneath her.

A full-pelt gallop ensued, chasing down the muddy path as she headed for the edge of the fields. The wide open space was too much temptation for such a skittish mare, and before I could breathe, she had reached the fence separating farmland from village. I closed my eyes tightly, leaning backwards as I desperately searched for control. She hurtled down the road, screeching up the drive, and back into the safety of her own paddock.

Breathless, and heart hammering against my ribs, I flopped from her back as a shocked Hannah came racing out of the house. "Oh, my God, Paige!" she shouted, grabbing hold of Georgia's reins and leading the heated mare into her stable.

Mark was not far behind her. "Jesus H., Paige!" He grabbed my hat, yanking it off my head as I gasped for air. "What the hell happened?"

"Rabbit," I wheezed. "Spooked her. I'm fine." I batted my brother away as he tried to pull me out of the paddock. "Bollocks," I hissed, rotating my left shoulder as the pain of taut muscle surged around my neck, blades, and bicep. Circling my head, the tendons stretched, pulled, and tugged, sending sharp pinches shooting into the joint. "Think I've trapped something."

Hannah stripped Georgia before dowsing her down with water and rubbing straw into her wet quarters.

130

"Hot bath," Mark ordered, pointing back to the house. "I'll help Hannah."

"Yeah, I bet you will," I teased, rubbing at the sore spots as I traipsed back into the house.

"What did you do this time?" Danny sang unsympathetically as I trudged up the spiraling staircase, but I ignored him, heading straight for the bathroom.

Dropping in essential oils of lavender, rosemary, and sage, I breathed in the herbal steam, hoping that the scent wouldn't cling to me too much before TDS arrived. Glancing at my watch told me that I still had half a day before he was due to arrive.

Sinking into the warmth, my mind wandered outside. I was unbelievably grateful for Hannah's help. I couldn't help but wonder if I had been too hasty in bringing Georgia back to the farmhouse. She had been spoilt on my mother's yard, but all I had succeeded in was neglecting the elegant mare.

I made a mental note to speak to my parents and return her to Holmes Manor until I was truly ready for the responsibility of such a powerful creature.

Of course, Georgia wasn't the only prevailing being in my life that I needed to let go of.

Mark and Danny insisted I take the rest of the day easy, and my brother did pry into whether I had contacted Dr. Franklin recently. I shrugged him off with an excuse of being tired and sore.

Soon it was early evening, and the summer sun was beginning to set earlier than it had of late. I ran my finger over the fine fabrics that adorned my wardrobe, struggling with the decision of which item to choose. I'd already decided on the black sandals with satin straps, so now had to find a dress to go with it. The rainbow of clothes taunted me as I wrestled with my thoughts. Eventually I settled on the cream pencil skirt with lace trims and a royal blue satin shirt, leaving several buttons undone to amplify my cleavage. After a thick layer of makeup to hide the yellowing skin around my eye and chin, and tussling my hair around my shoulders, I looked ready. It was a pity that I didn't feel the same way.

131

I wouldn't say I was dreading the evening; in fact, quite the opposite. I was excited at the prospect of ending in TDS's bed once more, but guilt and shame seemed to perfume the air around me at the same time.

He arrived as close to eight as he could without being bang on time, slowing the car to a halt at the bottom of the drive and standing by an open door, like the devil beckoning me into the mouth of hell. He could have even passed for Satan, the way he was dressed. Hair slicked back, slithers of silver woven into the deeply dark chestnut strands. Black trousers, black shirt, opened at the top button to show a small handful of thick, curly hair, and those black chukkas with which I first became acquainted.

Instantly on sight, I chided myself for being hot and ready for him. Then there was his scent; a deliciously striking woody aftershave, infused with crisp citrus flavors. I wanted to taste him as though he were some edible morsel. But the glint in his eyes, so dark that they almost matched his clothes, told me to be patient.

Suddenly, thoughts of Matt disappeared into the ether. The pain in my shoulder dissipated as though purely watching TDS was relief enough. All those contradicting thoughts cleared into one. I must have him again.

"I still haven't passed on your ideas to the board. I've been a bit tied up." I emphasized the last two words without meaning to.

"I don't want to discuss business tonight," he hushed as he slid in beside me and ordered his driver to take us back to Richard Courts. A sinister smile flickered across his lips, vanishing as quickly as I'd noticed it. Those few milliseconds were all my body needed to open up for him.

"What do you want to talk about?" I asked wearily, rotating my aching shoulders around as subtly as possible.

"My son." The words were said so casually. I opened my mouth to speak, but closed it again. I wasn't sure what to say, and from the sparks that fired from him, he knew exactly what I was thinking.

Crap. Does he know? How could he know? Did Matt tell him?

"He's a handsome boy." TDS sighed, his hands clutched into fists over his lap. "But that's all he is, Miss Holmes. A boy." With the final sentence, he turned his head to me, grabbing eye contact as though I was his to possess.

All my instincts screamed at me, ringing the alarm bells as loudly as they could. What was it Matt, Mark, and Danny had all warned me? That this man was dangerous? I could see that now, see it there in his eyes. What caught me as strange was my distinct lack of fear. Despite the internal alarms, the heart pounding against my ribs, the sudden jitter that trembled my knees, my head was cool and calm. Perhaps it was the adrenaline from the ride earlier that day catching up with me.

I broke contact and fixed my gaze straight ahead. Still, I couldn't help but melt slightly as his fingers reached for my thigh, pressing softly into the muscle.

The car stopped outside the hotel doors, and I waited impatiently for the driver to let me out. As soon as I stepped into the crisp evening air, I took a deep, cool breath as though it was my first. TDS was at my side, several inches above my height, with his arm wrapped around my waist. We marched swiftly towards the lifts without stopping for pleasantries at the front desk.

Once inside, I waited for the claustrophobia to take hold of me. Closing my eyes against the tight space, I counted in my head to ten before repeating the mantra. Had we not been accompanied by the man in the sharp grey business suit, I do think that either I or TDS would have moved to consummate our relationship further.

His fingers entwined into mine, tightening as we reached the first floor. The suit stepped out. I opened one eye in time to see the relief on his face as he escaped from the obvious sexual tension that weighed in the air surrounding us.

We were alone. My back was against the cold mirrored wall, a golden rail pressing above my hips. TDS turned on me. His head dipped to my neck. A finger moved the stray hairs as he sucked gently on my skin, like a vampire testing the sensitivities before taking that all-consuming bite. Immediately I fell apart in his grasp. Both hands swept down to my buttocks, hitching me until I was perched on the gold rail. He held me still as his lips fell to my cleavage, lapping up the taste of my skin and perfume.

This was not what I had wanted, was it? I couldn't think straight. Emotions toiled inside me like a ferocious whirlpool, as this man managed to seduce me without trying. His fingertips brushed against the bare skin below the hem of my skirt, sending bolts of electricity and heat soaring up between my legs.

Fingers began to creep beneath the stiff fabric of my skirt, stopping halfway up my thigh. Palms smoothed over my skin, causing every last nerve ending to pay attention to his touch. I threw my head back, allowing his mouth access to my throat and décolletage.

Disappointment settled in as the ping of the lift announced our arrival to his floor. I barely remember him pulling me towards the door, fishing out his key, and dragging me inside. My mind was still trying to digest the fast movements in the confined cage of the elevator.

Once in the room, he made short work of taking me into the sunken lounge area. The blinds and curtains were open, allowing the world to view our sordid pleasures. Later I would be grateful that the only voyeurs had been trees, grass, and woodland life.

We didn't speak as he took me into his arms, my back arching over the spine of the sofa. His hands gripped into the headrest as he kissed me hard. He pressed into me, and I could feel his erection, as hard as the marble floor beneath my heels. I gasped loudly as he dug it into my belly, groaning with delight, tasting my surface.

A hand reached between us, expertly slipping the buttons of my blouse loose before cupping my breast in its fine lace bra. Thumb and forefinger teased at me, and I responded proudly. His mouth trailed up my neck before teeth tugged on my lobe, a tongue playing with the gold ring in my ear. His voice was breathless and heavy. "I'm going to fuck you tonight, Paige."

I swallowed hard, gulping at the intent of his words. I was sure that listening to him alone could bring me close to the edge, if not falling over it helplessly.

His hands on my hips, he twisted me around so that I was overlooking the nighttime vista. I gripped into the headrest of the sofa, my fingers biting into the soft cushions as he moved my hair over my left shoulder, dipping his mouth to the arch of my neck. He nibbled lightly at the tender skin. I forced my pelvis back, my buttocks meeting with his firm member.

His hands moved gently over my hips until his palm was flattened against my bottom. He swatted me playfully but sharply, forcing an urgent gasp up and out of my lungs. He repeated those words again, but this time with more severity. TDS wanted me to beg for him, but I wasn't giving him that pleasure. Fingers moved over the fabric of my skirt, stroking the curve of my buttocks before tapping the cheeks softer this time.

"I want you to give in to me, Paige," he hissed.

I leant forward over the sofa, as much as I could. Fingers danced down my spine, sending shivers of anticipation through me. He reached the belt of my skirt, tugging the rest of my blouse free. I shrugged it over my arms, and he delved for the clasp of my bra, releasing me.

My skirt was hitched up over my hips as he moved my pants aside, feeling me ready for him. I heard the zip of his trousers, heard that familiar rip of foil before he reached forward and grabbed a handful of my breast as he slid inside me.

I groaned with pressure, circling my hips against him as he throbbed, filling me completely. A hand fell to my backside and spanked it, hard. I yelped with pleasure as he pushed further into me. The other hand groped wildly, pinching my nipple as he continued to press me. The hand moved to the nape of my neck, massaging at the tender flesh before clutching a handful of thick mane. I let out a shout, but it wasn't anything close to pain that surged through me like a tidal wave of pure rapture.

Both hands gripped around my hips. He pulled me back into him, moaning as he found his release. My muscles tensed around him, squeezing out his climax and my own before he relaxed and pulled away. He trailed his fingers down my shivering spine before spanking me once more.

"That was your appetizer. I want you in my bed now," he growled, leaving me in a state of half-undress.

Chapter Twenty-Two

It had been unexpected but needed, I decided, as I smoothed my hands down over my sore rump. Not the spanking, but the sex. There was nothing lovey-dovey about the way he had been; a complete change since our first experience together. But somehow, it seemed more appropriate to him. I had to wonder if there was a kinkier, darker side to my TDS, and whether I was willing to explore that part of my own appetite.

I lay on the bed, sheets covering my fully nude body, waiting for him to return from the bathroom. He'd ordered me to stay there. The curious I wanted to spy on him, but the obedient I stayed put. Frankly, I was kind of turned on by the sudden power he'd exerted over me. I could feel myself pool at the thought of him exercising his dominance. Still, the victim, the survivor inside me screamed to get out, internal bells clanging frantically.

As he stepped back inside the room, shadows cast down over his body. Splashes of moonlight glistened against the beads of water on his torso, reflecting on the silver strands that flecked his head, chest, and pubic hair. He was already proudly attentive.

"Stand up," he demanded. I swung my legs from the bed and made to stand, but he stopped me. "On the bed. Come here."

Standing on the bed, unsure of myself on the soft mattress, I trod across the sheets until I was close to him. My chest at his eyes, I wrapped my arms around his neck and pulled him into the valley between my breasts, urging him to take me in his mouth.

"Are you on the pill?" he asked sternly. I was taken aback, stuttering over my words. Looking fiercely, he repeated, "Are you on the pill?"

"Yes," I mumbled.

A hand swooped round and gripped on my tender skin. I winced, inhaling sharply as his fingers kneaded at the mounds. In one quick movement, he'd lifted me, wrapped my legs around him, and had my back against the wall as I sank onto his cock.

One hand held me up while the other scraped through my hair, fingers tangling into knots, pulling at the roots. He tugged me towards him, his mouth on mine, as he ate at me. Pressure built up in the pit of my belly as the thrusts grew deeper and harder into me. The tremble of his lips on mine forced me to groan into his kiss.

Palms braced against the wall, I had no choice but to cling to him as he urged further, his moans becoming louder, and spurring my own. He dropped his mouth to my collarbone, teeth against my skin, as he burst into me once more.

Beaded in sweat, I collapsed against him, my body slick with his. He moved us to the bed and lay me down, still inside me, wrapping my legs around his. He kissed my forehead before bending to my ear.

He left me, vulnerable and naked, heading back to the bathroom. Stopping at the door, he beckoned me forward. My legs were weak, wobbling beneath me as I tried to walk towards him. His hand around my waist, he led me in, sitting me on the closed toilet while he ran the shower, neither of us speaking. The water heated quickly.

Fingers around fingers, he led me into the glass confinements, taking some shower gel in his hand and soaping it around my curves. I did the same to him, my hands moving softly over the downy hair on his chest. His nipples were hard. I couldn't stop myself taking one in my mouth and sucking gently, releasing a deep groan from his throat.

He lifted his palms to my face, pulling me up and cupping my chin, kissing the lines across my brow and chin before sucking on my bottom lip.

I could feel him against my belly, hard with need again. This man was insatiable.

His hand dipped between us, finding my soft, sweet spot, massaging gently as I groaned into his chest. My own hands clung around his neck for dear life. A single finger slipped inside me, circling around, searching for my ecstasy. "Your pussy," he growled against my neck, reaching further for me. The words caught me off guard; shock jump-started my heart. "I am going to fuck it."

Hands moved beneath me, scooping me up again until the tip of him teased my entrance. I slid down over him slowly, with him taking all my weight.

Back against the cold tiles, the frigidity of the marble hitting every nerve, tensing my nipples against his chest as he slammed into me again and again. The water bounced off our corners, cascading between us, pooling in my cleavage as he pressed me into the wall once more. "This is how a man does it," he growled into my ear, pushing me up, fingers biting into my buttocks.

I grappled for my breath, gasping and panting, throwing my head back and only getting mouthfuls of warm water. I was so close to the edge I could taste it. I cursed, but it only came out as rushes of air. My voice got stuck in between the moans of utter lust.

"That's it, Paige." His voice was calmer. "Come for me." He thrust hard, grunting as his own muscles tensed beneath him.

My orgasm drowned me. Every bit of me ached and tensed, my inner walls tightening until it was almost excruciating.

"Louder," he ordered. I let out my yell of delight, my own screams shocking me. He throbbed and thrust harder, faster, still holding me up with one hand as the other moved to my breast, yanking it to his mouth. His teeth clamped over my nipple, toying with it. Electric bolts shot through me, hitting every sensitive spot. Fingers dug into my skin. "Again," he demanded against my breast, sucking hard.

"I can't," I moaned, panting for breath.

"I want to hear you." He found the crease of my buttocks, moving between the cheeks.

I screamed out in sheer delight. He echoed my glorious call.

Still hard inside me, he shifted his hips, pressing into me. Both hands on the curve of my buttocks, he pushed once more, calling my name as he reached his own crest. I fell against him, water still hitting my face and shoulders.

"Now you've been fucked," he murmured, kissing me deeply.

The sheets twisted around me as I lay on the bed, staring out the window. Clouds had covered the moon and I found it difficult to see beyond the glass. I was physically shattered, but couldn't find sleep. His head was nestled against my shoulders, kissing the skin below my hair.

"My son doesn't fuck like that, does he?" he purred.

I rolled over and tried to find his eyes, but it was dark to the point of being pitch-black. I couldn't find the words to voice my opinion on his blunt question. He moved his mouth to mine, finding me with ease, but I pulled away. "How can you ask that?"

"Don't play coy with me, Miss Holmes." He rolled to his back, pulling me into his arms. "I know you're sleeping with Matthew. Like I said, he's a handsome boy. But you need a man."

"You don't know what I need," I snapped, trying to break free of his tight grip.

"Oh, no? I think I found exactly what you need." He was on his side, looming over me. I could sense his power even though I couldn't see him clearly. His lips fell to mine, hands either side of my body. I wanted to fight him, but was helplessly within his control.

"You don't know anything about me."

"You are certainly an enigma."

"I should get home."

"It's late, and you don't have work tomorrow."

"How do you…"

"Know? There's not much I don't know, Miss Holmes. Just because something isn't made public knowledge doesn't mean there isn't a trail of breadcrumbs waiting to be pecked by the right person."

"Don't talk in riddles," I scolded, sitting up and straightening my back. I'd had enough of him. He may be good in bed, but he was not a talking companion.

Warm hands slid around my waist, pulling me back into him. "Do you really want to fight it? Why not give in? You know what you want."

Did I? Did I know what I wanted? Choosing between TDS and his son was like asking to choose between stilettos and slippers. Each had their good points, each had their bad.

"Does he know about us?" TDS asked, almost singing as though curiously playful.

"Yes." My head fell in shame.

"And he doesn't mind? Screwing his father's lover?"

"Is that what I am? Your lover?"

"You didn't answer the question."

"Neither did you." I sensed him smirk at my response. "I'm so pleased you find all of this amusing," I said sardonically, moving away from him, standing to find a light switch. I couldn't do this conversation in the dark. I needed to see his face, his reactions. But I was naked, and my nudity stopped me from doing anything until I'd hunted out my clothes.

Finding my pants, I picked up them up and immediately dropped them. Still damp from the excitement of earlier, I couldn't wear them. I would have to go commando. But what would that do to him if he noticed?

I tugged on my skirt, tucking my blouse into the waistband before searching for the lights. I hated dressing in the dark, but I didn't want him to see me in a vulnerable state.

He was still on the bed, lying on his side, a sheet loosely draped over his waist and legs. "Answer me," he demanded.

"Why don't you ask him yourself?" Marching into the living room, I fished my handbag from off the floor and tipped out the contents onto the coffee table. Thank goodness for my emergency makeup supply. Quickly applying mascara, eyeliner, and lip gloss, I didn't notice his presence until he asked if I wanted a drink, standing at the bar area by the lounge. "No, I do not," I retorted, snapping my travel mirror shut and tossing everything back into the bag. "But you can call me a taxi. I'll wait for it downstairs."

"No, you won't. I will have you driven back if you're so desperate to leave." He grabbed the phone and spoke to someone on the other end. It struck me that it must have been very early in the morning, and that there was still someone waiting on his beck and call.

"You are so bloody bossy."

"Get used to it." He handed me a glass of water. I noticed he was dressed in a pair of black trousers, but still had a bare chest. His stomach muscles were rigid, but not as toned as his son's. Age had taken its toll, alongside a hectic workload. The thought made me smirk, but I wiped it away before he could quiz me on my thoughts.

Placing the water on the table, I hitched the bag over my shoulder and made to leave, but found his fingers curled around my arm. "Unlike my son, I won't make you choose." His voice was stern, but not demanding, and his eyes had a sincere look about them. My shoulders relaxed at the warmth of his honesty.

"So you don't mind if I sleep with other men?" I wasn't sure how I wanted him to respond. I certainly didn't want to be his to possess, but I didn't want to be seen as some kind of slut, either.

"That's not what I said." He shook his head, soft strands of hair flopping over his eyes and ears. I wanted to move them away, but refrained from touching him in case I fell for him all over again.

"We can't be made public." He let go of my arm. "We can never go public. It wouldn't do either of us any good. Your parents would never understand, and neither would my children. I don't want, or need, a serious relationship. But I do want, and I do need, you." His mouth reached mine, leaving a trail of tender kisses across my bottom lip.

"He told me you were dangerous." The words came sooner than I could stop them.

"He's right. I am."

The bag slid from my shoulder, hitting the floor as I watched him, wondering if he was about to reveal some God-awful truth.

"Are the things I read true? Do you sleep with Matt's girlfriends?"

"Yes."

"Why?"

"Because I can. Matthew is weak, like his mother. He chooses weak girls who all need to be controlled."

"Great, so you're telling me you're into BDSM now."

"No." He shook his head with a laugh. "Nothing like that. But they do all need to be dominated in one way or another. Fragile little dolls," his fingers ran over my face. "Like you. Needing to be fixed."

"Screw you, Mr. Ellery. I'm stronger than you give me credit for."

A knock on the door alerted us to the presence of his driver.

"Secrets have a way of destroying lives." TDS opened the door and waited for me to leave.

My head was low as I walked by him, ashamed of my own truths even though I had no need to be. I stopped as I left the threshold. "Matt's not weak," I told him, shaking my head. "And neither am I."

Chapter Twenty-Three

It was gone three by the time I arrived at the farmhouse. Danny and Mark were snoring soundly as I trod up the stairs and into the sanctity of my own room. I wondered if I should tell TDS about my past. Would he understand? How would he feel? My mind trailed to the money that sat in some lonely bank account, waiting for me to take a firm bite on the bullet and either spend it or give it away.

There was something about his comment regarding secrets that scared me. He couldn't already know, could he? I was sure that my father had seen to it that it would never be traced. Of course, there were the court papers. His arrest, his trial... they were all trails that could easily lead back to me.

But what did it matter? I'd been telling myself for months now that I had nothing to be ashamed of, that it was not my fault.

I let the tears swell and burst, rolling down my cheeks as I watched the dark spot on the ceiling grow.

It was Mark who woke me with a cup of tea. The sun was shining brightly outside, although the distant grey clouds told another story. "We've got a photo shoot in London today and tomorrow. Are you going to be okay on your own? Perhaps you should stay with Mum and Dad." Pity spread across his face, and I hated him for it.

"No." I forced that smile that told everyone I was okay. "I have some paperwork to take over to the council, and Georgia needs riding. I'll be fine."

"I'll look after Georgia," called Hannah's pretty voice. I peered around the door to see her curls frizzed around her head in a golden halo.

"Really?" I raised an eyebrow at my brother. "What about Bianca?" I mouthed in a whisper so that Hannah wouldn't hear.

"What about TDS and Matt?" he mouthed back.

"Thanks for the tea. I'll be fine. And thanks, Hannah!" I called through the door before flopping back on my bed.

My eyes closed, I listened to the sounds of the village. We lived on the outskirts, so catching the hustle and bustle of the main street would have been near to impossible, but I could quite easily hear the tractors rumbling down the road and in the fields. Georgia whinnied as Hannah chucked slabs of sweet meadow hay over the rails into the field. A faint twitter of birds softened the air, but were lost in the clatter of metal on concrete that rang out as stables, sheds, and sties in neighboring farms were cleared out around us.

Clambering out of bed, I was aware that I was still dressed in my skirt and blouse from the night before. His scent clung to me like a second skin. Sandalwood, lemon, and sex. My weakness inhaled at the satin fabric, letting the smell revive my memories of our night, but my strength soon took over and tore the clothes from my body, tossing them into the linen basket in the corner by the door.

I showered quickly, scrubbing at the dead cells that refused to leave, exfoliating until I was nearly red and raw. Pulling on a pair of skinny jeans, a green tunic that floated around my hips, and my black ballet pumps, I grabbed at the file that he had given me the first time he'd taken me to

Richard   Courts   and tucked it under my arm, ignoring the tingling sensation that the vision of his skin on mine gave me.

The Golf fired into action, file and bag on the passenger seat, and I drove furiously towards the pavilion.

Lou, captain of the women's rugby team, was in the office when I arrived at the hall. I dumped the file on her desk and fell into the chair opposite her. "Tea?" she asked, standing without waiting for my reply.

Apart from Ken and Tyler, Louise Templar was the closest friend I still had, and we didn't see each other nearly enough outside of the weekly practice and occasional friendly get-together. I loved my sport, but didn't take it as seriously as Lou. She was constantly petitioning for women's sports to be as equal and professional as the male counterparts, as well as coaching the younger generation of the village and surrounding areas. She was also on the board of the committee, along with me, a couple of men from the football team, my father, several pompous asses that we tried to avoid if we could, and now Mr. Vance Ellery.

She returned with two mugs, white steam dancing above the rims, and placed one in front of me on a pile of papers already ringed with tea and coffee stains.

"Not playing today?" I asked, noting that she was dressed in jeans and a hoodie, and not her rugby kit. She lifted a hand and I saw that it was bandaged. "What happened?"

"Fell on the hockey field a couple of days ago." She scowled at her injury, thick dark brows crisscrossing above her long nose. "Some stupid cow went and trod on it."

"Ouch." I winced in empathy.

"What about you? No kit today?"

"I'm knackered. Had a long week, and got put on sick again," I complained, knowing that she would pry and eventually I would have a female shoulder to cry on.

"Are you okay?" she asked with genuine concern.

"Yeah, just things," I lengthened each word, "getting on top of me. I'll be okay." I nodded, assuring her. "I just, I need a break. Mum and Dad think I've pushed myself too far."

"They're probably right. I told you not to go head first."

Lou was one of the few people who had stuck by me after I threw everyone out of my life. She was the one who had encouraged me to go back into rugby, although she wouldn't let me play in any serious matches yet.

Dragging the file towards her, she flicked it open and began fingering the pages. I tried to ignore the earthy scents that seemed to drift from the paper.

"Okay, what's really going on?" she asked, slamming the file shut.

"Nothing. I'm tired, that's all."

"Yes, but why?" She raised a dark eyebrow towards the blonde roots of her hairline. "Come on, Paige. I can see it in your face. Something, or someone, is distracting you."

"I've met someone. Two someones." I caved easily beneath her probing inquisition.

"Paige Holmes, you dirty girl, you!" she teased. "Tell me all."

"You're as bad as Mark. He wanted all the details too."

"How is your bad boy of a brother?" Her voice flowed as she talked about Mark. Of course, there was another conquest of his. I also suspected he was as much a notch on her bedpost as she was on his.

"Bad doesn't really cover him."

"Depends how well you know him," she winked.

"Eww!" I squealed at the thought of my brother in any state other than fully clothed. Her capers with Mark were the only bedroom antics of hers that I hadn't had explicit details of.

"Come on, dish the dirt," she laughed.

"You know Matt Jackson?"

"The owner of Matieus? I wish I knew him. Oh, my God! You're shagging him?" she exclaimed in a voice so high-pitched that I suspected only dogs would be able to hear her. "Hang on. You said two someones. You're cheating on the fine and eligible Mr. Jackson?"

"He's sworn me to secrecy." My eyes fixed on the mug gripped in my hand. I wanted to tell her, but what would happen if it got out? He'd already promised me that he could be dangerous, and I had no reason to disbelieve him.

"I won't say a word," she promised.

"Vance Ellery."

"Fuck me sideways, Paige!" She looked around the room as though searching for a hidden camera spying on our every move. Lifting a long finger, she tapped on the file. "Then this is a conflict of interest."

"It's a frigging financial agreement, not a declaration of war," I argued.

"No, I can't have you shagging one of our prospective business partners."

"So what? You want me to call it off with him?"

"No." She shook her head. "No, I can see from the glint in your eye that whatever he's doing to you, it's working. But he's right. This can't get out. Not until the council have agreed to sign all paperwork, dotted the I's and crossed the T's. Fucking Branning is looking for an excuse to have us mowed down so he can build some new housing estate."

Philip Branning was as mean as he looked, and higher up in the chain of command than I cared to think about. He was also at my father's summer ball weeks earlier, spouting crap to TDS about how the sports pavilion was a waste of resources.

"Screw him. Ellery won't say anything and neither will I."

"What about your Mr. Jackson? If he finds out you're cheating on him, what's to stop him from going public?"

"It would hurt his business as much." I refrained from divulging the family ties that were also there.

"Well, stay safe. Keep it as under your hat, or bed, as you can. Do your parents know?"

"They suspect. But Mum's trying to convince Matt to propose or something just as silly."

"Would it be silly?"

"I barely know him, Lou! We've been seeing each other for, what, two weeks? Yes, it would be silly."

"Oh, I love you, Paige." She stepped around the desk and kissed the top of my head, hugging me into her chest, but being careful of her wrist.

I took the bandage in my hand and stroked it. "You should be careful too. We can't lose our captain."

"And it's time for you to leave before I ravage you as well," she teased, showing what she called her "lesbian tendencies." We'd often joked how the village must think we were a couple. "I'll make sure the board get the

146

paperwork. You go home and rest," she added, pushing me towards the door.

It would have been nice to be able to go home and simply rest. But I found myself driving towards the other end of the village, braking outside a familiar restaurant. I could see the white Audi parked at the back, in a space marked for the owner.

Sitting behind the wheel, refusing to move, I tried to peer through the tinted windows. It was closed. Matieus did open for lunch, but by appointment only.

I could go home, I thought to myself, humming to the pop tune that played out of the radio. I probably should go home.

Pulling the Golf into a spot by a wooden trellis fence, I sat for a bit longer. Glancing in the vanity mirror, I checked my makeup. Not too thick today, just a slick of tinted moisturizer, eyeliner, and mascara. The bruising was fading nicely, so I didn't feel the need to pile on the concealer.

A tap on the window made me jump. I turned and saw Matt's smile beaming down on me. Rolling the window down, I smiled back.

"I don't believe you have a reservation, Miss," he teased.

"I know the owner. I was sort of hoping he was around, perhaps he could squeeze me in?" What was I doing?!

"Come on." He opened my door. "They make the meanest tuna melt here."

His office could only have been described as plush. Cream velvety carpet spanned across the floor, reaching towards three magnolia walls and one feature wall painted in rich amethyst. A large painting of violets hung in the center, accentuating the purple colors that seemed to be the theme of the room.

Matt sat behind a glass desk and closed his laptop, offering me a choice of seats. I decided on the dark purple sofa that sat against a glass wall, shielded by thick wooden slat blinds. "Do you want a drink? What about food?" he asked, picking up a cordless phone and punching in a number, which I assumed led to the kitchen.

"Water," I said, unsure of what else to order. "The tuna melt sounds tempting," I added.

Matt raised an eyebrow, sensing the tension in my voice. "Bring two tuna melts and a bottle of still mineral water to my office, please," he ordered, allowing me a glimpse of the dominant genes he possessed. "I'm glad you came." The smile was shy, almost nervous.

Then I said those ominous words that held so much dread and fear. "We need to talk."

Chapter Twenty-Four

"Talk," he stated firmly, rising from his post and walking towards me. I wanted to shrink back into the sofa, hide away. He sat by me and looked squarely into my eyes. "Shit. You went to see him, didn't you?"

I couldn't answer him. I knew that if I tried to open my mouth to speak, I would blurt out something that I shouldn't -- either that or cry, neither of which would be good. I'd been crying too much recently.

"You have to cancel on my mother," I begged, trying to hide the wobble of my larynx.

"Your mother has been nothing but kind. I can't let her down, and neither can you."

"So we're going to go to a meal and pretend that none of this has happened?" I demanded, finding my inner strength and taking a firm hold.

"We're going to do exactly what you came here to do. Talk. And then make a decision."

I was grateful for the interruption of the maître- d' as he produced our lunches, even though neither of us were particularly hungry anymore.

"So, let's talk," he snapped, standing up and pacing back and forth across the creamy floor. His hands swept madly over his hair, gripping into a vice-like grasp at the back of his head. "Which one of us do you want?" He was furious, and he had every right to be.

"It's not that simple."

"Yes, it fucking well is," he spat.

"No, it's not!" I screamed, standing to face him, but falling short by several inches. "You don't know what it's like. Not being able to look at yourself in a mirror because all you see is those scars. Men that used to flirt with you suddenly hiding away, nobody willing to touch you in case you might break. People pretending they don't know, but then whispering behind your back, treating you like a victim. I'm not a fucking victim. I'm a fucking survivor."

I stepped back as my tirade settled. He looked shocked. His dark blue eyes had widened with an emotion I couldn't place. Tears streamed down my cheeks uncontrollably. Lifting a hand, I wiped them and the bleeding mascara away, smearing the back of my hand with black ink.

"I didn't think your father knew about everything. But he made it clear last night that he knows something," I said more calmly. "And he doesn't care. He knows I'm damaged, but he doesn't pussyfoot around me. He fucks me the way he wants to, without worrying about whether he's breaking me further."

The words were harsh, and unexpected, but they were out now. I sank back into the sofa, my head buried in my hands, waiting for Matt to either move or throw me out. To be honest, I didn't really care which he did. The truth was, I didn't know what TDS knew. For all I could have guessed, he may have been, and probably was, bluffing.

He moved. He came and fell to his knees at my feet. Hands gripped around the tops of my calves. "It makes me sick to think of you with him."

"Please, ring my mother and tell her you can't go. Make up a meeting or something."

"No, I won't do that."

"So you want to punish me? Don't you think I do that to myself enough?"

His glower darkened. "Why are you so determined to make me hate you?"

"I don't want you to hate me. I really like you, Matt. But I'm not ready for you yet."

"How do you know if you won't try?"

"Your father said he won't make me choose between you."

"Because he doesn't give a damn about you, that's why," he exclaimed, standing up.

I knew he was right. So why couldn't I walk away from TDS?

"I should go. I shouldn't have come here in the first place."

"So you can be alone and drink yourself to death again?"

"Don't worry, Danny and Mark have made sure that the only alcohol in the house is beer, and I can't touch that stuff."

"I'll make a note to remember that." I couldn't tell if he'd meant it sarcastically or not. "You're still not going anywhere. Eat." He pointed to the cooling tuna melt. "I have a meeting in five minutes, anyway. I'm going to Holmes Manor tomorrow whether you like it or not, but it will be a very boring lunch if you're not there."

"Perhaps we both need to cool off."

"Perhaps." He nodded, although I was not convinced he truly agreed.

I waited for him to leave, peering through the blinds as he swerved through the kitchen, avoiding bustling chefs and staff. Clearly, they had heard our disagreement, although I hoped it was simply loud mumbles and not actual words.

He disappeared into the restaurant. Staring at the sandwich, I contemplated taking a bite, but my stomach was unsettled. I needed to get back to the farm. Alone or not, I had to get out of this place.

Back at the farmhouse, I curled into a ball on the sofa, grabbing the remote to the TV and channel hopping until I found something mundane to watch, to ease the throbbing that pressed against my brain. There was no point in canceling on my mother -- she would only press as to why. It was like I was in a giant game of tug-of-war. Only I was on both teams and the rope as well.

I'd changed into my dressing gown; a thick white toweling robe that Mark had bought me for Christmas. Snuggling into it, I inhaled the comforting aromas of washing powder. Why couldn't life be simple? It was a stupid question, and one I damn well knew the answer to. It could have been, but I was intent on punishing myself for something that was beyond my control.

My iPhone kept me company, sitting loyally on the arm of the sofa. I considered sending an apologetic text to Matt, but I also considered sending one to TDS. Matt was right. He had been from the beginning. I needed to make a choice.

I'd gone to see him with the full intention of making sure I never saw him again, but he was determined to take my parents up on their offer for Sunday lunch, a date I knew I couldn't escape from, and one I couldn't even involve Danny or Mark in since they would still be in London. I couldn't feign illness. Two cases of a bad cold in the space of a couple of weeks would have even my father racing for the doctors. I couldn't use work as an excuse; Greg had seen to that. I didn't see that I had any choice. I would have to grin, bear it, and make the most of a bad situation.

The house phone rang. I nearly let it go to the answering machine, but picked it up on the last ring. "Paige." Matt's voice was weary. "Wait," he barked, obviously sensing that I was ready to hang up on him. "I wanted to apologize. I shouldn't have spoken to you in that way. I was angry, but not with you. Please come with me tomorrow. We should talk properly. Paige?"

"I'm here," I said furiously, angry that he insisted on chasing me like a dog and its tail.

"Will you come with me tomorrow?"

"Yes."

"Will you talk to me?"

"You can't scream and yell at me when I don't make the promises you want me to make."

"I won't. You have my word."

"Fine. We should meet there. As far as my parents are concerned, I barely know you."

"Yes. That sounds like a good idea. Are you okay?"

"Not really," I sighed.

"Do you want me to come over?"

"That's really not a good idea, Matt."

"No. Of course. I hate the idea of you being alone, though, especially when you're upset and angry." I hated the way he cared about me.

"I'm going to have a bath and go to bed."

"It's the middle of the day."

"I'm tired." And sore. My evening with TDS had left me aching in places I didn't know existed. But I couldn't tell him that. "Don't worry, please, Matt. I'm all right. I'll see you tomorrow." I hung up before he had time to argue with me.

Pushing into the sofa, I wanted to hibernate between the cushions, not waking until it had all gone away. I wished that someone could make the decision for me. Then again, I knew that the decision that any sane person made would be the one I really didn't want to. I liked Matt, I really did. But TDS had a hold over me that made me weak to fight him.

Action broke out across the screen, splintering a thousand colors across the room. But I couldn't concentrate on the script or figures as they fought for their lives. I was too busy battling my own internal war. Bath and bed. It sounded like a good plan, one that would wash away the loneliness, and one that was easy to fulfill.

It was still light when my head hit the pillow, but dark when I rose. The sound of the occasional car disturbed an otherwise silent night. Breathe in, breathe out. Why did Mark have to go away when I needed him? The blackness seeped into my subconscious.

Treading downstairs, I flicked on the lights. I wasn't afraid of the dark per se, but I was scared of being alone in it. In the living room, I searched through the DVDs, needing something easy to watch so that I may fall asleep to it. Lying with my head resting against the arm of the sofa, light broke from the TV and kitchen, shattering the darkness. There were a fair few hours between that time and the time that I was supposed to be at Holmes Manor. I didn't want to yawn my way through the meal, which would only cause my mother to quiz me, and Matt to worry further.

He was so kind and caring, much more than I deserved. Perhaps I could convince my mother to make him a project of hers, finding him a suitable mate within the village that wasn't me. Unlikely, since she seemed to have her heart on marrying the pair of us, despite the fact that, as far as she was concerned, we'd met only a handful of times.

Slumber found me within twenty minutes of the film beginning. Sunlight breaking through the window, shining into my eyes, blinding me. I stretched and yawned like an unsettled cat, trying to unkink the muscles and tendons in my neck and shoulders from where I had laid at an odd angle. Get dressed, I ordered, forcing myself to stand and head back upstairs.

I hadn't realized the sounds of the house until I was utterly alone. Steps creaked beneath my foot; old pipes clanged as the hot water woke. I washed quickly, rinsing away the remnants of sleep, and scraped my hair into a loose bun. Stray tendrils splayed out around my neck and hairline, sticking to my lashes as I applied plenty of mascara to darken them. Today concealer was needed to cover the bruised circles that showed a serious lack of sleep. Skipping breakfast meant that I arrived at Holmes Manor by ten o'clock.

Mother was fussing in the kitchen, ensuring that the roast dinner was being prepared to her exacting standards. My father was in his study working on some important papers that I didn't need to discuss with him. So I made myself at home on the patio, sipping at an iced tea, enjoying the warm sunshine that seemed to have broken the overcast and dreary spell we'd been having recently.

"Oh, there you are, darling," my mother called from behind me. I turned to see her linked, arm in arm, with Matt. "You remember Matthew," she beamed proudly. "Of course you do. I'll leave you two alone to get to know each other better. Lunch will be ready in a couple of hours. I'm sorry to be such a terrible host." She kissed the air by Matt's cheeks.

"Oh, that is quite all right, Mrs. Holmes."

"Lizzie, please," she giggled childishly. I couldn't help but roll my eyes. She left us alone.

"You look - " He glanced at my outfit of denim shorts and a black vest top with flip-flops. "Nice."

"Not really," I shrugged. "Thought I'd get the most of the sun and try and tan these pasty pins." I kicked my heels up onto a spare chair. "You can sit if you want."

He perched on the edge of the white metal chair. They weren't exactly the most comfortable of seats, despite the green gingham cushions.

"About yesterday," I said, my eyes closed against the burning rays. "I'm sorry. I wasn't even sure I wanted to go and see you."

"I'm glad you did."

"No, you're not. How can you be? I was awful to you. I am awful to you," I corrected myself. "You deserve so much better than me."

"Perhaps I don't want better." He tried to relax into the chair.

"But you agree that you could."

"Don't put words in my mouth, Paige."

I sniffed the air before pulling my sunglasses from on top of my head to shade my eyes, but not from the harsh rays.

"Are you two getting along?" my father's voice called from the doorway. I peered over my shoulder at him and shrugged. I heard him laugh before turning to Matt and saying, "Don't let her bully you. She's like her mother. She can wrap a man around her finger with one look."

"Yes, I gathered that," Matt responded. I pretended not to hear them.

Chapter Twenty-Five

After having checked that we were not sitting in awkward silence, my father returned to his study, leaving us alone again. I stared out across the gardens towards the fields and wooded areas that surrounded my parents' estate. From behind the dark brown visors, I was able to catch a glimpse of Matt watching me without him noticing.

I had to admit that I was attracted to him, and had I met him before everything that happened, then perhaps things would have been different. But the truth of the matter was that I hadn't. We had met long after the baggage and jagged edges had attached themselves to me, weighing me down and tearing at the fragile seams.

"I don't, by the way. Agree that I could do better." It was Matt who broke the silence. I inhaled deeply and loudly, biting my tongue against the lashing it wanted to lay upon him. Swallowing the words down, I searched for a more civil tone than I was sure I was capable of. Unable to find it, I remained quiet, waiting to see where he would go. "I'm not going to pretend that I'm okay with any of this. The thought of you with him, well, to be honest, Paige, it makes me want to murder him. I can't bear thinking of you two together. But I'm trying to understand what it is he gives you that you think I can't."

I was glad of the shades covering the sadness that filled me, and hoped that my bottom lip wasn't trembling too much for him to notice.

"I want to see you, Paige, and if that means sharing you…" His head dropped with a heavy sigh. "All I want is for you to be happy."

"Lunch is ready!" my mother's voice called through from the dining room. We both stood, face to face. He held an arm out, but I declined it, walking past into the house.

Dad sat at the head of the table with my mother at his side. I was next to Mum, and Matt sat opposite, trying to catch the eye contact I was desperate to avoid. Mum was the first to speak, asking Matt how the restaurant was going. "We do love dining there, don't we, Stephen?"

My father didn't answer, merely nodding between mouthfuls of deliciously moist sirloin beef. I thought I saw Matt smirk, probably sympathizing with my father's easy agreement. If he was going to keep pursuing me, it was something he would have to learn about the women in our family: We are stubborn, short-tempered, and judgmental. Although my mother wished I was also demure, elegant, and poised.

I followed my father's lead and kept my head down, savoring each bite of the meal, while Mum and Matt continued their polite conversation. It was inevitable that she would sooner or later ask the question I was dreading.

"So, Matthew, do you have a girlfriend?"

"Mum!" I exclaimed, slamming my fork and knife down a little too hard.

"What?" Mother asked in mock surprise, as though the question was perfectly innocent and without any hidden agenda.

"No," Matt chuckled. "I don't have a girlfriend."

"Oh, that's a shame." My mother smiled sympathetically. It was perfectly obvious from the tone of her voice that she didn't mean a word of it. "Paige is single too," she added.

"Mum!" I exclaimed again, after managing to stop myself from choking on the iced tea served with the meal. I glanced towards Matt, who had an amused smirk plastered all over his face. "Anyway, I'm not."

It was Mum's turn to slam cutlery against the table this time. My father stopped mid-forkful of vegetables. Matt's glare blackened, warning me not to say anything about TDS, something I had no intention of doing. I may be a cheat, but I still kept my promises.

"So who is the lucky man?" my mother asked, frowning at her plate. "Not…" she stopped herself, watching Matt. "Who I think it is, I hope." She knew precisely who it was. A ninja couldn't get past her.

I didn't answer.

"Well, we won't have this discussion at the table," my father intervened before Mum could cause a scene in front of company. Sophie and Rosa appeared to clear the dishes, returning with small plates with homemade apple pie and vanilla ice cream, one of my favorite desserts.

"So, Matthew." Mother distracted herself from the realization that I was sleeping with a man who was merely a few years younger than my dad, and not only that, but the father of the guest she had invited in a vain

SEVEN DIRTY WORDS

attempt to find me a prospective partner. "Are you planning on staying in Brookfield?"

"Actually, yes." He smiled politely. "I've bought a cottage not far from here. It's modest and quaint, but perfectly adequate for my needs, and it means I can run the restaurant more efficiently. I'm hoping to open a bistro for the daytime customers."

"Oh, I see. So you'll be expanding your clientele," she said disappointedly.

"Of a sorts. It's not financially feasible to limit income during a recession."

My father was nodding in agreement, and I cringed at the thought of business talk. Money was not my forte, unless it meant spending it on clothes, shoes, and handbags.

"And how's your car coming along?" mother added, as equally uncomfortable with the banking side of life as I was. Although I wasn't sure why she was turning the subject towards the Evo, since mechanics meant nothing to her. As far as my mother was concerned, all cars were the same: four wheels and an engine, painted in pretty colors.

"Bergin's is doing a fine job. It should be ready soon, actually."

"It's a pity that Paige isn't working there any longer. But then again, I guess that means that you are no longer her client."

"I am still working there. I've been put on sick leave, that's all," I disputed, not wanting to admit that the chance of me returning was lodged somewhere between slim and none.

"But Matthew is no longer your client, which means there is no reason why the two of you shouldn't get to know each other a bit better."

She may as well have just said it; she couldn't have been any clearer. Matt seemed to be finding it all very amusing. I couldn't have been more glad when the meal was finally over and we were allowed to escape from the dining room.

"I have some business to attend to, so if you'll excuse me." My father went into the study and locked the door behind him. I thought it strange; not only was he working on a Sunday, but he never locked that door. Mum seemed oblivious and floated into the drawing room, ready to pour drinks.

"Oh, not for me, thank you," Matt declined. "I have to drive."

157

She handed me a glass of soda and lime. No alcohol. "Perhaps you'd be kind enough to drive Paige home later?"

"I have my car here."

"I'd be delighted to," Matt interrupted. He stood by me, his head dipped to my ear while Mother had her back to me. "It will give us the chance to talk properly."

I closed my eyes and took a deep breath, reluctantly agreeing. I could see there was no way I was going to be able to avoid him. I suspected that he would have only followed me home anyway.

"Lovely," Mother declared, sipping from her martini.

It was four o'clock before we were allowed to leave Holmes Manor. I prayed that Danny and Mark would be back from London, even though I knew there was little chance of it being answered. I hadn't exactly done much to appease the Great Almighty of late.

"Paige, I really want to talk to you properly," Matt said as we drove back towards the farmhouse.

"We tried that and it ended in an argument."

"You can't expect me to be okay with the situation. Have you spoken to your doctor recently?"

"Why is everyone so obsessed with me talking to Dr Franklin?"

"Because we care about you."

"Do you? Do you care about me, Matt?"

"If you haven't figured that out by now, then you really do need to go and have your head read. I'm sorry, that was callous."

"No, you're right."

"I can go with you, if you like. As a friend."

"But you're not just a friend, are you?"

"Please don't push me away, Paige. I'm trying my best here."

"I know." I reached out and placed a hand against his arm. Immediately his bicep tensed beneath my touch and I felt that pressure build in my belly. I tried to ignore the chemical imbalance and invisible sparks.

He pulled into the driveway, parking behind Danny's red MR2. "Are they back now?" he asked.

"Not yet. They took Mark's car," I explained, getting out. "Do you want a coffee?" I asked, before laughing at the hidden implications. "I mean coffee or tea, a drink of some description. Not, well, you know."

"I don't think that's a very good idea, do you?"

"Probably not." I was more than aware that neither of us would be able to control our urges once alone and inside the comfort of my home.

"Promise me you'll ring your doctor tomorrow."

"As soon as the office opens."

"And stay away from my father."

"Matt, I…"

"Please. At least until you've spoken to someone."

"I'll try." It was the best I could offer, and he seemed to accept that, shifting the car into reverse and driving away. I watched and waited for him to disappear around the bend before physically entering the house.

As if he had some psychic ability to realize that I was now on my own, my phone flashed with a message from TDS. "Meet me tomorrow at Richard Courts. V."

I didn't respond. I'd promised Matt that I would at least try to avoid him. Instead, I made myself a cup of tea and took it to my room, leaving the iPhone in the kitchen.

The sun had set by the time Danny and Mark arrived home. "Hey, Butch," Mark greeted, as they both piled into my room like a pair of teenagers. Nobody would have ever have guessed that they were closer to thirty than eighteen. "How was lunch?"

"Painful," I groaned, falling onto my pillow, cuddling up to my big brother as Danny sat on the end, channel hopping through my TV. "You know, we have a bigger screen downstairs," I grunted.

"Yeah, but this way I can hear your gossip."

"God, you're such a girl."

His grin took over his wide face.

"Come on." Mark prodded me in the ribs, forcing a squeal out of me. "What happened?"

"Mum practically proposed to him for me."

"I doubt it was that bad."

"I spent the entire time trying to hide under the table."

"What about Dad?" Mark laughed.

159

"He just smiled and nodded before locking himself in the study."

"Oh." Mark was as confused by the locked-in-the-study scenario as I was. "Perhaps he was afraid that you would hide behind him," he chuckled.

"Hilarious."

"So what about Matt Jackson?" Danny chimed in. "Are you going to see him again? Anything to get you away from that twat of a father of his." The impression of Danny's hatred towards both men dented the air.

"Ellery isn't that bad," I defended, pointlessly since I was in the room with two men who were anything but his fans. "But yes, I am. He's made me promise to ring Dr. Franklin tomorrow."

Both Danny and Mark looked at me with surprise, eyebrows arched into their foreheads. It made me giggle. "And he's coming with me to see him. As a friend," I iterated.

Chapter Twenty-Six

I kept my promise, as I always did, ringing Dr. Franklin's office at nine o'clock on the dot. I was mid-conversation with his secretary, making the appointment, when my iPhone buzzed and screamed at me. I picked up and saw five unread messages, all from TDS. Each one could have been read as more serious than the last. But it was the more recent one that caught my attention. "Get dressed. Picking you up in ten minutes. V."

I finished my sentence and rang off from the clinic before dialing his number. "You can't just demand my attention like that!" I shouted before he had chance to even greet me. "I'm busy today. I can't drop everything to see you."

"And precisely what are you doing that is so important?" he asked, so sure of himself.

"I have a doctor's appointment," I lied, since my appointment wasn't until Thursday afternoon.

"I have a gift for you."

"Post it."

"It's not that kind of gift," he chuckled. "I will be with you in five minutes." Click.

"Bastard!" I screeched, dropping my phone to the table, flinching as it hit the wooden top with a clang. Rage and frustration burned my cheeks.

"What happened?" Danny was in the kitchen before I had a chance to gather myself.

"Fucking Ellery," I seethed. "Motherfucker!"

"Hey! Dirty words, as your mother would say," Danny soothed, taking me in his arms. "What did the bastard do this time?"

I picked up the phone and let him read through the messages.

"I'll kill him."

"No." I pulled out of his bear hug. "I'll deal with him." I hated the way TDS stirred such contradicting emotions in me. One minute I despised him, the next I was melting beneath his touch, and now he was buying me gifts unnecessarily. I doubted it was a simple box of chocolates or bunch of flowers, either.

True to his word, the familiar black car pulled up alongside the driveway five minutes later. I had refused to get dressed on principle, not even bothering to drag a comb through my tangled mane or apply a single scrap of makeup. He could take me as I was.

I forced Mark and Danny into the lounge, begging them to leave him to me. Their naturally protective nature meant it was difficult for them to agree, but eventually they conceded defeat and plugged themselves into the Xbox.

"So?" I snorted, arms clamped around my chest, as TDS towered above me. I didn't invite him in, although part of that was for his own protection against the brother figures ready to attack. "Where's this gift, so I can tell you where to shove it?"

"Paige," he purred, and my body reacted in the way he knew it would. Hairs on end, lightning bolts shooting down my core, it was all I could do not to kiss that wretched mouth of his. He stepped backwards and I could see the Aston Martin parked behind his Jaguar.

"You have got to be kidding me."

"I can't stand seeing you drive around in that death trap you call a car."

"I'll have you know that that death trap is only a couple of years old, and has been cared for better than some dogs."

"It's not exactly the sort of car a lady of your standing should be driving, though."

"I don't know if you've realized this, but I don't exactly aspire for wealth. If I wanted an Aston Martin, I could easily buy one with my own money."

"And where is this perfectly adequate car of yours?" he asked, glancing over the driveway.

"It's at my parents', if you must know."

"Well, now you can leave it there."

"I don't want your sodding car!"

"Be gracious and accept it as the gift it is," he said, through gritted teeth. It was nice to see that I could irritate him with my defiance. After our last conversation, the last thing I was about to do was simply bend to his every whim.

"Why don't you give it to someone who would be more appreciative? I'm sure your daughter would love it."

"My daughter wants for nothing, so this is not something she needs."

"Blinded by the love for her father, hey?" I echoed his own comments from the summer ball. "More like bought."

"A modicum of respect wouldn't go amiss," he growled, angrier. I had found the topic that riled him, and it pleased me. I couldn't help but smirk, a smile which disappeared as he stepped forward, his hand around my waist and his mouth upon mine. His tongue was hungry, desperately searching for any weakness. "Get dressed and get in that car. You need to be fucked again."

"Screw you," I spat, tugging myself free of his grip.

"I'll take you over my knee if you talk to me like that again." His tone was forceful, and even though I was sure he hadn't meant it in a good way, I couldn't help but feel the heat rise between my legs at the mere thought of his hand on my naked skin. My muscles tightened, clenching around his satin-smooth words.

"I am not a child," I said, refusing to succumb to my own desires.

"Then stop acting like one. Get dressed now. I'll even drop you off at your parents' so you can pick up that heap."

"I won't." But at least he had conceded that I wasn't going to swap my car with the one he had presented me with.

"Then I'll take you like that."

Seriously? Even in my least attractive state, he was still willing to provide his attempt at seduction?

"I'm busy today. I have an appointment," I stated, trying to hide my nervousness.

"I won't ask you again."

163

"I didn't think you were asking in the first place. I thought you were ordering."

"Damn it, Paige, why do you have to be so difficult?"

"Whatever happened to keeping this a secret? All that yelling and the neighbors will soon find out. And this is a village that likes to talk," I goaded.

"Get in that fucking car right now." He shot an arm towards the car, finger pointing to the open door. I flinched at the sudden movement, showing my weakness. "Shit." He stopped and rubbed a hand over his chin, coated in a fine stubble. "I have to have you." His voice was firm, but quieter.

"It's only been a couple of days since you last had me. Three times, if I remember correctly."

"Doesn't that tell you what sort of hold you have over me? Two days and I need you in my bed again."

"Mr. Ellery, please." I let my guard and my arms drop. "I'm tired, and I really am busy today. Thank you for the car, but I can't accept it. It's too much." I was tired of his games, but proud of myself for not giving in.

"I leave on Saturday for New York. I'll be gone for two weeks. See me before I go." He was almost pleading, but I figured it was probably a ruse to make me feel sympathetic towards him. It worked.

"Friday," I agreed. I would have spoken to Dr. Franklin by then, and perhaps have more courage to let him down for the last time.

"Friday," he echoed, leaning forward to kiss me. I turned my head so that his lips fell against my cheek.

I watched as he went back to his car, climbing into the Aston Martin and driving it behind the Jag. I couldn't help but feel a pang of sadness.

"I'm proud of you, Butch," Mark said.

"You were listening."

"It was hard not to," Danny added. "Are you really going to see him on Friday?"

"I don't know." It was the closest to being truthful that I could be at that time.

Looking in the mirror of the bathroom, I failed to see why TDS had been so attracted to me that morning. I looked like I had a bird's nest belonging to a golden eagle on my head. I forced the brush through the tangles and knots before spending at least twenty minutes beneath the powerful jets of hot water.

I hadn't many plans for Monday. Danny and Mark disappeared at lunchtime, heading for a photo shoot with some up-and-coming designer. I contemplated calling Greg to discuss my work contract, but guessed it would be better to wait until after Thursday.

Bored, I pulled on my leggings, baggy t-shirt, and trainers. It was a warm day, the sun hidden behind a cloud, but there was no wind to add any coolness to the air. Plugging my earphones in, I broke into a light jog and headed towards the sports fields.

The road from the farmhouse to the pavilion was nearly empty until I hit the crossroads that led to the center of the village in one direction and the dual carriageway in the other. I could see Lou waving frantically in the field across from me. "Hey!" she called, jogging to the boulders that lined the car park, leaning against a tree and stretching out the muscles in her back and calves.

"How's the hand?" I asked, noting that there was no bandage this time.

"Oh, yeah, it's fine," she said dismissively. "Actually, I wanted to talk to you."

"Lucky I'm here then." I pulled the plugs from my ears and let the white wire loop around my neck.

"The board approved the application." Lou handed me a sheet of paper.

"Oh, good!" I read down the contract, ready to place my signature on the lines that needed it.

"But there's some concerns."

"There's always a bit."

"Philip Branning is under the impression that there may be a…"

"Conflict of interest?" I finished for her, knowing exactly where this was heading.

"It's more than that, Paige. He's said that you're using your connections with Ellery to get the funding, and that it's unfair on the other areas that need the finances. We could lose this deal if Ellery doesn't convince him otherwise."

"Shit," I cursed under my breath.

"Any chance you could use and abuse the situation to swing it in our favor?"

"So you want me to do exactly what he's accusing me of? How the hell did he find out, anyway?"

"He's Branning! He's got his finger in so many pies, it's amazing that he's not his own conflict of bleeding interest. And yes. I want you to do exactly what he's accusing you of."

"There might be a problem with that."

"Shit. You two haven't split up, have you?"

"We were never together to begin with," I said pointedly. "We've had an argument."

"Lover's tiff," Lou teased.

"Slightly more than that. I haven't been completely honest with you."

"When are you ever?

"Matt Jackson…"

"Your other beau?"

"He's Ellery's son."

"Fuck me sideways, Paige! You're shagging father and son? I don't know whether to be impressed or appalled."

"Anyway, he knows. And it's now turned into this whole cat and mouse game. I don't know what to do anymore. Matt made me make an appointment with Dr. Franklin for Thursday. He thinks I'm using Vance as a way of blocking out what happened. Almost like a rehabilitation program," I scoffed nervously.

"I'm sorry to ask, but…"

"You want me to talk to Ellery." I nodded. "Can it wait until Friday?"

"I guess. But the sooner, the better."

"I'll see what I can do." I gave my friend a hug before plugging myself back into the iPod and jogging back to the farmhouse.

Chapter Twenty-Seven

I had several choices. I could go and find TDS right now, beg and plead, probably end up in bed with him, and hope that it would be enough for him to talk to Branning. Or I could go to my father, tell him the whole sordid tale, and hope that he had enough sway within the council to overrule any decisions that went against the sports pavilion. Or I could wait for Danny and Mark to return and ask for big-brother guidance. Or I could leave it until Friday, after I've spoken to Dr. Franklin.

I did none of the above.

Even though I'd already had one shower that morning, the sweat that had built from the jog and the realization that I was going to have to face TDS sooner rather than later stuck worse than superglue. I went over my options as I scoured away the grime and dirt, trying to concentrate on the aromas of orange blossom and vanilla, and failing miserably.

Still wrapped in a towel, wet rats-tails sticking to my neck, I picked up my phone and dialed the number of the one person who I felt I could trust at that moment.

"Paige?" he answered, with a delighted surprise.

"Hi, Matt. I need your help."

Before I'd even explained the situation, he informed me he would be round in less than twenty minutes. That gave me enough time to compose myself, and dress.

I thought he was going to burst through the door, the way he hammered against the wooden frame, calling my name. "What's happened?" He barged in, pushing me aside. "Are you okay?"

"I'm fine. No, it's nothing like that. I'm sorry, I shouldn't have called you, but I didn't know who else I could trust."

"Bloody hell, Paige, you had me worried out of my skin!"

"I'm sorry," I apologized again, suddenly feeling that he was the last person I should have called. "There's been a development, and I need someone who can be discreet and knows about the…" I circled my arms in front of me as though the word would come on a wave of intelligence. "Situation" was all that I could muster.

"What are you talking about?"

"Someone at the council knows about --" I stopped myself. I couldn't drag him further down. He was so kind and caring. The way he'd raced over to the farm on a single phone call was more I could ever have expected from TDS. "Forget it. It doesn't matter. I rang Dr. Franklin," I said, trying to change the subject.

"That's good, but someone at the council?" I could clearly see the confusion settled in his blue eyes. Then it dawned on him. "Someone's found out about you two."

I shouldn't have been surprised at his irritation and annoyance. "I'm sorry," I repeated myself, in a voice so pathetic that even that shamed me.

"What do you want from me, Paige? One minute you're pushing me away, telling me you want him. The next, you're saying it's me you want. And now what? You want me to clean up your… shit?" he spat. Hands rubbed over his face, through his hair, trying to push away the crud and debris that I had piled on top of him. "When's your appointment?" he asked, calming down.

"Thursday at two. It's in town."

"I'll pick you up at half-one."

"You'll still come with me?"

Reaching forward, he took my arms and wrapped them around his waist. "Whether you like it or not, I'm going to work on changing your mind about me."

"You're more than I ever deserve," I admitted sadly, nestling my head against his chest, listening to the steady drum of his heart.

"I'm also going to work on that negative attitude of yours."

"I still don't know what to do about --" I stopped, pulling out of his arms, catching the look on his face that told me to not go any further. "It's not your problem. I'll deal with it."

"We'll deal with it."

"What?" I asked, thinking I'd misheard him.

"Tell me what's happened. Perhaps there is something I can do. I have as much influence within the council as my father, if not more. I live here, after all."

I explained everything that Lou had revealed regarding Branning. "I can't tell my father, and I don't want to see Vance. Not after this morning."

"What happened this morning?"

"He turned up unannounced. With a frigging Aston, of all things! He expected me to dump everything, go with him, and take this bleeding car as a gift! You don't look surprised."

"It's one of his ways of making sure that he has control over you. No doubt the car would have a GPS tracker installed so that he can quite literally follow your every move. I told you before, he's a dangerous control freak. I can't tell you how elated I was when my mother announced they were getting divorced. I'm glad you didn't accept it from him."

"I didn't do it for you."

"I know, but still. I will speak to Branning. If he makes any noises about my father's money, I'll offer him enough to return the check."

"You'd do that?"

"Yes. The sports pavilion is a commodity this village can't do without. The last thing I want is bored children loitering outside my restaurant," he joked.

"Thank you. If it comes down to it, I'll put half of the money forward."

"You'd be willing to touch that money?"

"If it meant getting one over on Branning, hell, yes! I really can't thank you enough."

Matt bent down and placed a tender peck on my cheek. Without thought, my hands were clasped around his neck, pulling him towards me. I was left disappointed when he stepped back. "As much as I would like to take you right here, right now, I can't. Not until I understand everything. I'll see you on Thursday." Another kiss on my cheek and he left.

Immediately, I called Lou to assure her it was being taken care of. Then I spent the rest of the afternoon trying to distract myself, baking and cooking, reading and watching movies. I even found a can of polish and air freshener under the sink and started cleaning for a bit.

When Mark and Danny finally arrived home, I was exhausted and had collapsed on the sofa in a semiconscious state. They didn't disturb me, apart from pulling a blanket over my tired body, so when I woke, I was still on the sofa and with an awful crick in my neck.

By Thursday I'd managed to distract myself by involving myself in housework so much that the house was barely recognizable and resembled the scenery after Sophie and Larry had applied their magic touch.

"The last time you scrubbed this place to an inch of its life was after you got dumped," Danny remarked, although he wasn't entirely accurate. The last time I'd scrubbed the house clean was after I'd been released from the hospital, with a new scar across my belly. Still, I appreciated the sentiment.

"Nobody's been dumped."

"More's the pity," added Mark.

"I've had a lot on mind," I said through gritted teeth, shooting a glare towards my brother.

"So where is your TDS?" Danny asked. "It's been a few days since you've mentioned him." Only because I hadn't divulged the several text messages and emails I'd received with explicit comments that were not for their eyes.

"He's been busy, and so have I."

"I can see." Danny whistled, eyeing up the cobweb free beams.

I looked at my watch and swore. Only fifteen minutes before Matt was due to arrive for my appointment. I was dreading seeing Dr. Franklin as it was; I was even more nervous at the prospect of Matt Jackson sitting in on the conversations.

Mark handed me my jacket as the Audi rolled up behind the Golf that my brother had kindly reclaimed for me a couple of days earlier. Shrugging the animal print coat over my shoulders, I clutched the handbag in knuckles that were almost white. "You'll be fine." Mark kissed, followed by Danny.

"Jesus Christ, boys, I'm only going to the doctor's." I jumped out of their grips, trying to make light of it all.

"Make sure you call Mum when you get home. She's frantic."

"Yeah, yeah." I waved him off, clip-clopping over the concrete in ridiculous heels.

The drive into Andover was near silent, only the sing-song voice of the radio keeping it from becoming awkward.

Dr. Franklin's office was a mid-terrace white-fronted building that went up three stories and was snuggled between an optician and a dentist. Reception was on the first floor and consisted of a large Berber-carpeted room with a sweeping faux-wood desk. Dr. Franklin's secretary, a Liza Minnelli look-alike, was perched behind the desk chewing on a broken nail as she scanned through the appointments list. "Ya, take a seat," she said in quite possibly the most pretentious accent I'd ever heard, and that's saying something, considering the people my mother has as acquaintances.

I sat in one of the mint green chairs next to Matt, who looked as nervous as I was. I wanted to reach out and take his hand, needing the reassurance and comfort, but instead hid clenched fists under my bag, wringing them as though I was squeezing out every drop of moisture from my skin.

As usual, Dr. Franklin was running late and it was nearly quarter past before he called us into his office. "Paige, I'm so glad you've come back to see me." He held out a smooth hand for me to shake, but stopped short when he noticed Matt standing. "Who is this?"

"Oh, I'm sorry. Matt, this is Dr. Franklin, my psychiatrist. Dr. Franklin, this is my friend Matt."

"It's good to meet a friend of Paige's at long last." Dr. Franklin shook his hand firmly. "And I'm a psychotherapist, not a psychiatrist," he corrected.

"Potato, potahto," I sang, stepping into his room.

Timothy Franklin was a fairly average man, standing at probably no more than five foot nine, with platinum white hair that was receding at the

171

front, and icy blue eyes. He sat in his leather office chair, reclining backwards slightly, and offered us the two maroon leather chairs by his desk. "Now, before we go any further, I must mention that it is highly irregular having somebody in with the patient. I prefer to have one-on-one sessions unless there is an actual risk to said patient." He sounded like he was reading directly from a list of terms and conditions.

"Dr. Franklin, I've asked Matt to be here because I'd like him to hear what you have to say."

He paused for a moment, weighing up the options and considerations. "Fine, but as long as you are aware that anything that is said in this room must go no further. Patient confidentiality, you understand."

"I understand," Matt agreed.

"So what can I do for you today, Miss Holmes?"

Instantly my cheeks flushed, making my embarrassment known. I felt Matt take my hand, wrapping his fingers around mine. "If you would prefer me to leave."

"No!" I snapped too quickly. "No, it's important for me that you hear this. Dr. Franklin, Matt and I have only known each other a short time, but I really do feel like he's one of my best friends already." I smiled, but the hurt radiated from him like the rays of a dying sun.

"And does Matt know why you came to see me in the first place?" Dr. Franklin trod carefully around the subject.

I nodded. "Yes, he knows I was…"

"Raped. Paige, it's important that you are able to take hold of that word."

"Raped," I repeated, looking Dr. Franklin in the eye. Matt's finger tensed around mine. A lump grew in my throat.

"And what else does he know?"

"That's about it." Matt smiled at me empathetically.

"What about your relationship?" Dr. Franklin pointed between us.

"Complicated," I said.

"Describe complicated."

I looked at Matt, searching for permission. He didn't give it, but he didn't hold back either.

"I'm in a relationship with an older man," I started, trying to find the best way to describe it without upsetting Matt. "And I want to be in a relationship with Matt."

"This older man, tell me about him."

Matt took a deep breath. "He's my father."

Chapter Twenty-Eight

Dr. Franklin tried to remain impartial, but even I could see the disagreement behind those glassy eyes. I hung my head in shame.

"I think it's a good idea if Paige and I have a chat alone for a minute." He stood and opened the door, waiting for Matt to leave, but I kept my hand clamped around his.

"No." I shook my head. "I want him to stay."

"Paige, clearly we have a lot to discuss."

"It's okay, I'll be right outside," Matt assured me, kissing my cheek before leaving. I lifted a hand and wiped it across my nose, which had now begun to run, along with the tears that dripped down my face.

Alone, Dr. Franklin sat in front of me, and I told him the entire saga. Once I'd finished, he leant back into his chair. "You do realize that you're using this TDS as a means of punishing yourself, don't you? The fact that you don't even use his given name to describe him tells me a lot about the way you feel for him."

I nodded, tearing small pieces from the tissue he'd offered me.

"Matthew obviously likes you a lot, to stand by you, and to be here with you. If you want to be in a relationship with him, then you are going to have to remove yourself from his father, and tell him the truth regarding the rape. Have you told him what you remember?"

I shook my head. "I've told him bits…"

"Have you told him about the operation?"

I nodded.

"And he's still here, waiting for you. Doesn't that tell you how he feels?"

I nodded again. "Aren't you supposed to remind me that I've barely known him a month?"

"Would you like me to?" It was typical of Dr. Franklin to answer a question with a question.

"No, not really," I admitted.

"Tell me about work. How are you feeling now?"

"Greg laid me off. All this crap sent my head spinning, so he's told me to take some time, but I don't think I'll be going back."

"I did try to warn you, Paige, you were jumping in far too quickly. Never mind, there are other jobs," he said dismissively. "What about the sports? I can see from those new wounds that you are still playing rugby."

"They're healing," I said, lifting a finger to my jaw and brow.

"As long as you aren't locking yourself away in the house again. What about your brother and friend? Daniel, wasn't it?"

I nodded. "They're still with me."

"And the claustrophobia and panic attacks?"

"Under control," I fibbed. "I do my breathing exercises when I feel them coming on, and that does help."

174

"What about the nightmares?"

I sat back and thought for a while. How long had it been? I couldn't remember having one since I'd met Matt. I shrugged in response. "It's been about a month, I guess."

"Well, that's a step in the right direction. I've noticed that you haven't filled a prescription recently. You shouldn't just stop taking antidepressants."

"I've been doing fine without them," I stated defiantly, crossing my arms around my chest, but he ignored my childishness and turned to his computer, tapping out on the keyboard. The printer buzzed and whirred, spitting out a sheet of green paper, which he scribbled on before handing it to me with a stern look. I took it and glanced down at the prescription. More drugs.

"I want you to start taking these again." He tapped the end of a fountain pen on the paper in my grasp. "If you still feel the same way in six months, then we'll reconsider."

With a heavy sigh, and an even heavier heart, I plunged the chit into my handbag.

"Now, you're obviously here to discuss Mr. Jackson out there, so let's discuss him and where we go from here."

The session was typically half an hour long, and by the end of it, my hands were filled with disintegrating tissues. I thanked Dr. Franklin for his time and made another appointment for six months' time before acknowledging Matt's presence.

"So?" he pressed me. I didn't answer him, just led us out of the building and back towards the car park. Concern etched into his tight jaw and furrowed brows as I remained in silence until we were trapped inside the Audi.

"Please talk to me," he urged.

I shrugged. "Everyone was right. I've pushed myself too much too soon."

"Do you want to talk about it?"

I nodded. "But not now. I'm tired, and I need to go to the pharmacy." My head was tangled in a web of conflict. Deep down, in the pit of my being, I knew that Dr. Franklin had a point. I had to get away from TDS, but how could I distance myself from him if I was seeing his son? I wasn't very good at making decisions at the best of times. Perhaps I needed a break away from it all.

After picking up the prescription of antidepressants and muscle relaxants, Matt drove me back to the farmhouse. Hannah was riding Georgia back from a hack as we arrived. She waved and smiled, her wide smile taking over the entirety of her round face.

Walking in through the door, I found Mark awaiting my return. "Mum rang, she said call her straight away."

"Well, she can wait." I shrugged my jacket off and flung it over the back of a chair. Mark shot an apprehensive glare towards Matt, who returned it. I rolled my eyes. "For God's sake, I'm right here. If you have something to say, just say it already."

"Paige, we're worried about you. Mum is convinced you're going to end up being readmitted. You were doing so well, until…" He paused, aware that Matt was in the room. "You know."

"I can't take this anymore," I cried, throwing my hands in the air. "I can't take all this eggshell walking." Stomping my feet on the floor, I marched up the stairs, leaving them to their own conversations, falling onto my bed and staring up at that ever-growing dark spot.

They were wrong. I was wrong. Dead wrong. I wasn't being readmitted anywhere. I was doing fine. Vance Ellery wasn't a mistake; he was helping me rediscover parts of me I thought had died. If Matt wanted to hang around and wait for me to be ready for a long-term, monogamous relationship, then more fool him.

As much as I liked him, he was beginning to feel like a lovesick puppy, constantly dragging at my heels. Rolling to my side, I fished the iPhone out of my pocket and scrolled through to find his number. "I need to see you tonight. P."

Within moments I received his reply. "I'll pick you up at eight." Five hours.

I thought for a moment before responding. "No. You can't come here. Meet me at the sports pavilion."

"I'll be waiting."

Relief swept over me. Knowing that I would be able to take my frustrations out on him put me at ease in an instant. My emotional punching bag. No doubt Dr. Franklin would have argued that it was unhealthy, but…

A knock on the door startled me. "Come in," I called, quickly hiding the messages from my screen.

Matt peered from around the door. "I wanted to check that you were okay. Mark said it was okay to come up." As if he needed my brother's permission to speak to me.

"I'm fine. I'm sorry for storming off. I'm tired and, to be honest, fed up of it all."

"I was worried when you didn't ask me back in at Dr. Franklin's," he confessed. I wondered whether he was worried for my well-being or worried regarding what, or whom, I may have been talking about. I couldn't tell by the crisscrossed lines across his forehead whether it was genuine concern for me or him.

"What did Mark mean by readmitted?"

I rolled onto my back, lying prone and staring straight up at that black spot. It was definitely getting bigger by the day. "There is so much you don't know or understand."

"I can see that." He reached out and took my hand, stroking my fingers with his own. I didn't melt beneath his touch. Casting a glance down at the gesture, I realized at that moment that I felt exactly for him as I did Danny. He caught my gaze, holding it steady for a second. "You can trust me, Paige."

Therein lay the problem. Trust wasn't easy to give, but it was easy to smash and break down. He'd proven that the night he took me home and wrecked my mind, body, and soul.

Matt was right, I could trust him, but I was wary about giving it to him. At least with TDS I knew where I stood. I couldn't trust him in the slightest, and with that knowledge, I felt that I had control over our relationship. As bizarre as that may sound, it was the only way I could protect myself against being destroyed again.

"It's not about trusting you," I admitted quietly. "It's about being able to survive when you break that trust. I told your father that we were both stronger than he gave us credit for. In truth, I'm not convinced that I am."

"Why won't you talk to me? I mean, really talk to me. I can't, if you don't let me."

"Once you find everything out, you may not be so willing to stick around and wait for me." Perhaps that was the test I needed to give us both. If I told him the whole truth, and he stayed by my side, then I would know he was true to his word. If he left, then at least I would be safe in the knowledge that I hadn't let him get close enough to break my already fragile heart.

"Everything? Is there more?" he asked, confusion firmly pressed into his eyes and brow.

"It's not quite as simple as you think it is," I sighed, throwing my eyes to the heavens.

"Try me," he pushed, urging me to confess my darkest secrets.

I sat up, legs swinging down by his. He held my hand tightly, his deep blue gaze firmly fixed on me. "You should go and find someone who isn't as fucked-up as me." I tried to push him away one last time, but I sensed he wasn't going anywhere. "You can do so much better than me."

"How will I know unless you talk to me?" His grip was an anchor, ready to steady the boat as my storm threatened above him. Every muscle in his body was tensed, his jaw set into a hard line, his brow smooth without expression as he waited, preparing himself for the worst he could imagine.

"I don't think I can. I'm not ready to. Not yet."

"Please understand, Paige, it's not your past that worries me."

"I need a friend right now, Matt, that's all."

"You're having an affair with my father." The words sounded all too familiar, like a bad case of deja vu. "I understand, I really do, but…"

But. Always a bit.

"Please don't say it," I pleaded. "I'd like us to be friends."

He pulled away from me, fingers gripped around my arms, deep blue eyes sparking with fear, anger, and lust all combined into a heady mix. "I don't want to be your friend, Paige. I love you."

Shit.

Chapter Twenty-Nine

I was glad when he left without waiting for a response. I suppose I should have gone after him. Any sane woman would have done. When a drop-dead gorgeous, wealthy man confesses his undying love to you, you don't let him get away. But I'm not any sane woman, and I did know exactly what I had to do.

The evening sky was a sketch of contemporary fine art. Shots and sparks of burnt orange, crimson, and violet against a midnight blue backdrop with hot pink clouds surrounded the village. Dark trees cast their shadows down over the car park. I leaned against one, the bark prickled at my back, feet firmly planted on a boulder in front, making me several inches taller than my natural height.

Wheels belonging to the black Jag turned over the white lines, parking parallel with where I stood. My shoulders arched into the tree's body, spine straightening as I waited for him to exit. I think I held my breath as well.

TDS stepped out into the cool summer air. Instantly I felt the heat sear in the deepest part of me. No man had ever had this much power over my sexuality before. To think that I was about to dowse that flame was unbearable.

His expression was stern, with a rigid jawline and low brow. In the obscurity of sunset, his indigo eyes were almost black, hiding how his pupils reacted to my presence. Ice had replaced the fire that usually burned. As though he was emitting a cold wind, a shiver shuddered through me. Instinctively I lifted my hands to rub away the chills.

"I do not appreciate your childishness," he said angrily. Hands planted into the bark either side of my head, causing me to gasp. Something inside me stirred, the danger of this man igniting flames of desire. "You can't storm out and then expect me to come running each time."

"But you did," I pressed. His eyes sparked, a single glint in the darkness. He swallowed the truth; then, without warning, I could taste him. The tip of his tongue caressed at my mouth as a hand fell to my hair, pulling me deeper into him.

"So what brought on this sudden mind change?"

"I saw Matt today." Watching his reaction, I could see that he was by no means thrilled at the prospect of me spending time with his son. "He told me he loved me."

Disgust curled his bottom lip. He was not surprised by this piece of news.

"You could at least pretend that you care," I snapped. "Another man has just confessed that he loves me."

"Do you love him?"

"What? Of course not!"

"Are you sure?"

"Do you think I do?"

"You spend an awful lot of time together, and you have slept with him."

"I don't have to be in love with someone to have sex with them. I should think you, of all people, would realize that." It was a spiteful thing to say, and I was left disappointed that he did not react to my cutting remarks. "You really don't give a shit, do you?"

"You called me all the way out here, set up this whole clandestine meeting to tell me that my son has fallen in love with you," he stated without answering me.

I shook my head in disbelief. "No," I admitted. "I didn't."

TDS stepped back, giving me space to breathe, and pointed to the Jag. "Get in."

"I'm not sure I want to get in a car with you now."

"Miss Holmes, clearly there is something on your mind, and you're obviously not willing to discuss it here, or you would have spat it out already. So get in the damn car before I drag you in."

I did as I was told, following him like a little lamb would follow a wolf in sheep's clothing.

The sun said its good-nights as it dipped beyond the grassy fields. Inside the Jaguar, there was only the white glow from the moon as it climbed a star-lit ladder. I glanced towards the driver, aware of his ability to hear my every word as I prepared myself.

"Don't worry, Chalmers is as experienced in keeping secrets as I am," TDS tried to assure me. But it didn't work. My lips pursed tightly together, hair hanging over my eyes, shielding me from having to look at him too much. I noticed him nod to Chalmers in the rearview mirror. "Take us back to the hotel," he ordered.

"You still haven't answered me," I demanded. "Do you care?"

"Yes. I care." I had the distinct feeling he was only telling me what he thought I wanted to hear, but I didn't argue with his response.

His palm fell flat against my thigh; pressure built in my belly. I closed my eyes, concentrating on my mantra. His mouth fell to my ear. "You're going to tell me what is going on in that pretty head of yours, Paige Holmes."

"And what if I don't want you to know?" I snapped.

"I'm sure I can find a way of convincing you that I'm not such a monster."

"I don't think you're a monster." It wasn't entirely the truth. I don't believe in monsters and ghouls, but at the same time I had to take heed of my instincts when it came to this man. As much as he excited me, there was an element of fear to him as well.

Dr. Franklin had already told me that my past would try to break through, tar every man, as it were, but I wasn't so easily convinced that my reluctance around TDS was simply memories I desperately wanted to repress.

The only response to my reply was a tightening of his palm on my leg. I breathed steadily through the internal tumbling. I waited for him to take it one step further, to move those deft fingers closer to my warmth. But disappointingly, the only movement he made was to put his back further into the leather seats, and his hand on his own lap.

"Tell me, Paige," he urged. I didn't answer him, though, instead chewing on my bottom lip as I searched for a way out of this whole situation. He twisted in his seat, facing me in the darkness, not letting the sudden swerve of the car disturb him. "Don't play games with me, Miss Holmes," he said in a voice as dark as the night sky. "Either you tell me what is going on, what it is that is upsetting you to a point of distraction, or I am going to get my way." He didn't need to elaborate on the last part.

"Then you get your way whatever I decide."

He smirked. "One of the many perks I enjoy."

"God, I hate…" His hand swept into my hair. His lips stopped me from finishing my sentence. "You," I murmured as he pulled away from me.

"Just tell me, Paige," he kissed.

"First you. Tell me how you felt when I told you what Matt said."

182

TDS sank into the indentation of his seat with a heavy sigh, telling me all I needed to know. But I still wanted to hear him say it. I waited momentarily, watching as his hands rubbed over his face, through his hair, dyed jet black by the lack of light. The family resemblance was easy to spot, despite the darkness.

"Of course I care," he finally admitted. A wave of smug sadness brutally battered me as the words slipped from his lips. I moved closer to him, hooking his arm around my shoulder and nestling into his chest, inhaling that deliciously masculine scent. He stiffened against my movement as though instinct had made him cautious. After a while, he relaxed. His fingers tenderly stroked my arms as he kissed my hair. I didn't need to see him to know that he had closed his eyes, taking in my own floral femininity.

"Please talk to me, Paige," he pleaded softly.

"I'm scared."

"Of what?"

"You."

"You don't need to be," he said, seemingly unsurprised by my admission.

"I'm sorry."

"What for? Being scared of me?"

"No," I shook my head. "Of sleeping with Matt."

A deep breath raised my head. "Don't apologize. My son can be very convincing when he wants something."

"You don't believe it, do you? That he loves me."

"No. I'm afraid I don't."

"Why not?"

"Matthew is his father's son."

"He's nothing like you," I fibbed, unsure of whom I was protecting from what. The truth was that I had seen TDS within Matt.

"You've told him, haven't you? Whatever it is you're keeping from me, your little secrets."

"Yes." If he did know about my past, he wasn't going to say so.

"And how did he react?"

I didn't answer. How had he reacted? He'd been kind, understanding, and gentle. He'd taken me back to work, and then later on, he'd made utterly glorious love to me.

"I see," TDS nodded knowingly. "And how do you think I'll react?"

Again, I didn't answer, but this time it was because I didn't have one. I hoped he would be as sympathetic, but I suspected he would be as forgiving as a hurricane.

The car stopped.

"Shall we take this inside?" he asked rhetorically.

"I didn't want to get in the car with you. What makes you think I want go up there?" I asked, sitting up and straightening my clothes.

"Because you did get in the car with me." He had a point. Reluctantly, I let Chalmers help me out. I thanked him with a smile before leading us into the opening hall of Richard Courts.

TDS was a while behind me, giving me time to take in the gold and cream marble surroundings. It was then that I noticed the way the staff reacted to him as he entered. Again, he waltzed right past the front desk. I jogged after him, feeling extremely underdressed in trainers, jeans, and a t-shirt.

"Holy mother of fucking God. You own this place, don't you?" I snapped, stepping into the lift beside him. Chalmers threw me a smirk as he pressed the button for TDS's floor.

"Yes," he replied simply.

"Why didn't you tell me?"

"Why should I?"

Bloody hell," I cursed loudly.

"You really shouldn't swear."

"Fuck you," I retorted smartly. His hand landed on my backside with a slap. "Seriously, fuck you," I snapped, stepping out of his reach.

The lift stopped and we exited together. Once inside, TDS chatted to Chalmers quietly, no doubt giving him orders to ensure that I didn't leave. I marched towards the bar and poured myself a vodka and tonic, gulping it down in two swigs.

"When you're quite finished." TDS sat on the sofa, his arms stretched out across the back. The blinds had been pulled, and the lights were on and filling the room. If I hadn't known differently, I could have sworn it was daytime. He patted the seat next to him. "Come here."

"You can't just demand from me. I don't care if you do own this sodding place."

"Paige," he growled. "You're the one who called me, remember. Now, sit down and tell me whatever it is you're afraid to say."

I poured myself another drink, placing it on the coffee table in front of us, and did as I was told. Turning to face him, I prepared myself for the truths I was about to reveal so openly.

"Promise me that you won't hate me afterwards."

"I can't make any promises until you tell me." His expression was stern, but suddenly it softened with laughter lines. "You've eked this out long enough. Jesus Christ, Paige, it can't be that bad!"

"You have absolutely no idea."

Chapter Thirty

"His name was Evan Browne," I started, trying to grapple with the words as they spun around me in a daze. "He worked with my father, but I didn't meet him officially until the summer ball last year. He was only a year older than me, and was also the son of a man I was sleeping with. It wasn't anything serious with Rufus, his father. It was supposed to be a silly fling, but he was married. His wife found out that he was having an affair and divorced him."

I watched his reaction as he sank backwards, shoulders slumped, letting the realization settle. If he knew anything, it was not this. "It wasn't known as such that I was the other woman, even my own parents don't know, but Evan knew. He'd seen me leaving the house one night, and didn't tell anyone. I couldn't understand why at the time, but obviously, now I do."

He let go of my hand, but kept his eyes firmly fixed on mine, not fully understanding which road I was on. I inhaled sharply, preparing to continue, half-hoping that he would ask me to stop. But he didn't.

"As you know, my parents hold a fundraiser every summer, and they were all invited to the ball. I couldn't think of a good enough excuse, so I went as well. Evan saw me, dressed in very little, and started flirting. My parents thought it was fantastic. That this wealthy and affluent young man was showing me so much attention was more than Mum could have hoped for. Looking like I do, with the interests I have, boyfriends have been far and few between, so she was over the moon at the thought of me seeing someone.

"To appease her, I began to see Evan more often. It felt wrong, though. I'd destroyed his parents' marriage. I can't tell you how ashamed I felt. He kept pressing me to sleep with him, but I couldn't. Then, one evening, he took me out for dinner and invited me back to his house. I didn't want to go, but at the same time, he had some kind of allure about him. I can't describe it, but I felt utterly useless. A bit like I do with you."

I reached a hand out, but he recoiled from my touch. The lump in my throat increased in size.

"When we got back to his house, he offered me a drink. He must have spiked it with something, because the next thing I remember is being on the floor, underneath him. He didn't even undress me." I choked on the words, an acrid taste forming against my tongue. "He gripped my arms so tightly I couldn't move, and his knees pinned my legs apart." I stopped. Tears and mucus began to build up, blocking my voice. "I couldn't move." The sob was uncontrollable; salt-filled streams ran down my cheeks as the memories flooded back. "And it hurt so much." Words came through in spits and spats.

His arms moved around me, hugging me tightly. His lips fell to my hair, gentle fairy kisses, soothing as he hushed me. My eyes closed, but images shattered the blackness.

His lecherous sneer dripped down. Greasy paws groping wildly. The thin, jagged edges of Evan Browne blurred my tranquility.

"When he finished, he stood up and told me I was fucking shit in bed, and that he didn't know what his father saw in me. He called me all sorts of names, which I guess I deserved." Sniveling like a pathetic child, I scolded myself.

"No," TDS stopped me. "You didn't deserve any of it."

"I lay there for what seemed like hours," I continued, my head resting against his arm. "He even called my brother to come and get me. He told him we'd had an argument."

"You didn't tell anyone?"

"How could I? That would have meant admitting that I'd been sleeping with a man who was older than my father, a good friend of both my parents, and married with kids. "No." I shook my head. "I didn't tell anyone. Mark and Danny suspected something was wrong, but they didn't push the subject, so I didn't say anything to them. My Mum was heartbroken that I wasn't seeing Evan any longer. She had such a rose-tinted view of him, I couldn't destroy that.

"Then, about a month later, I realized that I was bleeding more heavily than normal. I went to the doctors and they did a pregnancy test. His baby.

"When I got home, Danny was there, but Mark was at Holmes Manor doing a location shoot or something. I didn't really have a choice, so I told Danny everything. I thought he was going to kill him. He was so angry." Guilt pulled at my fraying weakness.

His arms tightened around me as the tears began to flow.

"He agreed that he wouldn't say anything to Mark or my parents, but I think I knew that he was going to. Maybe that's why I told him, because I couldn't tell them myself. Danny's always been like a big brother to me, but there's that… I dunno… separation, I guess. Anyway, he did tell Mark, who told my parents, but things got left out, like my involvement with Rufus."

"So even now, your parents don't know?"

I shook my head. "They probably do, but they've never said anything."

"And yet I…"

"They see you as another Evan. Not that you would attack me or anything," I forced the words out, desperately backpedaling over the accusations. "Just that you are…" The words caught in a knot. I had to be honest with him. "Controlling and powerful, and very charming and manipulative. Everything that Evan is."

"I know exactly how people see me." His jaw was a solid mass, back teeth grinding against the venom and hate. "What happened? To the baby?" His words pained me, but I had to continue if there was to be a chance…

"I had a lot of pain in my stomach, and the bleeding got worse. The doctors insisted that I had scans and tests and talked to therapists. Danny came with me to every single appointment. I felt awful, but I found myself hoping that I was having a miscarriage. At least then it would save me having to make that decision. You have no idea what it's like to wish that your baby would die." Shameful fury burst from me, soaking his shirt. "Nobody will ever be able to hate me as much as I hate myself," I sniffed.

He swallowed hard, his Adam's apple bobbing as he fought to remain strong.

"One of the tests came back saying I had chlamydia. That fucking bastard hadn't just left me pregnant with his baby, he'd given me a fucking disease as well!" The anger seared through as I remembered the smell of antiseptic and bleach at the hospital, waiting with Danny's fingers tightly around mine, listening to the words that tainted me more than I already was. "And then when I did miscarry… Oh, God, I can't tell you how I felt. Sadness, regret, relief, everything and anything. I was completely overwhelmed by it all. They did an operation, an ERPC, to remove…" The words came out thick and fast, like a storming tidal wave threatening to engulf us both.

"It's okay," he assured me, his hands caressing my arms.

"To remove it. I don't know what happened then. I was in the hospital and perhaps I was in shock, I really don't know, but things got complicated with the chlamydia, the miscarriage, and the operation. I was left scarred. I ended up having a laparotomy." My hand moved across the scar on my abdomen. "They deduced that basically I'm a mess inside and out. If I ever have children, it will be nothing short of a miracle.

"Unfortunately, my hormone levels are messed up as well. They put me on the pill to try and regulate things, but the truth is, they're throwing whatever they can at me and hoping something works."

"Jesus Christ," he swore under his breath, raking it all in.

"They think I'll have to have a hysterectomy before I'm forty." Denial allowed me to become blasé.

I waited for him to ask me to leave, waited for him to tell me he was no longer interested, as I had imagined he would. But he didn't. He didn't move his arms as they clung around me. I looked up at him, watching as he stared into space, letting his mind consume everything I had said.

"My father called the police before Mark and Danny could find him. They arrested him for his own safety more than anything, I think. I didn't see him until the trial. My parents tried to petition the courts so that I didn't have to go, but the truth is, I wanted to. I wanted to prove to him that I wasn't going to be afraid of him, that he didn't control my life. I wish I hadn't, though. He sat there with this smug look on his face, as though it was all some kind of sick joke. His lawyers even tried to convince everyone that I'd made it all up, that it was consensual, and I'd lied about the…" I swallowed hard. "The rape, because Evan had broken up with me. They even used the fact that I hadn't told anyone against me. The problem is that I started to believe them."

"How could you believe that? None of this was your fault, Paige, none of it."

189

"You don't understand. My mind started to play over the events, and I realized that I couldn't really remember any of it. The lawyers started talking about my martial arts experience, and said that if he'd attacked me, I could have defended myself, but I didn't. I tried to remember why I hadn't kicked out, but there is nothing there. All I remember is him above me, but it's like an out-of-body experience. I can see my own face. How can I see my own face if it was a memory? It's almost as if I did make it all up. I thought he was going to get away with it." The memories, the truth, rasped at my throat. Fire burned against the delicate pink tissue.

"But he didn't."

"No. He had well-paid lawyers, but mine were more expensive." Money. Always money.

"And his father?"

"Rufus didn't show up to one single court case. Both he and my father made sure that it would never go to press. A couple of stories were , leaked. Evan's not important enough to become a headline, thank God. Once it was over, Rufus severed all ties. We haven't heard from him since my father sued Evan. They settled out of court, but that was more for their benefit than mine. I saw Rufus a few weeks after I was released from the hospital, but he blanked me. Probably for the best."

"There's more. Isn't there?" He trod carefully over the broken pieces of my shell, reaching for the finish line in the race to my past.

I took a deep breath. "I had a breakdown. I was admitted into the hospital, which is when I met my psychotherapist, Dr. Franklin. My father paid a lot of money for his services. I was only in for a couple of weeks, but they put me on all sorts of medication. I lost the majority of my friends and became reclusive. That's when the panic attacks and nightmares started. At first, it was almost like agoraphobia. I couldn't go outside without having an attack. Either Danny or Mark had to be with me at all times. I only felt safe when they were around.

"My boss, Greg, was very kind and told me to take as much time as I needed. And Lou, the captain of the rugby team, convinced me to go back and give it a go. Sports helped, a lot. My personal trainer and MMA instructors supported me as I rebuilt my fitness levels. The doctors were amazed at how quickly I healed physically, and they said that being so active stopped it from being worse than it was, if you can believe that. How could it have been worse?!" It all came out so fluidly, I could barely believe myself.

"You could have died," he said bluntly, as though not really talking to me. I gulped silently at the thought.

"Unfortunately, it then did a complete   360 and now I'm claustrophobic. I have a fear of loud noises, especially thunderstorms, and of being alone. I coped by drinking more, which pushed even more people away. Eventually Greg agreed that it would be better if I came back to work and kept myself busy. He even encouraged the lads to flirt with me so that I didn't feel completely broken. I was starting to get a handle on things. And then I met you." Anger, infuriation, and remorse bubbled beneath my surface.

We sat in silence after I'd finished, allowing each morsel of horrific detail to be digested. My stomach churned and twisted; bile bobbed in the base of my throat, waiting for his reaction.

"Say something," I urged after a moment or two.

"I'm not sure what to say." At least he was being honest. What could I expect him to say, or do? Did I think he would wrap his arms around me, stroke my hair, and offer to protect me for the rest of my life? Did I even want him to? I struggled to even find the reason I'd told him in the first place. The dark place inside hoped that the release would ebb away the guilt, shame, and degradation that stuck to me like thick tar.

"I would understand if you didn't want to see me again." My back teeth ground against each other, catching small films of cheek flesh. His silence was unnerving. The eerie ghosts haunted us both.

He was yearning to tell me he needed some space, some time to adjust. That would have been human of him, and expected, considering. I had unloaded a great weight onto his shoulders, no matter how broad they appeared to be. But then I saw a gentleman, a kind and caring soul who wasn't revolted by my misery, stayed by my side, arm clutched around me, fingers gently brushing against my skin.

Chapter Thirty-One

Waiting for the wolf to appear from beneath the sheepskin of concern, I stared into those indigo eyes, blackened as though we were still in the dark car. I watched as they softened from the harshness I was used to. It put me on edge, TDS going from smoldering to simmering. Now, he reminded me even more of his son. I closed my eyes, and waited for one of us to speak. The stillness was long and patient, but filled me with a fear I knew all too well.

I wasn't sure what I expected him to say. In another circumstance, I would have expected him to apologize. But he wasn't normal in any sense of the word. There was absolutely nothing average about TDS.

That was how most reacted to the news. They were sorry that this had happened to me. Sometimes there were tears, but they were never tears for me. Apologies and heartfelt sobs were always a selfish reaction to my trauma. I understand, though. The human's instant reaction is to try and put themselves in that position. How would they have coped had it been their body lying helplessly on the floor as they tried to push themselves mentally out of the room? Have my body, not my soul.

The only person who wasn't sorry, who didn't shed tears, was the one who really should.

TDS didn't, though. There was no self-pity, no guilt. There was only hatred. His eyes flamed with an intensity so severe I worried I may get burned if I looked long enough. His jaw and neck were a solid mass of muscle and hard lines.

I felt myself holding my breath, listening to the thump of my blood as it throbbed loudly in my ear, drowning out any thoughts I may have had. Still waiting.

An eternity passed before I finally broke the silence. "Say something," I pleaded, desperate to hear him speak. At that point I didn't even care if he screamed and shouted and blamed me. At least it would have been something other than sitting in the icy, bleak silence.

He swallowed, as though contemplating his thoughts. I closed my eyes, a lengthened blink, hoping that when I opened them, I would find myself in bed, alone, discovering that my admission had been some horrible dream. If it was a dream, then I could change my mind about telling him, and we could go on with the torrid affair of steamy sex and absolutely no emotional ties.

Ha. That was a laugh. No emotional ties. If I hadn't handcuffed myself to him, figuratively speaking, then I wouldn't be sitting here pouring my heart out to him. If I hadn't fallen so deeply and utterly for him, then I would have stayed with Matt easily. If I hadn't…

"Why have you told me?" He interrupted my self-chastising with the exact question I was asking myself.

Fuck if I know. It wasn't exactly the response that I could blurt out, so I took my time. Apparently too long, since he grabbed my shoulders and turned me to face him. He wasn't rough, though, certainly not as strong as he would have been before I told him.

"Why?" he repeated more sternly. "You can't push me away," he added, without waiting for my response. "If you thought telling me this would change how I want to be with you, you're wrong."

My shoulders sank, defeated by his obsession. The family resemblance was too strong for me to fight.

"Paige, if you don't want to be with me, all you have to do is say so. I will let you go."

"Let me go?" I snapped. "You really don't get it, do you? I told you because you deserve to know. I told you because if this is going to have any kind of chance, then you need to know."

"Is that why you told Matthew? To see if you two had a chance?"

"I don't know why I told him. Because he was there, I guess. I needed it out, and he was there."

"This can't work. You do know that, don't you?"

Tears sprang to my eyes before he'd even finished the sentence. "Don't say that," I stuttered.

"This is nothing to do with anything you have said tonight. You need to understand that. But if you're looking for a serious relationship, something long-term, or marriage, you have to know that it will never work."

I did know. I knew only too well.

"Why are you here, Paige?" he asked. I shook my head, but it wasn't the answer he was ready to accept. "Yes, you do."

"You will never ask me to give you something I can't give." I looked up at him, into those intense, deliciously hungry eyes.

"Children," he acknowledged. "No, that is very true. I will never ask you to give me that. But you can't stay with me to avoid a situation which may never happen."

"Why not?" I took his arm and wrapped it around me, snuggling into the crook of his elbow and chest. "Perhaps I want to be here." My hand dropped to his thigh, massaging gently at the thick muscle. Slipping my fingers over the bulge of his trousers, I caressed at him seductively. His palms moved over mine, fingers looping through mine, and slid them back to his thigh.

I couldn't help the disappointed sigh that escaped from me. He smiled, and placed a kiss on the top of my head. "Now is not the time."

"I think it's a very good time," I said shortly, trying to move my hand back, but he stopped me, gripping me around the wrist.

"No, you don't. You want sex to prove to yourself that I still find you attractive after you've told me about the rape."

I cringed, shuddering at the word.

"Don't do that," he said shortly. "Don't blame yourself."

"That's very easy to say."

"I know." He hugged me tighter, loosening his hands from around my wrists. "Why didn't you tell me before now?"

I shrugged, mumbling, "Dunno."

"Yes, you do. What did Matthew tell you about me that scared you?"

"I'm not scared."

"You're terrified, Paige."

"It's not just Matt. Everyone is warning me away from you. They say you're dangerous."

He laughed with a scoff. "In business, yes. But not when it comes to women. Especially you. Although I can understand Matthew's reaction. After the way I treated his mother..." he finished the sentence with a regret-filled sigh.

"And him," I added, perhaps a little harshly. "It was wrong of you to sleep with his girlfriends."

"Perhaps."

"Did you agree with me?" I teased. But the harshness of his frown stopped me from pushing it further.

"Thank you for telling me. Whatever anyone says, I do care about you." The softness of his voice, the words he spoke, settled my nerves, contradicting every thought.

"You're an enigma, Mr. Ellery," I echoed his own observations about me. "One minute you're colder than the bloody Arctic; next, you're making me hotter than the desert."

"I prefer you hot," he purred. "But it will have to wait. I am still attracted to you," he added, sensing my worries and concerns.

"But you still don't think I should be with you."

"It's..." He paused. Whether it was for effect or to find the correct word, I couldn't be sure.

"Complicated?" I offered.

"Complicated," he agreed. "You will eventually have to make a decision about Matthew."

"And you."

"No. Not me. That's a decision you don't get to make."

"Pardon?" I asked, thinking I'd misheard. "So only you can make decisions about our relationship?"

"Yes."

"And what if I decide that I don't want either of you?"

"It's not up to you," he repeated. Irritation itched at me, scratching my bones.

"Fuck you, it's not up to me," I snapped, jumping to my feet. I momentarily for something to throw at him, but the only things that came to hand were heavy, breakable objects. "I've just laid myself bare to you," I cried, fighting the scream that wanted to belt out of me and slap him hard. "I've given you everything that I have." Tears burned down my already hot cheeks.

In an instant he was on his feet in front of me, pulling me into a tight grip. I tried to push away, tried to break out of his chains, but I was too weak with exhaustion.

"I don't understand," I sobbed into his chest. "I don't understand how you can be so calm all of the time."

"I'm not," he admitted, sinking us both back into the sofa, embracing me with a strength I was incapable of. "Do you honestly think that I'm okay with you sleeping with my son? Do you honestly believe that I don't want to go and find this Evan boy and rip his fucking heart out? And I'm sure that I would have to stand in line to get my piece. But what would screaming and shouting about it do now?"

"It would show me that you care!"

"Have I given you a reason to think I don't?"

"You've given me hundreds," I snorted, not moving from his hug.

"Why are you here then?"

"The sex is good." It was all I could come up with, and it wasn't entirely far from the truth.

He chuckled at my response, saying, and "Is that it"?

"I need a break." I sighed heavily, shifting from beneath his arms. "And you're not making it easy for me. I don't care what you say about whose decision it is. I'm telling you that I need to get away from it all. From you and Matthew," I added, in case he wasn't sure what I meant. He'd already made it very clear that he wasn't going to let me go easily.

He blew out a thick, hot breath of disagreement.

"This isn't up for debate," I said, demanding my freedom. "I need to clear my head, get things into perspective."

"Come with me."

"Excuse me?"

"Come with me to New York on Saturday."

"No." I shook my head. "You don't get it. I need to get away from you."

"You can. I'll be busy with meetings the entire time. You can even check my schedule, if you don't believe me." It shouldn't have been any surprise that TDS had a strict itinerary, which I knew he would adhere to. Deviation would never be tolerated.

It was certainly tempting. A fortnight staying in what would no doubt be a luxury hotel, waited on hand and foot, because TDS would insist on it. I would have been mad to turn him down. But that was the problem. I was mad. Mad with him, at him, and for him.

Grinding my back teeth as I processed the options, I watched as he stood and made us both vodka tonics. I declined, knowing that one more drink and I wouldn't be leaving this room, which was probably his full intention.

"I can't." I argued with my own logic.

"Where are you going to go then?"

I shrugged. I hadn't thought that far ahead, although a week in the sun was tempting, and the Bahamas had not been ruled out entirely.

"At least think about it. I don't leave until Saturday morning." He pushed the tumbler with clear liquid towards me. Again, I declined.

"Can Chalmers take me home, please?"

"Promise me you'll think about it."

"I'll think about it," I conceded.

Knocking back the glass, he emptied the contents down his throat before grabbing his mobile and calling Chalmers up. "This doesn't end things," he stated firmly, walking towards me. I straightened my back, lifting my chin high into the air. His lips were on mine before I could turn my cheek. "Call me tomorrow with your decision. I'll need to make arrangements."

Chalmers appeared in the doorway, a warm and friendly smile showing. I smiled back, ignoring the tears that rolled down my cheeks.

Chapter Thirty-Two

He was expecting my call. He expected me to bend to his will and accept his offer of staying at an all-expenses-paid hotel in the center of New York City. If I was being honest with myself, I expected it too.

The empty suitcase lay on my bed, as I stared up at the black spot like I so often did. A sigh flared from my nostrils as I contemplated what I should pack. If I should pack.

"Talk to me." Danny stood in the doorway to my room, his voice as abrupt and severe as his body language. Arms crossed tightly around his chest, as though squeezing every breath out of his lungs. He couldn't have looked more Neanderthal if he'd had a prominent brow. "Tell me what the fuck is going on, because this…" He waved his arms around, gesturing wildly. "This isn't you, Paige. You were doing so well before either of them came into your life."

"Was I?"

"Yes!" Exasperation filled his voice. He wasn't the only one who felt exhausted by it all. "You were back at work, they come into your life, and now look at you. You're a mess."

"Gee, thanks." I still hadn't met his eyes. I knew they would be steely cold, and it was a frosty look that I could do without.

"If I can't be honest with you, who can?"

"Where's Mark?" I asked, finally lifting my head to look at him properly. I had been right. Steel-grey and ice-cold.

"Trying to undo some of his own damage." My raised eyebrow asked all the questions. Danny relaxed, rolling his eyes and falling onto the bed. "Bianca won't leave him alone."

Perhaps it's genetic and all the Ellerys have an obsession problem, I thought idly.

"You're going with him then?" Danny asked, eyeing up the still-empty suitcase.

Danny had been the first port of call when it came to TDS's offer of New York. Mark would have been, but he wasn't there, clearly dealing with his own Ellery-related issues. His Ellery problems didn't come close to mine, though. He wasn't sleeping with their mother as well.

"I don't know," I answered eventually. Turning to my chest of drawers, I pulled it open and stared at the contents. Sexy lingerie stared back at me. Feminine lace, satin, and silk, all wanting to be played with and chosen. The only pair of non-sexy pants I owned were the nude Spanx, and I had a feeling that even those would stir TDS to distraction. If I did decide to go, I would have to demand separate rooms. That would be the only way to steer clear of him. I hoped.

"Paige?"

"Huh?" Apparently I'd missed an entire conversation that I was supposed to be party to.

"I said, why don't you just take that trip to Nice back?"

"Nice?" Oh, yeah, of course. The trip I'd bought at the fundraiser, and then given to my parents. "Mum would be upset."

"Your parents can go whenever they want." That was true. The chateau they'd be staying in was owned by a close friend of theirs. "And I'm sure they wouldn't mind."

"I gave it to them as an anniversary gift! I can't take it back. Anyway, the South of France wasn't on my list of places to escape to." Isn't that where the ex-Mrs. Ellery now lived? The last thing I needed was to risk bumping into my lover's ex-wife and my other lover's mother. Did I know what she looked like? Bianca, presumably. There was no similarity between her and TDS.

As big a part of the world that France was, it would be my luck that I ended up staying in the same town, village, or street as her.

"And New York was?"

"No," I grumbled, falling down next to him. Leaning my head on my surrogate brother's shoulders, I closed my eyes. His arm looped around my shoulders.

"You could stay here," he suggested. "Lock the doors, close the curtains, and turn off your phone. Let me and Mark look after you."

"As great as that sounds, you two need a break from me as well. I know I'm disrupting your work."

"You're never a disruption. You've been through hell several times over, and we're all here for you. How about Holmes Manor?"

"Seriously? You think staying with my mother would be relaxing?"

"Good point. But is New York any better? You're supposed to be getting away from it all, and you're contemplating locking yourself in a room with him for two weeks."

"No." I elongated the word in self-defense. "I'm contemplating letting him pay for first-class flights and an upscale hotel on the other side of the world."

"Flights and a hotel that you can easily afford yourself."

"That's not the point. Please, Danny, I don't want to argue with you as well." I stood up and marched towards the drawers, hoping that the seductive fabrics had magically warped into over-washed, grey, worn cottons. Alas, I was stuck with sexy.

"It seems you've made up your mind." It seemed he was right. "If I can't talk you out of it, then I may as well help you pack. I'm going into town. Anything you need?"

"Umm, I'm not sure."

"Write a list. I'll be leaving in an hour."

"Thank you, Danny."

"No probs." He kissed me gently on my forehead before walking out on me.

I picked up my phone and opened a new message: "Do I get my own room? P."

It took a while for the reply to come through. I imagined him reading my text. Hard, set jaw; tense, muscular neck; and thick brows arcing into the bridge of his nose, indigo eyes flaming at my request. I smiled at the realization of how well I knew him.

"I'll pick you up at five tomorrow morning."

Typical TDS response. Throwing my head back and staring at the black spot, I wanted to scream to the gods. He was so infuriating! It was a sign that I shouldn't go; of that, I was sure.

Leaving my empty case, I trod down the stairs to search for Danny, and hopefully Mark. I found Danny in the kitchen, making sandwiches. "Decision made?" he asked, without even turning around.

"No." I sulked, plunking myself in a chair and eyeing up the soft white bread.

"You wanna talk?" He sat down in front of me, lifting the sandwich to his lips. Smirking, he offered me the other half, which I took gratefully.

"I was hoping Mark would be back," I said in between mouthfuls. "I need to clear my head. And I know I'm not going to do that in New York."

"So don't go."

"It's not that simple."

"Yes, it is. He's not worthy of you, Paige. Neither of them are. You're only twenty-six, and you've been through more than anyone should ever have to. They're not going to make it better for you. If anything, they're making it worse. If you need to get away, go, anywhere, travel the bleeding world if you want to, but don't go to New York with him."

"I can't be on my own," I said sadly, placing the crusts back onto his plate.

"Perhaps that is exactly what you need."

"I'm scared, Danny." A solid lump built in the center of my throat.

"I know you are." The chair scraped across the tiled floor as he moved to be near me. His arms hooked around me, tightly squeezing my shoulders and chest until the tears were flowing steadily. My bottom lip and chin wobbled as I let it all out in great heavy sobs. His hands were still on my shoulders as he moved his gaze to my own. "I'm here for you. I always have been and I always will." He smiled kindly.

The churning and squeak of rubber tires startled us both for a fraction of a second. "Mark's home." Danny nudged me up. The pad of his thumb wiped under my eyes as I sniffed and hiccupped. He gave me a final hug before stepping back to the kettle and making tea for three.

"You look like shit," Mark stated as he walked through the door. Danny threw him a sharp glare, while I stared at the floor. "Okay, what's happened?" he asked. I took a deep breath before catching him up on the day's events. He rubbed his chin as he took it all in. "You told him?" he asked, even though he already knew the answer. "It's good that you can talk about it." He nodded, ignoring that TDS had asked me to go away with him and, more importantly, that I was considering it. "You should talk to Dr. Franklin."

"No!" I shouted, the power of my voice shocking me as well as both men. "I'm tired of doctors and psychiatrists telling me what I should and shouldn't be doing." I glanced over towards the prescription, still in its white paper bag sat by the sink. "I'm tired of all the pills and potions. I want to be me again."

"Do you think running away is going to help?" Mark snapped.

"I'm not running away."

"Are you sure about that? It bloody well sounds like you are. And with him as well? Christ, Paige, what are you thinking? He's the precise reason you need a break!"

"You don't think I know that?" I exclaimed.

"What do Mum and Dad think?"

"I haven't told them yet."

"You should."

"Why? So they can try and stop me as well? Why does everyone think I'm incapable of making my own decisions? Why does everyone think they have a right to control me? Have any of you considered the fact that perhaps I need to get away from you lot as well?" I didn't wait around for another slinging match. Turning on my heel sharply, I stomped my way back up the stairs with the world weighing me down. My bedroom door slammed against the wall.

Clothes and toiletries were flung into the empty case. Fury built between my ears so much that I thought the metaphorical steam was probably visible. Inanimate objects quaked as I raged.

"Paige!"

I snapped round at the shout of my name. My brother stood in the doorway, filling it with ease. "I'm sorry." His voice was sharp, failing the meaning of the apology.

"No, you're not." I continued to pack.

"Yes, I am. We're worried about you. You're right. You do need to get away from us as well. But is New York with Ellery really the right decision?" Why couldn't they leave it and me alone?

"No. I don't think it is. But it's an offer that I can't turn down. I need to do this."

I ignored whatever else it was that he had to say, hearing only the part where he told me to ring our parents, something which I fully intended to do anyway.

The sun had set long before I'd finished my storming. Sinking into the soft duvet and pillows, I picked up the phone and rang Holmes Manor, grateful when it was my father who answered.

"Hi, Daddy," I sang, trying to sound as happy as possible. If my parents thought this is what I wanted, I knew I would get their support, whether they agreed or not.

My mother wept down the phone when I was passed to her. "It's only two weeks, Mum," I whined. "It's only a holiday."

"It's not that, darling, it's who you're going with. Come with us to France, if you need to get away."

"No. That's your holiday. I need to get away from it all, Mum. Mr. Ellery has promised that I'll have my own space. We're literally sharing a flight. That's all."

"I won't say that I understand, Paige. I won't say that I agree."

"I know, Mum. But please try."

The conversation ended as they always did, with me feeling even more guilty than before I'd picked up the phone. Refusing to cry, I finished my packing and went to bed, searching for sleep and peace that I so desperately needed. Neither came.

At two o'clock I realized there was one person I hadn't told. Did he need to know? He probably had a right to. No, I decided. It would do him as much good as it would me to have as little contact as possible over the next fortnight.

Chapter Thirty-Three

Chalmers and the Jag arrived precisely at five in the morning. There was no need to disturb Mark and Danny. Mark was still in his own turmoil, exhausted by his affairs. Danny would only try one more time to stop me from leaving.

The driver took my heavy suitcase from me and placed it in the boot. Once in the back of the car, I pulled out my mirror compact and examined my makeup. It had been expertly applied to cover the hideous red swelling on my chin that had rudely appeared overnight. Going through my handbag, I double-checked that I had concealer, foundation, eyeliner, mascara, and lip gloss to hand, hoping that they would be accepted by customs. There was no way I was sitting on a ten-hour flight without makeup.

I'd dressed in a dark teal shift dress with a pair of chocolate courts, but my hand luggage contained a pair of grey lounge pants, black vest, and ballet pumps. I didn't mind changing and slouching on the flight, but I was not being seen in public dressed so casually.

In the mirror I could see the lines on my brow and chin had faded to white once more, and the bruising was completely gone, not that it would have shown beneath the thick layer of creams and powders anyway.

"Where's Mr. Ellery?" I asked coolly.

"He had an early meeting," Chalmers explained.

"Very early," I said, glancing at my watch.

"Mr. Ellery works in many time zones." I figured that meant he was on Skype or teleconferencing somehow.

"He'll meet you at the airport. I've been asked to stay with you until he arrives."

"Am I unable to care for myself now?"

"Mr. Ellery is concerned for your welfare." It was the most Chalmers had ever said to me in one conversation. It was also a good hour's drive to Heathrow, longer if there was traffic. I wondered how much more I could extract from him.

"Do you ever drive Matthew?" I asked.

"No," he said bluntly. "Mr. Jackson has his own staff."

"What about Bianca?"

He cleared his throat. "Occasionally."

"Does Mr. Ellery know she's sleeping with my brother?" My scarred brow rose quizzically.

"There isn't much that gets past Mr. Ellery." I thought I heard a slight amusement in his tone. "Except you, of course," he added.

"Me? What do you mean?"

No answer. I sank back into the leather seat and stared out of the window. The grey morning sky filled my view. It wasn't cloudy, but it looked as though it may be later. Fields and trees and farms whizzed past as we hit the motorway.

Heathrow came into view before half-past six. Chalmers pulled up to a set of glass doors, away from the terminals. My eyes narrowed to thin slits suspiciously, as he helped me out and retrieved my suitcase. Standing by the door was a young man dressed in a smart suit, thick waves of black hair slicked to the side. He grinned widely at me and greeted me by name. I threw a confused look towards Chalmers, whose lips twitched knowingly.

205

"Miss Holmes, if you could follow me, please," the young man asked, his English accent smooth and fluent without a trace of his origins. Chalmers followed, pulling my suitcase.

We walked through to a private lounge. A burgundy carpet spread out before me, with a walnut-paneled wall to the side. The glass coffee table in the center of the room was laid with everything needed to make the perfect pot of tea, with a walnut rack adorned with magazines to suit every lifestyle.

The man took my passport and bowed out of the room, leaving me to take it all in. I rarely traveled out of the UK, but when I had, I had always gone through the normal routine of waiting in line at the terminal, listening to the rants of irate passengers whose flights had been delayed. I'd been a part of the cattle that were pushed through security and customs, asked ridiculous questions about who packed my luggage and whether I'd been asked to carry anything on, as if smugglers and dealers would so willingly hand over all contraband.

So, despite my wealth, I was still in complete and utter awe of the magnificence and care that was being readily placed at my feet.

"I'm glad you decided to come." TDS's voice was instantly recognizable. I swiveled around to see him relaxing in a black leather recliner, still reading the pages of a broadsheet.

"How was your meeting?" I asked politely.

"Interesting," was his only response. Folding the paper and replacing it on the side table, he stood and kissed me firmly on the cheek.

"Will that be all, sir?" Chalmers asked, returning with the man and my passport. No suitcase, though.

"Yes, thank you, Chalmers."

"He's not coming with us?" I asked. TDS gave me a cockeyed looked, skewing his symmetry. "Oh," I answered myself. "You have drivers in New York." The symmetry returned.

"Your flight will be ready in half an hour," the man offered before bowing out again.

"You're impressed," TDS stated. I remained standing, clutching my bag and jacket.

"No," I lied, shaking the severity of my stance and relaxing into the beige leather sofa next to him.

"Why did you come?" he asked.

"Do we have to go through this?" I groaned, rolling my eyes.

"No. You're quite right. We have two weeks to talk."

"I thought you had two weeks of meetings. I had fully intended to spend the fortnight skipping between shops and spas."

His lips thinned and turned upwards. Bastard.

"You don't have meetings, do you?"

"Yes, I do, but not for the entire time. I was hoping to wine and dine you, show you that I'm not such a monster that everyone claims me to be."

"I don't think you're a monster," I said quietly.

"Good," he smiled. The phone by his elbow began to buzz like an angry bee demanding attention. He frowned at the number. "I have to take this." He stood and walked out, leaving me alone.

I looked around the room, pursing my lips as I spied the large red canvas with yellow and purple splotches across it. I didn't get, or want to get, modern art. Give me a pretty landscape or cute baby fox cub any day.

"Miss Holmes?" The manicured man appeared in the doorway. "Your flight is ready."

"Should we tell Mr. Ellery?" I asked, standing and searching the room pointlessly.

"Mr. Ellery is going through security."

"Oh," I said simply, following Mr. Manicured to a single desk. The staff were so much more polite and caring than those I was used to. Smiles all around as they carefully removed the contents of my handbag and small holdall. I swallowed hard as they reached the makeup, praying that I wouldn't have to replace it once we reached New York.

"Thank you very much, Miss Holmes," Mr. Manicured smiled. "Mr. Ellery is waiting for you by the limousine."

Limo? Sure enough, beyond another set of glass doors, was a sleek black limo, complete with suited-and-booted chauffeur. TDS stood by the door, looking far from amused. The phone call had riled him somehow. This did not set a good precedent for the next fourteen days.

We sat in silence for the short drive from the lounge to the plane. Please don't ask me what type of plane it was. All I know is that it was smaller than the jumbos, but it was larger than a turboprop. It was pristinely white, and inside was decorated in cream with ridiculously smiley hostesses and only a few spacious seats. There were no other passengers on the flight, so I assumed it either belonged to, or had been hired out to, TDS alone.

He ordered a whiskey, but I asked for a bottle of still mineral water as the hostesses took our jackets and bags from us. They went through the routine process of describing emergency exits and showing me the bathroom (which, it turned out, really was a bathroom, complete with shower cubicle), and the bedroom .

"There's a bedroom?" I asked TDS, eyebrow raised.

"Of course, there is," he said, surprised by my lack of knowledge when it came to real first-class travel.

I sat down opposite him, thanking the hostess as the perfectly made-up blonde handed me a glass – proper glass, no plastic cups here – with water, ice, and a slice of lemon in it. "I could get used to this," I grinned, stretching out.

"Only the best," TDS smiled back, flipping open his laptop.

"Work? Really?"

"I never stop working, Paige. In time you'll come to realize that."

"In time? You think I'm sticking around? I've already told you. I'm here because I need a break. The fact that I'm spending it with you doesn't mean anything." This was going to be a long flight.

Over the intercom, our captain told us we were ready for takeoff. I clipped the belt together over my lap and closed my eyes, concentrating on my breathing.

"Are you okay?" TDS asked, almost concerned for my well-being.

"Fine," I said shortly. Breathe in. Breathe out.

"Don't tell me you're afraid of flying as well."

"It's been a while since I was last on a plane."

He laughed. "You're happy to be beaten to a pulp and tossed around as much as that rugby ball of yours, but when it comes to flying, you're terrified?" He didn't understand.

"It's about control." The laugh stopped. I opened an eye and peered at him. "I don't like being out of control."

The muscles in his jaw flexed as his back teeth ground against each other. Clearly this would be a problem we would have to overcome. We'd never spent more than a few hours together, certainly nowhere close to two weeks.

Make or break, I told myself, suddenly happy that I'd made the right decision. A fortnight with TDS would definitely give me all the information I needed as to whether I wanted to be with him or not.

After a few moments the seat belt sign flickered from a warning red to a dull grey, merging with its black background. Yes, even private jets have to follow rules and regulations. I pressed the button of the belt hard and it released me.

My stomach began to cramp. I rubbed a hand and grimaced against the ache that grumbled around my guts.

"Where are you going?" he demanded.

"Bathroom. Or perhaps you'd like to come and make sure I wash my hands to your exacting standards?" I snorted, reaching for my handbag.

"There is no need to be crude." At least I knew I had one hold over him. I would have swept away, had the bubbling not caused me to crumple at my waist. I felt a hand touch my arm. "Are you okay?"

"Yes," I snapped, pulling my elbow away from him. "It happens from time to time. I'll be fine." Since the operation, I was no stranger to stomachache and knew that it would pass. I didn't want him to see me break out in a cold sweat as my stomach and muscles twisted and turned. But as I reached the bathroom, the sudden warmth between my legs let me realize this was not just cramps. Shit. My period. That explained my grumpiness and the sudden breakout on my chin.

Despite the pills and operations, my cycle was far from regular, so I always had a supply of feminine hygiene products close to hand, as well as a spare pair of pants in my bag. It weighed on my heart that I had to be so prepared at all times, but the doctors were unwilling to do any further operations until I was past my childbearing years. I'd tried to argue with them that I was unable to have kids, so what did it matter? But there was no definitive proof as to my fertility. So I was stuck with an irregular cycle, mood swings, and acne until either I did miraculously become pregnant or I was over thirty-five. Roll on, the next nine years of my life.

Fixing myself, I checked in the bathroom mirror to ensure that my makeup was still firmly in place. No touch-ups needed, I made my way back to the lounge area.

TDS was on the phone, yelling at some poor secretary, no doubt. I rolled my eyes and beckoned towards an attendant and asked for another glass of water. She was dressed in a navy uniform, with white shirt and dark red ascot-type scarf. Her blonde hair had been sprayed into place so that not a single hair would escape the tight bun at the nape of her neck. With a dazzling, and forced, smile as equally glued as her hair, she handed me a refreshed drink.

Reaching into my bag, I grabbed at the medication and knocked back two painkillers. TDS raised an eyebrow, quizzing as to my ailment. I shook my head, telling him he didn't want to, or need to, know.

"Everything okay?" I asked, as he ended the call.

"Fine." Great. We had returned to monosyllabic answers. There was no point in pushing him further. It was a long flight.

He checked something on the laptop before his Jekyll-and-Hyde act meant I had the friendly TDS back. "Have you changed your watch to New York time?" he asked, reaching over the table and grabbing my wrist. He turned the dials until the hands mirrored the time on his Rolex. "Remember, you're going backwards. When we arrive, it will be two in the UK, but it will only be nine in the morning there."

"I can feel the jet lag already," I groaned.

"Don't worry," he chuckled. "At least you can just sleep. I have a meeting at noon."

"So how much of New York do you own? You seem to own most of Hampshire and London," I added.

"I have a couple of hotels and a publishing house in New York."

"I take it we're staying in one of your hotels then?"

He smiled.

"Surprise, surprise."

"You should get some rest." He motioned towards the bedroom at the back.

"I'm quite comfortable here, thank you."

"How did your parents take the news that you were coming to New York with me?"

"Not well. You really have to work on them. My father is the one place you can't throw money to appease."

"Do I need to appease them?" he asked. "You've already told me that there is nothing between us."

"Screw you." I yawned, closing my eyes.

210

Chapter Thirty-Four

I was trapped.

It was pitch-black and I physically couldn't move.

Restraints weighed down on my wrists. Frantically, I fought against them. Cold straps bit into my skin. I tried to scream, but my voice was muffled.

I could smell something, but struggled to inhale anything more than short gasps. Sweat, aftershave, and alcohol clogged up my senses. Gagging, choking, I heaved against the pressure that built in my chest.

Where was I? I had to figure out where I was.

Blinking wildly, I tried to focus on any sliver of light that might be in the room.

Nothing.

"Slut." The callousness of the word rained down on me, covered in spittle. "Fucking little slut." I knew that voice. Tremors racked through my body as I started to convulse. Bile and acid burnt my throat. "Show me what you've got."

The tear of fabric ripped through me as though it was my own skin. I cried, fighting against him. "No, please, no." I knew the sound of my own voice.

"Little bitch," he spat. Thick knees forced my legs open.

I was glad of the darkness.

"Get off me!" I screamed, kicking out, punching what air I could reach.

Tears and sweat mingled at the corner of my lips. The salinity mixed with the vomit that threatened to burst forward. I swallowed hard.

"You've been asking for this." Hard digits squeezed into the fragile bones of my hands.

"No," I sobbed, forcing the words out.

I opened my eyes.

Light blinded me.

There was nothing beneath me. Nothing above me. I felt… free.

Glancing down, I could see the yellow wooden floor sweeping towards equally golden walls. Below me, the light blue fabric moved violently. I narrowed my eyes, trying to focus. Honing my hearing on the struggle, I watched.

Grunts. Loud, pig-like grunts.

A head moved to the side. Light brown hair hid her face. A hand swept the sticky mane away, but before I could see who it was, his head was on hers, sucking the life out of her. He moved back, and I saw her clearly.

Me. I was watching me.

The scream ripped through as I dove down, hitting him with all my force. "Get off her!" The screech echoed around us. "Get off her!" A wild, invisible banshee.

"Fucking little whore," he grunted. His hips pushed forcefully. "Make me come, you fucking little slut."

Tears streamed down my ghostly face. I was helpless once more. I watched him abuse my body and soul. I could do nothing but watch.

"Paige?" There was a voice in the distance.

"Mark? Danny?" I called out, trying to tear my eyes from the horrific scene playing out in front of me. But my head was fixed in place. No matter how much I struggled, I couldn't stop watching. Like some sick, twisted voyeur, I watched. I watched him pummel her body -- my body -- with his force.

"Paige?" The voice called to me again.

"Get off me!" I screamed, closing my eyes tightly.

"Paige!" The voice snapped, shouting, yelling at me. He repeated my name over and over again.

"Such a tight little pussy," grunted the pig.

No words. Just a scream. A scream that could curdle blood reverberated through me, boiling every organ.

"Paige, wake up!"

My eyes shot open, widely searching. There was a woman to my side, a man in front of me. Neither of them were people I knew. "Paige?" the man asked. He knew my name. Why did he know my name?

"Get off me!" I pushed and ran to the end of the short hall, rocking back and forth. Was I on a train? Where the hell was I?

A door. I reached for the metal handle and yanked at it, throwing myself into the confines of the room. It was small, with only just enough room for a double bed. I leant my back against the door, sinking to the floor, sobs coming thick and fast, hot tears streaming down my cheeks. What the hell was happening to me?

"Paige?" came a voice from behind the door. "Honey, open the door." Fingers tapped against the plastic frame. "Let me in, please."

"Go away!" I screamed, hugging my knees tightly into my body.

Slowly my world came back into focus. The blurring edges of my dream mingled with the harsh lines of reality.

"I'm not going anywhere."

"Please just leave me alone," I cried, moving from the floor to the bed.

I heard the click of the door, but refused to look. Hands were placed on my knees. Shooting back up the bed, I scrambled to escape this stranger.

"What's going on, Paige?" I knew that voice. Looking up, I saw him. Indigo eyes, filled with a burning concern and anger all mixed together like a swirling, violent whirlpool. My heart stopped. No butterflies, no churning. Just stopped for what felt like an eternity. Exactly as it had done weeks earlier when I had first met him.

"Vance." His name came out with a rush of air. I threw myself over the blankets, falling into his embrace.

"Talk to me. You need to talk to me."

"Is everything okay?" the blonde asked, worry filling her voice.

"Fine," TDS snapped. My eyes stayed fixed with his. "Everything's fine," he repeated more calmly. The blonde backed away.

I gulped at the air. Breathe in, breathe out.

"What happened?" I asked, knowing that it was myself who needed to answer.

"You had a nightmare."

"Terror," I corrected, realizing. "Night terror. Jesus. It's been a while since that happened." I swallowed my fear down in a final gulp, inhaling the soothing scent of sandalwood and citrus.

"Evan?" he asked tenderly. I nodded. His arms tightened around me. "Do you want to talk about it?"

"No." I shook my head. "Just hold me, please." My fingers gripped into his shirt. "I feel sick," I groaned.

"I'll get --"

"No. Don't leave me. I'll be fine. I just need to rest."

"We'll be landing in about an hour." The blankets engulfed my aching body as he lay me down. "Sleep." He kissed my forehead, trailing down my nose until he reached my lips. His mouth sealed over mine.

"I don't think I can."

"Do you want me to stay?"

"Would you?"

He nodded, lying down beside me. Rolling onto my side, I tucked my hand beneath my head and shifted into his body, taking in the warmth. I closed my eyes. His lips rested against the back of my neck, tasting my skin. Arm draped over my hips, I breathed easy, knowing he was close to me.

A knock on the door disturbed us.

"Yes?" TDS asked gruffly, pulling away from me and sitting on the edge of the bed.

"I'm sorry for the intrusion," the blonde mumbled apologetically. "But the captain has asked that you return to your seats."

"Of course." He sounded so understanding. Reaching for my hand, he pulled me to sitting before guiding me back to my seat. I couldn't hide from the looks of pity and concern from the attendants as they checked my belt was clipped correctly. TDS sat back opposite me. His expression was just as probing.

"Please don't look at me like that," I mumbled, embarrassed by my own fears.

"I can't help it, Paige. I'm worried about you." Worried. Everyone was worried about me recently. Perhaps they had cause to be.

"It's kind of you, but unnecessary."

That brow arched again. "When we get to New York, I'm calling for a doctor."

"No," I snapped, red, puffy eyes staring. "I'll be fine. They happen. I'm in control. I'll bash it out in the gym."

He didn't agree, but he didn't argue, closing his laptop and switching off his phone.

Th landing was smoother than the flight had been.

Disembarking, security, and luggage was a bit of a blur, my mind still foggy with terror. I let TDS take the control he enjoyed, guiding me through the airport towards the Lincoln Town Car that waited patiently for us.

I paid no attention to the driver, who probably thought me a rude, stuck-up cow, sliding into the back of the car, trying to hide in the dark shadows.

Grumbles and aches still bubbled through my belly, and the sunspots in my eyes forewarned me of a migraine looming. By the time we'd reached our destination, the throb of my brain pulsed violently. Clutching at my skull, I tried to press the pain away.

TDS's hands slipped around my waist and moved me swiftly from the car to the room, my feet barely touching the ground, never mind stopping.

The curtains were drawn tightly. A golden glow shimmered through the thick fabric that cast the room in shadows.

I lay down on the bed, groaning as I clutched the pillow against my pain. What a great way to start my break.

TDS rummaged through my luggage, pulling out a variety of pills and placing them on the stand by the bed, along with a tall glass of iced water.

"Thank you," I moaned.

"I'm going to shower and change."

"Your meeting," I acknowledged.

"I'll have my mobile with me at all times. If you need anything, you call me. The front desk staff are under instruction to give you whatever you need. Are you sure you won't let me call a doctor?"

"It's a migraine. I usually get them after a terror. I'll be fine. I just need to rest." I swallowed a couple of pills, smothering myself in darkness under the sheets and pillows. I hadn't even bothered to get changed.

"If you're sure." He lingered by the door until I waved him away.

It always annoys me when people moan they have a migraine, when what they actually have is a bad headache.

I clenched my eyes tightly, waiting for the antiemetics to kick in, wondering whether I should give in and throw up. My womb and stomach tangoed, guts wrenching in a violent tumble. Reaching for the water, I sipped at the ice-cold liquid, quenching the burning thirst. My head was fit to explode, and I wished it would get it over and done with. Each movement forced the nausea to swell alongside the vessels inside my skull.

Forcing myself up, I shifted from beneath the heavy sheets. I stripped, leaving my dress and bra in a pile where my feet had been. My hands guided me blindly towards the door to the right of the bed. I only had half of my peripheral vision. It's hard to describe a blind spot. There is no grey circle or blob of either dark or light. Everything just merges into one, but you can tell something is missing. I held up my hand in front of me. My index and ring fingers sat neatly next to each other, but the middle was simply not there, yet I could still feel it. Like a badly edited TV program, I fumbled through the blurring images until I found the handle, opening the door to an ensuite bathroom.

The pressure of the water jetting from the shower helped to soothe my head, while the darkness of the room eased away the photophobia. No windows meant no disturbing sunlight.

Wrapping a towel around me and stepping into a pair of clean pants gave me some relief from the discomfort. I brushed my teeth as well, the minty paste acting on the sickness.

Clean, I climbed back into the bed wearing only my knickers, cocooning myself in the thick blankets, waiting for either sleep or TDS to return. I didn't care which.

Chapter Thirty-Five

"I don't give a damn what you think… Safe… Don't pretend you give a damn all of a sudden… If I catch you sniffing around… You're a goddamn liability, that's what you are."

"Who were you talking to?" I asked meekly, appearing from behind the doorframe, wrapping a cotton white robe around myself. TDS rubbed his face harshly, tossing his phone into the soft cushions of the sofa.

"Nobody important. How are you feeling now?"

I'd slept solidly for eight hours. By the time I woke, TDS had returned and was berating someone. "Much better," I thanked him.

"I have a dinner tonight, if you would care to join me?"

I shook my head. "I came for some space, remember?" I said, reminding him of our deal. He nodded, although I could tell he didn't truly agree.

"What are you going to do tonight?"

"The spa's open until ten. I thought I'd get a massage and some room service."

"Good plan." He walked forward and kissed my forehead. "I have to change." He walked to the opposite end of the suite. I followed.

"Oh," I said, stunned when I saw that the suite had two large double rooms. I'd assumed he'd ignored me when I asked for separate rooms.

"You can sleep here, if you wish," he offered.

"No. No, thanks," I stuttered, sticking to my plan. If I gave in now, I may as well just concede to the fact that it was him I wanted, and that was a decision I wasn't willing to admit to just yet. "I should ring my parents, and Mark. Let them know I'm here safely." To be honest, I was surprised that my phone hadn't been filled with concerned texts and missed calls.

"I rang them earlier," he explained.

"Oh. They were okay?"

"Yes. I told them you had jet lag and weren't feeling at your best."

"Oh," I said again. "Thank you. I guess," I added as an afterthought.

"I'll book you in for a massage when I go down."

"Make it about…" I glanced at my watch. My vision wasn't quite back to normal, and the Roman numerals were difficult to make out.

"I'll book it for eight o'clock. They'll ring you when they're ready for you. Go, get some more sleep. You look like you could do with it."

"Thanks," I grumbled.

"I didn't mean it like that." He changed quickly into a gunmetal trouser suit and dark blue open shirt that set off his eyes. Taking my arm, he led me back into the other bedroom before flicking on the television screen that almost took over the wall. "Watch what you like. Don't worry about the bills. I know the owner." He winked. I rolled my eyes. "I'll see you later." He kissed me before leaving.

The TV flickered nonchalantly, being watched by no one. I went into the bathroom and changed into the lounge pants and t-shirt I'd packed for the flight. The weight of my bloated belly was uncomfortable, but at least the painkillers had kicked in.

Grumpily, I climbed back under the sheets and picked up my mobile. Nothing. Not a single message. From anyone. Grabbing the receiver of the phone by the bed, I asked to be connected to the operator, giving them the number of the farmhouse. No answer. I left a message telling Mark and Danny that I had arrived, had a migraine, but they weren't to worry and I would ring them tomorrow. My parents were next on the list.

"Oh, Paige, darling, I was so worried. When Mr. Ellery told your father you were sick…"

"It's a migraine, Mum," I groaned. "My period started," I added by way of explanation. She knew that my migraines were usually connected to fluxing hormone levels. I didn't need to worry her with my terrors. "I'm going to go and relax in the spa. I've booked myself in for a quick massage."

"What are your plans for tomorrow?"

"I don't know yet. I thought I might do some sightseeing, a bit of shopping."

"Don't forget to take pictures!"

"I won't, Mum," I sang. "How's Georgia doing?"

"She's fine. Hannah loves taking care of her." I bet she did – more time at the farmhouse equaled more time with Mark. "Your father says hello," Mother added.

"Hi, Dad. I love you both."

"We love you too, sweetheart. Make sure you rest."

I contemplated calling Matt, but thought better of it. I still wasn't ready to face that hurdle.

Glancing through the room service menu, I decided against food. As mouthwatering as the club sandwich sounded, the remainders of the migraine and nausea left me without an appetite.

The front desk called me just before eight to tell me that they were ready for me in the spa. I made my way down and was surprised to find that I hadn't been booked in for just a massage, but for a full pampering experience including papaya facial and mani-pedi.

I lay face down on the couch, staring at the green carpet, listening to the sound of panpipes playing softly. Images of forests came to mind. I could even smell the oak, juniper, and fresh earth.

Two hands, belonging to Mia, my beauty therapist for the evening, pressed down between my shoulder blades. Mia was very petite, her slight frame looking as though it may snap under any amount of pressure. But as she weighed down into the depths of my aching muscles, smoothing out the knots that bulked against my tendons and skin, I couldn't help but wonder if her appearance was much like my own, and not at all warranted.

Rolling over to my back, Mia smeared a fruity paste over my cheeks, nose, and forehead. Fingers massaged at my temples before sweeping down my neck, over my shoulders, arms, and chest. If only I could have her live with me on a permanent basis.

Removing the mask, and finishing with a refreshing massage and cleanse, Mia helped me to sitting and offered me a drink of water before leading me to another chair, where I sat patiently. Closing my eyes and lapping up the calming atmosphere, I felt at complete ease as Mia finished my session by filing and painting my nails.

"Hope you enjoy the rest of your stay," she drawled as I left, floating on air.

I smiled at the desk clerk as I wandered past, towards the lift, stopping at the closed doors and groaning to the heavens.

"Hi," I smiled forcibly. "I seem to have locked myself out of my room." Patting myself down, there was a distinct lack of pockets or key card.

The man behind the desk, tall, skinny, and made entirely of sharp angles, grinned at me, although I sensed the distinct hatred seeping from him. How dare I put him out like this.

"Which room were you staying in?" Good point. Which room was I staying in? Suddenly it struck me that I hadn't bothered to note what door number, or even floor level, I was on.

"Umm… I'm with Mr. Ellery?" The smile disappeared, and he just looked – pissed off.

"I will have to call Mr. Ellery." He was curt and snippy, neither of which I appreciated. Didn't TDS own this building? Surely he should have been jumping through hoops to keep me happy.

"Oh, no, don't disturb his dinner," I cried. I didn't want an angry TDS on my hands. "Can't you just let me in?" I smiled as sweetly as possible. Unfortunately, I am not blessed with the talents of beauty and grace, so there was no surprise that it didn't work.

"Do you have any ID?"

"Do I look like I have any ID?" I snapped back at him, all manners washed away by the sudden grasp within my stomach.

"I'm sorry, but I wasn't here when you arrived, so unless you have ID to prove who you are, I will have to call Mr. Ellery."

"Is there a problem here?"

I groaned as I recognized TDS's voice from behind me.

"Mr. Ellery!" the receptionist exclaimed. "This young lady…"

"This young lady is my guest, and you should be aware of that."

"Yes, Mr. Ellery. Sorry, Mr. Ellery." The man backpedaled as fast as he could, while I threw him my best self-satisfied smirk.

"Try to keep your key card or ID on you," TDS grumbled, taking my arm and guiding me to the lift. "Did you enjoy your session?"

"Yes, thank you. It was perfect. How did your dinner go?"

"Fine." Yet again with one-syllable answers. "How are you feeling now?"

"Much better, thank you."

We stepped inside the lift, along with two other guests. TDS stood at the back, pulling me into him, keeping me as tight as possible. He bent his mouth to my ear and whispered, "I'm not sure this 'separate rooms' idea is going to work." Tugging me backwards, I could feel exactly what he meant.

The thick press of his erection into the small of my back sent a shockwave flooding through me.

I turned so that he was against my belly and looked up at him. "As much as I would love to, it's the wrong time of the month," I whispered back. There was a look of hurt in his eyes, followed by a shock of inspiration.

"There are other options," he mused. I giggled, slipping my hands between us and massaging the bulge of his trousers. Knowing that we weren't alone simply added to the excitement and anticipation.

"I'm not sure," I said coyly.

"I am." His lips were on mine, sealing in the promise. He stopped only to cock an eyebrow towards the woman who tsked and grumbled at our flagrant show of ardor.

The bell dinged to let us know we were stopping, the doors ringing open as the other guests stepped out. "Alone," TDS groaned, pulling me into him.

"Aren't there cameras in these things?" I asked, glancing around the ceiling of the car.

"The staff here are… relaxed."

"I don't like the idea of being watched," I stated, moving away from him. Still, I couldn't help but look at the swelling of his groin.

"But you don't mind watching," TDS taunted. My cheeks burned, flushing brightly. "You really are feeling better. I should send you to the spa more often."

"This isn't quite the break I was after," I sighed.

"I can't help being this way around you, Paige."

I moved to the mirrors at the back of the lift. I still wasn't at peace with the reflection, especially since the one staring back at me was plain with all scars and warts to see. Well, not warts. But there was an angry blemish barging through the pale skin on my chin.

"What on earth do you see in me?" I asked wistfully.

"The same thing all men do."

"A mess," I replied.

"Not at all. You're an intelligent and beautiful young woman. And you were right. You're a lot stronger than anyone gives you credit for."

"I'd like to believe you."

"Which part don't you believe?"

"All of it. Especially the beautiful part," I moaned, prodding at the spot.

"You are," he stated boldly, gripping my shoulders and turning me to face him, his fingers beneath my chin, lifting me to his lips.

"I don't feel it."

"Well, you are," he said shortly as the lift doors opened, releasing us. "Have you eaten yet?" he asked, checking the time on his Rolex.

"I'm not hungry."

"Paige, you should eat," he growled.

"Honestly, I think I'd just like to go to bed."

"You're not taking me up on my offer then?" he asked, pressing himself into me as we reached the door to his suite.

"Not tonight, stud," I teased, moving out of his grasp. "I meant what I said. I need some space and some time."

"I'll give you what I can," he compromised before moving back to me and kissing me hard. "Go sleep."

"Thank you. I really do appreciate it all."

"Sleep," he ordered before retiring to his own room.

Chapter Thirty-Six

When I finally woke, it was still dark. Moving to the window, I peeked from behind the curtains and looked out over The City That Never Sleeps. Orange and yellow lights flicked around buildings. Cabs below darted in and out lanes when they could. I half expected the moon to start crooning. The vista was such that it looked like something straight out of a musical.

I'd promised myself a sightseeing tour, although the promise of room service on demand was also tempting.

My stomach grumbled and growled, informing me of its starving state, and I wondered if the room service was twenty-four hours. Grabbing the menu, I took it into the lounge area and sat on a sofa with mahogany scrolled feet. Yes, it was twenty-four hours.

"Everything okay?"

"Are you spying on me?" I asked, jumping at the sound of TDS's voice from the corner of the room. I turned to see him sitting at the little workstation, laptop open. "And don't you ever sleep?"

"I'm still on UK time," he explained. I looked at my own watch. It may have only been three a.m. here, but back home it was closer to eight o'clock in the morning. "Business doesn't stop over there just because I'm tired."

"What are you doing?"

"Emails," he said, slamming the lid shut. "Hungry?"

"A bit," I confessed.

"I'll get some breakfast sent up." He took the receiver from the phone on the desk and mumbled something into it, which I couldn't hear properly. "Plans for today?"

"I wanted to go and see the Statue of Liberty, and I had promised myself a shopping spree at some point."

"Well, remember you're here for two weeks; don't rush yourself in one go. Why don't you let your clock readjust and I'll take you sightseeing later on?"

"I'd rather go on my own," I muttered.

"Are you sure? New York is a busy city. It's easy to get lost in the crowds." I knew he was referring to my panic attacks. Perhaps he was right. "I can organize a private tour, if you'd insist on going alone."

"No, it's fine. I'm sure I'll manage."

"I'm sure you will. But it would make me happier if I knew that you were safe." He didn't look convinced.

"You have to have control," I groaned, moving back into the bedroom.

"Paige," he called after me. I was lying face down on the bed when he walked in. "Paige, I know you wanted some space, but when I spoke to your parents, I promised them that I would keep an eye on you."

"Jesus Christ."

"Don't swear."

"Fuck you," I threw at him spitefully.

"Paige," he growled my name. I flipped over and stared up at the ceiling. "You're acting like a spoiled brat."

"Maybe that's because I am one."

"Don't be so childish."

"Then stop treating me like one!" I shouted, sitting bolt upright. "I am fine. I can look after myself. I told you I want to be on my own for a bit. I need to get my head straight and together. This whole fucked up mess is not doing me any favors right now."

"You can't even remember to take a key card with you down to the spa."

"Fine. I'll stay right here then." I sulked, folding my arms tightly around my chest. My nose pointed to the ceiling. No black spot here to stare at and watch growing.

"No, you won't," he growled again, grabbing my arm and tugging me to standing. "Get dressed. You're coming with me today."

"No, I'm not."

"I'm not leaving you on your own when you're like this. You can come with me and I will take you on a sightseeing tour, if that's really what you want."

"What I want is to be on my own." My teeth ground together, grating against each word.

"I don't believe you."

"I don't care whether you believe me or not."

"This is ridiculous," he snapped. "Get dressed. Breakfast will be here in five minutes."

I sulked for a bit longer in my room before returning to the lounge. It was still dark outside, and I was still in my pajamas.

"You're not dressed."

"It's only four o'clock in the morning," I pointed out. He couldn't argue with that. But he did point towards the tray of pastries and breads that adorned a silver table in the center of the room. Reluctantly, I sat in a chair and grabbed at a croissant, filling it with butter and jam. "Oh, my God," I groaned, savoring the pastry as it melted in my mouth.

"Good?" he asked more calmly.

"This is not me forgiving you."

"I haven't asked for your forgiveness," he smirked. The urge to slap him was almost overwhelming. "Will you come with me?" he asked more sedately.

"Are you going to take no for an answer?"

"No," he admitted. At least he was honest. At least with TDS I knew where I stood: somewhere between slave and maid.

"You promised me I could be on my own."

"I promised you I would do what I could. I can't leave you on your own, especially since I know that you will disobey me and wander around the city anyway. You'll get lost, you'll panic, and I will end up having to leave my meetings early to come to your rescue."

"I'm sorry I'm such an inconvenience." I pouted, not feeling sorry at all, finishing my delicious breakfast. He was right, though; not that I'd admit it to him, of course. If I did venture out alone, there was a very real risk of my panic setting in and disorientating me. Unlike Brookfield, I didn't know anyone here. I hadn't gone anywhere new or strange since…

Shaking the thoughts away, I said, "How about if I promise to stay here until you get back? Then you can take me on a tour tonight?"

He pondered my offer for a while before agreeing.

"Truth is, I don't feel particularly comfortable anyway." I rubbed at my belly to make a point before piling a plate of pastries and pouring out a glass of fresh orange juice, taking them back to my own private quarters.

A couple of hours later I was watching an Indiana Jones movie. TDS walked into the room and knelt by my side. He lifted the remote, turning the TV off. "Hey!" I complained. "I was watching that."

"Watch it later," he argued, kissing me firmly.

"What happened to my space?"

"If you didn't want this, then why did you come here? You knew that I wouldn't be able to keep my hands off of you." I hated that he was right all the time.

"I still don't get that."

"Why I can't keep my hands off you?" He asked my question. I nodded. "Stand up," he ordered. I obeyed. He took my hand and pressed it against the front of his trousers. His erection was thick and hot beneath my palm. "That's for you," he kissed.

Electricity spurred my nerve endings into action, firing all cylinders of my sex drive.

"Ever since I first saw you, there was something that sparked inside me." His hands slipped down to the small of my back, fingers hooking beneath my t-shirt and tugging it over my head. His lips were on mine, his palm cupping my breast as he squeezed gently. "I'm used to having women throw themselves at my feet. But not quite so dramatically," he laughed. His fingers dipped into my bra, releasing me from the constraints. Soon his tongue was encircling the dark flesh of my nipple. I tipped my head back, gasping wildly as he groped at me so expertly, sucking on me until I was rigid beneath him.

I moved my hips forward, feeling his thickness press against me. I wanted him so badly that I physically ached. Removing his own shirt, he pressed his chest against mine. Skin on skin, his natural heat stoking me further. "I want you," I whispered harshly.

"I know," he groaned into my mouth, hands tangled in my hair. "You are a remarkable young woman, Paige. No matter what you think, you are beautiful in ways I can't even describe. I want you in ways that I haven't wanted a woman in years. I want to give you control."

"Then let me have it," I said, bending beneath him.

"I can't." He exuded an animalistic moan as he pushed me onto the bed, landing on top of me. "If I give you that, then I have nothing." It was a selfish admission, and one I ignored, enjoying feeling his hands search my body, my nails scraping down his muscular back.

He may have been thirty years my senior, but that didn't mean he had any less stamina. His hands moved over the top of my pants, caressing me, his palm firmly circling the bud of my clitoris without even removing my clothes. He could bring me to the brink with his breath against my skin. His words ignited shots of lust. He stopped.

"No, please," I begged, refusing to release my grasp on his belt. I fumbled with the buttons of his trousers, springing him free, and taking him in my palm. "I need this," I pleaded, rubbing him firmly.

"Paige," he groaned my name fiercely.

"I want this," I mouthed, against his cheek. He moved off me, standing up at the edge of the bed. His indigo eyes burned furiously with desire. I knew exactly what he wanted, what he needed, and more to the point, what I wanted to do to him.

Crawling to the edge, I took him in my hand, stroking and pulling.

"Take me in your mouth," he ordered. The demand had me pooling immediately, and I grabbed him hungrily, taking him exactly where he wanted to be. I looked up, but his head was back, his eyes closed, and his mouth open as he sucked in the air greedily. His hands swept to my hair, guiding me to take him deeper.

I loved his taste. The saltiness of him trembled on my lips as I kissed down his shaft before licking my way up the throbbing vein. I mouthed at his tip, sucking gently, massaging his base.

"Fuck me," he groaned.

"Dirty words, Mr. Ellery," I teased, breathing over him before hollowing my cheeks and taking him as far as I could. His satin-soft shaft massaged against my tongue.

Spits of salt landed on my taste buds, the delicious pearly liquid that told me to slow down.

"Don't stop," he hissed, as I moved back.

"Patience," I taunted, pleasuring him with licks and kisses.

"Please," he begged, his fingers tangling in my hair, urging me forward.

228

"I said, patience." I enjoyed having this control. Massaging him, I pulled him to brink of destruction, stopping when I knew he couldn't take any more.

"Not fair," he moaned with a chortle.

"Now you know how it feels," I said.

"Fuck this." He pushed me back, mouth on mine, his hand between my legs. "I want this." He kissed me slowly.

"Not the right time," I said pointedly.

"Are you going to finish?" he asked.

"No," I giggled.

"Then I don't give a damn." Tugging my trousers and pants free, he guided himself into me. I threw my head back, enjoying the feel of him filling me so completely. He thrust forward, groaning with each movement.

No length of time passed before I was burying my face in his shoulder, squeezing my fingers into his back, urging him deeper with my legs wrapped around his broad waist.

"Fuck!" he cried out in one final gulp, exploding inside of me, collapsing against me in a hot, sweet, sticky mess.

Chapter Thirty-Seven

Sex is a good jet lag cure, I decided, as I showered away the remnants of our encounter. TDS had moved back to his own room to clean and change before his meeting. I had completely gone back on the promise I'd made to myself, but it had been worth it.

I wanted to sleep. The sun had only just begun to peep above the horizon. Yet my body insisted that I should be wide awake and making plans for lunch. So much for late night sightseeing.

Grabbing a small bag filled with spare clothes, I left the sanctity of my room, meeting TDS as he packed a black leather briefcase with papers.

He eyed the holdall, quizzing my intentions. "Gym," I said by way of explanation. "I can't go two weeks sat on my arse. I'll get fat."

"You haven't got an ounce on you."

"Are you seriously going to keep me locked in your tower for the next fortnight? Because if that's your plan, then I'm on the next plane back to England," I complained, throwing the holdall to the floor.

"No," he said, shaking his head and stepping towards me. Strong arms wrapped around my waist, hands slid down over the curve of my buttocks, gripping underneath so that he could lift me into a deep and passionate kiss. "I don't want you locked in my tower. I want you with me."

"I have absolutely no intention of listening to your boring meetings. I can't believe you even have one on a Sunday. Do you ever stop?"

"I don't want you there anyway. I just want you with me. If I could, I would stop. I would cancel every meeting I have to be with you.

"As flattering as that sounds, spending twenty-four/seven with you is not me relaxing. And remember, that is the reason I agreed to coming." I dropped a few inches to the ground, grabbing at my holdall as soon as I was free from his grip. "I am going to the gym," I reiterated.

He knew he couldn't stop me, so he stepped to the side and bowed dramatically.

"Arse," I sang, leaving the room. I was about halfway down the hall when I heard him call after me. Cross with myself for giving him the power, I stopped and turned to face my stalker.

"Key card?" he stated, handing me the little white piece of plastic.

"Shit."

"Precisely."

I took the card off him and shoved it into my holdall before throwing him a sardonic smile. The slap on my backside as I walked away from him caught me off guard. Swiveling around to give him a piece of my mind, I found that he had disappeared.

Twat.

The hotel gym was lavish, to say the least. A room of metal and white and crystal clear glass, filled with state-of-the-art equipment and seriously gorgeous personal trainers of both gender, overlooked a turquoise swimming pool with three whirlpool hot tubs at one end. There were no harsh fluorescent lights beaming down on those who were working out. Instead, small spotlights had been strategically placed within the metal lattice domed ceiling to cast a serene glow over the entire training areas.

I had already enjoyed the comforts of the changing rooms. Situated directly beneath the gym, the lockers had a beech finish and ran from ceiling to floor along two walls. Wooden benches split the room, but there were also two changing areas with curtains for those who preferred more privacy.

I tossed a cream hand towel over the rail of the treadmill, placing a bottle of mineral water and my phone on the tray in front of me, and plugged in the iPod. Alternative rock blasted through the earphones, blocking out any thoughts that may have considered creeping into my conscious mind. I couldn't help but spy the muscle-bound gym instructor sidling towards the stunning redhead who jogged beside me. I smiled to myself at his complete lack of discretion. Then he walked straight past her, and landed with his elbow on the rail by my towel! He mouthed something at me, but the music blared too loudly in my ears to hear him. Stabbing at the buttons on the panel in front of me, I slowed to a steady walk, and pulled one plug from my ear.

"Sorry?" I asked innocently.

"I asked if you needed any help." He grinned broadly. My gag reflex was almost too strong to control. Utter cheese. Did I need any help, indeed. He could quite clearly see that I was capable of using a treadmill. I shot a glance towards the redhead, who looked decidedly disappointed and disgusted at the same time.

"No, I'm fine, thanks." I smiled politely.

"If you need anything, I'll be at the weights."

Showoff. "Okay, thanks." I smiled again, praying that he would just leave me alone. I giggled at what Ken and Tyler might say about him when I told them, but frowned when I thought what TDS would make of it. The poor bloke would probably be out of a job before his shift ended.

I won't lie. I was utterly flattered by his attention, and it was no coincidence that I then moved to the multigym by the free weights. I glanced in the full-length mirror and wondered to myself what had attracted him in my direction.

My hair was tied high on my head, my brow was slicked with grease, and I had no makeup on whatsoever.

"So how often do you work out?" came a familiar American accent. I turned to find Mr. Muscles standing by my side, staring right past my face and straight into the black line of cleavage that burst from above my sports top. Ah… That was what he found attractive. Bloody men. Suddenly I wished to be back in Brookfield, surrounded by men who were only interested in each other. Still, despite his clogging cheap aftershave, he was luscious to look at.

I made a mental note to wear a baggy t-shirt and loose bottoms the next day, before answering with, "Quite often."

"I can tell." His glance moved down from my bust towards my stomach, an area of my body that was fairly well-toned. Instinctively my hand shot down towards the scar, even though it was hidden by the waistline of my black shorts.

"But I think I'm finished for the day." I excused myself, grabbing my phone, iPod, water, and towel, and marching towards the women-only changing room. Maybe being eye-candy wasn't enough.

My skin was crawling, itching at me like I was covered in bugs. It was an odd reaction that shocked me, since I usually enjoyed being flirted with. Primal instincts surged wildly.

The shower of the gym was warm and inviting. I think it's referred to as a rainforest shower – with a massive head that powered a waterfall down over my aching body. I squeezed the soft pink liquid into my hands, enjoying the jasmine and vanilla fragrances as I washed away the stickiness of the gym and the creepiness of Mr. Muscles.

I had intended to go for a swim, but now all I wanted to do was head back to my room and chill for a bit, awaiting the return of my TDS. He would be pleased that I had changed my mind regarding sightseeing alone.

Back in the hotel room, I dumped my holdall at the end of the bed and wondered if I should call down to the front desk. No doubt there was a laundering service, and TDS had said that they were there for my every beck and call.

Checking my phone, it was now lunch time. So I did ring down, but to the kitchen, and to order that tempting club sandwich with chips. Only when it arrived, I remembered the American-English translation of potato chips. Should have asked for fries, idiot, I told myself.

Never mind. It was still appetizing, and finished in about ten minutes. I was licking my fingers clean when the message came through on my phone: "Don't eat. I'll be back for lunch. V."

"Too late," I replied. A few moments later, another message came through. I grabbed my phone, expecting to be told off, or teasingly threatened.

"Been trying to call you. You're in NY, aren't you? With him. Call me. Matt,"

Shit. My thumb hovered over the Delete button, but pressed Call instead.

"Paige?"

"Hi, Matt." I failed miserably at hiding the guilt in my voice.

233

"Why didn't you tell me?"

"How could I? After what you said to me, I just needed to get away for a bit."

"Did you have to go with him?" The hurt in his words tugged at my chest, punching my ribs brutally.

"I needed to get away," I said again, as though it were excuse enough. "I'll be back in a couple of weeks."

"I could meet you out there."

"No." The word came quicker than I had intended it to. "No," I said again, more softly. "You have a business to run."

"I don't like the idea of you and…"

"We're in separate rooms. I literally shared the flight with him." The lie came out so easily, I was ashamed of myself.

"Is there really so much to think about?"

"Matt, you told me that you love me. It's all too quick."

"I'm sorry," he said. But I could tell he didn't mean it.

"Me, too. Please, I need some time to think."

"I'm worried, Paige," he admitted. "You're spending too much time with him. He's…"

"Dangerous. Yes, so you keep telling me." The anger filled my words like spiteful venom. "But you still haven't given me a reason to believe you. Sleeping with your exes doesn't make him dangerous. Arrogant, conceited, selfish, yes, but not dangerous."

"He'll hurt you."

"He won't, because he has nothing to hurt me with. I need a break, away from everything, and he offered me that. Let me think about this, get my head straight, and we'll talk when I get back."

"I won't wait around forever."

"I'm not asking you to wait at all," I pointed out before hanging up on him.

"Who was that?" I turned to see TDS standing in my doorway, shrugging his jacket off.

"Oh, nobody." I gave him a half-cocked smile and hoped he would leave it at that. It was too much to hope for, though.

"Matthew?" he asked. I didn't reply. "That boy is persistent, if nothing else."

"Can't think where he gets it from."

"And what did you tell him?"

I sighed heavily, not wanting to get into this conversation. I was still debating whether to tell him about Mr. Muscles or not. "He wants to come over here and whisk me off my feet, save me from his lecherous father."

"Do you think I'm lecherous or does he?" he asked, seemingly amused by the whole situation.

"We both do. Why aren't you bothered by any of this?" I asked.

"Bothered by what?"

"Oh, don't play coy with me! Matt is really hurt by what I've done, but still willing to fight. You," I waved a hand angrily towards him, "don't seem to give a damn whom I sleep with."

"If I didn't give a damn, I wouldn't want you here with me, where I can keep an eye on you."

I stepped back. God, I sounded like a complete and utter slut. "Well, for your information, I actually turned someone down today," I snapped, trying to salvage my own reputation.

"Who was he?" he asked sharply. His glare blazed furiously. Holy shit, he was mad.

"Nobody," I stuttered meekly.

"Who was he, Paige?" He marched towards me, grabbing my arms.

"Get the hell off of me!" I yelled, yanking myself from his grip. I watched as he walked away, rubbing his hands roughly over his chiseled face, through his thick mane.

"I'll kill him."

"Jesus Christ, calm down! He only flirted with me. And I think you'll find I told you I walked away!"

"Matthew, I can handle. He's just a boy. But if anyone else touches you…" I knew he wasn't mad with me, but it still felt like all the anger was pointed in my direction. My bottom lip trembled. I tried to swallow the salty tears down, but the emotion was too strong for me to battle. Turning, I marched into my own private room, the door slamming against the hinges.

Matt's words rang in my ears. Dangerous. Was he really? I'd seen fleeting moments where danger lurked, but I'd never felt frightened of him.

235

I wasn't frightened of him now, but I was scared by what he could be capable of.

Fuck. What had I gotten myself into?

Chapter Thirty-Eight

"Paige?" he called through the door. "I'm sorry." It sounded genuine, but I could never be sure with TDS.

Staring at the reflection, I could see every reason to avoid opening that door. Once brown eyes were puffy and bloodshot, and pale cheeks were now ruddy and blotched. The white lines across my chin and brow stared back at me angrily. I smoothed a finger over the hairs above my eye, trying to hide the gap.

"Let me in, Paige."

Closing my eyes, I reached for the lock on the door, twisting it open.

"Thank you." His hand was on my waist, caressing at the bone in my hip. "I'm sorry. I get so angry at the thought of another man being anywhere near you."

"But not Matt."

"I told you. That's different."

"I fucked him, and you don't care."

"I do care. I care very much."

"So what am I then? Another conquest? Just one more thing to hold over him. 'You can have her, but she's still mine'? I thought so," I added, when he didn't reply. Pulling away from his touch, I grabbed my suitcase from by the bed, flinging it open. "I knew this was a mistake. I should never have come here."

"Then why did you?"

"Because I wanted to be with you!" I shouted, shocking myself with the answer, the truth. "I want to be with you."

He smiled at my confessions. Oh, how much I despised him. And loved him, I realized.

"Why did you sleep with Matthew?"

"I didn't think you cared. I believed that all I was to you was another notch on your bedpost. I was angry with you, with the world. With myself. Matt cares about me, and I hate myself for not being able to feel the same way. I tried, I honestly did…" The sentence cut off with a great sob, as I turned and buried my face into his shirt. "But I don't love him. I love you."

His mouth sealed over mine in a fervent, hungry kiss. That familiar heat built between my thighs instantly. Hands hooked beneath my t-shirt, fondling me, reaching around and releasing the clasp. Soon my top and bra were in a puddle by my feet, and he pulled me into him. I fumbled with the buttons of his shirt, desperate for that skin-on-skin contact.

"Slow down," he cooed, hands caressing my shoulders and neck, his head bending towards me as he took in each and every breath, kissing away the tears that streamed down my cheeks. I ran my hands up his body, fingers dancing between the few hairs that dusted over rigid muscle, before scraping them around and down his back.

"Don't you have a meeting this afternoon?" I asked, my voice barely a hoarse whisper.

"They can wait." He kissed me, hands gripping my buttocks, as he turned me to the bed. "You can't."

I lay back and let him pull my jeans off, leaving me in nothing but a pair of dark teal pants. He teased the black lace trim, kissing my inner thigh. "You smell so sweet," he breathed. I looked down, just seeing his eyes peering up to meet me. "I want to taste you." He licked around the edge of my underwear.

Bending my knee, I hooked my leg around him, urging him into me. He smiled dirtily, moving his kisses to my navel, his tongue darting in and out of my belly button. I groaned as his hands moved up the curve of my waist and ribs, reaching for my breasts.

"I want you," I demanded hungrily. He smiled, a wicked smile, dipping his head back to my stomach, moving his mouth over the skin, trailing back towards the edge of my pants. I groaned in anticipation as one hand shot beneath me, kneading at my buttocks. "Are you still…"

"No," I replied, for once grateful of the unreliability of my body.

Fingers swept beneath the satin fabric, moving between my cheeks until he found my sweet spot, wet and wanting.

The pants were gone. Torn from my body, leaving me open and begging for him. His mouth was on me, kissing me hungrily, tongue darting where fingers had once been.

"Oh, my God!" I cried out in sheer ecstasy as he plunged into me, hands gripping my buttocks.

"Roll over," he demanded. I did what he said without arguments, lying on my belly. With his hands gripped to my hips, he pulled me onto my knees and towards the edge of the bed.

I was completely vulnerable to him, and utterly aroused.

The palm of his hand landed on my backside with a sharp slap, but it was the sound that made me jump more than the sting. I glanced back at him, lapping up the look of sheer enjoyment on his face.

"This," he hissed, dipping the tips of two fingers inside me. "This is mine." He claimed me with his hands before ripping off his own clothes so quickly, I blinked and missed it.

He pressed his erection firmly against my sex before gently moving the tip of him inside of me. I groaned loudly, wiggling backwards to take more of him. Fingers and palms bit into the flesh of my backside as he pumped into me, rocking me back and forth.

Before long, his movements became sharp and forced. I could feel him swelling inside me, filling me so completely I cried out, my own orgasm building to such heights I feared I may tumble to the ground in a soggy heap. It left me feeling shattered, but he didn't stop, reaching forward and taking a handful of my hair, rearing my head back as he slammed into me, again and again and again.

"I can't," I cried out, collapsing to my elbows, burrowing my face into the duvet beneath me. He slowed, becoming gentle. "I can't." My knees gave way, but his hand beneath my belly kept me up. He pulled out of me, still hard, and lay me down.

Curling behind me, I could feel his cock pressing into my lower back. "I'm sorry," I cried.

"Shhh," he hushed, moving the sweat- and tear drenched hair from my cheeks. "It's okay."

"No, it's not." I rolled over to face him, hooking a leg over his, pulling him closer. "I don't have the strength for that, but…" Pulling him over, he moved until he was on top of me, guiding himself back inside the warmth.

"Are you sure?" he asked. I nodded, chewing on my bottom lip, closing my eyes as he pressed into me and found his release.

"I better change," he said after a while of holding me in the heat of his body. "I'm already late."

"Sorry," I offered, although not feeling an ounce of guilt.

"What are you going to do today?"

"Sleep." I stretched out, yawning and claiming the rest of the bed as he stepped out and moved into my shower. If I were a cat, I'd have been purring. I closed my eyes and did exactly what I'd told him I would.

It was dark when I woke. I stretched out all of my limbs, enjoying the peace that I felt. I would tell Matt when we got back to Brookfield, I had decided. I was also going to tell my family, and they could like it or lump it. I only hoped that he was willing to take the public leap. No matter how complicated things felt between us, I was happy with TDS. He did care about me, and I cared about him. No. I loved him.

Flicking through the TV channels, I waited for his return. I even sent him a quick text to see how long he would be. But there was no reply. So I decided to head to the pool and take that swim that I'd wanted to earlier.

The joy of sleeping with the owner of the hotel meant that I was given access to the gym and pool even when it was supposed to be closed for the night.

A few spotlights shone down on me as I stroked through the water, enjoying the caress of warmth smoothing down my muscles. My fingers reached for the edge of the tile, pulling myself in. A bottle of water waited for me to take desperate sips after thirty lengths.

"You're out late," came an American accent, one that I knew to belong to Mr. Muscles.

"Oh, hi," I smiled. "Yeah, I prefer swimming alone. More space to splash," I chuckled.

"Mind if I join you?" He dove in beside me, flecks of water hitting my cheeks and lashes as he hit the surface. Well, actually, yes, I do mind. Which part of ALONE didn't you understand? I thought angrily.

"I was about to hit the showers." I smiled politely, hurling myself onto the side, legs still dangling in the water's edge.

"How about I join you there instead?"

"O…kay… This is awkward." I forced a smile. "Not interested."

"You sure?" he asked, reaching for my ankle and tugging me back into the water. I kicked out.

"Yes, I'm fucking sure," I spat, removing myself from his grip and back onto the safety of the tiles. I stood up, grabbing my water and towel, marching into the changing room. "Um, women only?" I pointed to the sign as he entered behind me.

"Oh, come on," he sang, swaggering towards me.

"No, seriously, fuck off now." Adrenaline began to pump through my veins, sparking every warning signal within me. RUN! My mind screamed at me. He sauntered forward, the light bouncing off the droplets that clung to his tanned skin. As his arm swung in front of him, I caught sight of a black tribal tattoo flexing over his bicep. Despite his drenched body, the cloying aftershave was still overpowering.

I sidestepped around him, but he moved in my way. "Move it or lose it," I snapped as his hand landed on my hip. He grinned down at me with a snarl.

My fingers twisted around his, bringing his wrist back with an earsplitting Snap! He screamed out, his free palm connecting with my cheek.

The floor beneath my palms and hip was cold and unforgiving. I gasped out for air, but it came in short supply.

"Bitch!" he spat. "You broke my hand!"

"Be grateful that's all I broke," I snarled, finding my voice. I jumped to my feet. This was not happening again. "Get the fuck out." My voice was low, deep, and filled with an anger I didn't realize I was capable of.

"Fucking bitch," he whined, turning on his heel and flouncing out of the room. I grabbed my water and towel, and marched out of the changing rooms, warm water dripping down my back and legs.

"Miss Holmes?" The angular man at the front desk called after me. "Is everything okay?"

I didn't answer him, desperate to get back to the safety of my room.

I reached the door. Shit. No key card. My palm landed on the frame with a slap. "Fuck!" I screeched, tossing the towel and bottle at the frame. My naked toes connected with the door, crunching against the wood. "Fuck." Sinking to the carpet, I hugged my knees into my body and sobbed.

And that was how he found me.

Chapter Thirty-Nine

Shivering, fighting the cold as the water evaporated from my naked skin, I gripped tightly onto my legs, chin resting between them, hiding me from any light.

His arms wrapped under me, scooping me up as we went through the open door. He placed me on my bed, wrapping the blanket around my shaking shoulders. "What happened?" TDS growled fiercely. I couldn't answer. Fits of sobs burst through every time I tried.

I peered above my knees, watching as he yelled something to the angular man standing in the doorway to the suite.

"They're looking at the security footage," he explained, stepping back over my threshold. "Please tell me what happened. It would be better for whoever if I found out through you."

242

Fear widened my eyes. "Leave it," I begged, shaking my head, pushing back into the blanket as though it may be able to swallow me whole and take me away. "I want to go home," I pleaded.

TDS sat on the bed, hugging me tightly. "I won't leave it, Paige. I can't."

"I don't know his name," I cried, staring up at him with dread-filled wide eyes. "This morning, in the gym. There was an instructor." The words broke through my tears. "He flirted and I turned him down. I went for a swim this evening. He was there. He wouldn't leave me alone." Fits and blubs drowned my voice.

"The same person from this morning?"

I nodded, "I… I think I hurt him."

"I'll kill him." Something in his tone made me aware that he meant it.

"Please don't leave me." I reached out and clung to his arm as he stood to leave.

"I won't. I promise. I'll be back in two minutes." He walked through the door, shutting it behind him. I sat in the darkness, repeating my mantra over and over. The iPhone buzzed. A message from Matt: "I'm sorry about earlier. I can't stop thinking about you. The car is almost finished. I'd like you to see it. We'll talk when you get back. Matt."

Tears drowning me, I flung the phone onto the pillow, falling down beside it. Cocooning myself in the sheets, I hid beneath the thick blankets and prayed for TDS to come back quickly.

Breathe in, breathe out.

The bruise on my cheek was inflamed; my teeth grated against the pain. Tears stung as they hit the red finger marks. I could still smell him. Cheap aftershave, chlorine, and salts abused my senses. Lumps of phlegm caught in my throat. I didn't want to close my eyes. Each time I did, all I saw was his hulking frame looming over me, the inky marks over his arm as he grabbed at me.

I grabbed at the air, sucking in the oxygen and filling my lungs. Pressure built in my chest, forcing my heart to beat painfully against its bony cage. My fingers clutched at the duvet, tugging it tighter around me. Sparse lashes fluttered like trembling butterflies against my cheeks as I fought the weariness that beckoned.

In through the nose, out through the mouth.

A shadow swept over me. Shoulders hunched around my ears, I cowered beneath the sheets.

"Paige?" He asked so demurely, at first I wasn't convinced that it was my TDS.

Cautiously, I pulled the covers back and peeked out from under them. He sat on the edge of the bed, blanketed by the darkness, watching me. "Let's get you dressed."

Forcing myself to move, I found myself between his solid thighs, wrapped in the sheets from the bed. He lifted a towel and rubbed each strand of hair gently until the dripping had ceased. Hands on my waist, he guided me to standing, stripping the damp swimsuit from my body.

Suddenly I felt more vulnerable than I had in over a year. Hands clasped together, protecting what dignity I had left, I let my head hang. My hair covered my face, attempting to hide my shame.

TDS knelt by my feet, lifting one at a time, sliding the clean, fresh pants up my legs. He made no attempt to take advantage of my naked body as he let the hem rest over my hips.

I held my arms out, and the bra glided up and over my shoulders, clasping tightly under the blades. I readjusted myself as he went to the drawer and chose a pair of pale pink pajamas adorned with lilac, cream, and mint butterflies.

Taking a hairbrush, he ran the bristles through the knots, sweeping the damp strands into a ponytail and tying it with a brown band. I turned to face him, to study him. His indigo eyes, usually so passionate and flamed, pulled down at the outside corners, deepening the hoods. His lips, swollen and kissable, echoed the look in his eyes.

I swallowed at the thought of the hatred and sadness being for me. He had seen me for what I was: a pathetic little creature, brash and harsh on the outside, but the blood that ran through me was as yellow as custard.

"Please don't hate me," I whispered so quietly that I doubted he had heard me.

His fingers hooked under my chin, forcing me to meet his stare. "I don't hate you," he said with short, abrupt words. I tried to believe him, but my stomach crumpled into a tight fist at the starkness in his voice.

"Mr. Ellery, sir?" came a female voice from the lounge.

"I'll be back in a minute." A tender kiss was placed on my forehead before picking up the remote control and switching on the television. "Wait here," he ordered.

My legs curled beneath me, I lay back into the pillows and watched as a rainbow of colors flickered across the screen. The volume was low enough that I could catch snippets of the conversation in the next room.

"...cameras...evidence...Miss Holmes...lying..."

Lying?? The word raced around my head. Oh, my God. He thinks I'm lying. Immediately I was torn away from the present and cast back twelve months.

I sat in a wooden box, being judged by twelve sets of penetrating eyes. A man beside me loomed over, peering above his wire-rimmed glasses with an icy cold stare. In front of me, a tall woman dressed in a severe black skirt suit, her blonde hair scraped into a strictly tight bun, scarlet red lips commanding the truth. The only color in a bleak scene. And Evan Browne, with that malevolent grin and narrowed stare, mocking every word I said.

"Just tell the truth, Miss Holmes," the woman demanded. "You were dating Mr. Browne, and agreed to go back to his home. It was consented, wasn't it?"

"No," I mumbled, shaking my head.

"It was consensual. And then, when Mr. Browne called the relationship off, you decided to get back at him, and his family, by ruining his reputation and crying rape. Isn't that right, Miss Holmes?"

"No." The tears rolled down my cheeks. My lawyers had warned me what would happen if I agreed to take the stand against him. But I was still mentally ill-prepared for the barrage that hurtled towards me.

"But when the hospital examined you, there was no sign of rape." Each time she said the word, a part of me died. Stinging, biting, snapping at my very soul. "Oh, of course. You didn't go to the hospital straight away, did you? You left it for several days, weeks even, before telling anyone. If my client raped you, why did you leave it so long to tell anyone?"

"I was afraid."

"You were pregnant. Isn't that the truth, Miss Holmes? You were pregnant and didn't even know who the father was." She would destroy my credibility, as though I was nothing more than an irritating cockroach beneath her Louboutin heel.

"No!" I screamed. The prosecution jumped up and yelled at the judge, at the defense lawyers, at everyone who would listen. Words jumbled together, but all I heard was her.

"I'm just trying to prove that she was lying. There is no video evidence, no taped evidence, no physical evidence that my client did, in fact, rape Miss Holmes."

Lying.

"Paige?" TDS stood over me, as I stared blankly ahead.

"I'm not lying," I stated defiantly, refusing to let that dam break.

"Nobody thinks you are," he assured me.

"I heard…" What had I heard?

"They're looking into the security footage now. They can see that he followed you into the changing rooms, but for some reason, those cameras weren't working."

"You don't think I made it up?"

"No."

"But I heard you say you thought I was lying."

"No, you didn't," he shook his head. "Arundel is claiming you asked him into the changing rooms and then attacked him."

"I didn't…"

"I know. This isn't the first time he's been accused of sexual harassment. But it will damn well be the last."

"What will happen?" I asked, twisting and knotting my fingers around each other. I couldn't go through another trial. I broke his fingers. What if they turned it around? Flipped it so that I was charged with assault?

"It's being dealt with." What did that mean?

"The police will think…"

"The police will think what I tell them to think," he said matter-of-factly. "Come on." He helped me up, arms wrapped around my waist, head bent to mine. Soft, supple lips embraced me, washing away the taste of chlorine. "I want you to eat something and speak to my head of security. Don't worry. I'll be with you all the time."

"What about your meetings?"

"Do you think I'm leaving you alone? I've got a couple of important ones I can't cancel, but they can cope with teleconferencing for the next couple of days. Then we're going back to England."

"You'd cut your plans for me?"

"I have cut my plans for you."

"I should call my parents. Let them know I'll be home sooner."

"Fine. But you'll stay with me for a few days." Good old domineering TDS, the one constant in my life. "You wanted a break for two weeks, you'll get a break for two weeks."

It struck me that I had no idea where TDS lived. I'd been to his hotel, both of them, but never to his home. I wanted to ask him, but my throat was red and raw. Each word rasped against the tender flesh, so I nodded.

He took my hand and led me into the lounge, where a woman I assumed to be head of security was waiting. She was no taller than I, with an abundance of flame-red circling her round face. Piercing hazel eyes smiled at me as she took my hand and shook firmly. "Miss Holmes, I can only apologize for…"

"Don't worry." I stopped her from the ridiculous pity and guilt she held over an act for which she had no control. She cast a confused glance towards TDS, who closed his eyes and shook his head.

"Miss Holmes is a strong woman," he explained, sitting me on the sofa and snapping his fingers to a man standing by the bar. Immediately a glass of ice-cold water was in my grip.

"This will be dealt with." The woman echoed TDS. "The police will be contacted --"

"No!" My whole body jumped with the word. "I don't want to…" My eyes darted to TDS, begging him to take control back.

"No police. We'll deal with this internally," he barked.

"But Mr. Ellery?" The woman was even more confused. "It's protocol. A matter of this… this nature needs to be… dealt with."

"And it will. Internally. Is that understood?"

"Yes, Mr. Ellery," the woman accepted, although her body language told me differently.

"Now, everyone out. Miss Holmes needs to rest."

Like mice, the staff scurried out of the room before TDS could grab a broom and start bashing them over the heads.

247

"Thank you," I muttered into my glass of water. "I realize that this is serious, and you have procedures that should be followed, but I don't think I could…" I paused and tried to catch my breath as it eluded me.

"From what I've seen of Arundel's hand, I don't think he'll be harassing anyone else," he smirked. "Those self-defense classes of yours seemed to have paid off."

"Why do you believe me? I get the feeling that nobody else did."

"You're not like that."

"But I slept with your son."

"Let me ask you something." He straightened his back, staring down at me over that straight nose. "Who seduced whom? Who started it?"

"Does it matter?"

"Yes."

"I don't know." I thought back. There was the thunderstorm. Crashing all around me. My panic attack. "He did."

"And why do you think he did?"

"I assumed it was because he was attracted to me." I raised an eyebrow. Where the hell was this going? "I'm tired," I argued with myself. "Can we leave this until tomorrow?"

"Yes. Just think about it." He leant forward and kissed me. "I have some things to take care of." He left me alone, only thoughts to comfort me. I didn't want to believe that Matt had seduced me simply to get to his father. I wanted to believe, desperately needed to believe, that he cared for me.

Chapter Forty

True to his word, TDS spent the next two days streaming through a laptop, never once leaving the room. We ordered room service, and I rested. A couple of times there were telephone calls and he gave me that look telling me to leave. Obediently, I stayed in my room until he retrieved me, and always with a warm kiss. He sensed my reluctance under his touch, though, and didn't pursue me.

On Wednesday morning he informed me that a flight had been booked to take us back to the UK. I couldn't help but be disappointed. Nearly five days in New York and I hadn't once set foot outside the hotel.

"I'll bring you back another time," he promised.

"What about --" I didn't want to say his name.

"Arundel?" he said for me. "Don't give him another thought."

There was something in his dismissive manner that scared me. It wasn't a fear I felt for myself, though. I'd hoped that broken fingers, lack of job, and damaged pride would be punishment enough, but I suspected that TDS thought otherwise.

The flight back to England was eventless. No night terrors this time. No awe-inspiring views over the oceans. I just slept. I felt like I hadn't slept in months. Exhaustion took over, and as soon as my head hit the soft, cushioned rest, my eyes shut tightly. I wasn't aware that it was possible for me to sleep so soundly and for so long.

I woke as the wheels came down and the engine began to roar. The landing was gentle, but there was still a jolt as we hit the runway.

"Are you all right?" TDS asked, genuinely concerned.

"I would have liked to have done some sightseeing," I moped.

"Next time," he chuckled.

He dropped me off outside the farmhouse, where Danny and Mark were both awake and waiting. "What happened?" Mark demanded as I strode through the door, dragging my suitcase behind me. "Five days is not two weeks."

"Nice to see you too," I griped. "I take it Mum called you?" I'd called my parents the day before to let them know I would be returning earlier than planned. But I refused to divulge a truthful explanation.

"You could have done that yourself," my brother snapped. "What happened?" he asked again.

"There was an incident," I said glibly. If they found out about Arundel, TDS would be on the plate for dinner.

"An incident?" I could see that neither of them would let this lie. "Stop being so fucking secretive, Paige. Ever since you got involved with that prick, you've done nothing but hide away. You were making good progress."

"I am making good progress!" I snapped back. "If you must know, some idiot got the wrong idea, tried it on, and I broke his fucking fingers. That's why we came back early."

"Shit," Mark hissed, grabbing me into his arms. I echoed his curse. Why had I told him?

"Okay. What's happened?" I asked, tugging free from his grip, quizzing the narrowed expression that set his face.

"You need to see Dad."

"What's happened, Mark?" I demanded loudly. Something was stopping my brother from ripping TDS apart, and whatever it was had to be serious.

"He's appealing."

"What?" I asked, confused.

"Evan Browne." Danny stood next to my brother. "He's appealing against the conviction."

My world went black. My body was floored. I waited for the ground to crack, swallowing me into the dark chasm of hell.

"He can't." My voice wavered over the words like a buoy in the midst of a tsunami.

"Your TDS is here," Danny muttered. I picked my head up and watched as his tall, dark figure marched to the door. He caught me through the window, brows furrowing as he saw the state I was in.

I cursed under my breath. "I told him I'd be out in a minute. I'm staying at his place for a few days."

"Jesus H., Paige!" Mark exclaimed. "You need to go and see Dad. His lawyers are already on their way."

Great. An army of men and women in suits who get paid far too much. Precisely what I needed.

"What about this bloke in New York?" Danny asked, picking up on my little tale.

"Umm…" I shook my head, trying to remember what had happened. "No charges were made. He's been dealt with, whatever that means." The grey cells within my aching skull melded the memories. Evan Browne was appealing. Could he do that? It hadn't even been a year since he was sentenced. There must have been a mistake.

251

"Are you okay?" He was the only one in the room who seemed concerned for my sanity. I smiled gratefully at him.

"I'm fine. Vance has told me to stay at his place."

"Told you," Mark chuntered.

"Asked me," I corrected. "Vance asked me if I wanted to stay with him since he's got meetings left, right, and center. Look, I can't think about this right now! I'll call Dad later."

"You need to speak to the lawyers."

"I need some peace and quiet and for everyone to stop treating me like I might break," I volleyed back to him. The door clicked. Our voices grew louder, until he stepped in between us.

"Paige," TDS growled at me.

"You need to leave." Mark squared up to him, matching his fiery stare with an icy blast.

"Grow up." I shoved Mark away. "I will deal with this in my own time."

"Talk to me." TDS again.

"It's none of your business," Mark snapped.

TDS swirled around, hands against my brother's shoulders.

"Vance," I called out warily, as I watched the two men in my life begin the battle of stares. "Come on, please." I placed a hand on his arm, the muscles flexing beneath my touch. I caught sight of Danny as he urged Mark backwards. He whispered something in his ear. "Vance," I said again.

"I'll take you to see your parents." He relented, breaking the hold and walking towards the door.

"Thank you. Wait for me in the car." I twisted on my toes, growing as tall as I could. "What the hell is wrong with you?" I threw the words callously towards my brother.

"Paige, he's worried about you," Danny offered, as Mark flounced past me.

"Well, he needn't be. I can handle myself."

"We know. But we love you, and we can't help it."

"I'm sorry, Danny, I really am." I gave my good friend a squeeze.

"You made your choice then."

I cast a glance over my shoulder towards TDS as he stood by the car door, spits of rain beginning to soften the edges. "I think so."

"Have you spoken to Matt Jackson yet?"

"No. I'm not sure what I'll say."

"Greg called," he said, changing the subject. "He wants you to go in for a meeting once you're back."

"I'll ring from…" Of course. I hadn't got a clue where TDS lived. Wherever the money is; isn't that what Matt had told me? "I'll ring him later."

"You're happy, aren't you?" he asked.

"Yes." I smiled. "He makes me happy."

"I'll talk to Mark," he proffered. I responded with a half-smile and nod, reaching up to place a kiss on his cheek. Danny's arms wrapped around me, hugging me tightly. "We're always here for you, Paige." His lips brushed past my cheek as we pulled away from the embrace.

I grabbed my suitcase and took it back to TDS. "I didn't have time," I explained, handing it back to him. I felt the vibration of the phone against my thigh.

"I'm sure I can have them washed for you. Or buy you a new outfit or three." He grinned, in a vain attempt to lighten my mood.

"I better see Dad." My shoulders heaved with a breathless sigh as I clambered back into the Jag. Chalmers tipped his head towards me as I directed him to Holmes Manor.

"I will speak to your father," TDS declared. "Between us, we can make sure he never sees the light of day again."

"I think you've done enough," I said, my hand on his arm. "Just believing in me is more than I could have ever asked for."

His teeth ground together, contracting the muscles along his razor-sharp jawline. I closed my eyes and exhaled a tightly held breath. "You hurt him, didn't you?" I asked. "Arundel. You did more than have him fired."

"He won't be touching anyone any time soon."

"What did you do?" I asked, not wanting to know the answer.

He turned his gaze to mine, a long finger stroking over the white line across my jaw. "Nothing you need to concern yourself with. You have more important things to worry about right now."

Chalmers halted the car outside the front door of Holmes Manor. I expected my mother to greet us, but it was Hannah who came racing around the side of the house, arms spread open wide, and lifting me into a

253

tight squeeze. "Are you okay?" she wheezed, catching her breath. "Mark rang me and said you'd come home early. I was worried."

"I'm fine," I lied, removing myself from her bear hug. "How's Georgia doing?"

"Missing you. But I don't mind spending so much time at the farm," she giggled with a wink. She stopped and took a step back as TDS appeared by my side.

"Hannah, Vance Ellery. Vance, this is Hannah," I introduced.

"Your parents are waiting," he said, taking my arm. "Nice to meet you, Hannah."

Hannah didn't respond, her mouth hanging slightly loosely.

"You're drooling," I whispered with a wink. "I need to ask you a favor. Could you take Georgia on?"

"Of course," Hannah squealed excitedly. "She's brill!"

"Thanks. You can bring her here. Or leave her at the farm. It's too much for me right now."

Hannah squeezed me tightly.

"I better go," I said, turning to follow my guide.

My parents were both in the drawing room. Mother was wringing the worry and guilt from her hands while my father paced back and forth, yelling down the telephone. He stopped as TDS stood opposite him. "I'll call you back," he barked, placing the phone on the sideboard with a light thud.

"Stephen." TDS nodded.

"Ellery." My father was not so polite with his greeting.

"Paige, why don't we go and see if Rosa can rustle up something to eat. You must be starving after your long flight." Mother's soft arm slipped around my waist and led me out of the drawing room.

"Mum," I started, trying to think of some pathetic excuse or reason as to why TDS was with me.

"You don't have to say anything." She smiled sweetly. "I assume Mark has… explained?"

I nodded. "Please tell me it's not true."

"I only wish I could, darling." I thought she might cry, but Rosa rescued us as we reached the kitchen, placing a white pot, with painted pink and blue flowers trailing around its fat waist and spout, in front of us with two matching cups and saucers. Mother poured the tea out diligently.

"What happens now?"

"Hopefully nothing," she said, handing me my cup and saucer. "Your father has his solicitors looking into the matter. Why did you have to bring Mr. Ellery with you?" she asked with a saddened sigh. "What happened to that lovely young Mr. Jackson?"

"It didn't work," I fibbed, placing my phone on the table, and seeing the words "New Message" glancing up at me. "Please be happy for me, Mum," I implored.

"Have you spoken to Mr. Bertin recently?" She changed the subject so smoothly.

"No, not yet."

"Your father has been talking to him while you've been away. And the sports council. They're all happy for you to return once you're fully rested."

I'd forgotten all about the committee. I should give Lou a ring and see how the plans were developing. That would give me something to concentrate on.

The phone vibrated against the wooden grain. "Two New Messages."

Shouts echoed down the hallway.

"And how was New York?" mother asked, seemingly oblivious to the arguments across the house.

"Fine." I strained to hear what it was that TDS and my father were "discussing," although I had a fairly good idea already.

"Why did you come home early? Did you see much while you were there?"

"Not really. It was too muggy to do anything." I lied with a disturbing amount of ease. "Mr. Ellery had some important meetings, so we had to leave." Again with the lies. But these were for her own good. Mother would never cope with the knowledge that I had been attacked. Again.

My father appeared in the doorway. For a split second I thought TDS had told him everything, but as my father pulled me into a hug, kissing the crown of my hair, I knew that my trust had not been betrayed.

255

Chapter Forty-One

I sat in the back of the Jaguar, Chalmers up front, waiting for TDS. I stared at my phone, unsure as to whether I should read the messages. I knew who they were from.

"Where does T -- I mean, Mr. Ellery, live?" I asked as casually as I could. Chalmers glanced back at me through the rearview mirror. He didn't respond as TDS slid into the seat beside me.

"Richard Courts, please, Chalmers," he instructed. The car was shifted into gear before ambling down the drive, gravel crunching under the wheels as the tires churned into the ground. I was disappointed that we were going back to the hotel and I wasn't about to discover where he resided.

"What were you and my father arguing about?"

"It's nothing to worry about."

"If it's about me, then I think I have every right to know." His dark look threatened me not to pry further. My scarred brow flickered into a high arch. "Tell me, or I go back to the farm."

"We disagreed as to how to handle this situation."

This situation?! How could he be so blasé? "And what did you finally agree on?" I asked snappily. "This is my life you two are tossing around. It was me he…" My tongue tied around the word, refusing to let it leave.

The muscles in his jaw and neck tightened. "Your father made it very clear that he does not approve of us spending so much time together. It appears Matthew has been spending rather a lot of time seducing your parents into the idea of…" It was his turn to stumble at the end of a sentence.

"What? What does Matt want? And what does he have to do with… him?"

"Matthew wants to marry you. He's asked your father's permission, and he's given it."

"He's what?" I exclaimed, the yell rasping against my already sore throat. "What the hell does he think he's playing at?"

"He was also there when your father got the phone call regarding Evan Browne's appeal."

"So he knows. Oh, great." I picked up my phone and scrolled into the messages. I was right. They were both from Matt, asking me to contact him A.S.A.P.

257

"Of sorts. Your father didn't go into too much detail other than to warn me away from you."

"I'm sorry." I hugged his arm. "I'm sorry for everything."

"You have absolutely nothing to apologize for."

"I'm such a mess," I confessed, sniveling into his sleeve. He pulled it from my grasp, hooking it around my shoulders.

"You're an enigma," he agreed. "Can I assume that you won't be accepting Matthew's proposal?"

"No. No, I won't."

He twisted to face me, his mouth encompassing mine, tongue parting my lips. His fingers entwined through my hair as he drew me into him, devouring me entirely. I gasped for air between kisses, each time inhaling and tasting the sandalwood and citrus scents. Here is where I belonged.

Richard Courts came into view, but I didn't notice until Chalmers broke in front of the steps that led up to the open double doors.

"Mr. Ellery, so pleased you've returned." The doorman grinned and bowed. "Miss Holmes," he acknowledged with a nod of his head.

"Sir?" called the front desk clerk, as TDS marched briskly past him. He swiveled on his heel, leaving me by the golden doors of the lift. I saw him grab a cream envelope, shoving it into the inner pocket of his jacket.

"Everything okay?" I asked, but he didn't reply. We waited for the lift, his hand slipping down over the mound of my buttocks. My cheeks heated at the thought of everyone seeing his blatant show of sexual prowess.

Chalmers brought my suitcase and laid it on the bed for me while TDS made us both drinks and I sat in the sunken lounge.

"You should call him." He handed me a short tumbler filled with fresh orange juice and ice. No alcohol, I noted. "Matthew. You should call him and put him out of his damn misery."

"That envelope?"

"Nothing. But his mother has left several messages for me to contact her." The elusive ex- Mrs. TDS.

"Will you?"

"No. We have nothing to discuss. She gets her maintenance. Bianca's education is fully paid for until the end of term. Matthew has made it quite clear that he wants nothing from me." He gulped his drink down in one swig. "You should rest as well. I have to let London know that I'm back."

He marched out of the lounge into the bedroom with the phone. Evidently he did not want to be disturbed for a while.

I picked up my phone and hit Matt's number. And waited.

"Where are you?" Not even a hello. Yes. I had definitely made the right decision.

"Hi. I got your messages."

"Where are you?" he asked again.

"Matt, I…"

"Can you meet me? I need to ask you something." I knew exactly what he wanted to ask me, and the answer was…

"No. I've just got off a plane, I've had a really long day. I want to sleep."

"Tomorrow then."

"Matt." It came out like a lengthened whine. I rubbed at the corners of my tired eyes.

"The car's ready."

I had to admit, I did want to see how the Evo had turned out. It had been weeks since I'd stepped foot inside the garage, and I desperately wanted to see Greg and the boys again.

"Tomorrow," I agreed. It would give me an excuse to discuss my job with Greg anyway.

"I'll be there at ten."

"I'll see you then," I said reluctantly.

Tossing the phone to the side, I leant back into the sofa and enjoyed the relaxing comfort that surrounded me. TDS's voice was loud in the bedroom, but then again, when wasn't it? It seemed that all he did was bark orders to everyone, including me.

I must have fallen asleep, because the next thing I remember is TDS standing over me, hands on hips, with a wickedly delicious glint in his eye. He ran a hand absently over his dark hair, silver flecks catching the light.

"Have you spoken to him?" he asked. I nodded. "Good. Tell me. Where do you want to be, Paige?"

"Here." It was joyous to have my authoritative TDS return. He gave me a half-nod, lifting his head to the ceiling in agreement with my decision. A flicker of a smile teased at the corner of his lips.

"I want you. Now." My insides turned to cream at the depth of his order. "Stand up." I did as I was told. He took my hand and led me over to the floor-to-ceiling windows that gazed out across the lush gardens, still green from the wet summer. "I want you here." His voice was a harsh whisper. I closed my eyes, hands braced against the cold glass as I felt his fingers trail down my spine, reaching the waistband of my skirt. The elastic twanged playfully against my skin, nipping me. His hand fell between my legs. "You're wet," he noticed. "This is mine." Adroit fingers moved the cotton fabric aside, sweeping over me. I groaned, hot breath misting in front of me.

Gripping my hips, he lured me into his groin, pressing his full rigid length against me. I heard the zip of his trousers being ripped, and suddenly the satin softness of his erect penis was pressing against my naked thigh. Fingers swept my pants aside once more while he guided himself inside me.

We rocked back and forth, hands pressed against the glass. He moved my hair to one side and tasted my skin, nibbling at the back of my neck and shoulders as he urged himself deeper. One hand moved beneath the belt of my skirt, palm pressing against my pelvis as his long fingers played with me through the cotton.

Passion built beneath my skin, crying out for release. My skin was on fire as he tickled my every nerve. I thought I heard him call my name, but my ears were too blocked with the sound of my own pulse as it bashed at the walls of every vein.

At last I reached the brink of eternity, and with one swift movement, he pushed me over it. We tumbled together down our spiral of ecstasy. I threw my head back, opening my neck to the world.

Collapsing against him, my body sagged wearily. His teeth nibbled the lobe of my ear, expertly avoiding the golden stud. "This is how I want you," he breathed, claiming my very soul. He didn't have to demand it; I gave my all willingly.

"Thank you," I said, grateful for washing away the thoughts of Matt, Evan, and the past month from my consciousness for a few enjoyable moments.

I woke before TDS. He lay, sprawled out, across the crisp cream sheets of the hotel bed. I couldn't help but take in his naked body. For fifty-six, he still looked good enough to eat. A brief thought of biting him crossed my mind, making me giggle aloud. The sound stirred him. He glanced over his shoulder with a quizzical expression.

"Just admiring the view," I tittered, before traipsing towards the shower. I had to wash the smell of pure, unadulterated sex from my pores if I was going to see his son. Not that I had any intention of succumbing to his charms again.

As the soapy bubbles ran down my body, desperate to escape to the dark depths of the drains, my mind skipped and hopped over the past few weeks, stopping abruptly as it reached Matthew Jackson.

Stepping out of the shower, I was met by the delectable sight of TDS in all his glory, lying prone on the bed. "Don't you have a meeting?" I asked, trying to ignore the sheet between his thighs, pitched like a pyramid tent.

"Not until eleven," he purred, patting the pillow beside him.

"I have to go to Bertin's. I need to make sure I still have a job."

"You're choosing cars over me?" he pouted childishly.

"No," I chortled. "I'm choosing a career over homelessness." He frowned, rolling onto his elbow, the sheet slipping away. My eyes rolled in an exaggerated circle as I pulled on a striped Bardot top.

"You do realize that you don't have to work. You won't be homeless."

"It's the principle. I don't want to be some little rich bitch, or a kept woman," I added, before he had chance to claim ownership over me. "This is part of my survival. I have to be able to stand on my own two feet."

He understood that. "Do you want me to drop you off?"

"Chalmers can take me to the farm, and I'll pick up the Golf."

"You deserve a better car."

"I deserve one that I can buy using my own money, and a Golf is what I can afford on my wages." If he wanted me to accept that he was going to be domineering in this relationship, he would have to accept that I can be stubborn and pigheaded.

"I won't be finished until three. And afterwards, there is something we need to discuss."

"Discuss?" I echoed, studying the glint in his eyes. I glanced down at my watch, and impatience got the better of me. "I still have a bit of time."

"Move in with me."

"What?" I sat down beside him, stunned, but not really, by his request.

"Move in with me," he repeated, kissing the naked skin on my shoulder.

"Vance, I don't even know where you live. I don't want to be some nomad hopping from hotel bed to hotel bed." He raised an eyebrow. "Even if it is yours," I added.

"You won't have to. Once the sports pavilion is finished, and the mergers in New York are complete, and some… other business… is taken care of, then I will be all yours."

"All mine?" I teased. "I get control?"

"Let's not push it."

"And where will you be when you've finished this other business?"

"New York. One of the meetings I had over there was finalizing the sale of an apartment. I spend a lot of time in America, so it seemed to make sense."

"New York? You want me to move, permanently, to New York?"

"You said you wanted to do sightseeing and shopping. I'm sorry you didn't get the chance to."

I shivered at the memory.

"I spoke to your father, and the one thing we did agree on is that you need to get away from Brookfield. You've been trapped here for far too long, and now, with the appeal, we both think that you would be better if you were to move away."

"So you both thought it would be okay to collude against me, and decide my own future?" I snapped.

"Don't twist my words, Paige," he growled.

"Fuck you!"

"Do you have to use such foul language?" He rubbed his hands tiredly over his face and hair, the sight sending bolts of electricity firing through me as the muscles in his arms, chest, and stomach flexed with the movement.

"I have to go." I stood up, yanking on a pair of jeans, slipping my feet into a pair of teal Jimmy Choo courts. All seven dirty words whirled around my head. They somehow felt apt.

Before I had the chance to walk out on him, his fingers were wrapped around my wrist. He turned me in to him, his mouth on mine. "Three o'clock. Here," he demanded, palm moving to my chest, cupping me perfectly. "You need to be fucked."

"Is that your answer to everything?" I asked, trying to resist melting into him. "I defy you, so you shag me? And how come it's okay for you to swear, but not me?" Tipping towards him, I let my mouth sink onto his, tasting the scent of maleness that exuded from his every pore. His eyes widened for a microsecond, forcing his brows to rise suggestively. I groaned, "Three o'clock." He dropped me, and I scooped up my bag before walking out reluctantly.

I'd never trodden on that fine line between love and hate before I met Vance Ellery. Now it felt like I was jumping on it, smashing it in the ground, and kicking dirt over it for good measure. I hated him for having so much control over me, but as I climbed into the Jag without him, I couldn't help but ache for his touch.

God, how I hated him.

Chapter Forty-Two

A shiver shook my entire body, goosebumps prickled my skin, as I pulled up outside Bertin's Body Shop. It was nine o'clock, so I had a good hour before Matt would arrive. I pushed the reception door open, stepping through as quietly as my heels would allow, hoping not to be noticed by the hulk of man standing on the other side of the glass window that peered into the workshop.

Alek Zubek turned and smiled, although it did not quite reach his eyes. He turned and yelled up to the office, over the whirring and buzz of machinery. I clip-clopped through the side door, making my way up the metal steps and into Greg's office.

"Paige!" he exclaimed, embracing me. "This is Yvette." He introduced me to the young raven-haired girl sitting at my desk. "She's temping for us until you get back."

"Hi," I offered, but it was only returned by a look of concern. Clearly this job meant a lot to her. I turned back to Greg. "I heard the Evo's finished."

"Mr. Jackson spoke to you then?"

"Yes. He said he was picking it up today, and I wanted to see it."

"Come on." He hooked an arm through mine and led me back down the metal steps. "I hear you've been to New York?" Trust the grapevine of Brookfield to keep everyone up to speed. "Did you have fun?"

"It was… eventful." I forced a smile, not wanting him to press the matter further.

"Mark rang me," he said seriously. "He told me about Evan Browne. We're all hoping that the bastard is rejected."

"Thank you." I nodded slowly, eyes cast over the ground.

"Here she is!" he said more cheerfully, whipping away the dustcover that sheltered Matt's beauty from any debris.

The car was stunning. She'd been lowered, with a carbon-fiber body kit added so that she looked only inches off the ground, painted in a striking turquoise and violet flip-paint, with privacy tint on the windows.

The front lip spoiler grinned proudly, while the rear spoiler set the look like a pair of wings, ready to fly down the motorway.

"Matt will love it!" I cried, proud of the boys I had once worked with.

"I hope so," Greg said, pulling her blanket back over, tucking the car in as though she were a newborn baby. "Tea?" he asked, leading me into the staff room. That familiar smell of grease, WD-40, and rubber circulated around, comforting me with memories of a life before Vance Ellery and Matthew Jackson.

"Coffee machine still on the blink then?" I joked, taking the mug of steaming tea from him. Greg gave me a wide grin that instantly settled any nervousness I'd felt earlier.

"You're not staying, are you?" Greg asked, seeing my despondency.

I shook my head. "It's all too... complicated."

"The rumor mills have been working overtime. Vance Ellery?" He cocked an eyebrow at me, although with Greg it tended to be both brows that raised.

"He's asked me to go to New York with him. Considering the appeal, I think it might be best."

"When will you leave?"

"I don't know. I'll write out my official notice and bring it later."

Greg looked over my head. The set muscles along his cheeks beckoned me to turn. Matt Jackson strode in. Inky black hair spiked at the top, dark blue eyes coolly staring ahead.

"I should go." I stood up and walked out, narrowly avoiding landing in his firm chest.

"Paige," he purred with a voice smoother than melted chocolate.

"Matt." My greeting was not so friendly.

"I will be back in five minutes." He pointed to Greg, fingers clamping into mine, and pulling me into reception. I cast a look towards Greg, who simply rolled his eyes, arms crossed firmly around his chest.

"Everyone can see," I said, nodding towards the dirty glass windows.

"Come to lunch with me. I'll get the Evo, and we can talk at Matieus. I have something to ask you."

"No. I don't think so, Matt." I knew only too well what he wanted to ask me.

He huffed a short, quick breath. "Please, Paige, it's important."

"I can't marry you, Matt."

He stumbled backwards.

"Your father told me. He said you'd even asked my Dad's permission. Very gallant of you, but you should have waited until I got back."

"I wanted to surprise you."

"I'm surprised. I'm surprised that you even thought I would say yes. I care about you, Matt, I really do. But I don't love you." I crumbled inside at the hurt he felt. I hated myself as I watched his heart break into two pieces. "I'm sorry." It was all I could say.

"Do you love him?"

"Yes," I said. "He's asked me to go to New York, to get away from the appeal and everything else." I stated each word clearly, hoping that it would strengthen my convictions. "I'm going to go."

"When will you be back?"

"I don't know that we will, Matt. He's bought an apartment over there. I'm sorry you had to find out like this, I truly am, but I can't be around you anymore. I thought we could be friends, but we can't. You want more than I can give you, and that's not fair on either of us. I want you to be happy, Matt, and you never will be with me."

"He didn't tell you, did he?"

"Tell me what?" I sighed, exasperated.

"I rang while you were in New York."

"Why would you do that?"

"I needed to know you were safe."

"Why would you think I wasn't?"

"You can't stay with him, Paige."

"Why? Give me one goddamn reason why." My voice raised several pitches, seething at his audacity.

He stepped closer; my breath caught mid-air. There was still that pull between us, a polar attraction I fought to break. "You don't feel this?" he asked.

"Of course I do. Which is why I have to go."

He nodded, knowing but not agreeing that I was right.

"I'm sorry," I said once more, before walking away from him. I hesitated as I reached the door, wondering if I should look back, wondering if I had made the right decision.

The lump in my throat doubled in size. I closed my eyes, turning my chin to my shoulder. But swiftly turned it back. Breathe in, breathe out.

The farmhouse was my next stop. TDS would have only just reached his meeting, and I really didn't want to be on my own at that point.

Danny was at the kitchen table, laptop open, editing photos, I assumed. "Hey," I greeted. He looked up from the screen, grey eyes judging me. "Please don't," I said, holding up my hand to stop the barrage of "I told you so."

"I wasn't going to say a word," he fibbed.

"Where's Mark?"

"Banging Hannah, I should think." He nodded towards the back of the house.

"Fantastic." I slumped into the chair opposite him.

"What's up?" he asked, taking my slouch as a sign I wanted to talk.

"Everything. You were right. I have royally fucked up this time."

"Don't be so hard on yourself," he backpedaled. "You've been going through a rough time."

"He wants me to move to New York."

"Your TDS? Are you going?"

"Probably."

"Forever?"

"Dunno," I sighed, my head falling onto folded arms on the wooden table.

"When does he want to leave?"

I shrugged. "Before the appeal, I guess."

"It was on the news."

"What?"

"Evan's appeal. It was on the news earlier. He's claiming that you had an affair with his father, and accused him of…" He paused over the word. "He's saying you lied to hurt his family after his father dumped you."

"Fuck," I spat. "Does everyone know?"

"No. I wouldn't do that to you."

"Thank you," I cried, tears of anxiety spilling over my lashes. "I don't know if I can do this anymore."

"Mark told me that they'll know in a week whether the appeal's been rejected or not. Why is he bringing all this up now, Paige? Why has he waited twelve months?"

"I don't know. I honestly don't."

"Do you want some lunch?"

I laughed. "I'm not hungry."

"You should eat," Mark said from behind me. "You're wasting away."

Standing, I couldn't help but fall into my brother's broad arms. "I'm so sorry, Mark," I sobbed. "I'm so sorry."

"Don't," he hushed. "I can't stand seeing you like this." He sat me back down, kneeling at my feet. "This isn't the Butch we know and love. He's ruining you."

My phone buzzed and sang out to me. I looked down at the flashing screen.

"That's him, isn't it?"

"Yes." I nodded, pressing the answer button. "Hi," I said sweetly through the tears. "What? How?" Mark and Danny exchanged confusion. "Shit." I hung up. "Mark. I need to tell you something."

He sat down in the chair next to me, gripping my fingers in his. "Evan's telling the truth. I did have an affair with his father. You need to hear this from me, before it's made public knowledge."

"What the hell are you talking about, Paige?"

"Shit," Danny cursed from the corner of the kitchen.

I swallowed the truth whole. It was time to face my past and my demons.

"He has pictures," I explained. "Somehow, Evan has gotten hold of photos of me and his father. He's going to use them against me. He's told his lawyers that I made it all up just to get back at the family."

The look that spread across Mark's face destroyed me. Hate, confusion, guilt, judgment, disbelief, everything that I had had thrown at me during the trial, wrecked my soul. My innards torn to shreds by my own brother. I grabbed at each breath. "I didn't make it up," I cried, great sobs bursting from my lungs. "I promise you, I didn't."

"We believe you," Danny said, watching Mark as his face fell.

"Why didn't you tell anyone?" he asked. I glanced up, begging for Danny's help. "Holy shit, you knew!" Mark jumped to his feet, hands planted against his best friend's chest. He shoved hard; Danny stumbled backwards. A clenched fist poised above his face. But Danny didn't retaliate as the blow connected with his jaw. He took the punch that should have been mine.

"Stop it!" I screeched, throwing myself between them. "If you're going to take it out on anyone, it should be me!"

Fury burnt in Mark's chestnut eyes; rage bulged from every vein. My stomach rippled, losing control over the pent-up guilt. "I'm so, so sorry," I sobbed, the words virtually inaudible.

"And what has Vance Ellery got to do with this?" my big brother spat down at me. Danny stood, lip bleeding, cursing to himself. I dabbed at the open wounds we bared so proudly.

"He's trying to get the photos back. I didn't know what he was doing," I pleaded. "He told me he had business. If I'd known…" I broke off. What would I have done if I'd known that all this time had been spent searching for photos that I didn't want him to see? TDS hated the idea of me being with anyone. How would he react to those?

"We should speak to Dad."

"I don't know if he knows…" My voice trailed as I raked over the events since we'd returned. The argument at Holmes Manor. The abruptness of TDS. Of course, Dad knew. Is that why he'd been willing to let me leave with a man he despised? Because he was going to use what power he had to put an end to any scandal that could leak through from this appeal?

I nodded. I was at a loss as to what to do. I hated myself. I hated him even more.

Was this why TDS had told me to leave with him, to return to New York? If he was able to retrieve photos from Evan Browne, a case where the personal attachments were unknown, what had he been capable of in New York?

A heavy weight hung in the pit of my belly. I was about to lose everything. I knew it.

Holmes Manor loomed over me imposingly. My heart leapt to my throat as I noted the black Jag in the driveway. A heady mix of fear, nerves, and shame grew in the pit of my belly.

Mark and I got out of the Golf. Nobody greeted us as we stepped over the threshold of our childhood home.

My father's voice bellowed down the hallway, bouncing off the walls. "Paige," my mother cried, rushing towards me. "Please tell me it's not true."

I couldn't lie to her any longer. I couldn't fake the strength. "I'm so sorry, Mum," I sobbed.

"Mark, did you know?" my father yelled.

"No. I didn't have a clue." I waited for him to betray Danny further, but he didn't.

TDS stood in the doorway to the study, dressed entirely in black. We exchanged looks, but nothing more.

"What happens now?" I asked, head hanging with guilt and disgrace.

"You're lucky that Mr. Ellery knows some extremely powerful people," my father barked.

"Stephen, let's not forget how this ended." My mother protected me. At least she still believed. My father stopped dead in his pacing.

"The appeal will be rejected." TDS stepped in. "I've seen to that."

How had he seen to it? I wanted to ask, but daren't in front of my parents.

"Dr. Franklin should be informed," my mother said to the older adults in the room.

"No. No more pills, or therapy," I stuttered.

"Perhaps it's a good idea, considering New York." Mark rubbed my shoulders.

"New York?" my mother inquired. I closed my eyes and told her the truth. After I'd finished, my mother was near to collapse. Dad helped her to a chair in the lounge before storming into the office with TDS.

I couldn't cry anymore. All my tears had dried, leaving me empty and sore.

"He's good to you, isn't he?" Mother took my hand, patting my shaking knuckles. She looked towards Mark, who nodded in agreement. "I was wrong," she admitted. "I want you to be happy, and I can see that you are with him."

"I'm sorry, Mum." Apologies were all I seemed to be capable of recently.

"Go with him, Paige," she urged. "But remember to come back to us. Hannah will care for Georgia. I will see to that. You concentrate on getting better." Tears brimmed over her thick lashes. I smiled and kissed her cheek, soft with foundation, clutching at her hand.

"Paige," TDS's voice called from the doorway. My father stood behind him.

"Dad?" I asked, walking towards him. My father softened, his arms dropping by his side, granting me the permission I desperately sought.

"Did you see the photos?" I asked later as TDS drove the Jag, followed by Chalmers in my Golf.

"Yes," he said firmly.

"What's happened to them?"

"They won't be seeing daylight again."

"Can you do that?" I asked, convinced he'd committed some kind of crime. His brow arched, telling me not to question him further. But my stubbornness prevailed. "Should I be afraid of you?"

The car jolted to a sudden stop, the belt slamming against my chest, as his foot jumped on the brake. He turned towards me, one hand clasped under my chin. I heard the click of the seat belt only seconds before his lips were on mine.

"The only people who need to fear me are those that hurt you. Put your seat belt back on," he added, shifting the Jag into first and pulling away slowly.

"I love you," I said softly, watching him stare straight ahead, as the whisper of a smile danced across his harsh expression.

And in that moment, I knew that he loved me too.

ABOUT THE AUTHOR

Born in Oman, Charlotte moved to the UK in 1989, settling in Somerset in 2008. She lives with her husband, two children, and growing menagerie of pets, and works as a makeup artist and a freelance writer. She loves learning new skills and keeping fit, always looking for ways to keep her brain and body active. Her career as a writer started at an early age when she began writing poetry, short stories, and flash fiction. "Seven Dirty Words" is her first published full-length novel.

Made in the USA
Charleston, SC
29 August 2013